IN PLAIN SIGHT

A Novel

by

Elizabeth Schmeidler

This book is a work of fiction. While it contains some factual data, the characters and events described are fictional. Any similarities to real life persons/events are purely coincidental.

IN PLAIN SIGHT

©2019 Elizabeth Schmeidler
ISBN: 9781790869961

DEDICATIONS

~As always, I dedicate my work to my Father, as a humble offering in thanksgiving for all He has given me. Each time I think You are finished with me, You show me a different side of You, and a different side of myself. Thank you for giving me the opportunity to be Your Voice and to share Your love through my works.

~Thanks to my husband. Your hard work has allowed me the freedom to do my work, do God's will. I will always be grateful to you and love you forever.

~Thank you to all those in my family and to the friends who have supported what God has given me to accomplish. Thanks for understanding my heart and the mission that calls me to speak and write what needs to be said. You have blessed me and lightened my burden and I love you.

"The Truth is like a lion.
You don't have to defend it.
Let it loose. It will defend itself."

St. Augustine

Prologue

January 19, 2025
Fremont, California

Why do you profane what I have made perfect?
Maryn's eyes flew open, putting an immediate end to a nightmare that was recurring much too often of late. With her thoughts and heart racing, her gaze frantically scanned the dark room and finally connected with the alarm clock on the table next to the bed. She stared at the time for several seconds before it registered that it was 5:58 in the evening rather than time to start her morning routine.

Relief flooded her senses, slowly pushing back the anxiousness that had become part of each day. She reached up and touched the lamp. Immediately, the room filled with light. She tossed the last towel she'd folded before falling asleep onto the top of the other clothes in the basket and murmured, "I better get dinner started. Thomas and the girls will be home any minute."

Just as she stood, she heard a loud bump from below. She smiled. "Thomas!" she called out. "Lily...Pearl...I'm up here...be down in a sec."

Maryn placed a stack of neatly-folded towels on the shelf in their adjoining bathroom. While hanging up a blouse in the walk-in closet, she noticed that the house was eerily quiet.

Apprehension steadily crept up her neck.

"Thomas!" she shouted again, as she lifted her wrist and pressed a button on her LockTight monitor.

Security alarm is solid.

She exhaled a sigh of relief, just as the familiar squeak of the second step on the staircase cut through the silence. Inwardly, she laughed at her jittery behavior, and then forced herself to laugh out loud to break the tension her imagination had created.

"I don't know which one of you is sneaking up on me, but *I heard* that!" she called out playfully, despite her slightly increased heartrate.

The silence continued. She ignored it and placed a freshly-washed blanket onto the shelf of the hall closet. Playing along with their game, she announced, "One of these days I'm going to get you *naughty* people back for all the times you tried to scare me...."

Her words were cut off as she turned to find herself looking down the barrel of a gun. She screamed and dropped the clothes basket.

Maryn didn't recognize the man coming toward her. Shaking her head, she slowly backed into the bedroom. "What are you doing? Why are you here?" she demanded.

Her voice sounded tight and unfamiliar to even herself. The pounding of her heart in her ears was nearly deafening. She wanted to scream but fear twisted her voice into silence.

The man was talking to her, but she couldn't quite process what he was saying. Just like in her nightmare, she couldn't separate reality from fiction.

He was telling her to stay calm. He reassured her that no one would get hurt if she cooperated.

I am dreaming. This is a nightmare. Thomas is coming. He will help me. Oh God, my babies! Where are my babies?

The man reached for her and she twisted away, but not before feeling the cold steel clamp onto her wrist.

Terror filled Maryn's being as she screamed in protest, "NO! What are you doing? *NOOO!*"

The shrill, desperate sound of her own voice was the last thing she heard before her body crumpled to the ground.

Chapter 1

"What?" Gavin Steele growled into the air as he slammed a file onto his desk. "What *the hell* do you expect me to do?"

"What you can," the voice on the speaker phone answered calmly. "You're the man of steel, remember?"

"Very funny...you're a comedian, now?" he asked dryly as his thumb popped two pieces of nicotine gum through the foil and into his mouth.

The room remained silent for several seconds while Gavin chewed furiously on his new habit. *Next thing they're going to tell me is that I'm not allowed to chew this frickin' gum either.*

"You're going to give it some thought, right?" Sister Helena persisted.

Gavin ran a shaky hand through his course, dark hair. His computer screen was off, so his reflection gave him a good look at how far back his widow's peak had recessed. Just as unsettling was that the few grays he once sported at his temples had forged new trails throughout his hair.

God, I look old.

"Well?"

Gavin swore under his breath. He was already a day's worth of consults behind and it wasn't even nine yet. "Look, Sister, I am due in court in an hour. I've got so much shi...work backed up that I really don't know when I would have time..."

"But you'll do it," Helena answered with confidence. "I *know* you'll find the time. This one's important, Gavin."

He laughed caustically. "They're *all* important to you, Sister."

"You're *right*, they are. Glad we agree. So when can we go?"

There was no point in arguing with her, she would just keep needling him until she got her way.

Sylvie can call her later and cover for me.

"And don't have your secretary call me with some lame excuse," she stated bluntly, putting a quick end to his scheme. "Just call me when you're ready, please—and as soon as possible. I'm praying for you."

Gavin stared in annoyed disbelief at the now silent landline phone—the Dinosaur, as Sylvie loved to call it. He didn't give a crap if it was archaic, he was fully convinced that cell phones and most communication devices were responsible for a multitude of health problems and the reason he could never really take a vacation.

His irritation with Sister Helena increased. "Everyone thinks they have a right to my time," he grumbled.

He plopped down onto his plush, oversized office chair. After taking a big swig of his coffee, he stared at the picture of his kids.

Lucas's graduation was just months away. Brenna turned sixteen, three weeks ago. He'd been so busy that he resorted to having Sylvie send her a gift in the mail. When he texted her late that night, she hadn't responded, but he could hardly blame her.

What kind of lame father doesn't show up for his kid's birthday?

Their innocent, happy faces smiled back at him, reminding him of better times. Instantly, he thought of everything he'd lost, including their mother. His stomach knotted. It had been almost a year since he'd had any real conversation with Annie. He wondered if she was seeing anyone.

For all I know, she's engaged.

Suddenly, irrational anger at Sister Helena resurfaced. "She's going to just have to find another lawyer. I've got my own screwed-up life to fix. Why the hell does she always have to call me when someone needs saving?" he spat into the empty room.

Maybe it's because she saved YOU.

He groaned at his conscience. "There are days I wish she hadn't," he grunted truthfully, just before a knock on his office door forced his gaze upward.

"I'm *busy*," he growled, before Sylvie could even speak.

She ignored him. "Judge Burton is on line one. He sounds *pissed*."

Gavin rolled his eyes. "He's *always* pissed. Why would today be any different?"

"True. And I hate to add to your *fun*, but I have to go pick up Jack from school. He's got a fever and just puked all over everything. Hopefully, the worst is over, and if I can get him settled, I'll try and come back—that is if my mom can keep both boys until I get off. Just let the machine pick up your calls while I'm gone. You're due in court soon anyway."

She tossed a phone message on his desk and added, "I sure hope Kade doesn't get sick too." Then, releasing a weary sigh, she added, "Lately it seems like they've been sick more than they are healthy."

Sylvie was gone before he uttered a response.

She'd been his personal assistant for almost a year. After multiple failed attempts to find an assistant with half a brain, who was willing to put her smartphone down long enough to complete a sentence, Sylvie Morris fell into Gavin's hands like a well-thrown pitch.

On the day he'd hired her, she stood in the doorway of his office with his Sub 'n Salad hoagie in hand. Dressed in a ridiculous striped uniform—hat and all, she offered him an entrée of loathing, garnished with a side of humiliation.

Gavin almost smiled at the memory. Apparently, his poker face wasn't quite perfected, because she glared at him with fire in her eyes. Then, mustering every ounce of bravado she possessed within her skinny frame, she declared, "You better not say a word—not one *single, freaking* word! I've got twin boys to provide for…and their dad, the *asshole*, has decided that women and weed are what he chooses to spend his money on. So, do you want this damn sandwich or not?"

To this day, he still wasn't sure the reason he offered Sylvie a job on the spot was because he'd just fired his worthless legal assistant, it was the last shred of decency he possessed, or out of blatant admiration for her chutzpah.

Admittedly, she was a good worker, but she was gone a lot because of her boys. Still, he would gladly put up with Sylvie's absences rather than subject himself to the task of wading through the typical, tech-zombie Millennials or even worse, the Generation Z's raised by them.

Hiring had officially become a discrimination suit just waiting to be filed by a multitude of ambitious, money-hungry, ass-wipe lawyers, just like him. No matter who applied—Black, White, Hispanic, Asian, old, young, single, married, divorced, gay, straight—including those who refused to acknowledge or determine their race, gender, or planet of origin, there was always the potential threat of becoming entrapped by the PC police. Asking a potential employee simple questions felt a little like wading through a mine field. The mere thought of ever having to hire someone else made Gavin want to give Sylvie a raise.

The shrill ringing of the dinosaur startled him from his ponderings. *Judge Burton.*

"*Damnit!* I forgot he was on the line. He's going to have my ass for lunch," he grumbled before picking up the receiver.

He was hoping it was Burton's assistant, but the booming, caustic voice assaulting his ears belonged to the Judge himself. The man always sounded like an enraged coach yelling at the players from the bench. Gavin held the phone away from his head as Burton proceeded to rail him about being hung up on and a plethora of other perceived offenses.

Wincing at the pain throbbing behind his eyes, Gavin mused, *Sister Helena, you can forget about praying for me. I'm already in hell.*

Chapter 2

Gavin slammed his empty glass onto the bar and gave the bartender a nod for another.

Despite the grueling day he'd had, the idea of going home was about as appealing as rolling naked in broken glass. At least at the bar he could pass the time pretending he had a life worth going home to.

The acid in his empty stomach churned with the scotch, causing a burning sensation. He knew he should leave and get something to eat, but then he'd have to face the prospect of dining alone or picking something up to take back to his apartment. Either option increased the feeling of emptiness he'd been experiencing lately.

A sweet-smelling blonde slipped onto the barstool next to him. She offered him several obvious gestures to convey the message that she was interested, but strangely, he wasn't. There was a time he would have been—too many times—and it had cost him everything. Now, being enticed by pouting red lips and several inches of cleavage only made him want another drink and a cigarette.

And Annie.

He cursed aloud and popped two pieces of nicotine gum into his mouth. At this point, Gavin wondered if he would ever quit craving smokes, ever stop missing Annie, ever quit feeling empty and worthless. He tossed down the remaining scotch in his glass, swallowing the accursed gum in the process.

Hot, vaporous acid rose to the back of his throat. He suddenly felt like vomiting and wondered if he was getting sick with whatever Sylvie's kid had.

She never did make it back to work.

"That's the least of my worries," he grumbled.

He should have been celebrating the huge court case he'd won in court. Eduardo Rojas, a wealthy cannabis grower, was tried for felony possession and intent to distribute methamphetamines. Piece by piece, Gavin had effectively shredded the evidence against Rojas, knowing full-well that the bastard was guilty. His client walked out of the courtroom a free man. Gavin walked out of the courtroom nearly half a million dollars richer.

Afterwards, he was congratulated by his colleagues. Even Judge Burton gave him a nod. Though his defense was brilliant— by the book and perfectly legit, Gavin couldn't squelch the all-too-familiar feeling of self-loathing. He wondered how many young kids like Lucas and Brenna were hooked on meth or cocaine because of scum like the client he'd just set free.

It was too much to think about. The war being waged in his conscience caused his stomach to roll.

I really am going to puke...

Hoping to get to the bathroom before he embarrassed himself, Gavin tossed a couple of twenties on the bar and slid off the stool. He didn't get very far before his eyes locked with a familiar face. He groaned aloud before demanding, "What are you *doing* here? How did you find me?"

"I called you at the office, but since you failed to call me back, I called Sylvie's cell number. I admit that I fibbed to her a little in order to find you, but it was worth it. Look at you...you're a *mess*."

Gavin couldn't argue. His head was pounding with the intensity of a determined woodpecker on crack. The burning in his stomach seemed to increase with her every word, but the urge to vomit was temporarily waylaid by the shame that washed over him.

He hung his head.

Despite the loud music and party crowd around them, he could still hear her voice as she questioned him. Though his vision was blurred from the scotch and clouded with humiliation, his gaze zeroed in on a large pair of worn, black, hi-top tennis shoes. Slowly, his eyes rose to take in the voluminous folds of her black habit before coming to rest on the giant crucifix that hung at her waist. His gaze continued upward until he finally looked her straight in the eye.

I'm really on a roll now...meeting nuns at the bar.

Sister Helena was a big-boned, tall woman, whose rectangular eyeglasses rested atop rounded cheeks as though they were sitting on a shelf. Strangely, considering their modern style, they didn't look out of place, even considering her age and old-school habit. Her expression was a mixture of anger, sympathy, and disappointment. Seeing it caused instant remorse to course through his body.

"Good work, Gavin," he mumbled.

"I *asked* if you've eaten anything yet," Sister Helena repeated loudly.

He didn't answer. She was acting like his mother. His remorse was quickly replaced with resentment. Admittedly, he was drunk, but not drunk enough to let a nun in high-tops get the best of him.

At the thought, he threw his head back and laughed. "Do you make a *habit* of wearing tennis shoes underneath your *habit*?" he joked, his words slurred. "Aren't those shoes *converse* to the proper attire of a nun?"

"Very funny. So you're a comedian now?" Helena responded with a slight grin, mimicking his words from the conversation they'd had that morning. "C'mon...you're leaving with me," she barked resolutely. "We're going to get you something to eat. You're a *mess*," she reiterated.

Gavin didn't need to hear it twice. Hearing the words come from her mouth sobered him. In that moment, he couldn't agree more. He felt like the fat kid on the playground no one wanted to play with. Before him stood his no-nonsense teacher urging him to get up so they could go in and "have a talk."

It was as if he had stepped back in time. All he could do was put his hand in her outstretched soft, aged hand one more time.

*****

Gavin stared at his plate of food in silence. The nausea had passed, but the guilt and resentment he was feeling seemed to have lodged in his throat.

"Well," Sister Helena began, after swallowing a forkful of pancakes, "are you going to eat, or would you rather tell me why you're drunk again? Doesn't matter to me which comes first, but you need to make up your mind and get on with it."

Gavin was grateful that the late-night party crowd at Frank's Place had yet to arrive for their breakfast sober-up. He certainly didn't want an audience to witness the tongue-lashing she would surely give him for falling off the wagon. Even now, her piercing green eyes bore into his soul like arrows. As uncomfortable as her never-wavering gaze made him, he noticed that her skin was nearly flawless—her face, almost wrinkle-free. "For your age, you sure don't have a lot of wrinkles," he blurted.

She chuckled. "Ever see a wrinkle on a balloon before?" she asked, while forking a sausage link.

He shook his head and tried to smile. "Nope." In reality

"Precisely. So, if you're trying to flatter me, I'm not," she teased with a wink. "We have lots to talk about…like what's eating you. Kids okay? Annie?"

He nodded and pushed the food around on his plate. "As far as I know."

"Have you talked to them lately?"

"No."

"What do you mean, *no*? You're their father, aren't you? No matter what your relationship with their mother is like, you still need to be their father…"

Gavin held up his hand, "I know…I *know*! I *get* it! But you have no idea how hard it is. Their schedules are so busy and all they care about is their friends…and *I'm* so busy…"

It was Helena's turn to cut him off. "Nope. Not buying it, so just stop. No excuse is good enough. You need to *make* time and so do they. *Insist* on setting time aside. Take them to a ballgame or a concert. You're going to have to go above and beyond—stand on your head and blow bubbles out your nose if you have to, but in the end, you have to be the one who tries the hardest. If you don't keep trying, they will start to believe they are dispensable."

"And what if *I am* dispensable?" he asked in a voice so low it was almost a whisper.

Sister Helena stared back at him. His eyes were downcast, but she didn't need to see them to confirm the despair he was feeling—she could hear it in his voice. It was palpable. Gavin needed both a kick in the pants and a hug of mercy, and she wasn't quite sure how to effectively deliver them both at the same time.

She paused several moments before saying, "*No one* is dispensable—and especially not a brilliant man like you. If you are feeling dispensable, it's because you have *chosen* to live a life that is out of order."

He lifted his gaze but said nothing.

"I asked you earlier what was eating you. Are you going to tell me or not?"

When he didn't answer, she did. "Gavin, you can't turn back the clock and take back the affair. We can't take back our words or our actions. What's done is done…but, we can atone for our mistakes and *choose* to do better by giving what we can and living a life we can be proud of."

Gavin's eyes unexpectedly hardened. She watched as his previously sad countenance transformed into anger.

"You really don't *get* it, Sister, do you?" he declared, his words clipped. "I don't really give a *damn* about *anything* right now, including your advice and what you think of me. I don't happen to live in the same butterflies and roses world you do—the world where everything turns out for the better of *humanity*.
"Give me a *freaking* break! I'm never going to be the choir boy you want me to be and you're never going to convince me that life is much more than a damned social experiment."

Sister Helena slowly raised her glass and took a drink of water. His irrational anger was a sure sign that she was right—he was definitely feeling guilty about something.

Her mind flashed back to the night she found him passed out on the walkway of the church rectory. Reeking of alcohol, his clothes were filthy and torn and his wallet and pride were both missing, which is why he accepted her help. Afterward, she met with him several times to talk about his issues, and eventually, he joined AA.

Now, he was staring at her defiantly. If he wasn't so cranky and vulnerable, she would have told him that it looked like the wagon he'd fallen off of must've ran over him.

She waited for a few minutes to give his harsh words sufficient time to convict his heart of his irrational mood, and then said, "You *know* better than that. Those words were like that of a belligerent teenager—nothing more than a temper tantrum meant to get me off your back. But I'm not going anywhere, and you're going to hear me out whether you want to or not...so here goes."

She reached over and put her hand on his forearm. "You are *important* to this life, Gavin. To your kids...to your clients...to *God*...to *me*. You are *miserable* because you are not fulfilling God's plan and purpose for you. You cling to relying on laws and statutes that will win your cases, yet you discard the laws and precepts that will bring you *lasting* victory. You know how the saying goes...you can lead a horse to water, but you can't make him drink. Well, you well-know where the water is that will refresh you, but instead, you always resort to partaking what will always leave you thirsty."

Shaken and still red-faced, Gavin stood up. "I don't have to listen to this."

"Well, you're right about that," Sister Helena answered calmly, taking a bite of her scrambled eggs.

Gavin threw several bills on the table and turned to leave.

"I drove us here, remember?" she asked.

"I'll get a cab."

"Okay...just make sure that you don't get lost along the way."

Gavin stared at her for several tense moments before he turned and silently walked away.

"Lord, have mercy on him," she whispered sadly.

Chapter 3

Maryn blinked her eyes in disbelief. Thomas and the girls stood off in the distance. Lily, the six-year-old, simply stared questioningly, but four-year-old Pearl smiled broadly and immediately ran toward her.

Thomas remained flinty, like a statue, his face, unreadable. Still, with her sweet Pearly drawing nearer, Maryn could hardly focus on him. She reached out her arms to welcome her baby, her body literally aching in anticipation of the sheer joy that would come in feeling Pearl's small, but strong, warm body against her own.

Just inches away from her grasp, Thomas's strong arms reached out, grabbed Pearl by the waist, and held her just out of her reach. Pearl began to cry.

Thomas's badge glinted in the sun, blinding Maryn's eyes from fully seeing his face. Confused by his actions, she held her hand up to shade her eyes. Behind him, Lily peered around his torso and called out to her, "Mommy why? Please Mommy...tell me why! Why did you do it? I thought you loved us! Why?"

Her voice continually called out to her, but slowly, Maryn became conscious that the voice was one she didn't recognize. Immediately, she rejected it and tried desperately to go back to sleep. Even the nightmares of sleep were preferred to the real-life terrors that would flood her senses upon awakening. The cold. The despair. The loneliness.

Her babies were gone. Thomas was gone. She was alone. *Completely alone.*

Like a simmering volcano, the pain rose up inside Maryn once more, threatening to erupt into sobs that burned her soul.

In an attempt to press the despair back down into the pit of hell where it belonged, she took several deep breaths, but the pain would not subside. She was sure she didn't have the strength to cry a single tear, but slowly, the tears rose inside her just as steadily as the eastern sun.

God, I want to die. Please. I can't do this. It's too much.

Maryn lay as still as possible on the threadbare cot and thin pillow that was still damp from her last cry. Chilled to the bone, but numb, she prayed that whoever was there calling to her would go away so she could go back to sleep and never wake up. Still, the voice persisted.

A touch on her cheek made her recoil. "Please," she croaked, her voice so hoarse from crying it didn't even sound like it belonged to her. "Please let me sleep. Go away. *Please!*"

Sister Helena swallowed hard to keep the tears from her own voice. "Maryn, it's me, Sister Helena. May I please pray with you today?"

"No!" she cried in anguish, her emotions violently erupting. "God...has...abandoned me!" she choked out, in between sobs. "I don't...know...who...he...is...anymore...or...what...to do!"

Sister Helena sat onto the cot and pulled Maryn to her chest with such force that she nearly toppled them both over.

"There, there. It's going to be alright...I *promise*," she crooned, patting her back lovingly. "You're not alone, honey. God *knows*. He knows all about it and is here with you. He hasn't abandoned you! He has promised never to leave you, and He *won't* forsake you...and neither will I. Shhh...shhh...calm down now. I'm here to help. We'll get through this...*together*."

As if against her will, the prisoner in Helena's arms began to relax, her sobs eventually slowing until they had dwindled to an occasional hiccup. Helena was doubtful that Maryn Pearce was even aware of a single word she prayed. She felt so small against her ample frame—almost like a child. The intensity of her desire to protect and help her was completely unexpected and powerful. Helena couldn't explain it if she wanted to.

She reached up and cupped the back of Maryn's head and continued to pray.

Dear God, how can I help this woman? I don't even know what she has done.

Immediately, her mind flashed back to when she had found Gavin. He, too, had been broken, but in a much different way. This woman's despair was indescribable. She was slipping away. Helena was sure of it.

She prayed harder still. *God help me know what to say, what to do. I don't know how to help her.*

Helena dared a glance down at the women she held. Her eyes were closed. Dark, spiked lashes, wet with tears, greatly contrasted skin so pale, it looked almost translucent, the spattering of freckles across her nose and cheeks, almost imagined. In the dim light, despite its matted appearance, she thought it looked like Maryn's hair was a dark shade of strawberry blonde. Contrary to the common perception that redheads were feisty and confident, this woman reminded Helena of a waif—lost, like so many others.

She thought she'd seen it all. The women's prison ministry was nothing new to Helena. At times, her attempts to help or pray with an inmate was met with sheer hostility, other times, she was wholeheartedly welcomed. Many of the girls had zero real knowledge of Christ, thinking they had no need of prayers. Other had the, "I was saved eight years ago when I accepted Jesus Christ, so my salvation's a done deal," attitude. This false-perception caused her the most grief. Without accountability to God for one's own actions and disobedience to God, the sins would be repeated, resulting in multiple incarcerations, and eventually, land them in the worst prison imaginable—hell.

Nearly always, the common factor that landed the women behind bars was drugs, including alcohol—they either got messed up using them or mixed up with a man who was using or selling them. Abusive relationships were common among the women, as was the frequent tale of childhood sexual abuse, which often led to the drug scene and prostitution.

The woman in her arms seemed different. Previously, when she had visited the prison, Maryn had been in the infirmary because she was on suicide watch. Helena didn't know much about her case—just that she'd been charged with at least one federal offense to warrant her imprisonment.

God, you already know this...but I admit, I'm worried. Help me to help her.

She had no more finished the thought when she caught the faint sound of a whisper.

She said something!

Energy pulsed through her body at the breakthrough. "What dear?" she asked gently. "I didn't hear what you said."

Silence filled the space as Helena's ears strained. All her senses collectively willed Maryn to speak again, until at last, she whispered, "I killed him."

It felt like a brick had just landed at the bottom of Helena's stomach. Her heart was pounding furiously now. "Who?" she asked with a calm she wasn't feeling.

"David," Maryn answered so softly, that if Helena hadn't been listening so intently, she would have been certain she imagined it.

Dear God...no! Helena lamented silently, struggling for the right words to say after such an admission. Swallowing hard, she squeezed her eyes shut and prayed for wisdom.

"They're all gone," Maryn added quietly, now in a state that almost seemed robotic.

"Who are *they*?" Helena asked quickly, increasingly alarmed at her use of the plural reference.

"My family...my friends...*everyone*," she answered flatly.

Helena's mind raced at her declaration. She'd been told that the woman was charged with multiple crimes, but not a breath had been spoken about any killing.

"Your parents?" Helena asked, hoping Maryn was simply distraught that her parents were not with her. *Surely, I would have heard about the murder of an entire family.*

Slowly, Maryn's head moved from side to side.

Helena fought back tears. She really had no desire to ask Maryn to explain—her expression was so empty, she feared the admission would be the end of her. In truth, she looked so utterly void of life, she already looked like she was near death.

Several moments passed. "I've done something terrible, and now they're all gone," Maryn admitted woefully, her previously blank expression now transformed into the most sorrowful expression Helena thought she'd ever seen.

"My husband...my...*babies*," Maryn choked out, finally, burying her head into the crook of Helena's shoulder once more.

Helena held her, rocking her back and forth, gently patting her back to soothe her, but she still couldn't bear to ask what had happened. No words of comfort seemed sufficient to give hope to such a tormented soul. All she could manage to get out was, "God knows. It's going to be okay...He is with you."

Despite her assurance, a niggling fear had worked its way into Helena's confidence. *God, help me. I don't know what to do for her. Please...help her!* she pleaded in silence.

After what seemed like forever, the sound of footsteps caught their attention. Maryn's body went completely rigid.

Despite her state, Maryn found the strength to lift her head. "Thomas?" she whispered questioningly.

There was such hope in her voice that Helena's breath caught in her chest. As the steps grew closer, she silently prayed that the footsteps belonged to whoever Thomas was. The raw hope in Maryn's voice made Helena worry how she would handle the disappointment.

"Well, I should have known I'd find you here."

Maryn's body immediately went limp again at the sound of the man's voice, but to Helena, the sound was like a symphony. "I knew you'd come," she declared with a broad smile.

"No you didn't," Gavin shot back.

"Okay, so I didn't," Helena admitted. "You're like the son who said no to his father, but then ended up doing the right thing after all," she said, as relief coursed through her.

"Yeah, whatever. I'm an ass and you know it, and I don't want to be compared to bible stories. I'm here to look at her case if she wants me."

"We want you," Helena answered, bobbing her head up and down affirmatively.

Gavin almost had to laugh. He wondered if the woman in Sister Helena's arms had any idea that she was being held by an official Rottweiler of faith.

Chapter 4

"Okay, so let me get this straight—you fully admit that you withheld medical treatment and falsified medical and government documents?" Gavin asked, inwardly shaking his head.

"Yes," Maryn answered firmly, her red, swollen eyes never leaving his face.

No shame whatsoever, Gavin silently noted. "Okay...so, do you have a reason for doing this?"

"Yes, I'm sure she does," Sister Helena quickly affirmed, nodding her head profusely.

Gavin raised his eyebrows. "I was asking *my client.*"

"Sorry," Helena offered sheepishly.

He focused on Maryn once again. "So can you tell me why you made these decisions? Were you under a great deal of stress?"

Maryn shook her head slowly. "It was a nightmare. *All* of it," she whispered.

"Okay, then tell me about the nightmare," he persisted.

Maryn stared back at him for several tense moments, and then said, "It was a nightmare I experienced every single day."

"Do you mean you had been experiencing nightmares that caused you to break the law?" he asked, inwardly rolling his eyes.

She might need a shrink more than a lawyer.

"Maryn, just start at the beginning," Helena coaxed gently, hoping to make up for the impatience in Gavin's voice.

Again, several moments passed. The silence seemed to grow louder than the sound of activity outside the room they'd moved to for counsel.

Gavin would have preferred her jail cell to the tiny, windowless room they were presently sitting in. His stomach was rolling, and he was sweating profusely. Everything about the moment made him regret coming. The woman already admitted she was guilty. It would be an uphill battle—more like a mountain. Of that, he was sure.

Finally, Maryn stopped shaking her head and said, "I just couldn't do it anymore. I've lost everything for what I've done, but I just couldn't do it."

"Do what?" Helena asked before Gavin could.

"I started to notice," she answered, looking directly at Helena, avoiding Gavin altogether.

"Notice what?" Helena asked.

"The eyes," she answered quietly, fresh tears rimming her own eyes.

"Go on," Helena pressed, now sitting so far on the edge of her chair that Gavin wondered if she was going to tip it.

"I see kids every day," Maryn began. "I *love* my job. I *love* the kids…I love *my* kids."

She stopped, her throat clearly clogged with emotion.

"I'm sure you do," Gavin offered, but his tone was laced with impatience rather than empathy, "but I need to know what happened."

Once again, Maryn ignored Gavin and looked into Helena's eyes and said, "The new immunization schedule requires that we give the kids the Lunatia both at a year to eighteen months and one more dose sometime before they enter pre-school."

Gavin gave his head a slight shake. "Wait…Lunatia? Help me out here—my kids are grown."

"Well, you're lucky you don't have to deal with this—for now anyway," Maryn answered quietly.

Gavin let out a grunt. "Yeah, I feel *real* lucky," he answered dryly, before Sister Helena gave him a look he was sure a Catholic nun should not know how to give. "Okay," he began again, "can you tell me more?"

"Lunatia is supposed to prevent the Lunavirus, which is spread through certain mosquitoes common to South America."

"Okay...yeah, I guess I have vaguely heard about it on the news. Go on."

"Well, I started to put two and two together that the Lunatia might be causing some sort of neurological problems."

"Like what?" Sister Helena blurted, completely enthralled.

"At first, we dismissed it as just a temporary reaction. Then the reactions started happening more often—like every other month or so, and the usual symptoms...fever, crying...you know, the usual side effects, didn't seem to go away like we had anticipated. We had kids coming in who could no longer focus on their school work—some had lost their hand-eye coordination..."

"So you decided, on *your own*, that you would not give them the shot," Gavin interrupted, "even at the risk of the kids dying from the virus?"

"Yes," she stated flatly. "I did what I thought was right. It was all I could do."

"Counsel time's over, Pearce," the prison guard announced before Gavin could get another question asked.

"Can't we just have a few more minutes?" Helena pleaded.

"No. You'll have to wait until tomorrow. Everybody out."

Gavin swore under his breath. They had hardly scratched the surface.

"You're coming back tomorrow?" Helena asked in a way that was more an order than a question.

"I'll see what I can do," Gavin answered without emotion. "If she wants me for her attorney, that is, she'll have to sign this waiver of her previous counsel and acceptance of me as her new counsel."

Sister Helena, though clearly annoyed by his attitude, ignored the hesitation in Maryn's expression and said, "Of course she will sign it."

She then leaned toward Maryn and gently touched her cheek. "He is a bit of an ass, I know...but he'll do a good job for you, I promise," she whispered, deliberately loud enough for Gavin to hear.

He wasn't offended at all by her comment—it was true, and in a strange way, it ignited a small spark of pride in knowing that she trusted him despite knowing his weaknesses.

Maryn chose that moment to look up at him questioningly. The faded orange prison attire nearly swallowed up her thin frame. Several seconds ticked by before her eyes locked with his. *"Please...help me."*

Chapter 5

Gavin peeled back the protective covering to expose the adhesive on his nicotine patch and slapped it onto his upper arm. "There, now all my problems are solved," he muttered sarcastically.

It was after seven by the time he got back to the office. He was tired, hungry, and irritable as hell. Not only was he further behind than ever on his current cases, but Sylvie hadn't been there to shuffle his schedule and run interference for him, so he would have to listen to all the B.S. on the answering machine himself.

Thinking of her made him feel a little less sorry for himself, but only a little. *I hope her kid gets better soon. She could sure use a break and so could I.*

He blew out a gust of air and then tossed Maryn Pearce's file onto his desk. Including his travel time, he'd invested almost four hours on his newest client already.

Reaching into the bag of food he'd picked up, he stared at the receipt. *Twenty-two bucks for the grub, almost four bucks for tax, and another four bucks for the health tax.*

He shook his head. "Thirty dollars for a lousy burger and fries," he lamented. "Frickin' health tax. Those bastards can tax me all they want, but I'm still going to eat whatever I want."

After taking a giant bite, he leaned back into his posh leather chair and wondered for the hundredth time why he let himself be guilted into taking the Pearce case. He was certain he would never see payment for most of it.

Maybe taking this case for Sister will finally even the score.

As soon as the thought came, the memory of the pain he saw in Maryn's eyes surfaced. He would be a liar to say her despair hadn't affected him.

Still, in reality, there was only so much he could do. The woman had pretty-much bitten off the leg of a rabid dog. Government mandated vaccines were highly approved of and heavily enforced. Now more than ever, they were considered necessary due to the open border policy that had been implemented in the previous administration. Full compliance with the immunization schedule was one of the non-negotiable requirements for illegals already in the U.S. to prevent deportation and one of the few requirements for those seeking entrance. Moreover, to further ensure the "herd immunity" would proliferate, the vaccinations were provided free of charge to all immigrants.

White, black, rich, poor—no one wanted disease brought into their homes and schools. Gavin understood the concept. He understood the passion behind it all—the desire to be immune to as many illnesses as possible, but the mandates were unsettling and down-right unconstitutional. The minute the initial mandates passed, a push for legislation surfaced which would require full immunization for every American, including booster shots—regardless of age, gender, or potential physical risk, and regardless of moral objection.

Those with compromised immune systems would be allowed to receive their shots in a spaced-out time schedule, but they would no longer be exempt. Proponents of these mandates maintained that full participation was necessary for the greater good of the nation. Last he heard, the bill had been written and re-written several times, but a vote was anticipated to take place before summer was upon them.

I guess the powerful have chosen to deem the weak collateral damage...again, he mused, before chasing his food down with lemon-infused tea.

He stared at the bottle in his hand. "Organically-grown green tea, dairy-free, soy-free, sugar-free, gluten-free, all natural. Contains caffeine."

He scoffed and added, "Won't be long and caffeine will be nixed too…oh wait, they'll just tax it."

After shoving several fries in his mouth, he wiped the salt from his fingers and picked up Maryn's folder. He looked over the notes from their earlier meeting, and then the notes from her file that he'd managed to get his hands on before heading back to the office.

The court appointed attorney who had accompanied her to her preliminary hearing had been almost giddy to turn the case over to him. So anxious, in fact, that Gavin wondered what the guy knew that he didn't.

"What a rookie jackass," he muttered, at the memory of the attorney's demeanor.

Due to several new clauses written into the new vaccine mandate, one of the charges against Maryn Pearce was treason. Gavin shook his head. The crime of treason had all but been erased from California law in recent years, due to its "potential to discriminate against those who feel radically opposed to constitutionalism."

Ironically, Maryn's disobedience to the government mandate was considered treasonous. It was the first case he'd heard of so far, but he suspected there would be more, eventually. Even though bail was almost always denied in treason cases, it didn't look like the first attorney had even attempted to plead for an exception, based on her actions being due to her fear for public safety and her low flight risk.

"Her husband's a *cop*," he declared aloud. "How much risk could she possibly be?"

The dinosaur rang, startling him. The caller ID showed it was Sylvie. He grabbed the phone with gusto.

"How's Jack?" he barked.

"Uh…yeah…hello to you too," she answered dryly.

"Humor me, would you? I'm a little out of small talk at the moment."

"No more fever and no pukes for several hours now. I should be in tomorrow if Kade doesn't come down with it. I hope I don't get it too...I could puke just thinking about it."

"Well don't bring it here. Keep that crap at home. Do what you have to, but I don't have time to be sick. By the way, have you heard anything on the news about a woman named Maryn Pearce?" he asked, rubbing his tired eyes.

"You're kidding me, right?" she scoffed. "Of *course* I've heard of Maryn Pearce...*who* hasn't?"

"Well, I hadn't until this afternoon." *I still wish I hadn't heard of her,* he added silently.

"Wow, you need to get out more," she answered with a chuckle. "It's been all over the news. She actually worked at the pediatric clinic I take my boys to, so I was really weirded out to hear that she'd been fudging the immunizations. There's a kid—David—something, would still be alive if she had given him the Lunavirus shot."

"That's the accusation, anyway," he challenged.

Sylvie ignored his comment. "Glad my boys weren't affected by it. We usually see the other nurse at the clinic," she added. "Why do you ask?"

Gavin didn't answer.

"Are you still there?" Sylvie asked.

"Yeah...just thinking."

"Wait a minute...don't tell me you've been approached to take her case...and if you have, good luck with *that*. I mean, what she did will cause people to question their healthcare at every level. She's really opened a can of worms for everyone. Her name might as well be Satan as far as parents are concerned—probably among the medical community too. She should *never* be tried around here, that's for sure. I guess even her husband has ditched her."

"What?" Gavin blurted, suddenly re-entering the conversation.

"Yeah. Her husband's a cop, but he's mad as hell. Showed up at the preliminary hearing and asked that the judge *deny* bail. I guess he found out that she didn't give their girls their shots either."

Stunned, Gavin swore under his breath and then said, "How in the hell could I have missed all this?"

Sylvie gave a short laugh. "Probably because you've been too busy defending the drug dude or because you're a self-centered ass—maybe both," she teased.

"I've gotta go," he muttered and slammed the receiver down.

He immediately shuffled through Maryn's file and skimmed several more pages before he searched the caller ID until he found Sister Helena's number.

Gavin took bites of his burger while he impatiently waited for some nun who answered the phone to go and find Sister Helena.

It seemed more like an eternity than minutes before she answered, "This is Sister Helena, how may I help you?"

"Did you know that her husband is pressing charges too?"

"What? Who is this...Gavin?"

"No, it's the Pope. Of *course,* it's me," he answered, immediately cringing at his lame joke. "Did Maryn tell you her husband showed up at the preliminary hearing and requested that she be denied bail?"

"Dear Lord, no!" Helena gasped. "No wonder she's so distraught. That must be what she meant when she said that her family is all gone."

"Oh yeah? So what else? Exactly what has she told you?"

"Nothing more than what you heard today. The first time I met her she was curled up on a cot looking like a discarded rag. She was so drugged up that I didn't even know if she heard a word I said. I prayed for her and that was it. I called you right afterward to see if you'd help—remember? She was the reason I went looking for you at the bar. I thought she was going to die. I really did."

Gavin let out a low whistle. "*Geeezus...she is screwed.*"

"Gavin *Steele!*" Helena exclaimed much like his mother would have. "I better not hear the Lord's name coming from your mouth unless you're praying or giving thanks. We've had this conversation before."

"Okay...*sorry,*" he interrupted, hoping to waylay the lecture he'd heard almost a dozen times, "but do you have any idea how much trouble she is in?"

"No," Helena answered quietly. "Is it really that bad?"

"Well...for starters," he began, reading the charges aloud, "One count of voluntary manslaughter. A hundred-seventy-eight counts of child-endangerment. A hundred-seventy-eight counts of withholding of medical treatment to a minor. A hundred seventy-eight counts of felony falsification of records. A hundred-seventy-eight counts of felony medical malpractice. One felony count of willful endangerment of community. A felony count of willful misconduct against the residents of the state of California, and a felony charge of *treason.*"

"Treason?" Helena exclaimed, how could she have committed treason?"

"Basically, the new vaccine law declares that anyone who interferes with or impedes the implementation of mandatory vaccinations, resulting in the compromise of the country's herd immunity is guilty of treason."

"Oh, dear *God,*" Helena groaned. "So...you're not calling to tell me you're quitting, are you?" she asked, clearly riled before he answered.

Gavin paused. He was tempted to feel a little insulted at how quick she was to believe the worst of him, but he knew he deserved it. "No. I was calling to figure out what the *hell* is going on. I was hoping that you could fill me in a little more."

"Well, I'm thankful you're not bailing on me. I always knew there was good in you."

"Yeah, well I don't know how good I will be on this case...I've got so damn much work backed up..."

He ran his hands through his hair several times in frustration before realizing he'd just coated his hair with French-fry grease and salt.

"Gavin," Helena said firmly, "we *have* to help her. You saw her...imagine the pain she must be going through. She's lost everything."

Gavin stared at his reflection on his computer screen. When Annie left him, the pain was unbearable. At times, the agony got so bad, the only thing that kept him breathing was the thought of his kids and winning them back.

As if Helena had read his mind, she added, "Imagine your despair if you had lost, not only Annie, but your kids too—especially when they were so little. At that age, you miss out on everything."

"Okay! *Enough* already...I *get* it."

"So, will you keep her?" she pressed.

"Yes! Stop asking me that...it's really pissing me off. And you better get used to the idea of her staying in prison for a long time. I'm no freakin' magician."

"Don't give me that crap," she shot back. "You just got a known drug-dealer off, and Maryn's motivation is *completely* different than his."

"Y'damn right, it's different!" he barked. "She messed with the big-dogs—government and big pharma. In my opinion, those entities are potentially more dangerous than drug-dealers and users *combined.* They have *all* the power. They've got the money, control of the news-media, the internet, and..."

Gavin stopped talking and stared at the dinosaur. "Sister, what kind of phone are you talking on?"

"The phone here at the convent."

"I *know* that. What *kind* is it? Is it cordless? Mobile?"

She chuckled. "No it's an old-school phone. Sister Mary Frances thinks that even with the new laws that were passed to protect our privacy on phones and the internet, the people who want to do us harm can still find a way to listen in on those smart type of phones."

"I agree. Sister Mary Frances is a *smart* woman," Gavin affirmed.

"Yes, she is..."

Gavin cut her off. "Don't talk to *anyone* about Maryn's case...and I mean, *anyone.* Are we clear? That's all I need is a bunch of vultures swooping down on me for a story every damn time I step foot out of my office. That'll happen soon enough."

"I understand your concern," Helena answered. "So, just to confirm, are we meeting with Maryn tomorrow? I signed up for the two o'clock slot for ministry because I saw that your counseling slot was at three. That would give us two hours."

Gavin silently cursed the strict limited counsel regulations for prisoners accused of treason. They would be hard-pressed to get done what was necessary in the allowed time, but it would have to suffice.

"It's all we have at this point," he declared with a sigh.

"Not true...we have God's help."

"Then you better start rolling those beads."

Helena chuckled. "That's how much *you* know. I've been praying for her from the instant I met her...and I pray for *you* the same."

Suddenly irritated, Gavin rolled his eyes. "Well so far, your prayers don't seem to be worth a *shit*."

"You really shouldn't call yourself that," she shot back without missing a beat.

It took him a few seconds before he caught her sarcasm. "See you tomorrow, Sister," he answered with a chuckle.

Chapter 6

Maryn stared up at the cracked ceiling of her cell, her gaze tracking each line, as if there was a purpose in doing so. The task was simple, requiring zero effort or thought, and allowed her mind to drift back to happier times.

Lying there on her back reminded her of better days. As a young girl, she'd laid on the trampoline in her backyard, soaking in the sun and watching the clouds roll by. How she wished that, like the clouds, the cracks in the ceiling would come together to form something magical—something beautiful and whimsical for her to dream about. But the wonder and promises of those carefree days in the sun were gone now. Only darkness and shades of gray remained with her now.

Growing up as an only child and then losing both parents to cancer just two years apart, Maryn had grown accustomed to solitude—until Thomas and the babies came into her life, when her life had turned completely around. Now, the isolation she'd once felt when her parents died was back and unbearable. Torturous. At the thought of what she had lost, her body began to tremble.

She was cold. Always so cold. It wasn't the room temperature, it was deeper, she knew—a chill of conscience that permeated her bones.

Maryn turned over and squeezed into the tightest ball possible, wrapping her arms around her body and tucking her chin onto her chest. The effort eased the trembling just enough to prompt her to offer up a few words of gratitude to God.

The very instant she uttered His name, however, the tears began to trickle. In just seconds, they gushed forth like a dam that had burst. She felt so betrayed, so abandoned. She had trusted God. She had trusted Thomas. There was no one now. No parents. No siblings. No cousins. No in-laws. She was certain that the hatred Thomas had shown her at the preliminary hearing had been instilled in his sister as well.

My girls will grow up without me. Hating me.

At the thought, a guttural moan of pain bellowed from deep within her being.

This is my punishment for killing David. His parents will never get to see him grow up, either. I can only imagine how they must despise me.

The revelation caused a fresh jolt of hot pain to rise up inside her, punching her heart with an iron fist, twisting her insides into knots so tight, the urge to vomit was overpowering. She quickly rolled to the side of the bed and dry-heaved.

Afterward, she resumed her fetal position. Her mind raced with guilt she could not appease, questions she could not answer, sorrow she could not bear. Before she was arrested, she would have never—could have never, pondered such things, imagined feeling such agony and abandonment. The intensity of these emotions was as foreign to her as the prison cell in which she now resided.

Oh God...what have I done? Why didn't you show me? How could you have allowed me to take a life?

Maryn rocked back and forth until she no longer had the strength to continue. The thought of going to sleep and never waking up was appealing—until she realized that hell could very well be the punishment that awaited her. Initially, her mind rejected the notion, but the thought would resurface on occasion to torment or entice her, depending on her mood.

It felt impossible to even think straight anymore. She tried to pray but couldn't. God seemed far away. Unreal. A stranger who had once been her friend, confidante, and Savior.

"Who will save me now?" she whispered woefully.

Still, because of her girls, she made every effort to conjure up a glimmer of hope. *Maybe Sister Helena and my new lawyer can help me.*

Help you how? The darkness mocked her. ***You have no life to return to. Your husband hates you. You betrayed them all.***

The voice of doom crashed down upon her sliver of optimism, smashing it to smithereens. The rolling of her stomach returned.

She squeezed her eyes shut to block out thoughts of how she'd hurt the only man she'd ever loved and the precious girls she had given birth to. She'd loved them even before she ever laid eyes on them.

The minute she closed her eyes, their sweet faces appeared. Maryn cried so hard she was certain there were no tears left.

Afterward, she lay there spent in the now-dark room, shivering violently, aching to the marrow of her bones. "God, help me," she croaked weakly.

It is not the healthy who are in need of a physician, but the sick.

Luke...chapter five, verse thirty-one.

Maryn's heart pounded wildly at the voice that had spoken deep inside her. The reasons behind her actions immediately surfaced. She couldn't deny that sometimes a child's well-visit was the last time they were ever well.

The eyes. The tiny lump. The dreams.

I am the Lord, your Healer. I am near to the brokenhearted and I save those who are crushed in spirit.

A soothing warmth spread over Maryn. Gradually, her trembling ceased. A single tear of gratitude slipped down her cheek as she drifted off to sleep.

*****

Gavin lay wide awake, his head cradled beneath his hands. Sleep was something that rarely came easily to him.

He wanted a drink. He wanted a smoke. He wanted the peace and contentment that always seemed to elude him.

The plush penthouse suite he'd purchased when Annie threw him out was stunning. Modern and sleek, it provided everything he could want or need, including valet parking, a professional chef, housekeeping staff, and laundry services. But it wasn't home. It never would be. He avoided it as much as possible. It was a reminder of what he'd lost and that he was alone.

I hate this place. It feels like a prison.

Immediately, he scoffed at the absurdity of his comparison. "Dude, you need to get a grip. Look around," he grumbled.

His eyes canvassed his bedroom, taking in the expensive furnishings, the sixty-five-inch, wall-mounted television, and the skylight above him.

Yeah, asshole, I'm sure the cell Maryn Pearce is going to spend the rest of her life in looks just like this.

Her case continued to make him uneasy. After he'd hung up with Sister Helena, he poured over the notes from the preliminary hearing. Clearly filled with hatred and anger, her husband's testimony against her was brutal. Burton's denial of bail, even considering the extenuating motive behind her actions, was proof that Thomas Pearce's testimony weighed in heavily on the decision.

While he could understand the guy being upset and angry at his wife for creating such a mess in their lives, Gavin found Pearce's behavior odd. Admittedly, however, he probably wasn't the best judge of character, since he was also quite adept at creating messes in his own family's life. Still, Pearce's behavior didn't settle right with him.

You'd think that since he was a cop, he would have a greater sense of loyalty to his family.

Again, his failures with his own family mocked him, but he forced the thoughts from his mind and tried to focus on Maryn's welfare.

"I still need to figure a way to get her out of there," he whispered, punching his pillow and turning onto his side.

Along with the change in his position, his mind also took an unexpected turn, as a memory of his father surfaced. Joseph Anton Steele served for almost twenty-five years for the San Francisco Police Department, until he was fatally shot by a drug dealer during a bust.

The man who shot him was a convicted felon who had previously been deported six times. Just months prior to the incident, the thug had re-entered the country illegally and made his way to San Francisco, a sanctuary city. Presently the need for sanctuary cities no longer existed. The battle against illegal immigration had been hard-fought, but the borders of the U.S. were open to all.

The puppet masters have the immigrants just where they want them. They'll offer them government programs and entitlements to ensure their votes each election cycle.

Gavin shook his head. *Democracy and justice are all but dead.*

His father's death had been the deciding factor in his choice to be a lawyer. At the time of his tragic murder, Gavin felt patriotic as hell—determined to mete out justice without getting killed in the process. He'd been smug about it then and still felt smug in the knowledge that he'd chosen the wiser path. In fact, he was more certain now than ever. There was just no way he could have followed in his old man's footsteps—dealing with the dregs of society, watching good, decent people being pushed back into their homes, having to look over their shoulders while they went about their lives terrorized in their own neighborhoods. Clutching their children's hands to prevent them from being snatched and sold into sex-trafficking.

As if our country didn't have enough criminals on our own. Now, thugs from other countries can walk right in with the decent people and collect entitlements until they can find a better way to get rich through committing crimes.

"Glad my old man smoked that bastard before he hit the ground," he grumbled.

You mean like the bastard you just defended?

He hadn't even finished the sentence when the truth smacked him in the face.

He lay there, still. His heart was pounding, his stomach churning. With the intensity of a sledgehammer, his blatant hypocrisy dealt him a heavy, crushing blow. The stillness of the room allowed him to hear the thundering of his treacherous heart.

There was a very good chance that Maryn Pearce would rot in jail because of her misguided attempt to prevent a medical injury. He, on the other hand, helped Eduardo Rojas walk out of the courtroom a free man, able to resume the countless illegal activities, of which, he swore he had no knowledge. The irony was brutal.

I lie here complaining about a crooked system and government, full-well knowing I've worked it toward my own good a thousand times.

Gavin nearly sprung from the bed. There was no way he was going to lay there with nothing to think about but his own debauchery.

The bar in the master suite was empty, except for the half-full bottle of scotch he'd put there after leaving Sister Helena at Frank's Place. Just the sight of it flooded his senses with relief.

His hand shook with anticipation as he poured the first drink. By time he'd downed his third, it was as steady as a rock. After his fifth, he'd all but forgotten what a hypocritical loser he really was.

"TV on," he commanded.

It was late. A male enhancement commercial preceded an erectile dysfunction commercial. Gavin looked down at his lap. "Sorry pal, none of that for you," he mumbled. "You already got me into enough trouble…I'm not falling for that again."

He quickly changed the direction of his channel surfing away from the dozens of adult-rated programs available at the click of his remote or simple voice command for porn. He'd blocked the adult channels in the rare hope that Lucas or Brenna would stay the night with him at some point, but every so often, more were added to his cable package without his knowledge. It was hard to stay ahead of it.

"Let's see here…infomercial…sitcom reruns…gory crime scene shows…nut-job, psychic. Oh…and here's the Spoiled Housewives. They're so dysfunctional, they even make me look good."

He shook his head. "Three hundred friggin' channels and nothin' wortha damn to watch."

Suddenly, he stopped channel surfing and stared at the screen. A vague memory surfaced of news footage aired during the recent court battles over mandated vaccination. The footage featured a celebrity who, nearly thirty years prior, shot out of the gate with accusations that her son's Autism was caused by his vaccinations. Despite her celebrity status and valiant efforts, she stood nearly alone in her fight. Presently, he couldn't recall her name, but recently, during the unsuccessful fight against the passage of mandatory laws, she was joined by hundreds of thousands of others who also claimed they had experienced vaccine injury.

In Gavin's estimation, the problem was that every time a credible vaccine-injury report surfaced, it was quickly debunked by government studies showing no correlation to the vaccines, so any validation for the skepticism quickly turned into disdain and ridicule. *In a nutshell, most people are scared to death of viruses and even more petrified of those who are unvaccinated.*

The more he thought about it, the more sheepish he felt. He'd been so caught up in his divorce, the Rojas case, and trying to stay sober, that he'd paid little attention. His kids were fully-vaccinated and were fine. He could at least take comfort in that, but his stomach instantly tightened at the real possibility that the passage of the mandatory vaccination laws was already wreaking the havoc so many had predicted.

He downed the remaining scotch in his glass and reached over to pull his briefcase off the table. Grabbing the legal pad inside, he scribbled down a reminder.

If she's back tomorrow, I'll have Sylvie research this celebrity's claims. Maybe by tomorrow I'll be able to remember her name.

He stared at the television screen. As sauced as he was, he was still sober enough to be paranoid. No amount of government assurance would ever convince him that the Feds and industry giants had quit spying on people of interest—and more than likely, everyone, through "smart" devices that were listening to their conversations and tracking every move they made. It would seem the American public couldn't get enough of intrusive devices, as long as they tantalized their senses or seemingly made their lives easier.

After the Info-leaks blew the scandal wide open in 2015, it took congress several years before new legislation was signed that supposedly prevented it from happening again. Now, almost ten years later, Gavin remained unconvinced.

Despite the promised hi-tech programs developed to stop hackers and alert systems to suspicious activity or signals, he didn't fully trust *any* technology. There was too much money involved for it to be unaffected by corruption. For that same reason, it shouldn't have come as a surprise to anyone that the mandated vaccine bill had passed almost immediately with the newly-elected president, his liberal agenda, and his power-hungry minions.

Gavin figured it would take a major collapse of the economy or another national tragedy to bring most, including himself, out of their apathetic stupor. Still, there were times when he wondered if the country could even survive—if it was only a matter of time before the good ol' USA no longer existed as it once was. Too few politicians seemed to remember why they were elected. Freedoms were forfeited in favor of political correctness, bartered like trading cards on the playground.

Meanwhile, much of the youth were being raised by social media and television, forcing educators to dumb-down the curriculum to accommodate waning attention spans and lack of parental influence and support. Consequently, the average college-age person might not be able to come up with the name of the current vice president but would confidently declare Socialism as the fix-all for the country because it meant free tuition. Ironically, these same advocates wouldn't be the ones to have their own wealth redistributed for decades to come, because they had none.

No wonder I drink.

Disgusted and overwhelmed by it all, Gavin got up and staggered to the linen closet. Grabbing a sheet, he walked into his bedroom and made several clumsy attempts to hang it over the screen.

When he'd finally succeeded, he gloated triumphantly. "Take *that* ya dirty bastards…and I'm gonna have Sylvie do th' research at th' library. That way, ya can't spy on her or see what we're researching."

Despite his bravado, a seed of remorse for getting soused took root in his gut as he headed back to bed. With each wobbly step, the guilt increased. By the time he'd crawled under the covers, Gavin's heart and head were pounding.

The escape he'd recently enjoyed, now eluded him. Anxiety filled his being, pushing out any semblance of hope. An accusing voice rose up inside him to point out his failure, his continued weakness. The voice reminded him that he hadn't been there enough for his kids, either. They hadn't returned his calls even though he'd left messages. The voice also reminded him that Annie left him because of his own failure to control himself.

How can I expect the youth to know better, do better, when I don't?

A bitter tear escaped from his closed eyes and trickled down to pool in his ear. "When am I ever going to get my act together?" he whispered. "I'm sucha loser."

The voice immediately urged him to take some pills for his headache. ***Lots of pills.***

The urge to comply was strong. Gavin's head was spinning. The callous words he'd thrown at Sister Helena regarding her useless prayers came back to punch him in the gut. Even so, he sensed she was praying for him at that very moment and was certain she was the only soul on earth who would ever exert herself to pray for him.

I have called you by name and you are Mine.

Though silence filled the room, the voice that spoke inside him was commanding, yet very different than the accusing voice. Imagined or not, Gavin felt comforted.

The skylight allowed him to stare up at the stars blanketing the sky. The vast beauty made him ponder his smallness in comparison, yet he recognized the significance of the moment at the same time. He was free to embrace the infinite or choose the finite. The decision was his.

His mind drifted to another whose life was hanging in the balance because of her choices.

How backwards is that? I helped set a guilty man free, but Maryn Pearce is rotting in a prison cell because she tried to save lives. It's going to cost her everything unless I can find a loophole. The pharmaceuticals and government agencies are a modern-day Goliath...but the problem is, I'm no David.

The truth was sobering.

"God, help me to not mess this up," he whispered woefully.

Gavin repeated the request several times before the alcohol and sheer exhaustion won out, and he fell into a deep, drunken sleep.

Chapter 7

Thomas lay intertwined with her, his breath on her cheek, their sand-covered feet mingling, caressing one another. Despite the cooler temperature, both were warm, a little sunburned, actually. Neither cared.

Maryn was so happy. She looked deep into his eyes and saw her reflection. "I am so happy, Thomas," she whispered, "so happy that I can't believe it's real—that *you're* real."

He grinned back at her. "I'm *real*," he assured her, his sky-blue eyes suddenly appearing much darker with his passionate admission.

She reached up and smoothed back the sandy blonde hair from his forehead. "Are you sure I'm not going to wake up one day only to realize this is a dream?" she teased, but in truth, wanting reassurance. The thought of ever losing him was terrifying.

Thomas sat up and reached into the cooler beside him. Pulling out two glasses and a bottle of champagne, he grinned and said, "Let's celebrate!"

Taken completely by surprise, Maryn's mouth dropped open. For several seconds, she was speechless and then giggled delightedly at his resourcefulness. "What? How did you sneak this by me?"

Thomas shrugged and answered mischievously, "You don't have to know *all* my secrets."

Maryn eyed him suspiciously, just to tease him, and then answered truthfully, "Well, I don't need to know *all* of them, but I sure do want to know the important ones...like why we are celebrating!"

"Okay...so here's the most important secret I will *ever* reveal to you...I love you, Maryn. I *really* do. And what we're celebrating is our future together...if you'll have me."

He reached down and took her hand. Before she could even absorb what was happening, he slipped an engagement ring onto her finger. "Please say yes, Maryn. I could *never* live without you. That would be like trying to breathe without my lungs...trying to see the world without my eyes."

The tears in his eyes, mirrored her own. "I'm a simple man...and I know I don't have much to offer you except my love, but my love can be trusted. It's *forever*."

"Forever," Maryn repeated.

Her eyes snapped open at the sound of her own voice. It took her a few moments to realize where she was, to separate the dream she'd just had from the reality of her shattered existence.

The cell was still dark, but a glance at her watch told her that the morning alarm would be blaring in a matter of minutes.

Normally, she would have enjoyed waking from such a surreal reenactment of their remarkable engagement. Now, it only served as a reminder of Thomas' betrayal. Waking up made the fairytale into a nightmare.

Though the dream had been about Thomas, as usual, the first thing on her mind was her girls. *I must have told the girls at least a hundred times that I would love them forever and a day.*

The realization was hard to bear. "They surely must feel as betrayed as I do," she whispered achingly.

Valiantly, she made several attempts to force the thoughts from her mind, but they remained, like an anchor weighing down her chest, pushing her to the bottom of an ocean of despair.

"Jesus, help me!" she choked, forcing herself to sit up.

In truth, the memory of Thomas' broken promise to love her was more painful than being locked up. If he was angry enough to want her dead, his rejection and testimony against her had almost succeeded.

The pressure in her chest from the heaviness of pain became so intense that she wondered if her heart would simply stop beating. There was a part of her that wished it would.

I should have known, she lamented.

Even in the beginning, she worried whether it was all too good to be true. Thomas was the perfect knight in shining armor of her dreams—handsome, humble, funny, loyal and brave.

Maryn was so proud that he was a police officer, especially so because he'd chosen his profession in spite of the rioting against law enforcement that had gone on for nearly two previous decades. The hate-speech, marches, name-calling, and execution-style murders of police officers were detrimental enough, but the lack of government support and the threats of lawsuits continued to take its toll on the number of men and women willing to risk their lives. Law enforcement numbers had dropped to less than half, while crimes of all nature had more than tripled. Still, Thomas' determination to enter the police force, despite the high risk he would face every day, was impressive and patriotic—or so she'd believed.

Now, she felt betrayed by his status. His treachery rose up within her like steam from a geyser, causing an eruption of resentment to push back against the anchor's pressure.

Who are you Thomas Pearce? What has become of you? You promised to protect and uphold the law, but what about when the law is not just? What about your vow to love and honor me? What about protecting me? Our daughters? The innocent?

Anger slowly took the place of the heartache, rejection, fear, and insecurity. Her dream, which would have normally left her longing for his love and to be in his arms again, forced her to grasp the depth of his betrayal. Upon reflecting upon his empty promises, her heart, previously broken in a thousand pieces, suddenly felt like a cold, hard stone.

Maryn tried not to feel anything at all as she forced herself from the bed to use the toilet. It was important that she be stronger than ever. Because she'd been on suicide watch, she had been kept from the worst of prison life, but she was smart enough to realize that it was about to change at any moment. Ironically, concern over what the day would bring helped push back the devastation she felt from Thomas' betrayal.

Maryn realized, as she set to the task of making her bed, that she had officially transitioned into survival mode.

From now on she would be forced to do what was asked of her by those in charge at the women's facility. Her life, and all that she'd known, was gone. Strangely, a powerful yearning and determination had blossomed within her at the grasping of her fate. With it came a force of will so strong she was sure nothing or no one could take it from her. In that moment, she became fully aware that she must be resolutely determined to survive—long enough to write down the truth for her girls or explain it in person when they were older.

My girls will know their mother. I will make them understand—one way or another, how much I love them and why I made the decisions I made.

They can take everything away from me here, including my life, but they cannot take the truth from me. They can't take away my love for my babies.

With great resolve, she neatly tucked the corner of her scratchy, worn blanket under the mattress.

"I am going to fight these charges," she whispered into the dark cell. "Lily and Pearl are going to know what *real,* forever love looks like."

Sister Helena and my new lawyer will help me. I have to believe that God sent them because He knows what I've been through. He knows my heart.

The morning alarm sounded, startling her and putting an end to her thoughts and newly-found courage. The high-pitched frequency shook every inch of her body, causing her heart to hammer with anticipation of what the day would bring. It took every ounce of her will to say a prayer rather than panic.

After Thomas gave his testimony in court against her, she couldn't really pray. Her hope and love had been trampled underfoot. Thomas had become a stranger, and God seemed like a stranger as well—or part of a fairy tale that was as unreliable as Thomas's promise to love her. Now, however, she couldn't deny that she felt His presence when Sister Helena prayed for her, and again during the night, when she was certain she heard His reassuring voice speaking to her soul to give her peace.

The memory now encouraged her to pray for the strength and endurance to face all that lay ahead. She prayed also that Thomas would not turn the girls against her. The trauma that they had already endured would only worsen if he chose that route.

At the very thought, the emptiness she felt without Lily and Pearl was indescribable. Her arms ached with the need to hold them. They were in her thoughts constantly.

What have they been told? Are they scared? Are they asking for me? What will I say to them when I finally get to see them?

If she closed her eyes, she could still see the angry, unshed tears in Thomas's eyes and his red face as he shouted accusingly at her in the courtroom. The recollection quickly squelched any hope that he would have softened his heart by now. Her heart squeezed in her chest.

Maryn turned on the faucet and waited until enough cold water trickled into her hands to splash onto her face.

Afterward, she stared at her reflection in the rusty, broken mirror. A jagged crack in the glass separated her eyes from the rest of her face. She was almost unrecognizable. With the swelling and dark circles beneath them, her blue eyes look colorless and haunted—as if the pair belonged to someone else, in a different time and space. Her expression was pained, her mouth turned downward.

"There is nothing pretty about this face," she whispered sadly, immediately thinking of Thomas's handsome face, his fit frame.

The urge to blame her haggard appearance as part of why he'd betrayed her was powerful. She cringed, acknowledging that she had never quite gotten back down to her pre-pregnancy weight. Her body had shifted and gotten soft in places she wasn't at all proud of.

Thomas never said a word about my extra weight, but, then again, he also told me he would love me forever.

Despite her earlier resolve to be strong, hopeless tears threatened to fall again.

"God please," she begged, "I just *can't* start crying again…I don't have the energy. Please renew my hope and give me the strength to carry on."

Maryn had no more finished her prayer when the door to her cell opened. A stocky, pinched-face woman stepped inside. She glanced quickly around the cell and then gave her the once over.

"Time for breakfast," she barked, without looking her in the eye. "Follow me, get in line, and keep your mouth shut, if you know what's good for you."

Chapter 8

The first annoyance of the day Gavin could have avoided and didn't was his hangover. The second was forgetting that Eduardo Rojas had left a message stating that he was sending in his cousin, "who needed some extra help with a serious problem."

Hoping to work on the Pearce case, Gavin arrived at the office earlier than usual, only to find another message from Eduardo on his answering machine.

"Damnit! I'm an *idiot!*" he growled into the empty room.

I forgot to call him back and let him know I'm unavailable. His cousin's probably another worthless drug dealer, and now, Sylvie's not here to get rid of him.

He groaned at the thought and swore a string of cuss words that almost made him blush.

After his tirade, which did nothing more than to prove he had a mouth as filthy as a sewer, he blew out a deep, shaky breath and stared down at the mess he'd left on his desk.

Reminds me of the mess I've made of my life.

Before he'd started drinking the previous night, he had texted both kids. Lucas still hadn't answered back. Brenna threw him a bone and texted him a thumbs-up emoji. When he saw it, the temptation to throw his smart phone in the toilet was fierce. Instead, he decided the better response was to cancel the kids' phone plans.

That'll get their attention.

With that very intention, he did a quick search for the phone number, and in just seconds, was punching numbers on the dinosaur to carry out his threat.

"Press one for Spanish...Presiona uno para español. Two for German...Zwei für Deutsch. Press three for French...Appuyez trois pour le français. Press four for other languages, five for English. If you would like to check your account balance..."

Gavin ground his teeth in annoyance. "Why the hell isn't English the first choice?" he growled into the receiver, wishing he was talking to a human being rather than going postal on a recorded voice.

"Excuse me..."

Gavin's head shot up to see a petite, dark-haired woman standing in the doorway, with a wide-eyed toddler on her hip. Holding her free hand was a little girl that looked almost identical to her mother.

He glanced at the clock. It was 8:15.

Inwardly, his own chastisement began again. He cursed himself for being careless enough to forget to lock the doors behind him. The oversight was dangerous. It could have been any of the thousands of addicts and thugs mulling about the city looking for a hand out or an easy target to rob.

His office was located on the 5th floor of a six-story high-rise, in the heart of Palo Alto. The building housed everything from private accountants, insurance agents, chiropractic services, to shrinks and more. He sincerely hoped against all hope, that the woman was just lost. Either way, he marveled at her nerve to walk through the front office and into his private office, like she had a right to be there.

"This office doesn't open until nine," he blurted, without so much as a hello or an ounce of regret. He had way too much on his plate to do otherwise. "And you'll need to call during office hours to set up an appointment," he finished, clearly dismissing her.

"I'm sorry, but I was told that Gavin Steele was expecting me," she responded, undeterred.

"Well, that's not the way it works here," he grunted, opening a file cabinet and pulling out a file. "There are no appointments made before office hours. So, like I said, call the office."

Something about the look on her face made him think she was about to cry. *That's all I need...*

He was wrong.

She squared her shoulders and stated, "My name is Isabella Sanchez, my cousin is Eduardo Rojas. You are his lawyer."

Gavin would have paid a lot of money to be able to get away with groaning aloud at that moment. Not only had he meant to distance himself from Rojas, but the last thing he wanted to do was deal with his relative, and particularly, the woman standing before him. Something about the look on her face made him certain he was walking a fine line between her dissolving into a fit of tears or having his name added to a hit list.

Gavin shrugged. "Yeah...well, I *was* Eduardo's lawyer, and he did mention a cousin on a message, but I never got back with him to confirm my availability."

"So, you *are* Gavin Steele," she declared triumphantly.

He cringed. *Me and my big damn mouth.*

She didn't wait for his confirmation, but rushed to explain, "I've been to fifteen other lawyers. None of them would take my case."

Isabella stared him down. "Cousin Eduardo said you are no coward," she challenged.

Gavin let out a sardonic chuckle. "Well, your cousin *was* my client, but he doesn't know my work schedule or my level of courage for that matter. I'm sorry, but I really can't help you. Now if you'll excuse me..."

"My son's *life* is in *jeopardy*," she replied. The tone of her voice was grave, driven.

He felt a slight twinge of sympathy for whatever she was going through, but answered firmly, "I'm sorry, I wish I could help, but I can't."

"If I do not give him the shot, he cannot go to daycare or start school when it's time," she declared without pause.

It didn't take but two seconds for him to grasp her issue.

Marveling at the irony, he softened his tone and said, "I am sure you are talking about the immunization requirements. If your child has a potential issue, you can file a medical exemption. The form can be downloaded on the state's website or filled out and submitted online. Now, if you'll excuse me, I have a lot of work to do, and my office is *closed*."

"I know all about the exemption," she shot back, her eyes boring into him. "Do you think I would have gone to so many lawyers if this was a matter of an *exemption*?" she spat. "*Look* at my *daughter*! Look at her *closely*," she added pleadingly.

Before Gavin knew what was happening, Isabella had positioned her little girl right in front of him.

Gavin couldn't deny that she was a beautiful child. Dark hair, perfect olive skin and rosy lips. "You're a beautiful little girl," he said softly, giving her as much of a smile as he could muster.

"Look at my Sophia's *eyes*!" Isabella demanded, "It is like she's not there anymore."

He would have to be blind to not notice what she was talking about. The little girl was completely emotionless. She appeared to be looking right at him, but then suddenly, her eyes moved slowly to one side and then appear to sort of slip and catch, like the skipping of an old movie reel.

Poor kid.

"Look," he began, "I *do* feel sympathy for you…and your daughter. It's obvious that she needs to see a doctor, and if they determine that her condition was caused by the immunization, your physician will more than likely give you a medical exemption for your son. There are lots of malpractice lawyers who deal with this type of thing who are much better qualified than I am."

Isabella's lip began to quiver, but the look in her eyes made him sure that her anger eclipsed any other emotion she was feeling. "And you think I don't *know* that?" she hissed, not even attempting to hide her irritation.

"I'm *sorry*, but I can't help you."

"You *can* help me," she countered, angrily. "You *won't* help me. You're just like all the rest—either too lazy and rich to care, or too afraid of what will happen…and I *get* that, but…"

"What do you mean, *afraid* of what will happen?" Gavin answered defensively. "I'm not *afraid* to take your case. I just know that it would take a lot of money and time to get your case heard. I don't have the time right now, especially considering the new mandates. We'd be swimming against the tide."

"You *are* afraid!" she accused. "Either that, or you are worried I can't pay. You *know* who my cousin is! Even though we don't conduct our lives the same, surely you must know that he would help with the money! We are *family*! He called you and told you I was coming! You are *afraid*!"

"Why do you keep saying that? What in the hell would I be afraid of?" he asked again, now, not only irritated, but highly curious.

Isabella got very quiet. Her baby boy had fallen asleep on her shoulder. Despite her small stature, she never shifted his chubby, all-boy frame, even once. She glared defiantly at Gavin for several seconds before a single tear slipped over her bottom lashes and slowly rolled down her cheek.

"That they'll kill you," she answered soberly.

Even if he had tried a hundred times to guess her answer, he would have never gotten it right. "*Kill me? Who* would kill me... why would anyone even *care* that I was defending you?" he asked dismissively. "Immunization injury cases are litigated all the time."

"I don't *know* who's doing the killing," she admitted. "I only became aware of it when I started looking for answers to find help for my Sophia. But make no mistake, those who speak out against this vaccine are dying."

Gavin looked at her in disbelief. "What exactly led you to believe this? What do you mean, they're *dying*?"

"Accidents...heart attacks...car wrecks..."

"People have heart attacks and accidents all the time," he interrupted, "you can't make that leap to say that someone has killed them because of some common, childhood vacc...ine..."

He stopped mid-sentence. Pure adrenaline pulsed through his veins, mostly because it had taken so long for him to realize the possibility that she could be talking about the same vaccination that landed Maryn in jail.

"What vaccine are we talking about here?" he demanded.

"Lunatia."

Chapter 9

Gavin was never so happy to see Sylvie walk through the door—even if he was a little leery of her dragging along her sons' flu-bugs with her. All things considered, he'd gladly put his germaphobe paranoia aside to have her help.

In less than an hour, he was due in court to represent two different clients, back to back. He also hoped to squeeze in a meeting with Judge Burton to see if there was anything he could do to get Maryn released.

Isabella Sanchez's visit had changed everything. Even though he had squat for proof, there was enough to her story that rang true to spur him forward with greater intensity. Still, even though he'd come up with a plausible argument to file for Maryn's release, the chances of getting the judge to change his mind was slim—her husband's testimony was highly persuasive, and Burton's ego was massive.

"Sylvie, I need you to do some research for me," he blurted the minute she took off her coat.

"Hello to you too," she offered dryly. "My boys are getting better. Thanks for asking."

"Sorry," he answered sincerely, "but I'm up to my ass in alligators this morning, and to say that I really need your help is the understatement of the year."

Sylvie tipped her head to one side and took a good look at him. In the entire time she'd worked for him, she'd only heard him apologize once, when she overheard him on the phone with his ex.

Whoa. This must be serious.

"Okay, what do you need?" she asked.

He grabbed the legal pad he'd written on the night before, flipped the page, and scribbled on it for a minute or so. He tore it out, handed it to her, and said, "I need you to research this at the library."

"The *library*?" she chuckled, sure he was joking. "Why not here?"

"I don't want the searches on our computer system…just trust me, okay?"

He was clearly on edge. "Okay. You don't have to get all worked up about it. I'll do it."

She glanced down at the paper. "Gavin…this is all about vaccines…oh my *god!*" she gasped. "Are you *really* going to get mixed up in that woman's case?"

"I don't have time to get into the details," he offered, ignoring her question. He couldn't deny that a part of him wanted to avoid the discussion forever, "but to make a long story short, a woman named Isabella Sanchez—a relative of Eduardo Rojas, showed up at the office this morning. She believes her daughter Sophia was severely vaccine injured—and from the looks of her, something happened. I just need to know what's out there on the net regarding what I've given you to research. I've got a lot going on and have to be in court this morning," he continued, glancing at his watch. "I'll try and touch base with you on your discovery as soon as I can. I really want some back-up in case Burton gets stubborn…and yes, I *am* taking the Pearce case."

Sylvie's mouth hung open for several seconds. "Wow…good luck with *that*," she finally offered sarcastically.

Gavin closed his briefcase and grabbed his coat. "Don't talk to *anyone* about this. No one. I mean it, Sylvie. If you do, consider yourself *fired*. Don't use your cell phone to call or text me about any of it, either. I'll talk to you in the office…or when I can."

Her dark-blue eyes widened. "Well, *geez*…now you're sounding a little weird—and *scary*. What's going on?"

"No need to be scared. I just don't want reporters hanging around here. I also don't want anyone getting wind of what we are researching. If they do, then Maryn Pearce will have a much harder time being exonerated."

"Yeah, like impossible already," Sylvie scoffed.

"Don't be so quick to judge—that's always the first mistake. I had a visitor this morning that gives me reason to believe that Pearce might have had good reason to do what she did. It's all conjecture at this point, of course, but keep it under your hat."

Still trying to take it all in, Sylvie merely nodded. "What about your schedule for the rest of the week?" she finally asked.

"Don't schedule *anything*. I'm full. *Nothing*. In fact, don't commit to anything for the rest of the month, unless you hear from me otherwise."

Her eyes widened. "Are you *serious*? Like, are you going out of business or something?"

He laughed. "Oh, how I wish it would be that easy, but no. Your job's secure. All is well—for now, anyway. Oh…I almost forgot…if Sister calls, don't talk about the Pearce case with her. Just assure her that I still plan on meeting with her this afternoon."

Slightly unsettled, Sylvie robotically slipped her coat back on and grabbed her purse while he held the office door open for her. "Okay, I'll do my best," she replied with sincerity.

"That's all I ask," he answered soberly, before heading in the opposite direction toward the stairwell.

At the sight, a niggling feeling of apprehension washed over Sylvie and settled into her bones. *If he's too impatient to take the elevator, whatever's going on must be big.*

With the legal sheet tucked into her purse, she protectively pulled the bag closer to her waist and looped her thumb around the strap.

The thought of Maryn Pearce being in jail gave her pause. She thought of how awful it would be for her boys if something like that ever happened to her.

I sure hope this turns out to be nothing, but if there's something to be found, I hope I can find it.

The elevator doors opened. Sylvie was relieved it was empty. Despite her determination and Gavin's reassurance that all was well, she couldn't help but feel as though something monumental was about to happen. After his adamant warnings to be so cautious, she sincerely hoped that her boss knew what he was getting into—for all their sakes.

*****

Gavin's jaw literally ached from chewing his nicotine gum so zealously. Even so, he popped two more pieces into his mouth as he waited for the elevator to open on the 4th floor.

Though his cases for the morning had gone remarkably well, they took longer than he'd expected; and unfortunately, the meeting with Judge Burton had been a complete waste of time. He was kicking himself for not waiting until he had talked to Sylvie to see what she had uncovered before approaching the hard-headed old goat. A text from her indicating that she had some information to share with him had caused him to jump the gun. Now, he deeply regretted jumping in with both feet, especially after how close-minded and downright angry Judge Burton was at even the mention of reconsidering Pearce's bail.

Gavin sighed at the memory. The excitement he'd initially felt in knowing Sylvie had found something had turned into dread. If they couldn't find a similar case, wherein a person's conscience gave them valid cause to break or postpone obeying a law directly related to an individual's health or welfare, Maryn Pearce could very well be toast. On the other hand, if Sylvie uncovered even a smidgeon of evidence backing up what Isabella Sanchez claimed, the potential for unimaginable chaos was more than tangible—it was a given.

He looked up to see Sylvie waiting for him in the doorway and his pace quickened. *Whatever she found must be good.*

Before he even got a chance to say hello, she literally pulled him inside and locked the door.

Straight away, he noticed that her coat lay draped over her computer screen, and the door to his office was closed—something completely out of character. Sylvie always kept his door open when he was gone so she could enjoy the natural sunlight from the wall of windows behind his desk.

"What the hell did you find, Sylvie? You've got this place locked down tighter than Fort Knox."

He'd said it just to tease her, but one look at her expression convinced him she believed whatever she'd uncovered was serious business. Her face was pale, a stark contrast to her dark brown hair. Her arms were crossed as if she was warding off the cold.

"I did what you said, and I haven't told a soul," she declared, her deep-blue eyes shadowed with worry.

"Okay…what? Go ahead, I'm listening," he urged, crossing to the coffee table to lay down his briefcase.

"I don't even know where to start," she admitted. "First of all, I want to ask…did you know that more than ninety natural medicine and chiropractic doctors have died in the past several years? Most of who were very vocal about their concerns regarding vaccinations—and more recently, one in particular…called *Lunatia*. Twenty-four docs have died in the past year *alone*."

His eyes locked with hers. "Actually, I only recently was made aware of the deaths," he answered, trying to sound and remain objective. "I hadn't heard that kind of number. Is it a credible source?"

She shook her head. "No—nothing mainstream, anyway. It was mostly anti-vax, prepper sites—you know, the anti-government, right-wing conservative type," she explained. "But there were a few natural medicine and blogs that sure seemed credible."

"So then, we have *nothing*," he blurted, disappointed, but slightly relieved.

"No! We have *everything* to worry about," she countered, her expression so filled with angst that his pulse quickened.

"Without valid news sources or studies, we have *zero* proof, Sylvie!" he argued. "I can't build a case on quirky anti-vaxxers or paleo and vegan enthusiasts. Most of this country, and I'm certainly including Judge Burton, consider these groups to be a little whacky. There are *mountains* of evidence to prove that vaccinations have saved entire populations, so if the media ever had a chance to break a story like this, they'd be all over it."

"Are you referring to the *mainstream* media that you're always assuring me is *biased*?" Sylvie shot back smugly before continuing. "I assure you, the media isn't going to touch this shit with a ten-foot pole! *No one* is going to want to get involved with this. It's seriously the biggest scandal I could ever think of…and I'm pretty sure that it's the biggest cover up since the beginning of time."

Gavin really wanted to laugh out loud, but refrained. Obviously, she wholeheartedly believed she'd found something significant. Still, he had a hard time imagining that a few hours spent at the library could have uncovered the biggest scandal in history.

He pulled out her chair. "Have a seat. Let's discuss this. Want something to drink?" he asked, pulling two bottled teas out of the bag he'd carried in.

"No thanks."

Gavin shrugged, unscrewed the lid, and tossed his gum in the trash. After positioning a chair opposite her and settling in, he took several much-needed swallows and said, "Okay, so tell me…if there weren't any credible news sources, why are you so convinced?"

"Because," she began, reaching over with a trembling hand to grab the tea she'd just declined, "There were so *many* of these fruit-and-nut-type articles—as you call them, that I started doing obituary searches on random natural medicine doctors. By the time I'd searched six, maybe seven, I found a natural medicine doc that died six months ago."

"What'd he die from?"

"*She.* Dr. Kelly Browerton, fell over dead in a restaurant in Dallas. Supposed heart issue."

Immediately, Isabella Sanchez's assertions surfaced, causing him to feel an eerie chill down to the bone. Regardless, he had to be reasonable, remain objective. "Okay, so that's *one,* but what makes you think she is tied to Lunatia and that it wasn't just her time to go? People die from heart disease all the time."

Sylvie began cracking her knuckles nervously. "Yes, I *know,* but after reading the articles, I started to have my own worried thoughts creep in, so I kept searching articles on Kelly Browerton."

"I know I've heard the name before, but can't remember where…but go on."

"Browerton actually wrote multiple articles a couple decades ago on the Protecta vaccination."

"What's that one for?" Gavin asked.

Sylvie's mouth dropped. "If you really don't know then I have to say…you really dropped the ball, because your kids probably got it," she answered with a look that made him feel even more stupid than guilty.

"Anyway," she went on, "it's supposed to protect against a certain type of sexually transmitted disease that can lead to cancer."

He nodded. "Okay…I remember now. There was a big stink as to whether it should be included in the mandatory vaccination schedule. Go on."

"Yes, and with good reason. Dr. Browerton claimed that the vaccine had been prematurely pushed through the government regulatory agencies for approval. She also maintained that, not only was the vaccine ineffective against most strains of the sexually-transmitted virus, but it was also causing Guillain-Barre type symptoms in an alarming number of pre-teens and teens who were given the shot during their random school physicals."

Gavin thought a minute. "Isn't Guillain-Barre Syndrome the injury some claim to have gotten from the flu vaccine way back in the Seventies?"

"Yes!" Sylvie exclaimed, obviously thrilled he was getting her drift. "Dr. Browerton talked about that! Numbness, tingling, and paralysis are all a part of GBS—but there's more. Literally *hundreds* of symptoms related to Protecta were reported to VAERS—that's the government's vaccine reporting site, but it was never pulled. The *scariest* part is that some of the patients *died* from it."

Gavin blew out a gusty sigh. "How many?"

"I couldn't find anything that gave me a concrete number— just a couple of testimonies from grieving parents and one affidavit from a medical examiner who did an autopsy on a fourteen-year-old boy who keeled over at basketball practice.
"Apparently, the kid had received his immunization less than forty-eight hours prior, and the medical examiner discovered extensive swelling in his brain, which he believed was caused by the Protecta."

"So, is this *same* formula still on the market and part of the mandated vaccine schedule?" he asked, worriedly.

"Yes! And the really stupid thing is, they are giving it to patients as young as nine!" Sylvie exclaimed. "That's just plain crazy! And it's one thing to *offer* a vaccination for protection against sexual diseases, but another thing to *mandate* it for school! I mean…it's not like the virus is *airborne* or something contagious like a cold. It's *sexually* transmitted, so to require it for school is a complete violation of parental rights and an infringement on religious freedom. Despite all the reports to VAERS, nearly every state includes it in the mandated schedule for school immunization!"

Gavin wanted to swear a blue streak. He hated every aspect of the government's overreach with a passion. Things had gotten so out of control in the past years that he had to just quit talking about it. Rational thinking had ceased to be the norm.

"Okay, I *get* it," he finally answered, immediately wondering if his kids had received the Protecta.

"No," she argued, interrupting his thoughts. "I'm not sure you *do* get it…I'm not sure you are connecting the dots," she lamented, shaking her head.

Gavin wanted to laugh again. She was like a super-sleuth wanna-be. "Okay, Detective Sylvie, connect them for me then."

She answered without any indication that his teasing had even registered. "If the government agencies and pharms blew it that badly on the Protecta, why should parents trust them to get it right with the Lunatia…or *any* vaccine for that matter? According to what I found, the government pays out millions and millions every year to compensate the vaccine-injured."

Gavin nodded. He'd heard the claim before but dismissed it because his kids seemed to have breezed through most of their vaccinations with not much more than an occasional fever and crankiness afterward. Admittedly, he'd been gone more than he was present during their teen years, but he couldn't remember Annie talking about the Protecta or any side effects.

He pushed the guilt from his mind. "Okay, I get your point," he began again, "so back to this Dr. Browerton…what makes you think her death is suspicious…or connected to Lunatia?"

"Oh yeah," she said with a nod, pausing to take a drink of her tea. "First of all, one of the last articles she wrote was about the Lunavirus and how the Lunatia vaccine was not only unnecessary but potentially dangerous. She claimed that most who contracted the Lunavirus would have a mild fever and rash that would come and go as more of a nuisance than anything. Only in rare instances would it be a problem—mostly because of an already-challenged immune system. She also contended that, like the Protecta, Lunatia hadn't been through enough testing."

"Okay. Go on...proof...I need *proof*."

"Gavin...the woman was in *tip-top* shape! She was a runner and nutrition *freak*. Seems really odd that she would just keel over of a heart condition, right?"

Gavin raised his eyebrows.

Sylvie went on without waiting for an answer. "Anyway, there's more. After I found her obituary and the article, I did a search on her name with the words, vaccine and injury. Sure enough, I found multiple articles and even some videos of her giving testimony of her beliefs and findings. So then, I went back to the articles and searched names that were mentioned in them. Each natural med doctor led me to more articles and more names of natural doctors. Sure enough, when I searched for obituaries, I found at least six more—car wreck, freak accident, suicide, and...get this...one doctor and his entire family were found murdered in their home. No arrests made to date. Another doc was found floating head-down in a lake—a bullet hole to his chest. They've ruled it a suicide, even though they have yet to recover the gun he supposedly used, despite dragging the lake repeatedly."

The two stared at each other for a while before Gavin asked, "So you found seven. Where'd you get the idea that there were twenty-four recent deaths?"

"From the multiple articles written by the less-credible sources. I figure that once you've found six, twenty-four doesn't seem loony at all. And...I did happen to find a *legit* newspaper article about a researcher who worked for the CDC a decade or more ago. He had reportedly made statements that the current flu vaccine was *causing* a flu outbreak. That part is rumor, I know, but the story about this guy disappearing all of the sudden was covered by multiple news sources—both hardcopy and on the web. Weeks later, he was also found in the lake. No foul play was suspected. Yeah...right, like most people kill themselves by drowning themselves," she added, rolling her eyes.

"Anyway, I wrote his name and everything I could find down for you," she said, handing him the legal pad she'd used.

Gavin's mind was racing. He reached into his coat pocket to grab more nicotine gum and then thought better of it. His heart was pounding so hard he worried the nicotine might just put him under.

"Sylvie, you've done a great job," was all he could think of to say.

After several anxious moments of silence, Gavin blurted, "I just want to remind you again, don't talk to *anyone* about any of this. I have to figure out what to do...how to proceed."

"What *are* you going to do?" she asked, completely dismissing the fact that he'd just admitted he didn't know what to do.

He mustered a small smile. "I just *said* that I don't know."

She nodded and chuckled nervously. "Sorry. I'm just so rattled. This is freaking scary. I mean, *really* freaking scary. I just can't believe that it's all out there in the wide open, but covered up...like, it's in plain sight but no one's paying any attention. I haven't heard a whiff of it on the news or any of the social media outlets. Have you?"

He rolled his eyes. "Are you *kidding* me? *No*. I don't do social media, and you know that I quit listening to most of the news media a long time ago."

I don't even know if my kids got the Protecta or the Lunatia, he lamented silently.

"I know," she admitted, "but *seriously*, don't you think it's just crazy that we haven't heard *anything* about this string of natural doctors dying? The other doctor that supposedly committed suicide was touted to have tried to prove a cancer-causing link in vaccines due to carcinogenic adjuvants used in them. The doctor whose entire family was killed with him had just released his findings on the link between the DNA from the aborted fetal cells in vaccines and increased autism."

"*DNA?* What are you talking about? Why would an immunization contain DNA—you can't mean *human* DNA..."

"Yes!" she exclaimed. "From what I read—and I *did* find legitimate sources for this, including the CDC's list of ingredients, that originally all vaccines were created from aborted fetal cells and many still contain them. There is even a *set amount* of human DNA that's allowed in each vaccine."

Gavin pulled a face. "I'm trying to wrap my head around this...another person's DNA has been directly injected into our bodies? I feel like I surely must have known about this, but for the life of me I can't remember discussing this with Annie."

"Not *has been*...it *is* being injected! When the truth came out about the aborted fetal cell lines, pro-life advocates were disgusted and *livid* that this had not only been going on but had been kept quiet. Truth was, most doctors didn't even know about it—a few still probably don't. They just do what they've been told and taught to do in medical school—that's what some of the sites said, anyway.

"But now that the *baby's out of the bag*, so to speak, the vaccine makers are using animal cells more, pig, monkey, and bovine, but there are *still* many vaccinations that contain human DNA—the chickenpox vaccination, for one."

Gavin thought a while before answering. "Our DNA is so individual, so I just can't wrap my head around this. What in the *hell* does that do to our own body's immune response? I mean...doctors don't mix one blood type with another...you know what I mean?"

"Exactly! Autoimmune diseases have exploded in recent decades—you know, like celiac disease, rheumatoid arthritis, asthma, ALS...the list is *staggering*, and some doctors who are studying these diseases are certain the increase is directly correlated to the increase in vaccines, so you have to wonder if it's the DNA exchange or the other toxins that could be contributing. From what I read, the vaccination program has been one giant experiment from the get-go, and geez, if this is all true..."

Gavin slowly shook his head before saying, "I can understand a coverup of a recent drug or vaccination like Lunatia, but how would it be possible for this type of massive collusion? I know for a fact they've done studies on the Autism risks and vaccine safety..."

Sylvie let out a grunt. "You're the one who told me one time that you can get the results of a study to say anything you want them to say as long as you can manipulate the data and controls."

He gave her a wry grin and raised his eyebrow. "So...you really do listen to me on occasion."

"I try hard not to," she shot back teasingly.

Gavin would have laughed, but his head was swimming with the implications. "Sylvie, if what you've uncovered is right...if the twenty-some physicians—or even *one* of them has been somehow snuffed out because of what they know, then this cover-up is so big that it would take a miracle bigger than the Resurrection to bring everyone involved to justice."

Sylvie nodded and said soberly, "Then you better start getting in shape."

"For what? I'm not following," he admitted.

"If you take on Maryn Pearce's case and the manufacturers of Lunatia—which will threaten all big pharmaceuticals, we both know that you'll be taking a bite out of the ass of one of the biggest, scariest dogs I can think of. You better get used to running...and *fast*."

Chapter 10

Gavin's senses were on high-alert as he walked through the door of the Almeda County Women's Correction Facility. He felt more than a little silly for his occasional urge to look over his shoulder and suspiciously eye his surroundings. Still, he continued a state of increased awareness.

He cursed the fact that he was even a few minutes late. He needed all the time he could get with Maryn Pearce—especially in light of what Sylvie found and the fact that Judge Burton flatly refused consent to another hearing to discuss new evidence. He really had hoped the judge would at least allow her to be released under house arrest until the trial. He dreaded telling Maryn that he'd failed to change the judge's mind but knew that her disappointment in him would be nothing compared to Sister Helena's ire.

Thank God I've got some hope regarding her defense to offer them both, he mused, as he approached the body-scan.

Gavin hated the damned things, even if they served a valuable function. The scanners at the correction facility checked for weapons, confirmed visitor identity, and logged arrival and departure times. Nonetheless, he was still unconvinced of their safety.

He'd been wondering for quite some time about the radiation and energy forces from so many devices—including wi-fi signals everywhere, and what part, if any, the exposure contributed to cancer and other auto-immune diseases that used to be so rare.

Moreover, he felt completely vindicated in his convictions when, in early 2020, citizens were advised to return to using landline phones and hardwire computers, and to use cell phones and wi-fi computers for emergencies only, due to their potential carcinogenic and neurological damage. Unfortunately, the cautious approach lasted less than two years before the supposed "new and improved" devices hit the market. The new "safe electronics" not only were touted to make lives much easier, but their return helped to revive the floundering economy—mainly the technology giants who had grown so accustomed to inexhaustible income.

Something is making people sick...maybe it's a lot of things.

Gavin groaned aloud at the thought while he walked through the scanner.

Next year, they'll come out and say, "Sorry, we fried your insides and gave you dementia, but for those of you who survived, enjoy a free year of service for your trouble!"

Still, despite his caution and indignation, he was trapped into using nearly all modern devices just like everyone else in the rat-race. The reminder made him recall that he had failed to cancel Lucas and Brenna's phone plans.

He swore under his breath. He hadn't had a real conversation with either of them in weeks. If he didn't have Maryn's case consuming his mind, the reality would have crushed him. They just didn't need him anymore.

And you're to blame, he reminded himself.

Shame filled his being at the memory of his recent drinking binge, but he pushed the negative thoughts aside, assuring himself that it wouldn't happen again. He quickened his pace down the long corridor toward the facility's meeting room.

A uniformed guard with spiked-up short hair stood outside the door. Terry, the name on the ID-tag made him nervous—mainly because neither the name, nor the appearance, revealed a clear-cut gender. If he had to guess, the guard was female, but the last thing he needed was a citation for using the wrong pronoun.

Gavin needn't have worried. Terry didn't even look his way until he was standing right in front of her. He held up his arm so that she/he could see the plastic wristband that served as added proof he had gone through security. Without so much as a grunt, the door was unlocked for him.

Once inside, the door wasn't even fully closed before Sister Helena blurted, "*Well*...what'd you find out?"

Gavin had to chuckle. *She is something else.*

"Sister, you get an F for welcome greetings, but an A+ for determination," he declared, before nodding a hello to Maryn.

"Ladies, we've got work to do," he began, hoisting his briefcase onto the table and unlocking the latches.

Sister Helena didn't even smile at his teasing. Her demeanor was all-business. She was sitting on the edge of her chair, her elbows on the table. It felt like her eyes were literally burning holes into him as she waited to begin their discussion.

Gavin was glad to see that Maryn's appearance had improved—her coloring was better, and she had pulled her hair back into a ponytail.

She's actually very pretty. Further proof her husband's a real dumbass.

He hated to have to break the news to her, but there was no other way. He gave his head a slight shake and blurted, "Maryn, I'm sorry to tell you but the judge refused to grant you another hearing. You won't be released before the trial."

"What?!" Sister Helena exclaimed, "That's just *terrible*. Did you tell him how *unjust* this all is?"

Gavin nodded. "I *tried,* but he wasn't buying any of my argument."

"Did you tell him she was *afraid* for those kids?" she asked, grabbing Maryn's hand and squeezing it tight.

He tried not to be irritated by her questions and said, "Sister, I *assure* you, I tried *everything*. I even lied and told him that you would take her into the convent and be *personally* responsible for her until the trial. He wouldn't budge."

Helena raised her eyebrows. "You *didn't*?"

"I *did,*" he confirmed. "I told him I had evidence that would possibly negate Maryn's responsibility to give the immunization, but he still refused."

"Did you…"

"Yes!" Gavin interrupted her next query. "Sister, *believe me*, I tried it *all*. Burton threw me out of his office—not physically, but he warned me to get out or he'd hold me in contempt. That's a pretty big no."

"He *didn't*!" Sister exclaimed, clearly fuming at this point.

"He *did*," Gavin assured her again, secretly wishing that the judge would have to face Sister Helena's interrogation just once. In truth, he'd pay money to see it.

Utter disappointment blanketed the previously-hopeful faces of both women. But for Maryn, it was clearly much more than disappointment. She was suffering unjustly amidst a very real nightmare.

Gavin immediately thought of Isabella Sanchez and was reminded that she was also living a nightmare she didn't deserve. His stomach churned at the thought of what lay ahead for poor little Sophia—for them all, but he had no time to waste feeling sorry for anyone, including himself.

"Before you get too downcast, I want to tell you that my office has come across some new information that may be very pertinent to your case."

Sister Helena pushed her up fogged-over glasses and said, "Well what in Saint Francis are you waiting for? Let's hear it!"

He looked around the room suspiciously. Thankfully, there was no glass that could be used as a two-way mirror. Picking up his pen, he scribbled a few words onto his legal pad and slid it across the table to where they both could see that he'd written: "Checking for bugs. Quiet."

With his elbow, Gavin pushed his pen until it rolled off the table. When he leaned down to retrieve it, he checked beneath the table for any wires or anything that could be a bug. Having found nothing out of order there, he used the flashlight on his phone and examined each chair.

Finally, he felt safe to say, "Okay, this place looks clean, so listen up."

Both women sat still as stones as he told them of Isabella Sanchez's visit to his office. Tears spilled from Maryn's weary eyes as he described Sophia's blank stare and the erratic movement of her eyes. Isabella's insistence that it was the Lunatia was nearly Maryn's undoing.

"She's *right!*" Maryn confirmed, "The vaccine caused Sophia's symptoms and her son *is* in danger! When a patient reacts with sensitivity to immunizations—great or small, the chances of it occurring in one or more siblings is significantly higher. The greatest damage from the Lunatia seems to come with the second shot rather than the first, but there's just no telling with any of the vaccines."

Gavin shook his head.

A quick glance at Sister proved what he already knew—she was livid. "Gavin, you have to do *something*."

He sighed. "Of *course* I have to do something! But I also have to do it *right*. I can't just rush back into the judge's chambers making wild accusations. I have to find the proof."

"What do you mean you can't rush in! You *have* to!" Helena insisted. "Every day those kids are being injected…it's like playing Russian roulette!"

Gavin blew out a weary sigh. In the worst way imaginable, he wanted a cigarette and a mug of beer the size of Texas.

"Sister…*listen* to me. I *know* this is serious. It's *more* than serious, but you need to trust me when I tell you that this is potentially bigger than any of us."

"I understand that, but why can't you just march into that obstinate, pompous, Judge Jerk-ton's chamber and tell him you've got new evidence that needs to be heard? Take Isabella and her daughter with you. *Make* that pig-headed, tax-payer-paid servant listen!"

There wasn't a single thing that was funny about the predicament they were in, but Gavin chuckled anyway and said, "His name is *Burton*, and though I agree with you, there is more to consider. *Much* more."

Maryn dried her eyes on the sleeve of her prison shirt and asked, "What is it? What aren't you telling us?"

Still apprehensive, Gavin looked around the room again and said, "What is spoken in here must remain in here. I *cannot* emphasize this enough—don't talk to *anyone* about your case. Trust *no one*—not relatives, not your friends, your doctor, or the President of the good ol' U-S-of-A. *No one*. Do you both understand me?"

Sister Helena nodded so profusely that she reminded him of a bobblehead. "Yes! *No one*," she declared obediently.

"My husband hasn't talked to me since the first time he confronted me after I was arrested," Maryn answered sadly. "I still haven't even seen my kids yet—but even if I get to see them, they are much too young to discuss this, and I would never talk to them about something that would scare them. I don't have any other family that will be coming or calling. According to my husband, I deserve to be hated."

The pain in her voice was palpable. Her soulful admission was one that Gavin, even in his worst misery, could not relate to. Annie had left him and had taken the kids with her, but all of them still communicated with him. His kids still told him that they loved him, even if it wasn't often. They were still in his life.

Maryn was experiencing a pain that most would never be able to comprehend. She'd lost her husband, her children, her home, her friends, job, and her reputation, all because she believed she was doing the right thing. The awareness made Gavin even more determined not to waste another moment of their time together. If he was going to help her, he needed answers.

Quickly, downplaying it as much as possible, he told them what Sylvie had found, giving great emphasis to the fact that most of what she found came by way of internet sources that were not necessarily valid.

Still, it was obvious that the news of the mysterious deaths shook both women. For several moments no one said a word, until Sister Helena broke the silence. "In the gospel of St. Luke, Jesus said, 'the man who is distrustful in small things is distrustful in much.' The devil thrives in deceit."

"Keep in mind," Gavin interrupted quickly, before they were subjected to a longer version of her sermon, "this is *all* conjecture at this point—there is a great deal we don't know and much that will have to be substantiated before I can use any of this to defend you, Maryn. Isabella Sanchez assured me that she tried to secure as many as a dozen lawyers, but no one would take her case."

"Why?" Maryn asked, clearly devastated to hear that bit of news. "I would think this type of case would be a potential gold-mine."

"Yeah. Normally, I would agree," Gavin answered, "but you have to remember that vaccinations are *overwhelmingly* advocated in most every country. It goes without saying that parents don't want their children to get sick, and they also don't want their children getting sick because of the unvaccinated. So, in the court of public opinion, which can, and often does, impact certain cases, this would be a slam-dunk win for vaccine mandates and ultimately, the pharmaceutical companies."

"If the vaccines work, then how can the unvaccinated get anyone sick?" Sister Helena asked.

"Precisely," Maryn answered, "but unfortunately, the immunization mandate argument is based on a concept called *Herd Immunity*, meaning that most everyone has to be vaccinated for the disease to be under control. This theory has been debunked by researchers, and considering what I've witnessed, I really don't know if I trust it or any of the protocol anymore."

"Why," Gavin interjected.

"Because…in the years since I've been practicing, the number of booster shots needed has increased several times, so obviously, the vaccines must not be providing lasting immunity. We also know that viruses are mutating, yet to my knowledge, the cause hasn't been pinpointed. Moreover, most people are unaware that recently-vaccinated individuals can actually *spread* the viruses to others for six or even eight weeks. It's called *shedding*. This is considered rare, but it does happen."

"Are you *sure* about that?" Gavin asked, his eyebrows raised.

"Yes. It's listed right in the vaccine inserts—which no one reads because they are never given to the patients. Feel free to contact any major cancer treatment center and you will find this clearly stated in their policies and procedures. They all ask those recently vaccinated to refrain from visiting their patients for eight weeks."

"Wow!" Gavin shook his head disbelievingly. "I've never heard of any of this, which leads me to ask…approximately, how many people would you estimate know these facts?"

"Well, anti-vaxxers know all about shedding, the dangerous potential side-effects, the injuries and lack of lasting immunity, but the average person has no idea. I would say less than five percent—possibly fewer, but I'm just guessing based on my experience with patients and parents. For the most part, parents just show up and do whatever the doctor or nurse tells them—which is what I would have also done, if I hadn't witnessed so much. What choice do they have anyway? It's the quandary Isabella Sanchez is facing—if parents want their children to go to school or attend day-care, they *must* get them vaccinated."

Sister Helena's expression was filled with utter shock. "I knew about the aborted fetal cells used to make them—most anyone who is active in the pro-life cause understands the gravity of using slaughtered human beings to develop vaccines, but how can any doctor or nurse feel good about *saving* lives if they know this and can see these side effects with their own eyes? This is complete duplicity…malpractice…*immoral*!"

Maryn gave her head a slight nod and said, "It is for *some maybe*, but in all fairness, up until recent years, I don't believe that most doctors and nurses knew all the dangers or about the potential for transmission of the viruses through vaccination. We were also unaware that the vaccines have had a long history of containing harmful ingredients like mercury, aluminum, formaldehyde, animal and human DNA—not to mention that in 2018, a high level of a popular weed killer was found in them as well. I'm sure I don't have to explain why this would be highly toxic."

"In the vaccines?" Helena gasped.

"Yes," Maryn answered. "The exposure of all these issues has steadily increased for decades now, but with each revelation there has always been great reassurance given to the medical community and public that the risk of vaccine injury was small in comparison to the risks of contracting the viruses."

Helena and Gavin both shook their heads in disbelief as she continued.

"We are all basically taught and trained by the same institutions. Because of the massive amounts of pro-vaccination propaganda fed to the public at large, most people have become so fearful of even common childhood illnesses, that they go along without question. Well, all except for the holistic doctors, anyway," Maryn admitted.

Gavin's head shot up at the mention of the natural doctors. "I think you just hit the nail on the head. Lest we forget the seemingly high mortality rate of those who disagree with the vaccination concept. It's no wonder Isabella Sanchez cannot find anyone to represent her daughter. Even I have to admit that it's pretty unsettling to realize that natural medicine professionals are suddenly dropping like flies. Uh, it's not exactly an attractive case to jump into."

Sister narrowed her brows and scowled at him. "You're not thinking of turning Isabella down...turning *us* down, are you?"

Gavin paused. He couldn't deny that he really wished he could just walk away. He didn't need the money, didn't want the attention, and sure as hell didn't need the stress.

Several long moments ticked by before he gave her an answer. "Look...I really need to be straight with you both, but especially with you, Maryn. I want you to know this going in, because this is *your* life, *your* kids, *your* career and future on the line. I am *not* the best litigator for this type of case. There are hundreds of lawyers with more experience in settling medical injury lawsuits. Not to mention, I'm a workaholic, alcoholic, who just relapsed *again* last night, so you better think very hard before making the decision to move forward with me."

For several moments, awkward silence filled the room like smoke before Gavin continued, "And one more thing...if the deaths of these doctors are related to some sort of medical malpractice cover-up, then that makes us all potential threats, including both of you, the Sanchez family, and even Sylvie, my assistant."

"Dear Jesus in Heaven," Sister Helena whispered.

His words came down on them like an avalanche, every aspect of the implications weighing heavily upon their hope in his ability and a victorious outcome. Gavin knew hearing the truth would be difficult to swallow and would shake them. He felt both shame and a bit of relief at having confessed his relapse, but it was imperative they knew the risks going in. There was much to consider.

Finally, Sister Helena gave her head a shake and said, "Maybe we are reading too much into this. Common sense tells us that not *everyone* in the government, or all people who work in the pharmaceutical companies, or medical clinics are bad. Mistakes happen. Bad drugs are made. Errors are overlooked, and yes, sometimes covered up, but do you really think these deaths are *murders*? Is this *possible*? Is it *plausible*?"

Gavin couldn't help but notice she completely sidestepped the admission of his relapse. It was her way of showing him she still believed in him. He cringed at the thought of disappointing her, but he was grateful.

"Of *course*, not every drug is bad," he answered, "and not everyone involved with vaccines is bad, but even just a *handful* in key positions can wreak widespread damage."

"I believe every bit of it," Maryn declared firmly. "There is *something* going on. If it was happening in my clinic, it's happening elsewhere."

"Then what's next?" Sister Helena asked. "What can we do and how can I help?"

"I have a great deal of research and work to do, but I am beginning to believe that this could potentially be much worse than any of us can imagine. While I was driving here, it also occurred to me that the drug companies have such strong ties to mainstream media. Think about it...how many commercials for prescription drugs do you see in any given television timeslot? It doesn't matter what you're watching—a baseball game, a movie, the news...there's always a commercial for medications or treatments. Imagine the lost revenue if the drug companies quit advertising?"

Maryn's nod was mechanical. She looked completely overwhelmed, but he had to press forward and make her understand what they were all up against.

"Where there is great potential for money to be made, there is great potential for corruption," he continued honestly, shaking his head slightly. "Unfortunately, I'm speaking from experience here."

His eyes locked with Sister Helena's before he went on, "The government entities involved with the pharmaceutical companies are like a two-headed monster—one feeding the other. Both are determined to devour anything that gets in the way of their common goals, which are to make money, safeguard their secrets, and remain in power and good-standing in order to influence the public at large. Combined with a fearful, angry public that's convinced vaccines are the way to ensure they won't get sick, the monster grows another head."

His gaze shifted to Maryn. "We are up against a near impossible feat—a force so potentially destructive that you could very well lose more than just your freedom."

Maryn's gaze never wavered, but the fear in her eyes was palpable. Gavin blew out a sigh. He really wanted to give her hope, wished he could assure her that everything would turn out right, but he just couldn't.

"I'm sorry, Maryn, but I have to be honest with you. I have no idea if I can help you...and at this point, even *how*. As I said, this is not my area of expertise, but I have a sneaking suspicion that Isabella Sanchez was right...she was unable to obtain a lawyer because no one wants to take on this three-headed serpent. If you decide you still want me to represent you, the only thing I can promise is that I will do my best to try and figure out a way to proceed. For now, that's all the assurance I can offer."

Tense silence filled the air for several moments before a single tear rolled down Maryn's face.

"Without you and Sister Helena," she began, "I have *zero* hope of being free and zero hope of exposing Lunatia's dangers. Sister believes in you…I *do* want you to try."

"It's settled then!" Sister declared with great enthusiasm.

"Thank you, Gavin," Maryn offered, her voice filled with heartfelt conviction. The hope that lay bare in her eyes made Gavin wish Sister hadn't believed in him so much. He was petrified of failing.

"God help us all," Sister prayed passionately.

From the depth of his weary soul, Gavin silently answered, "Amen."

Chapter 11

Gavin shoved the last bite of his take-out burrito into his mouth before flopping back onto his bed. He was exhausted. Physically. Mentally. Emotionally. He couldn't get Maryn Pearce off his mind, nor could he forget the sweet face of little Sophia, whose eyes could no longer focus. The day's events left him feeling overwhelmed. Powerless.

If the numbers from the past years were even close to correct, approximately ninety professional, conscientious men and women, including some of their family members, met their Maker because of their efforts to expose the truth. He had no idea how to even begin to expose a potential cover-up of such magnitude.

If even one of the bunch was snuffed out because of what they knew, this is some serious shit.

The realization struck a chord of fear deep down inside him. Normally, he relished any quiet time afforded him to think things through, but in that moment, the silence mocked him. He felt completely alone.

The urge to drink was powerful, consuming. His temptation grew with each moment, leaving him feeling as though his free will was no longer even a part of him. The problems of so many, along with his own worries, were squeezing his head like it was in a vise.

Before long, his need for comfort and escape was strong. The familiar pull to make a trip to the liquor store prompted him to reach into his pants pocket for his car fob. What he found instead, was a prayer card.

Sister Helena had put the Saint Michael prayer in his hand earlier that day when he walked her out to her car after the visit with Maryn.

"You better get it in your head that you're up against the devil himself. He knows you're weak and knows just where, when, and how to get into your head to make you fall. But greater is the One that is in you, than the devil who tempts you in this world."

"Gavin, you are a baptized, adopted son of the Living God, the Creator of Heaven and earth, who will never leave you, nor forsake you...and don't you ever let anyone tell you different! Ask your Guardian angel to protect you as you fight your demons and the evils that have come against these women. Say this prayer to St. Michael when you're tempted or scared, so he can go to battle for you against the evil forces that seek to destroy your soul."

The memory of her passionate expression, the sincerity with which she spoke, and the hope that lay bare in her eyes gave him the strength to drop the key fob and pick up his phone to call his kids, instead.

Brenna didn't answer, but just seconds later, a text came through to say she would call when she got out of cheer practice. After the day he'd had, he was satisfied with at least an answer.

Lucas, blissfully unaware that his phone service was perilously close to being discontinued, answered on the third ring.

"Hey Dad! What's up?"

For some reason, just hearing his voice made Gavin's throat thick with emotion. He swallowed hard and said, "Well, nothing's really up. I just hadn't heard from you for a couple of weeks and I...well...how are things going? How's school? Are you working hard?"

He hadn't intended to bombard him with questions, but his emotions had turned his brain into mush. All he could picture was little Lucas, the toddler who wanted to have a "gweat big head wike my Daddy," when he grew up. The kid who used to beg him, non-stop, to play ball in the backyard. The kid who used scissors to trim several inches off half-a dozen of his business ties so that he could wear them too.

Thankfully, Lucas didn't seem to mind his questions and proceeded to give him the lowdown on his life. Gavin listened intently, grateful for the time to swallow back the unshed tears and clear his voice, so he could respond.

"Sounds like you're enjoying your last year, Son. I can't believe you'll have your business degree in just months."

"Yeah, I know what you mean. It's gone by so fast. I still don't know what I'm going to get my master's degree in or whether or not I want to go to law school, but I'm keeping my options open."

Gavin smiled sadly. He couldn't, in good conscience, encourage him to become a lawyer. The temptations that came with the lifestyle and income had nearly destroyed him and their family.

"Well, I know you'll do well at whatever you choose. You're a good kid, Lucas. I mean...a good *man*."

Lucas paused on the phone. "Dad, are you okay? I mean...you're not drinking, are you?"

Gavin squeezed his eyes shut to keep from crying. It pained him to know that his son felt the need to ask, but he was also thankful that he'd said no to the booze and could answer honestly. "No...haven't had a drop tonight."

"Oh good!" he answered so relieved it further pierced Gavin's heart. "So...I mean," Lucas continued, "is everything okay otherwise? You're not sick or anything, are you?"

As if the effort would give him strength, Gavin pinched the bridge of his nose and replied, "No...*really*. Everything's *fine*. I just got to missing you and wanted to hear your voice. How about you call me once in a while to let me know how things are going...okay?"

"Oh...yeah, sure. I'll do that."

Several moments of awkward silence ensued before Lucas said, "Okay, well, some friends and I are going to watch the Lakers play tonight, so I'll talk to you later."

"No problem. Have fun."

"Yeah, you too. Bye Dad."

"Bye...hey Lucas...are you still there?"

"Yeah, what's up?"

"What did you ever do with your old laptop? If you didn't sell it, I know of someone who could really use it."

"No, I didn't sell it. As a matter of fact, it's probably in the closet at your place, remember? You kept it for me and had the hard-drive erased so I could sell it, but I forgot it. If someone else can use it, give it to them. It's really yours anyway," he added with a laugh that sounded more like the little boy Gavin remembered. At the sound, his heart squeezed in his chest.

After he hung up with Lucas, Gavin thought of Isabella's young son, and how desperate she must be to protect him from what had happened to Sophia. He imagined what it would be like to watch Brenna or Lucas disappear into a state where they could no longer be reached. It was hard enough dealing with Brenna's peanut allergies and Lucas's asthma. As severe as these illnesses could be at times, they paled in comparison to Sophia's symptoms.

He walked over to his hall closet and pulled open the doors. Sure enough, Lucas's laptop sat on a shelf next to several boxes of unopened golf balls.

The idea to ask Lucas about the laptop had come to him out of the blue. Years back, his college roommate, now CEO of an electronic company in Oregon, had contacted Gavin to ask some legal questions. The following week, the laptop had arrived as a thank you.

Paranoid as hell and hoping the machine would be untraceable, Gavin plugged in the charger and connected it to the machine. It would take a couple of hours to fully charge. Until then, he figured he'd try to catch a nap before making his way to wi-fi hotspots to do some web searching.

If the Lunatia scandal was as big as he guessed, those with a vested stake in it were likely to have either professionals, or some basement-dwelling techie watching for unusually high activity related to the vaccine and pertinent sites. Either prospect unsettled him. He certainly didn't want to set off any red flags, especially so early in the game.

Feeling satisfied that he'd at least figured out a possible way to sink his teeth into the case, he closed his eyes, but his mind was far too busy to rest. Maryn's reference to her husband's hostility came to mind, and before long, he was stewing.

Thomas Pearce's statement to the judge regarding the "deliberate and potentially life-threatening danger she'd brought upon their daughters," was puzzling. Gavin could understand Pearce's anger, especially because Maryn had failed to immunize their girls, but what he couldn't fathom was why he hadn't cooled down yet.

Either I'm missing something, or the guy's got a screw loose.

"So much for those pesky wedding vows," he grumbled.

Then again, I guess I shouldn't have much to say about Pearce's failure. I blew my own wedding vows...and Annie dumped the whole till death do us part concept too. But if I hadn't screwed up, there would have been nothing to forgive.

Just thinking of Annie made his stomach burn, so he quickly pushed her from his mind. He was still perilously close to drinking like a fish until he was numb. Thinking of her would all but guarantee it.

Thoughts of his own failed marriage caused his mind to wander back to Thomas Pearce.

Maybe, since he's a cop, he's got some over-the-top scruples and just a little too much pride to have to admit his wife broke the law.

He shrugged and looked over at the clock. He'd already wasted more than ten minutes of his nap time.

Is it possible that he just wants to distance himself and his family as much as possible from any liability in case of civil lawsuits? I mean, they're trying to hang David Adam's death on her, and if she's found guilty, there is sure to be a big lawsuit coming. Hell, there's potential for multiple suits from all the patients she failed to immunize.

"I have *got* to make sure that Judge Burton can see that the motives behind Maryn's actions are credible. If I don't get those charges dropped or drastically reduced, they could very well use her case to make an example of her."

Just speaking the words aloud caused his worry to build. His thoughts shifted from Maryn to Isabella Sanchez and her children, and his frustration increased.

He could smell the scotch. Taste it.

Reaching into his pocket, he fished around until his fingers connected with what he sought. He pulled out the prayer card and stared at it. The image seemed laughable at first—an angel with a sword, the devil under his feet. The concept of God, Heaven, and Hell always seemed much more like a fairytale than anything.

In fairytales the good guy wins. In real life, good guys finish last.

In that moment, he felt more connection with the dude under St. Michael's foot. His chest suddenly felt as tight as a drum. The sensation had been occurring more and more of late; he was hoping it was his acid reflux. He grabbed the antacid from the table next to him and chugged a couple of gulps.

Antacid—one. Scotch—zero.

Knowing that he couldn't drink away his worry and failures made him almost wish his heart would give out. He closed his eyes and pondered the end of his life. He thought of Lucas and Brenna and wondered if they'd be a little relieved if he was out of the picture. Still, the afterlife was the great unknown. If Saint Michael was a fairytale, he had nothing to worry about. If God was real, he was in serious trouble.

Behind his closed eyes, Sister Helena's kind face appeared, and he remembered the love and confidence in her eyes when she'd given the card to him.

He squeezed his eyes shut to keep the tears in check and whispered, "God, if You haven't already given up on me, I could sure use some help."

*****

Maryn lay atop her cot mulling over everything her lawyer had laid at her feet. The information had been both frightening and exhilarating at the same time. She was certain that Isabella Sanchez's visit to his office that morning was God's way of intervening for them all.

For the first time since the horrible night of her arrest and Thomas's complete rejection of her, she felt a glimmer of hope that somehow things could possibly work themselves out. To realize that Gavin Steele not only believed her, but also understood why she'd faked the immunization records, helped to heal some of the brokenness in a way she couldn't fully convey.

Even so, the remembrance of Thomas's hateful words, the intensity of his wrath, still haunted her. The fact that he'd raged at her in front of his peers—people who had been to their home for dinner, whose children had played with their girls, added insult to injury. Her heart pounded at the memory and fresh tears filled her eyes. The hurt rose inside of her like a tidal wave, threatening to pull her under, to a place from where she'd never return.

There were times that she really wished it was possible—that she could be swept away and never have to feel the pain, the rejection and disappointment again. But then, she would remember that her daughters' lives were at stake. Many lives were at stake. If she allowed her sorrow to kill her, who would remain to testify? How many more children would be injured?

She thought of David. Her heart squeezed at the memory of his sweet little face. It was still hard for her to believe that he'd died of the Lunavirus. Like the measles or mumps, most people ran a fever, developed a rash or other minor symptoms, and then in a few days, it was over.

So tragic. He was so healthy otherwise. How could he have succumbed to such a mild virus?

The unanswered question only served to bring up more questions. *Who told the authorities that I wasn't giving the shots? It had to have been either Mandy or Dee, or maybe even Carol. The patients wouldn't have known the difference.*

Her mind drifted back to the day of her arrest. She was covering the 8:00 a.m. to 4:00 p.m. shift, and the day had been hectic as usual. Strep, along with an unnamed virus that mimicked strep, made the day especially busy.

As hard as she tried to remember, Maryn couldn't be certain as to how many vaccinations she'd given that day. As far as she could remember, it was no more than five or six younger children.

There wasn't a patient due for the Lunatia that day—of that, I am certain. So, when…and who turned me in?

Though the questions remained unanswered, now more than ever, she had hope that God would help Gavin Steele expose the truth about the dangers of the vaccines and why she went to such extremes to prevent more harm to the children.

"God, You are my hope, my strength, and my shield of protection. I believe You sent Sister Helena and Gavin Steele into my life to not only help me, but Sophia Sanchez and all the victims. Help me to place my trust in You. Help me to push away the pain I feel from Thomas's rejection and anger. Oh God…I so desperately miss my girls…"

She stopped praying. She wanted to be brave, but just the mention of her girls broke the dam that was still so very fragile. It had been nine days since she'd seen Lily and Pearl. She had never been away from them for even a full day. Never. She wondered what they were thinking. Wondered if they were asking for her when Thomas tucked them in each night. She could almost see their wide, questioning eyes. The way Lily would knit her brow when she was confused. The way Pearly always reached up to stroke her cheek when she said goodnight.

Maryn longed to hold them close, to feel their arms around her neck and smell the sunshine in their silken hair. She'd give anything to hear them say, "I love you, Mommy…forever and a day."

For the hundredth time, she wondered if they were scared, devastated by her absence. Imagining their anguish was as painful as a sledgehammer blow to the chest. Yet, in thinking of her children's woundedness, her anger also flared.

How could Thomas do this to them? To me? How could he be so enraged that he could abandon me and hurt our children so terribly? Surely, he must see how damaging this is to them!

A trail of indignant, hot tears turned into full-fledged sobbing that lasted until she could cry no more.

Maryn got up and grabbed a wad of scratchy toilet paper. After blowing her nose, she crawled back onto the cot. Curled tightly in a fetal position, she squeezed her eyes closed to shut out the ugliness of her cell, her fear, the hatred, her pain.

"God, help me," she rasped, in a voice so weak she hardly recognized it. "*Help* me, Jesus. I'm so tired. I don't have a tear left to cry."

Do I not keep track of all your sorrows? I have collected all your tears in a bottle. I have recorded each one in my book. I am the Lord, God. Is there anything too difficult for me?

The Word of God spoke firmly and tangibly within her. Immediately, she calmed.

In the darkness of her cell, with only God to hear her, Maryn reaffirmed a scripture she had discovered when she made the decision to withhold the immunizations until the dangers were uncovered, "So let us not grow weary in doing what is right, for we will reap at harvest time, if we do not give up."

I can't give up. I will carry this cross that's been given to me so others won't have to suffer this evil.

"Guardian angel," she whispered, "carry my heart and my love to Lily and Pearl. Tell them I love them and miss them, and that I only wanted to protect them…thank you."

After pulling up her threadbare blanket to her shoulders, she turned over on her side and tried to sleep, but her heart would not let her rest.

One last tear squeezed from the corner of her eye as she whispered, "God, please bless Thomas. Help him to understand. Soften his heart…*please.*"

Chapter 12

The traffic was heavier than usual. Gavin marveled at how it always seemed slowest when he was in a hurry.

Before long, the movement turned into a crawl as three lanes of traffic merged into one. When the line came to a complete standstill, it became obvious that a pile-up had occurred up ahead.

His phone rang. After quickly hitting the hands-free button, he barked, "Yeah…what's up?"

"Good morning to you too," Sylvie offered with a laugh.

"Sorry, I'm stuck in traffic."

"I figured. Anyway…you're not going to believe this, but Burton's office called and said he cleared the way to ensure that Maryn Pearce's kids will get to visit her—tomorrow at the latest."

"Wow…That's unbelievable. I wonder what the hell changed his mind?" Gavin answered, completely stunned. "He was as cold-hearted as Hitler last I talked to him."

"Who? I've heard the name before, but not really sure who Hitler is…he was pretty bad right?"

Gavin stared at the phone disbelievingly. He would have rolled his eyes but then realized he wasn't sure his kids would know who Hitler was either. Inwardly, he sighed at the deliberate erasing of history that had been sneakily taking place over the past couple of decades.

"Yes, he was very bad," he finally answered, but that would be a long subject for another day. I just wish I knew what changed Burton's tune—maybe I did get through to him a little…"

"I have no idea," she answered, "but there's *more*. He also increased her time allowance for legal counsel—and I quote, 'Up to three hours per day, to be used either consecutively or split during the normal operating hours of the facility as long as counseling sessions do not overlap or interfere with routine or mandatory prison obligations.'"

Gavin couldn't believe his ears. He let out the deep breath he hadn't realized he'd been holding. "Considering the treason charge against her, this is really unheard of, but we'll take it."

"Exactly!" she answered, obviously happy to give him the news. "I'm not a religious person at all, but if there are such things as miracles, this *has* to be one. I wanted to let you know in case you wanted to head over there first. I called the facility. She's already had breakfast and is doing her chores now. She will be free for two hours after that."

"What's on my schedule this morning?" Gavin asked, more than anxious to ask Maryn the dozens of questions to which he needed answers.

"Nothing that can't be postponed or that I can't take care of. Uh…except…that one woman…you know…the one that came to the office yesterday."

Isabella Sanchez. "Yes…I know the one you're talking about."

"Okay, well she called and left a message. I think you already know what she's asking."

Gavin's heart immediately quickened at the thought of being responsible for both cases at once. He'd be a liar not to admit that part of him wanted to press the accelerator down and drive away from it all.

"Tell her I'll do it…but she's going to have to be patient."

Sylvie's squeal interrupted him. "I *knew* you wouldn't turn her down. I'll help you any way I can, I *promise*."

Gavin could picture her smile and enthusiasm. Sadly, he knew she wouldn't be smiling if she knew that last night he'd confirmed at least three more deaths of natural medicine advocates all within the past eighteen months. The news would have to wait until he could tell her everything in person.

"Yeah, I know. Tell her I'll try and file a motion just as soon as I can. And in the meantime, remind her to keep it all to herself. *Warn her*, Sylvie. In fact, tell her that if I find out she's even talking about it in her *sleep*, I'll bow out faster than Obama at the RNC."

"Obama...oh yeah..." she laughed. "Is that dude even still around?"

"Depends on which news media outlet you're listening to," he retorted dryly.

She laughed again. "True. Okay, I'll make sure she understands the confidentiality and seriousness of it all. See you later...and Gavin?"

"What now?"

"Nothing...I'm just so happy you're doing this. And...be careful, okay?"

*****

Sitting across from Maryn Pearce and Sister Helena in the same tiny, windowless, meeting room they'd previously met in, made Gavin anxious. Still, he was grateful for the extra time he'd been given to interview her. Moreover, Sister Helena's presence somehow gave him the extra kick in the pants he needed to do his best.

He pushed the record button on his phone sitting on the table in front of her and said, "Okay, Maryn...start from the beginning. Tell me why you quit giving the Lunatia to your patients. You work at a pediatric clinic that does mostly immunizations, virus screening, and bloodwork, is that correct?"

"Yes. That is correct. There are no physicians in our office. The pediatricians are available in the offices next to our clinic. They see the patients after we have finished our assessments and only when needed and for emergencies."

Gavin shook his head. "Seriously? There's not even a doctor there?"

"As I said, they are in the building next door. We are there to do all the vaccinations, strep-screening, blood-work, urine tests, weight and height checks, chart their physical and emotional progress, and other minor things, like colds and ear infections—stuff like that.

"With the continued influx of migrant groups and other immigrants, and to keep up with the continually increasing vaccination schedule, clinics like ours have become necessary to keep abreast of the patient volume. The nurses used to work as a team when we gave vaccinations—so it's over with quickly, but now we work alone and do the best we can."

Dressed in faded orange prison clothes that looked a lot like hospital scrubs, he could absolutely imagine Maryn as a caring pediatric nurse. She had worked her strawberry-blonde hair into a braid that came over one shoulder. For the first time since they'd met, her vivid, blue eyes held a spark of hope.

It scared the hell out of him.

She was facing treason, manslaughter, and so many more charges, that he wondered if she really had any idea as to how slim her chances of being exonerated really were.

He forced the reality from his mind and said exactly the opposite of what he was thinking. "Makes sense," he muttered, not wanting to take the time to explain his objections.

"Go on," he urged.

Maryn didn't need to be told twice.

"The trouble began several years ago when Lunatia was first added to the vaccination schedule as an optional vaccination. Even though we didn't have many parents asking for it, because it prevented such a mild and preventable virus, we noticed an increase in the number of parents calling in and reporting really high fevers after their child received their first dose of Lunatia—and especially if they had received other vaccinations the same day."

"But isn't that common with vaccinations?" Gavin interrupted. "I mean, isn't it standard to give more than one shot at a time and for fevers to develop afterward?"

"Well, yes...and no. Yes, it's common to give more than one shot to a child, and low-grade fevers are common, but high fevers are *supposed* to be rare. Admittedly, they happen more than we'd like them to, especially in the past several years."

"Okay, so when did you get concerned enough to take action?"

"I took action *immediately*. I went to my supervisor."

"Her name?"

"Carol White."

"Can you prove that you discussed this with her?"

"I don't know...I guess so. I told one of the nurses I work with that I was going to talk to Carol."

"What's her name?"

"Mandy Baines."

"Okay. Go on...if we need more information about her I'll get it later."

"So, when I talked to Carol, I expressed real concern about the fevers and shared what I had observed—that the reactions seemed to be the worst when children were given the Lunatia in combination with other vaccinations. I told her that I was wondering if it was the Lunatia or just that their small bodies were incapable of the overload of vaccinations with the increase number in the schedule. I also mentioned that I thought my observations should be reported to VAERS and, of course, I told the parents the same when they called in with concerns."

"What is VAERS?" Sister Helena asked.

"It's the government's vaccine site. It stands for Vaccine Adverse Event Reporting Site."

Gavin nodded. "So that was the clinic's protocol?"

"Well normally, yes, but we didn't contact VAERS because Carol informed me that it had already been reported, and that the CDC along with Welprox, the manufacturer, were already working on a replacement vaccination that would address these issues."

"Okay...so if you knew this, why didn't you just keep giving the shots?"

"I did—at least for a while, anyway," she assured, "but then the *supposed* new and improved formulas came in."

"Formulas—as in plural? There is more than one formula?"

"Yes...five. Apparently, genetics are suspected to play a factor in the efficacy rate, so Welprox developed different immunizations to cover each of the five ethnic groups. When I was still giving the shots, I was always extra cautious to make sure the kids got the right one."

"I see...but since we live in the great melting pot, can you explain what kind of criteria was set for choosing which formula would work?"

Maryn nodded. "Many times we could tell which dominant ethnic group the child was in—Caucasian, Native American, African-American, Asian, or Hispanic, but still, we were always told to double-check the genetic code on their chart and match it with the corresponding Lunatia immunization."

"Genetic *code*? I've never heard of such a thing."

"Yes. New government regulations require all individuals to be tested and provide their DNA. Without the DNA code, we cannot vaccinate—anyone."

Gavin was immediately annoyed. "I hate *everything* about the idea of mandatory DNA reporting."

Maryn gave a sad nod of her head. "They say it's not mandatory, but it *is*...because kids can't go to school or daycare without the vaccinations. I can't work in any healthcare facility without a yearly flu vaccination and any other booster they insist I need."

"So how do you get around it...or do you just go ahead and take the vaccination?"

Maryn's face colored. Her gaze went from Gavin's to Sister Helena's, and then back to Gavin, before she admitted, "I have falsified my record for about four years now. I think vaccinations are toxic and that they damage our natural immune system."

Sister Helena was quick to defend her. "I don't believe in them either!" she declared. "They never pin down the right flu virus anyway."

Gavin shrugged and admitted, "I haven't gotten a flu shot for years because I always seemed to get sick afterward. Okay...back to the CDC and big pharma...it sounds like they went above and beyond to ensure that their bases were covered."

"That's what I thought...initially, anyway."

"Why, initially? Why did you quit giving the shots *after* the improved formulas?"

"Because—not only did the incident of high fever *increase*, but that's when the problems I mentioned to you earlier began, especially with the second dose."

"Loss of hand-eye coordination, trouble concentrating…if I remember right," Gavin confirmed.

"Yes. Kids just like Sophia, previously healthy children— some we had been caring for since birth…"

Her words were cut short by the tears that lodged in her throat. She swallowed hard and continued. "Slowly, but surely, we saw more and more delightful, smart children slip into a world where they couldn't be reached. Their parents were confused and distraught, wondering what had happened and demanding answers as to how they could help their child."

With her glasses fogged over with unshed tears, Sister Helena reached over and gently patted Maryn's hand.

"What did your supervisor say?" Gavin asked, now leaning forward, hanging on every word.

"She reported it all, just like she should have, and her supervisor at the pediatric clinic reported it to the doctors."

"And no one did *anything*?" Sister Helena exclaimed, unable to keep quiet a moment longer.

Gavin shot her a look to remind her that he was the one who was asking the questions. Still, he understood her angst. He was growing angrier by the minute.

Maryn looked from one to the other before she answered, "The pediatricians contacted the higher-ups and demanded to see the injury data and the clinical trial studies on Lunatia. Turns out, the reports were *clean*. Side effects were minimal—well, *some* would say they were minimal—you know, like any other vaccination we give. Unfortunately, there will *always* be children who have terrible reactions, but I guess the government has decided that these kids are just collateral damage, because of their belief that without herd immunity, the health of our society will rapidly decline."

"What do you *mean*, that the government has *decided*?" he asked, clearly enthralled.

"It's been that way for a long time," Maryn answered. "I didn't know it until I started researching…but I discovered that, in 1982, four pharmaceutical companies went before congress and threatened to stop providing vaccines unless their liability was removed. This led to the passing of the National Childhood Vaccine Injury Act in 1986. Drug companies and health care professionals were released from *all* liability for harm caused by vaccines. The pharms were in trouble. Their initial whooping cough vaccine, part of the DPT shot, was causing brain inflammation and death in multiple children, and their live oral polio vaccine had crippled both children and adults with vaccine-strain polio. Naturally, the injured and their families were filing lawsuits to hold the pharmaceutical companies responsible, both for compensation, and to ensure that their products were improved or taken off the market."

Visibly flabbergasted, Sister Helena asked, "So, you mean to tell me that congress actually *waived* their responsibility?"

"Yes…and in 2011, the Supreme Court upheld the 1986 ruling stating that no drug manufacturer could be held liable, since vaccine injury was an unavoidable risk—vaccines were declared "unavoidably unsafe."

"Holy Mother of God," Sister Helena whispered, crossing herself. "You've got to be kidding me…*unavoidable?*"

This time, Gavin was so engrossed, he didn't even blink at the interruption.

"Yes. There will *always* be those who have reactions to vaccinations—sometimes mild, but sometime serious—even deadly."

Gavin wanted to swear a blue-streak. He knew several injury lawyers that worked on vaccine cases. He just assumed that they were suing the manufacturers. "So, let me get this straight," he began indignantly, "Americans can sue tobacco companies, seatbelt and automobile manufacturers—just about *any* company when it comes to matters of public safety, *except* the vaccine manufacturers?"

Maryn nodded. "Unbelievable, I know."

"But I thought there were lawyers who specifically took vaccine-injury cases…I guess I'm not quite following," Helena admitted.

"There are," Maryn assured, "but the *government* has taken over the task of paying out compensation for injury—but ultimately, the money comes from American consumers."

"How?" Gavin asked, skeptically.

"Through a surcharge on yearly flu shots and other vaccinations."

Gavin let out a long, frustrated sigh. The information was not only disturbing, considering the government's involvement in keeping the pharmaceutical companies in the game, he felt even less confident in any real success in defending Maryn's actions. He would have to prove intent to deceive or reckless neglect and intent to deceive on the part of the pharmaceutical companies and/or the medical community. In truth, he wasn't sure what charges he'd have to hit them with to prove Maryn's actions were reasonable.

"The scary part of all of this is that I wholeheartedly believe that the mandates are unconstitutional, but as clueless as I've been, I'm certain that other lawyers surely have attempted to prove this and failed," Gavin finally admitted, running his hands down his face in frustration. "Go on, Maryn…let's hear the rest of it."

She nodded sympathetically as if she understood the blow he'd just received and continued, "After reviewing the documentation, the CDC and the FDA agreed with the safety data findings, and declared Lunatia safe, stating that reactions were more than likely caused by genetic or other outside factors. But, as a precaution, their recommendation was that the second dose should not be combined with other vaccinations."

Gavin was livid. "Did the FDA or CDC do any comparison studies of vaccinated and non-vaccinated children?"

Maryn shook her head, sadly. "No. To my knowledge, there has *never* been an official study done to compare non-vaccinated children with the vaccinated. From what I know and have seen, it's because the findings would be explosive."

"How in the *hell* could anyone just dismiss these severe reactions as being *genetic* or *outside factors* without thoroughly studying these issues to make sure?" Gavin asked, clearly disgusted.

"Exactly! But those in the medical profession are in no position to argue, myself included—especially because they had just added the Lunatia to the *mandated* schedule for children attending any public school or daycare setting. Remember, anything mandated by the government is protected. My hands were tied."

"What did you do with your own girls?" Sister Helena asked.

"Well, I didn't have to bother with the daycare mandate because my co-worker, Mandy, and I take turns watching each other's kids, and Thomas stayed with our girls whenever he was available. But if an overall mandate is passed, parents' choices will soon be non-existent. Right now, upon school enrollment, the state gives parents a thirty-day window to get caught up, so that meant my girls would eventually have to get the Lunatia as well. This petrifies me…*literally*. I have had so many nightmares about the Lunatia and frankly, all the vaccinations, because of what I've witnessed, and so I have just kept making excuses and putting it off."

"Then it was after this finding that you decided to falsify your daughters' records?" Gavin asked.

"No, that started when I began to realize that the other vaccinations weren't even really working."

"What do you mean they weren't working," he interjected.

"We were having outbreaks of measles and mumps, and the number of kids coming down with the viruses who were vaccinated was pretty even with the unvaccinated. I figured, if the vaccines weren't going to give my girls real and lasting immunity, then why risk the side effects?"

Maryn looked from Gavin to Sister Helena, searching for even a glimpse of judgment, before she added, "I began to wonder…how many vaccinations would they eventually mandate for my girls—my patients, to ensure their theory of herd immunity? How high would the number have to reach? The current schedule requires eighty-seven vaccination doses. Would the number go to one hundred soon? One-fifty? Some vaccines, given as early as six weeks, cover *six* viruses in one shot. Will they start giving kids five shots in one visit to cover thirty viruses?"

Maryn woefully shook her head. "I mean...I had just seen too much! Kids were suffering. The parents were suffering. I started to question even the chronic ear infections. We give kids a vaccination to prevent an intestinal flu that is mild to serious for up to a week, but the intestinal issues caused by the vaccination can last a lifetime. What about the increase in asthma, the peanut allergies? The pharms never told the public that peanut oil had been used in the vaccinations."

"I didn't know about that either," Gavin admitted.

"Peanut allergies were almost unheard of in my day," Helena interjected, "and my parents said they had *never* known anyone allergic to peanuts."

Maryn nodded. "That's because your parents were unvaccinated...Sister, you probably received very few vaccinations. It's just a crapshoot, but the more we give, the greater the risk.

"We hardly see kids who have chickenpox, but we are now seeing kids with *Shingles*, which is much worse! How can we continue to ignore the irrefutable jump in autism and autism-like symptoms that has continued over the past several decades? The pharms never said a word about the aborted fetal cells used in them. How can we be sure that another person's DNA doesn't adversely affect our bodies? As nurses we were told to assure our patients that vaccines were *safe*, but as time went on, I could see with my own eyes that kids were suffering from them."

No one spoke a word for several seconds as Maryn wiped her eyes on her sleeve. Eventually, when she reigned in her emotions, she said, "Suddenly, everything I had been taught to believe in— had *relied* on, seemed false—or at the very least, skewed. But ultimately, the decision to withhold the Lunatia and falsify the records of my patients was when I noticed the first lump."

Gavin's head shot up. "Lump? What lump? Where?" he asked, before trading his thoroughly-chewed nicotine gum for an entire handful of antacids.

"On the top of a little boy's head, right where his soft-spot would have been. I'll never forget it. He—I'll call him Sam, was just as cute as could be. When Sam came to the clinic to receive his Lunatia shot, his mother had just buzzed his hair for summer. Sweet little Sam was adamant that I feel his *whiskers*, as he called them."

Maryn's eyes misted again at the memory. "Then, just two days later, he came in with an extremely high fever and his muscles were twitching. His eyes didn't seem to focus on me when I talked to him. I tried hard to get him to look at me, but he just wouldn't, so I tried to bring him around by asking him if I could feel his whiskers...and that's when I noticed the lump."

"Describe it," Gavin ordered.

"It was about the size of a dime, but more oblong and not much protrusion. It felt different than a typical hematoma—it was much harder."

"So, the kid had a lump on his head—I would think that could be a lot of things," Gavin offered.

"Yes, it could, but because of the fever alone, we sent him to the pediatric clinic to be seen by a doctor and put the discovery in his chart to be reviewed."

"Then what? What happened to the kid?"

"We never saw him again. When I asked about Sam, Carol told me that he'd been diagnosed with DSM-62, which is in the spectrum of Autism. He was transferred to the specialists of course."

"So *that* was what convinced you that you shouldn't give the Lunatia?"

"No...not even that did it. I got convinced that the Lunatia was causing these problems when I decided to pull up this kid's chart and review it. I wanted to see if there was anything else in his history that could have caused it. I needed to know for *sure*. It was possible that my girls were going to have to be injected soon."

"So, what did you find?"

"Nothing. A whole *lot* of nothing. Someone had deleted the data entry that indicated he'd received the Lunatia. In addition, the notes I'd entered during the last visit—the high fever, the odd hematoma were all *gone*. The DSM-62 diagnosis code was the last diagnosis entered."

"Well, computers have glitches a lot. It could have been accidental."

Sister Helena let out a harrumphing gasp so loud, it was as if she had been holding her breath for an hour.

Maryn nodded at Sister Helena, and then looked at Gavin to explain. "Initially, I thought the same thing, sincerely hoping that it was all just a series of unfortunate events, but I had to make sure. We always keep a hard copy that gets printed from the computer entries, so I went into the file room and pulled his folder. Imagine my complete distress to discover that my supervisor signed off on the altered record. Her signature was right there on the page that was incorrect."

"Would she have known any different?" Gavin asked, anxiously, "I mean, she can't know which patients you see every day."

"She *definitely* knew about this one because I had already voiced my concerns about Lunatia. When Sam came in with the fevers and the lump, I talked to her about it before I went home that night. I was worried. She was too."

"So that's it? That's when you chose to withhold the Lunatia?"

"No. I went to Carol *again*, hoping for an explanation as to why she signed off on an inaccurate record, when Sam had clearly had a reaction to the Lunatia."

"And?"

"She said that she erased it herself because she found out that Mandy forgot to give Sam the Lunatia on his earlier visit."

"I thought you had given it to Sam that day," Gavin interjected.

"No. I normally would have, but I had to step out to take a phone call, and Mandy said she'd finish for me."

"So...I'm still not following. If Mandy forgot to give the kid the shot, then he didn't get the symptoms from the Lunatia vaccine."

"She gave him the shot. Carol lied."

"Can you prove this?"

"No. I'm only hoping that I'm right."

"Not good enough. Explain yourself. We can't build a case on hope. I need facts."

Maryn took a deep breath. "I can only prove it if Mandy tells the truth. Well...after everything I had seen, I was just so puzzled—Sam had all the signs, so I just played dumb and said to Mandy, 'Considering poor Sam's diagnosis, it's a good thing that he didn't get that Lunatia after all.'"

That's when she looked at me really weird and said, 'What do you mean? I *gave* him the Lunatia, he was *due*, remember?'"

Gavin's expression hardened. "Did you question or challenge her?

"No."

"Did you discuss Sam and his reaction to Mandy or to Carol or anyone else after that?"

Maryn shook her head. "*No*. Not a word. I was scared to *death* by then. I knew one of them was lying and I needed time to think about what to do. The only person I talked to about it was Thomas."

The mention of Thomas caused Gavin to quit scribbling notes. "What did your husband tell you to do? I need you to try and remember his exact words. What he said to you might impact your culpability."

Maryn didn't hesitate. "He said I should just try and forget about it and that I needed to trust that the new batches were okay. In the end, he said I needed to just let it go because we had no other choice."

His argument made a lot of sense at the time. Thomas also reminded me how many kids get run through there and all the outside factors that could play a part in adverse reactions, genetic and otherwise, and he also told me that Carol was more than likely just trying to save all our asses because the higher-ups were probably trying to keep the clinic from being sued."

Gavin locked eyes with her. "But obviously, you didn't listen to him...*why*?"

She shrugged. "My mother's instinct? I can't explain it exactly. I just *knew* in my heart that the Lunatia was bad news...especially when I began getting the recurring dream."

Gavin groaned inwardly. The last thing he wanted to hear was that she'd made her mind up to commit a crime because of a dream.

The prosecution will have a field day with this one.

On the other hand, he realized that her dream could be elevated to mental distress—a possible legitimate, albeit long-shot, defense. In reality, he knew damn well that Maryn Pearce was anything but mentally incompetent. Reluctantly, he asked her to explain.

"Well," she began, "I kept *praying* that God would show me what to do, especially when it came time to vaccinating our girls. I was just so desperate for answers."

"I can imagine," Sister interjected sympathetically.

Maryn nodded sadly. "One night, I fell asleep praying, and I had this dream about when Lily was born. For the most part, what I dreamed had really happened. It was like I was sent back in time, but I knew I was dreaming all at the same time. Does that make any sense?"

Sister Helena nodded and patted her hand. "It does," she assured comfortingly.

"Well, anyway," Maryn continued, "Lily was just a day old and I was absolutely thrilled that she had figured out how to latch correctly and was nursing so nicely. I could hear her literally gulping my milk."

Maryn's face glowed at the memory. Gavin couldn't help but smile. He remembered Annie being just as thrilled when their babies nursed successfully. Melancholy washed over him at the thought, but he forced himself to stay focused on what Maryn was saying.

"Thomas was looking down on us with such love that my heart literally ached—both then, and in my sleep, during the dream. It was like…like I was re-living the love I had for them *both*."

Clearly emotional, she paused to swallow hard before continuing.

"I said to Thomas, 'Look at what God has given us…a beautiful, healthy baby girl. Ten toes, ten fingers, feather-soft blonde hair…she's *perfect*.'

Thomas smiled and crawled onto the bed beside us. He kissed Lily and then me, and said, 'She *is* perfect…just look at her…drinking like a champ…perfect milk from the most beautiful mother and breasts any baby could ever hope for.'"

"Did he really say that, or was that the dream?" Gavin asked, interrupting her.

"He really said it. I'll never forget it. Like I told you, it all really happened—except in my dream, a nurse suddenly appeared out of nowhere. She was carrying a hypodermic needle and the needle was inching closer and closer to Lily's chubby, little thigh. And that's when the voice inside the room boomed like thunder...'Why do you profane what I have made perfect?'"

"Whose voice? Thomas'?" Gavin asked confused.

"No. Remember, this part was just in my dream, but it was a big, booming voice that shook the room. Then the dream ended with Lily crying uncontrollably as the needle went into her leg."

When I woke up, I felt literally *sick* thinking about all the toxins we'd injected into both Lily and Pearl," she finished sadly.

"Did you ever tell this dream to Thomas?" he asked.

She shook her head. "No. Thomas always got really agitated when I would talk to him about the Lunatia incident and my doubts, so I just kept it to myself. I mean, Thomas felt like most people—all the experts tell us that if we don't follow the vaccine schedule, we are irresponsible and putting our children in danger. And besides that, no one really has any choice in the matter if they are working people—because all daycares and schools require it."

Knowing that their session was quickly coming to an end, Gavin pressed forward. "So, Thomas *wanted* you to give the girls Lunatia, despite what you told him?"

"I really don't know anymore. At the time, I honestly thought he was worried too." He finally told me to just put it off as long as I could, since the disease it prevented was relatively low risk."

Maryn looked from one to the other with great sadness in her eyes as she said. "I truly believed he was sincere when he told me he was hoping that more information would come out that would either cast enough doubt to ban it, or prove the new formula was safe. Frankly, I had the same hope, because if I was noticing these adverse reactions, other people were seeing things too."

Gavin nodded. "Right. But if Thomas told you to wait as long as you could...well, I am just so surprised that he is as pissed off as he is at you. I mean...his statement in court is the reason you haven't seen your kids yet, and why the judge didn't give you leniency regarding the treason charge—which, in my opinion, should have been thrown out immediately."

Tears quickly filled her eyes. "I know...I *know*. It's like...well, I don't even know him anymore. The Thomas from my dream—from my *life*, has become a complete stranger. Sometimes I wonder if it's because he's a cop. Maybe he didn't want to lose his job over what I'd done. He really prides himself on keeping the law. I just don't *know*. Maybe he was just really scared and...well, even more scared and mad when he realized that I faked giving Lily and Pearl their other booster shots after the Sam incident."

"And why did you do that?"

"Because...I just figured," her voice began to crack, and her bottom lip began to tremble like a little kid's. "I just didn't trust *anyone* at that point. The pharmaceutical companies have made so many mistakes and recalled so much medicine...even the Lunatia was on its second revision. I mean...as a parent, what guarantee do I have that a vaccination being injected into my child's body is not worse than getting the measles or chicken pox? Some government *study*? How can I have confidence in government studies when so many entities have a financial interest and they keep getting caught in one scandal after another?"

By now, Maryn's voice was shaking with righteous anger that ignited a fire in her eyes that replaced her tears. Her gaze went from one to the other before she continued passionately, "Lily and Pearl are my *children*! When do *I* get the right to decide what's best for them? How did this *ever* happen? To allow our government to force us to do something we don't agree with, especially when it could hurt or kill our children, is *communism*, not freedom."

Her declaration floated through the air, but the truth of it was weighty, pressing down on all of them. In that moment, Gavin couldn't think of a single argument to negate her concerns. But then, there was the matter of David.

His stomach rolled just thinking about it. He hated to bring it up, but he had to know for sure. "Maryn, I am sorry. I am really beginning to understand where you're coming from. I've been oblivious to these issues for the most part, but the sheer number of lawyers who specialize in vaccine injury tells me that there is a great deal of controversy surrounding vaccinations. Isabella's experience with her daughter proves that you are definitely not alone in your concerns. We can certainly use this to help defend you. But...there is still the matter of David. As much as I hate to, we need to address it."

At the mention of his name, fresh tears sprung up in Maryn's eyes. "Oh, Dear God...that *poor* boy...that poor, sweet boy! What's ironic is that I gave him all his shots, *except* for the Lunatia. I figured that he wasn't going to be going to the beach any time soon...I mean, it's way too cold. I just wanted to buy some time and spread them out as best I could..."

She broke down, crying so hard that Gavin could not stay in his chair. He walked around the table and pulled her into his arms.

The tears in Sister Helena's eyes matched his own as their gaze connected. Sister shook her head woefully. To see her sadness was even more unsettling to Gavin.

God, I am in way over my head. What the hell do I do now?

Chapter 13

After his session with Maryn was over, Gavin sped back to the office, his mind racing almost as fast as his BMW. To say he was rattled was a gross understatement. Consumed with all he'd discovered, he could now thoroughly relate to the concept of feeling the weight of the world on his shoulders. All he could think of were the masses of kids at risk—and at the top of the list, were his own. He was adamant to do everything possible to protect them from future vaccination risks. This time he wouldn't blow it.

Brenna had texted him the previous night explaining that practice had run late and that she would call him the first chance she got. Even though he knew she wouldn't answer because she was in school, he felt the need to connect with her in the worst way. Using voice command, he called her number, and as expected, her voicemail picked up.

Gavin groaned with disappointment. *My baby girl is growing up so fast...without me.*

Marveling at how emotional he was at just hearing her voice, raw determination made him swallow his guilt and leave a message.

"Hey baby girl, I just wanted to hear your voice and make sure everything's going okay for you."

I need you to help me survive.

"I know that you're busy..."

You learned that from watching me give up everything for money.

"But be careful not to get burned out and take on too much. And just remember that I'm here if you need me..."

I'm waiting for you to love me again. I need you so much.

"I miss you, honey."

Some days I feel like I'm going to die without you.

"I love you, Brenna."

More than you'll ever know.

After he ended the call, pain like a hardened fist landed a punch to his stomach. His guilt twisted tighter and tighter until it was difficult to breathe.

Annie went through all the vaccinations and their health issues with our kids by herself. I was completely oblivious for the most part. I vaguely remember her worrying about their fevers...but it was so long ago. My God, I hope she isn't thinking about getting them the Lunatia vaccination. Maybe they've gotten it already.

At the thought, he immediately sent a text.

"Hey Annie, just in case it comes up for the kids, or for you, please don't get the Lunatia shot. I'll explain later. Hope you are well."

After he'd finished, a great sadness added to his already heightened anxiety. *What is happening to us? We communicate on every device and yet, we are further apart than ever.*

He thought of Maryn's torment. She was suffering losses hard to voice, to even fathom.

At least I still have my kids. She can't even text her kids.

"God help us. This world's a mess," he blurted into the silence of the car's interior.

His clumsy half-prayer, half-lamentation caused him to think of Sister Helena.

She must be praying herself nuts. Between Maryn, the Sanchez family, and me, that rosary of hers has got to be smoking.

Normally, he would have smiled at the vision he'd conjured up, but everything Maryn had revealed was devastating—almost too much to grasp. As he pondered the reality, fear slowly began to rise up inside him, intensifying the tightness in his stomach and chest.

There is surely much more destruction to come.

He made every attempt to take slow, deep breaths to push away the thought and forced himself to focus on the fact that he had found the strength to keep from drinking the previous night.

At the traffic light, just blocks from his office, he reached into his pocket and retrieved the prayer card. Staring down at the visage of God's most powerful angel was strangely comforting but fleeting, as flashing red lights in his rearview mirror shattered the moment.

Gavin let out a hailstorm of swear words as he pulled over in the parking lot of the Kwik-Fill fuel & charge station. His mind raced to think of what exactly he had done wrong.

The phone calls.

He swore again and reached over to the storage compartment to retrieve the information he knew would be asked for. By the time he settled back into his seat, an officer was knocking on his window.

Gavin pushed the electronic button and watched as the glass disappeared. The face of a young, clean-shaven officer came into view. Without saying a word, Gavin thrust his driver's license, registration, and insurance cards toward him.

Despite his boyish appearance, the cop's face was stoic. "Mr...uh...Steele," he began, reading Gavin's name from the driver's license in his hand, "I am sure you are aware that phone use while operating a motor vehicle is prohibited."

Gavin nodded. "Sure am, Officer...uh...Johnson," he replied, snarkily, imitating the officer's stumble with his name.

Johnson gave Gavin a sharp look in response to his sarcasm. "So, either you were talking to *yourself* or you were on the phone—which is it?" he retorted flatly, while his eyes scoured the interior of Gavin's vehicle.

Completely annoyed, and ever the lawyer, Gavin countered, "How do you know I wasn't *praying?*"

His intention was to simply get a dig in at the overconfident rookie, but he looked over to find him staring at the prayer card on the console. In spite of his dour mood and high anxiety, Gavin wanted to laugh. It was positioned perfectly to give Officer Johnson pause.

Gavin stayed quiet, as though he was waiting for an answer. Finally, Johnson said, "I'm going to give you the benefit of a doubt today, Mr. Steele. Make sure you keep your eyes on the road at all times—even when you're *praying*."

His tone indicated that he didn't believe for a minute he was praying, but before Gavin knew it, Johnson handed him his information back and was walking back to his car.

That's it? What just happened here?

Gavin knew the hands-free phone law was yet another excuse for the police to be able to stop anyone—targeting especially, those suspicious of criminal activity, but the fact that the guy let him go without so much as checking his phone log, left him dumfounded.

"He didn't even run my driver's license," he whispered.

As he merged back into traffic, Gavin marveled at what had just occurred. With a plethora of serious worries pressing in on his mind, it never would have occurred to him to try and get out of a minor ticket for being on the phone—he could afford the fine and it would have taken less than a minute and a credit card to take care of it. Still, he was on his way without a hitch.

He glanced over at the card next to him. St. Michael seemed to be staring right back.

"That was fast work, Mike," he quipped. "Thanks."

*****

With his coat still hanging from one arm, Gavin punched the speaker button on the dinosaur and dialed Isabella's number. He hoped to get her to the office ASAP, so they could discuss whether she had ever noticed a lump on Sophia's head after the Lunatia shot.

When her answering machine picked up, he hung up and came unhinged. "NO! I don't want to leave a friggin message at the tone—or *ever*," he barked, before filling the room with a few choice cusswords.

Sylvie heard his ranting and stuck her head into his office. "Uhhh…is there anything I can do to help? Your little tantrum may have just broken the sound barrier."

"No…nothing," he muttered, rubbing his tired eyes, "I'm just so *pissed!* Why don't people answer their damn phones?"

"You mean like how you answer yours?" she asked dryly.

"Touché, Smartass," he shot back. "Have you eaten yet? I'm starving. Order us some food, would you?"

Sylvie laughed. "Mexican or burgers?"

"Burger Shack—no onions. My gut is on fire."

"Gee, I wonder why," she answered, raising her eyebrows. "When my boys are upset, my mother tells them to take a deep breath," she teased, before her face turned serious. "So, what's going on that's got you so postal? Isabella Sanchez is going to call eventually—you know that, so what gives?"

"More than I can explain right now," he admitted, "and if you knew, you'd understand how it is to start building a logical case that I can use to help both Maryn *and* Isabella. Sophia could be the key that just might be able to give me the ammo I need to march right into the courtroom and shred Maryn's charges so completely that the CDC will immediately become the Center for Damage Control," he gloated.

Then, sobering suddenly, he confessed, "You just might have been right, Sylvie…we may be on the verge of exposing one of the biggest scandals in history."

Her eyes widened and then quickly narrowed when he didn't elaborate. "Wait just a *minute*…after everything I found out, don't you *dare* dangle that big juicy morsel in front of me and then not tell me what you're talking about!"

Gavin thought about telling her everything. In truth, it was a little overwhelming to know so much and not be able to discuss it. After giving it some thought, he said, "To be honest, Sylvie, I'm a little concerned that telling you wouldn't be the wisest thing to do. I don't want you involved in this thing any more than you have to be, especially until I can get a handle on it. I'd be lying if I said I knew how I'm going to make it happen. In fact, as soon as I eat, I'm leaving. I've got a lot more information to collect."

Her face showed an array of mixed emotions. "Well, part of me is frustrated to not know what's going on, but the other part of me is scared just enough to trust your judgment and stay out of it. But, if you need me to go to the library again, I will. There's so many people hanging out on the computers there—weirdos included, that no one's going to even notice me."

"Thanks, but I've got a laptop I can search on. I've been driving to different wi-fi locations, so all the inquiries don't come from the same server."

"Wow, you're really serious."

He got up and started pacing the floor.

"Am I serious? *Yes*. Paranoid? *Yes*. Worried? *Yes*. I feel like I'm the star of a conspiracy theory movie where every move I make is being watched."

"Are you for *real*?" she asked, her face paling a little. "I mean, do you *really* think that's happening…for *sure*?".

He sighed. "Not yet…but that's why we have to be so careful. No discussing either case, *remember*?"

"Not a word. It scares the hell out of me, especially now," she answered convincingly.

"Good. If Isabella Sanchez calls, use the dinosaur to talk to her and tell her I'll call her back as soon as I can, and then text me something generic about my call coming in. If someone comes in looking for me, I am out for the day—tell them I'm sick or at the doctors, or something they can't get pissed about."

She nodded. "Okay."

"On second thought," he interjected, scooping up the coat he'd only just taken off minutes ago. He pushed his arms through the sleeves. "Forget about ordering food for me," he said, tossing a twenty on his desk. "Get yourself something. I'll eat while I'm researching."

He was out the door so fast that Sylvie wondered if he heard her say thank you.

Chapter 14

Gavin woke to the faint beeping sound of his fax machine. It was pitch dark in his bedroom, so initially, he thought he'd imagined it. He looked over at the illumination on his wall that told him it was 3:45 a.m.

"Who in the hell is sending me a fax at this hour?" he groaned.

The fact that he'd been asleep for just a little more than an hour added insult to injury. "Whatever it is, I'll be damned if I'm going to look at it now," he grumbled.

For the first time in more than a year, he'd fallen into bed without wondering whether he'd be able to sleep. The reason had to be sheer exhaustion; his mind and emotions had been put through the ringer, and then some. Now, thanks to the beeping fax machine, the events of the day were bouncing around his head like the silver ball in a pinball machine.

He'd spent most of the afternoon and night listening to internet videos of various doctors and those claiming to be vaccine-injured and their families give testimony of their experiences and findings.

Even though Gavin was also able to find reports debunking these claims, the testimonies he'd listened to were wholly unnerving—especially the testimonies of parents who didn't give a crap what the experts or reports said, because they had literally watched their child suffer or even die after being immunized.

The stories were all different, but really, all the same basic pattern—a vaccination experience that resulted in a reaction, followed by the worsening of symptoms, then culminating with delayed or denial of treatment, before injured victims and parents are left to live life as best they can.

In some rare instances, there was admission of the connection by medical personnel and so-called experts, and he did find one testimony where the attending physician was able to make the connection right away. One set of grateful parents gave testimony that their concerned pediatrician immediately advised them to report the sudden onslaught of rheumatoid arthritis in their three-year-old daughter to VAERS.

It was brutal watching the couple come to grips with the knowledge that their toddler would battle crippling arthritis for the rest of her life, Still, Gavin was glad to hear that their physician was supportive and was sure there were more dedicated professionals like him out there. Unfortunately, finding them was like looking for a needle in a haystack. He suspected that ignorance and fear of retribution were factors, but with the recent deaths of so many outspoken physicians and researchers, the number could very well decrease rather than increase.

One of the most disturbing, yet convincing, videos he'd watched was from a nurse who'd gone undercover. An older RN with decades of experience to her credit, she had risked taking screenshots of patients' files at her OB-GYN clinic to illuminate the connection between the sudden death of unborn babies in correlation to recent immunizations given to their pregnant mothers. Gavin was stunned to hear her report that many of the unborn babies who died suddenly were third-trimester, otherwise-healthy babies. Most of the mothers had very low pregnancy-risk factors.

Sometimes, the mother received the flu shot, sometimes the DTAP was given, but seeing the words: "Fetal Demise" on chart after chart, made Gavin certain that the nurse was on to something. There just had to be a connection—the number of occurrences just couldn't be a coincidence. It just wasn't probable.

The nurse's testimony greatly stoked the fire for justice in him. He'd always believed that most medical injury lawyers were just money-grubbing dirt-bags like he was, but now he was more than convinced that there was a legitimate need.

There should never even be a need.

Still, he knew Maryn's case would be an uphill battle—brutal in fact. The liability would be tough to prove. Witnesses would scatter like roaches when they began to feel the financial burden and real pressures associated with coming forward—especially if the unexplained deaths of vaccine opponents continued or was exposed somehow.

The brave nurse whose testimony he'd watched had risked a great deal—but only if she was believed. Due to confidentiality, the patients' names had been blacked out. He understood that anonymity was necessary, but without names he was still without concrete proof of the nurse's claims. He would be unable to use the video as credible evidence to sway a jury. Vaccinations were currently considered the Savior of every nation.

I wonder when they'll begin calling the vaccine schedule, SAVIOR?

"Scheduled, Administered, Vaccination, Implementation & Obligation Regimen," he declared aloud.

If the concept wasn't so disturbing, he might have laughed at his cleverness. His mood was dark.

I've got to figure out a way to contact that undercover nurse so I can subpoena the records and get her to testify.

He yawned. It had been a long, exhausting day. After driving miles and miles to different wi-fi spots to do the research, he was now, officially, paranoid as hell—to the point of taking the extra time to drive to two separate, smaller suburbs where security cameras didn't line every street. Still, he knew that anyone watching for these types of red-flag searches could eventually track him down if they were determined to do so.

Even more frustrating was that the more he learned, the more he felt he didn't know. Everything he'd ever been told regarding immunizations appeared to be skewed, or simply omitted. So much so, it appeared that the pool of common knowledge most had come to trust looked more like an oozing swamp.

It was mind-blowing to learn that the dreaded disease of Polio, which most everyone feared because of the potential for paralysis, was not an air-borne virus but is spread through fecal matter.

Moreover, one data chart he stumbled onto showed that the decline in the Polio rate came before the immunization was ever introduced. He discovered that cleaning up the water and sewer systems was the real key to control of the malady, and why under-developed countries relied so heavily on the vaccination. The truth made him livid.

All these years we have prided ourselves on being the country that provides impoverished nations with vaccinations to save their lives...

"How about cleaning up their frickin' water and helping them to get nutritious food?" he grumbled, rearranging his pillow and turning onto his side.

Once more, he squeezed his eyes shut to try and sleep, but his mind would simply not shut down. Pieces of hard-to-accept truth surfaced along with his anxiety. The Cutter Incident, a study from 1955, revealed that the first Polio vaccinations caused forty-thousand children to come down with the disease, paralyzing two hundred children and killing ten.

To come across these such monumental findings, which he had never even heard a whisper about, made him feel like he had awakened on another planet—in a different place and time. It was mind-boggling to discover the plethora of information available for the public to see; and yet, very little of it was known by the vast majority.

I wonder if Maryn knows about The Cutter Incident. I had to look through a lot of searches before I finally found it. The propaganda bombs we've been spoon-fed for the past century or so have been unbelievably effective.

The report about the World Health Organization and UNICEF lacing the immunizations of Kenyan girls was kept quiet. I never heard a whiff of it before I stumbled on it yesterday. I wonder how long it had been going on before those Catholic bishops who discovered it caught on?

"UNICEF and W.H.O. are supposed to be the good guys," he grumbled. "Our children have been a part of an enormous, ongoing medical experiment."

Still, considering the fact that for years and years social media giants and search engines had been spying on the world, using their technology to manipulate elections and thinking in general, it was a miracle that he was able to find anything at all to shed light on vaccine damage. New regulations restricting these types of manipulations and collection of personal data were more of a joke than a real solution. It would be near impossible to put a screaming cat back inside the bag.

For the time being, Gavin was grateful for the internet—even if his gratitude would probably be short lived. He would have never stumbled onto any of the controversial information without it. It was troubling, however, that despite all he'd uncovered, he had come up empty-handed regarding recent VAERS reports or patient testimonies on Lunatia—both the original or improved formulas. This was unsettling. In his estimation, it meant one of two things—either there were none out there, which would make everything harder to prove, or they had been removed from government and media-sharing sites. The latter possibility, while it scared the hell out of him, seemed to be the only credible explanation, because Maryn was sure that VAERS initially cited Lunatia injury reports.

Welprox came out with a revision of the original Lunatia formula for good reason. It sure as hell isn't the norm for pharms to willingly admit problems, so the issues with the original vaccine must have been significant. Or is there something else I'm missing?

"Where have the reports gone to?" he whispered, as he lay there wondering where to go, what to do next. He had a mound of potential evidence, but most of it could not be backed up by medical documentation.

In reality, if the case was about any other topic, Gavin was certain it would be enough to sway a jury as to possible extenuating circumstances surrounding Maryn's actions. But the subject of vaccinations was untouchable—the medical community's Holy Grail. Considering the increasing number of suspicious deaths, it appears that those who dared question the schedule, or got too close to the data, were either snuffed out or made out to be lunatics. But without a smoking gun for evidence, Gavin was leery of exposing his clients and all involved, to a circus event that would quickly turn ugly—not only in the press, but in the eyes of the public at large.

If that many doctors are dead, there is no predicting the magnitude of opening this can of worms. I'm going to have to be very sure of who the enemy is, and very sure my evidence will blow this whole thing so sky-high that people will come raining out of the sky to testify.

"They can't kill us all."

In the darkness, his declaration fell flat. Thoughts of his kids and the potential impact his involvement may have on them, quickly gave him pause.

His mind drifted to his earlier conversation with Brenna. Considering how long he'd waited for her call, she must have sensed something in the message he left, because the first thing she had asked him was whether he was okay. He hated the idea of her worrying about him, but admittedly, he was glad she cared enough to call him back. Small as it was, it was a breakthrough.

Regardless of the outcome of these new cases, I've got to do what I can to stop all this vaccine crap. I don't want my kids putting anything into their bodies that could harm them.

"I need to know the *truth*, damnit!" he growled into the dark.

I need some help, but I don't know who to ask. I sure as hell don't want to throw anyone else into this fire.

He looked at the clock again and groaned. He'd lost another thirty minutes of sleep. Worse than that, he was now wide awake.

Swearing in frustration, he threw off the covers and rolled out of bed. *I might as well get up. I'm never going to be able to go back to sleep with all this on my mind.*

After using the restroom, he headed to the kitchen to brew a cup of coffee. As he passed by his office, he noticed the light on his fax machine was still blinking, causing him to remember the reason he was awake in the first place.

"I guess I *didn't* imagine it," he mumbled. The room lit up immediately as he passed through the doorway and crossed the space to the fax machine. He yawned as he retrieved the fax and shoved it into the wide pocket of his robe. He needed either a stout cup of coffee or a shot of scotch and wasn't about to start working until he had one or the other. Thinking of his kids, he chose to go for the coffee and quickly headed into the kitchen before he changed his mind.

The soft lights came on as he passed through the entryway, illuminating the modern, but hardly-used, space. He grabbed a mug from the open shelf next to the coffee maker and placed it into the Insta-Brew. After choosing his favorite coffee blend, he hit "strong" on the brew level. He needed it. By the time he got back from the fridge with his cream and honey, his mug was steaming with coffee.

After stirring in all the "nonsense" as his old-man called it, Gavin padded to the spacious living room and sat on a plush, black, easy chair. He then traded his coffee for the remote on the table beside him. With two clicks, the sky-light above opened, the sleek, gas fireplace instantly danced with flames.

Now comfortably settled, he placed the remote on the table and reached for his mug. After a few satisfying, much-needed sips, he pulled the fax from his pocket. The very instant his eyes focused on the page, his arm robotically reached out to set the mug on the table next to him, but he missed. The mug fell to the ground and shattered.

Gavin hardly noticed the broken pieces of ceramic, or the hot steaming liquid that was seeping into the plush area rug on the hardwood floor. All his senses were focused on the message:

To: Gavin Steele
Subject: David Adams
Cause of death: Aortic aneurysm; genetic abnormality.
Autopsy record altered.

Chapter 15

Hoping to ease the pain and stiffness in her joints, Sister Helena slathered a generous glob of arthritis cream onto each calloused knee. Having just finished her morning prayers and with breakfast still waiting, she was a bit surprised to hear a knock on her door. She put an end to her regimen by hastily rubbing in the last of the pungent liniment before pulling up her support stockings. After tossing her skirt down over her knees, she answered cheerfully, "Good morning! Come on in!"

Standing in the open doorway was Sister Joanna, one of three remaining retired nuns living at the convent. She was a tiny little thing—complete opposite of Helena in stature and personality. Her small, heart-shaped face, and clear-blue eyes still reflected the beauty of her younger years. Since her voice was always soft, her demeanor, unhurried, the fact that Joanna blurted, "You have a visitor," confirmed what Helena already knew. Something was up. She had sensed it all night.

Without a word, Helena hurriedly made her way through the creaking, wooden hallways of the convent, all the while hoping that whoever was waiting wasn't bringing bad news. Among other things, she was worried about her beloved cousin, Father Anthony. A priest for more than sixty-five years, he had suffered a stroke two weeks ago, and she wondered if the prayers she'd been awakened in the night to offer up had been for him.

She hadn't meant to throw the heavy wooden door to the visitor's center open with such gusto, but the doorknob banged loudly against the thick wall, startling both Helena and her visitor.

"Jah-eez…"

"Don't *say* it!" Helena warned, cutting him off.

Still holding his chest, Gavin blew out a sigh. "Can ya give a guy a little warning before you give him a heart attack?" he barked, shaking his head.

"No such luck," she answered teasingly. "You have way too much work to do. No trying to cut out early on me."

"Very funny," he answered dryly.

"Speaking of *early*…what brings you here at this hour?" she asked, "Even the birds are wondering what you're up to this morning."

"We need to talk," he answered, nodding to the open doorway. "Is this the best place to have a private conversation?"

Helena quickly shut the door behind her. "What's going on?"

"I'll take that as a yes," he replied, before placing his briefcase on the floral couch cushion next to him. "Have a seat," he ordered, flipping the locks open with his thumbs, "I don't have much time."

Helena obeyed without pause. Gavin's early visit and his demeanor made her certain that whatever he needed to discuss was very important. With one finger, she pushed up her glasses and took the paper from his hand.

It took just seconds for the content of the fax to sink in. The message was nothing she could have ever anticipated, but at the same time, Sister Helena knew it was an answer to prayer. She looked up and said, "Lord Jesus, we thank You," her voice thick with emotion

Gavin raised his eyebrows and answered, "Well, I'm glad you're so thankful…this scares the *hell* out of me. Do you understand what this means?"

Helena looked up at him with a happy grin. "Yes! It means that Maryn will be exonerated in any wrongful death charge regarding David!"

"Yeah…well, let's not jump the gun here. *If* this information is correct, don't you realize that our biggest fear is about to become a reality—whether we are ready for it or not?"

"*Your* biggest fear, not *mine*," she answered calmly, placing her hand over his to still its trembling. "*My* biggest fear is that so many are suffering needlessly and are in jeopardy of losing their *souls*."

Gavin gave her a look that clearly indicated he thought she was loony for talking about souls when it was obvious that something very sinister was happening in their midst.

"Sister...I know that souls are your business, but I don't think you really see the potential danger here..."

She cut him off. "I *do* see the potential danger, Gavin. What has taken place is not just dangerous, it's *evil to the core*. Learning of the evil that Maryn uncovered was just the beginning. The injuries that innocent children and their families are being subjected to is also evil at its worst—*I get that*. I am just trying to calm you down enough to make you realize that someone out there is working on our side—someone on God's side who wants the truth uncovered."

"You don't *know* that!" he exclaimed cynically. "We don't know *who* sent this fax to me! I tried looking up the number and it's unlisted. Probably was disconnected after the fax was sent."

"Okay, so we don't know who sent it, but what would be the motivation except to help Maryn? Obviously, whoever shared this with you is sticking his or her own neck out for the sake of justice—or for a motive that we don't understand, but I see it as all good."

"Well, I'm glad you're so certain. I'm about as confident as a Jew having dinner with Hitler. Seems to me, he enjoyed playing God, too."

"Oh poo!" Helena exclaimed, waving his comment away. "Whoever sent this message is on *our* side. I *know* it. Have you told Maryn yet?"

Gavin slapped his forehead with his palm and said, "No! I received this in the middle of the night. I've got to figure out how to proceed...and frankly, I really haven't a clue. I don't know *who* to trust. You're it. I can't trust another single soul with this information. Take that as a compliment."

"Sad as that is, I *do*," she answered with a compassionate smile. "God will guide us."

Gavin turned his head and rolled his eyes, but Helena saw his expression anyway. She chose to ignore it and asked, "Gavin, do you know anyone in the medical profession? We need someone to confirm this. We need access to David Adam's file...and the coroner's report. Goodness, if we just knew who sent this...wait! Is it possible that Maryn's co-workers are trying to help her? Can we even trust them? Remember, Sam's records were altered too."

"I thought of that," he admitted, "and what if we approach either of them and are wrong about their involvement. There's no way they'll keep our inquiry a secret. I just told you—I don't trust *anyone*."

"Good point. So...let me think..."

Helena sat quiet for several seconds before Gavin blurted, "Don't *you* know anyone in the medical profession who can be trusted? I mean, you're a nun...and well, you're old. You should know those type of people."

She wanted to laugh out loud but didn't. He was oblivious of the humor in his words. "I'm sorry," she answered, shaking her head, "but I really don't. I don't go to the doctor much. As long as my heart's still ticking, I just leave the rest up to God. But if the Holy Spirit tells me to go, I do."

Gavin put his head down and rubbed his eyes. "Sister...with all due respect, I don't think you really understand the gravity..."

"Of *course* I do!" she interrupted with a snort. "I'm just telling you the truth. I don't know any trustworthy physicians. When I do go in for something, I end up seeing a nurse practitioner or someone different every time, anyway. But I do have a cousin who may know someone. He's a priest so we can trust him. The only problem is that he's in the hospital. He had a stroke."

Gavin threw his head back and laughed sardonically. "Ohhhh great! I feel so much better now! We've got a brain-damaged priest for help now."

Sister Helena stared back without blinking. "Let me know when you are you finished acting childish?"

"Childish?" he asked disbelievingly. "Sister, what you don't understand is that once this case explodes we will *not* be able to *contain* it, and we won't be free from the fallout no matter *where* we hide. We must have *clear, foolproof* evidence so strong that we can blow the doors off Maryn's jail cell. Right now, I don't know how to get that evidence! And if what we know gets leaked somehow, we all could be quickly joining the fateful doctors who are six feet under because they failed to thoroughly and powerfully expose the coverup. My concerns are not *childish*, they are *real*."

"I *know* they're real!" she countered, louder than she had intended. She lowered her voice and said, "The concerns are *real*. It's your attitude that is childish. Open your mind, Gavin! You've just been given information that you didn't even know you were looking for! Have faith! God is our ally here! He *hates* deception and all manner of evil. If we pray and trust Him, He'll help us. *Believe* it."

Gavin sat quiet for several moments before saying, "Well, God's going to have to pull out all the stops on this one, cause I've got *nothin'*."

Helena shook her head and corrected him. "You've got *everything*. You've got God on your side…and you've got *me*."

She let out a chuckle and added, "You have *no* idea how determined I can be."

Gavin shook his head. "If things weren't so damned serious, I'd be laughing. I *do* know how determined you are. You've driven me nuts with your dogged meddling ever since we met."

Her expression soured a bit until he sheepishly added, "Thank you."

She gave him a smile and said, "You're welcome. We'll find a way to get this information. I'm sure of it. After my prayers, I will go and visit my cousin. You go visit Maryn and update her on this news. I'll call the office when I get something."

For the third time, Gavin stared at her before asking, "Since when are you calling the shots?"

"Got any better ideas?" she countered.

He marveled at her tenacity and answered honestly, "No. But I need to emphasize two things—remember to trust *no one*. When you are at the hospital or wherever, make sure you're alone, cannot be overheard, and are not being watched."

"I know. I'll be careful. What else?"

"Secondly, I'm going on the record as saying…if you can pull this off, you can officially call me a believer."

Helena grinned broadly. "Perfect."

Gavin shook his head. "That was not a statement of confidence, Sister. I think you are dreaming."

"And you don't think I know that?" she asked flatly. "I don't put my faith in dreams, but in the One who makes them come true."

Chapter 16

Gavin put the bottle of pastel-colored antacids to his mouth, gave it a good shake, and then chased them down with the rest of his ice-cold coffee. He was starving, yet sick to his stomach, and very irritable.

Getting stuck in traffic for nearly two hours was only the beginning of his exasperating commute. Just when traffic had started to move again, a three-car pileup brought four lanes of bumper to bumper traffic to a complete stand still.

It's already after ten. If I can't get to the facility soon, I will have to wait until this afternoon to see Maryn.

He swore loudly and couldn't resist joining in the actions of the drivers who were laying on the horn to show their displeasure. "That'll really show 'em," he grumbled, mocking his own juvenile behavior.

Impulsively, he checked his phone for any messages or missed calls from Sylvie or Isabella.

Nothing.

He swore again. He really didn't want to be forced to drive to Isabella's house to confirm whether she had noticed a lump on Sophia's head after her Lunatia vaccine.

Gavin blew out a sigh of frustration.

This is rich…Isabella comes to me for help but then won't answer my calls. In the meanwhile, I'm racking my brain trying to figure out how to get Maryn off and yet I have no freaking idea as to where she'd go or how to keep her safe until the trial. She'd need protective custody for sure.

On the other hand, I can't say I'm going to feel really confident with the cops protecting her against this level of corruption. Whoever found a way to kill those doctors will eventually find a way to shut Maryn up. Not to mention that the cops may not exactly be thrilled to protect her if their loyalty is with her dirt-bag, traitor husband.

The gravity of it all was staggering, especially since he was stuck in traffic. Feeling helpless, he turned on satellite radio to listen to the news. It took about fifteen seconds for him to search for something else. It was always the same. Politics, war, economy, the ridiculous, all from the same mechanical, phony, rating-driven, talking heads. How anyone could listen to people blasting their opinion, especially about things they knew little to nothing about, was beyond his comprehension.

Bunch of liberal drivel and crybabies I can do without. If there's a conservative channel out there, it's probably one in a million, and I sure as hell wouldn't know where to find it.

Gavin snorted derisively. "What would it matter anyway, these days many of the conservatives are as goofed up as the libs."

The thought made him even more agitated as he considered the present state of the country. Besides the ever-present threat of terrorism, drug overdose—including opioids, was now the number one cause of death, second only to abortion. Guns had been outlawed, but crime was at an all-time high. Along with the crime, racial tensions worsened every day, largely due to the P.C. police who ensured that any criticism of anyone for any reason be considered hate speech. Contrary to the effect they'd hoped to achieve, politically correct policy enforcement seemed to just add fuel to the fire.

Thanks to government funded tuition, most college campuses had become breeding grounds for overindulged, lazy kids with entitlement attitudes, who believed that everyone should be tolerant of their behavior and ideals. Heralded as the "future of America," many of these "champions of tolerance" destroyed, burned, and looted everything in sight on their campuses, while protesting every injustice, including a hangnail someone found offensive.

Sadly, this pattern of destructive behavior, which had started more than a decade ago, had now grown to epic proportions. Protests were seldom peaceful. Instead, using fear of retribution, they were used to control and manipulate any dissenting institution or person.

"No wonder I drink," Gavin grumbled.

Traffic was now inching along at a snail's pace, but he was glad for even that. He mindlessly pushed the scanner button again and glanced at his gauges. "This damn traffic better start moving soon. I only have about fifty miles left on this charge," he murmured, turning down the heat just a bit to conserve energy.

"CWTN Breaking news ..."

Gavin's ears perked up at the announcer's declaration. He glanced up to see which news station was reporting and had to chuckle. *I knew that station sounded familiar.*

"Boy, Sister Helena," he declared, as the traffic began to move along, "you must be pulling in some big favors from the man upstairs to hook me up with a Catholic news station..."

"Breaking news...Former Congressman, Roger Allen Townes, has died of apparent heart failure. Townes, recently appointed by President-elect Moore to oversee the formation of the Vaccine Safety and Injury Prevention Council—VSIPC, has died at the age of fifty-nine."

Gavin sobered immediately. Just the mention of the word vaccine made his heart beat faster. He immediately turned up the volume.

"Townes was in the process of putting together a team of physicians and researchers to oversee vaccination procedures and provide Americans with an advocacy to ensure the highest standards of safety and efficacy for all vaccinations."

The racing of Gavin's mind now matched his rapid pulse as he attempted to absorb the implications.

How could this possibly be happening? What are the chances?

The CWTN announcer continued, "Townes, a pro-family, pro-life advocate, will be sorely missed by his family and community in Bellevue, Washington. Those who served alongside him in Congress will remember him fondly as a man of integrity and good will.

Townes leaves behind his spouse Laura, of thirty-three years, four children, and two grandchildren. May his soul rest in peace."

*****

Despite his proximity to the correctional facility and his relief to be moving through traffic again, Gavin pulled off the freeway and into the nearest station to charge his battery and backup cell. By the time he got on the road again, his nerves had him cracking sunflower seeds faster than a chipmunk.

The death of Congressman Townes left him shaken. From his perspective, the timing was highly suspicious. On the other hand, many would think the possibility was too farfetched for even the wildest conspiracy theory.

I need to chill. The coroner said it was his heart. So the L.A. Coroner's part of the conspiracy too?

The idea was laughable. Still, considering Towne's new position, the timing left Gavin trembling inside. Either way, he was convinced that the trip to see Maryn wasn't nearly as important as gathering evidence from Isabella.

Earlier, Sylvie had texted him that she had been trying to reach her all morning, but so far, hadn't gotten an answer. Ultimately, Isabella's silence, along with the news about Townes, made up his mind. He made a U-turn, and in just seconds, was on his way to the Sanchez residence in San Bruno. His visit would either tie everything together or add to the increasing knot of misinformation and deception.

The extra miles and time will be well worth it if Isabella noticed a lump on Sophia's head. There wasn't a single mention of that side-effect in the package insert or in any of the Lunatia literature I found online. This is pertinent. I can feel it.

"And if the shots are given in the upper thigh, why the swelling of the head?" he wondered aloud, spitting an entire mouthful of shells into an empty paper cup he'd gotten at the charging station. "Could that indicate that the brain has been affected somehow?"

He took several gulps of his tea before grabbing another handful of seeds. When he tipped his head back to toss them in his mouth, it was then that he noticed a black Lexus in his rearview mirror. Nothing about the car should have made him uncomfortable, but strangely, it did. Though it was following at a respectable distance, something about not being able to clearly see the passengers through the tinted windows left him with an eerie feeling.

Silently, he mocked his nervousness. *I'm so damned paranoid. There are hundreds of thousands of cars on the road with tinted windows, mine included.*

He sped up slightly.

The Lexus matched his speed.

Gavin quickly emptied his mouth, so he could focus all his attention on the car behind him. He engaged the hands-free function on the steering wheel and dictated a text to Sylvie:

I may be in some trouble. On Highway 880, heading north, to San Bruno. Near Union City. Stand by.

Hoping the car would pass so he could get a look at the tag, Gavin signaled and switched into the right lane used for exiting.

The Lexus followed.

The highway was full, but not overly busy. He should have been happy to be traveling without delays. Suddenly, he felt foolish for worrying. To prove to himself that he was overreacting, he sped up and crossed two lanes to the left and drove in the passing lane.

His heartbeat finally slowed when he realized that the car had not followed him. He almost laughed at his paranoia, but the flash of black suddenly re-appeared in his rearview mirror.

Gavin swore nervously and sped into the center lane. Putting some distance between himself and the Lexus, he changed lanes again, positioning himself in front of a semi. He then lowered his speed to ensure that the Lexus could not get between the truck and his car.

Less than a minute later, his pursuer appeared in the lane to his right, nose to nose with the semi. The sight threw him into full-blown panic mode, prompting him to press the call button and have Sylvie call the highway patrol to send a drone out to investigate.

Before the line had a chance to connect, however, he changed his mind.

Maybe this guy is just messing with me. On any other day, I would just chalk this up as road-rage. It's possible I pissed him off somehow. Maybe I cut in front of him at some point. What would I have Sylvie tell the cops anyway—a mean black car is following my boss? A mean car that's done nothing aggressive?

"I'm losing it," he groaned aloud.

What are the chances that the driver of this car is anything but a jerk? I'm just paranoid.

Still, a drop of anxious sweat rolled down his temple. With every passing moment the Lexus remained, his fear intensified. It grabbed hold of his stomach and twisted it tighter and tighter, as the feeling of doom increased.

The highway noise he was accustomed to hearing each day now seemed to be pulsing, growing in volume, until the vibration of the semi behind him was almost deafening. Deep down in his bones, Gavin sensed the driver of the Lexus was purposeful in his intent, and the last thing he wanted was to be followed to Isabella's home.

At the thought, his angst increased, causing him to feel detached, as though he was on auto-pilot. Still, enough self-preservation pulsed through his veins to keep him engaged.

"God, what should I do? I'm in *trouble*..." he choked.

Seconds ticked by but felt like minutes; his own words seemed to float through the air in slow motion. Though his eyes were fixated on the side mirror, he suddenly felt a strong urge to look up ahead.

A dairy truck had just eased onto the highway in front of the Lexus. Just ahead of the dairy truck was a massive eighteen-wheeler.

Acting on adrenaline and sheer instinct, Gavin sped up, crossed between the two trucks and into the far-right lane, just as an agriculture truck merged behind him.

Exit now.

Gavin didn't think twice. With the trucks obstructing the Lexus' view, he floored the gas pedal and took the exit ramp at a speed that made his stomach flip over. Getting nailed for speeding was the least of his worries. At that point, he would have welcomed police presence.

As quickly as possible, he disappeared into a residential area and continued to weave through adjacent neighborhoods until he was sure he was not being followed. After about twenty minutes, he pulled over in front of a house that almost looked like it could have come straight out of a storybook—picket fence and all. A porch swing swayed slightly in the January breeze. Christmas lights, garland, and decorations, which had become almost unheard of in the area, still framed the windows and graced the porch and railings.

Gavin stared at it all. A nativity scene next to the front door was kept safe inside a metal container with bars that sort of looked like the Holy Family was in prison. The sight both warmed and stabbed his heart at the same time. Since the celebration of Christmas was now viewed as potentially discriminatory against non-Christian faiths, fines for Christmas decorations left up past January 2nd were hefty. Of course, the day after New Years' deadline was unreasonable to most, so rather than pay the fines, many people just quit decorating at all.

In that moment, he realized that his parent's porch would probably look the exact same way if they were alive. His mother, Sarah, would have also carried the tradition on, no matter what, even after his old man had passed.

There are still good people trying to do what's right. But how in the hell has it come to this?

The thought was sobering. Too sobering. He felt cold to the bone. Rattled to the core, he ran trembling hands through his hair and rested his forehead on the steering wheel. If there had been a pack of cigarettes in the car, he would have smoked every last one. A bottle of scotch, he would have consumed every last drop, or at least until he warmed up or passed out, whichever came first.

He had absolutely no desire to go anywhere, especially to Isabella Sanchez's home. Fear had officially won the day.

I am failing everyone. I am scared shitless and don't even know if I need to be. I have absolutely no idea what to do next.

His phone buzzed.

He jumped so high, his head hit the roof of the car.

"*Please*, let this message be Sylvie telling me that Isabella is at the office," he begged aloud, as he reached to for his phone on the passenger seat.

It's from Sylvie.

His pulse calmed a bit as he keyed in his passcode and read:

Are you okay?? What is going on?

Gavin cringed. He'd forgotten all about the alarming text he'd sent her nearly half an hour ago. "I'm such a jerk. She must be really worried." He texted her back:

Sorry. I'm okay.
Probably just worrying for nothing.
Anything new?

Within just seconds, she texted back:

No word from your client, but Sister called.
She said to tell you that Father Anthony is doing well
and was very talkative. She is filled with hope.

That means she has something!

Relieved, Gavin blew out a gusty sigh. Still, he couldn't afford to feel too hopeful. Being followed had changed everything. What had started out as disappointment and annoyance at Isabella's lack of communication was now slowly turning into an unsettling worry for her welfare. It occurred to him that she could just be getting cold feet about pursuing her case. He certainly hoped that her reasons were that simple.

Either way, I have no choice but to get back on the road and try to reach her again. Even if Isabella has changed her mind for some reason, I need to be in contact with her. I will have no choice but to subpoena her to testify, but I would much rather have her as an ally. If she isn't home, I'll head to the corrections facility to continue with Maryn.

His phone buzzed again. The sound startled him and made him realize that he had completely let his guard down.

Swiftly, he looked around in all directions. The neighborhood was perfectly still, the Lexus was nowhere in sight.

Gavin exhaled the nervous energy trapped inside him and then opened another text from Sylvie:

Eduardo Rojas is dead.
His body was found floating in the bay.
Gunshot wound to the head.

Chapter 17

Maryn paced back and forth in her cell, making every attempt to pray, but failing miserably. It was impossible to concentrate on anything, especially since both Gavin and Sister Helena failed to make an appearance for their scheduled morning appointment.

After their last meeting, a genuine spark of hope had ignited within her to boost her confidence and give her courage to carry on. Now, the loneliness and rejection, that had previously almost killed her, was slowly seeping back into her heart. Like the threat of rising flood waters, it seemed to be only a matter of time before her newfound hope was completely swept away.

If the pain of all she'd lost wasn't enough to pull her under the tide, she was now also filled with anxiety over the possible reasons her only two allies had yet to show up.

Gavin was a wild card—she really couldn't read him or his motives completely. One minute he seemed sincere, the next, he seemed restless, anxious, and downright rude. She realized, as she pondered her unease concerning Gavin, that Thomas' behavior was already affecting her trust of men.

Sister Helena was another story. Sister seemed fully in touch with not only her torment at losing her children and husband but every hurt she was experiencing.

Gavin could have simply gotten tied up but, having Sister Helena not show up is really unsettling.

The longer she paced, the more if felt like the ominous dark cloud had reappeared, swirling around her, threatening, pressing her down, and shrouding her with doom.

Maryn shivered and wrapped her arms tightly around her midsection. Thoughts of Isabella Sanchez's plight, including the lawyers who turned down her case, caused her further grief. It was utterly terrifying to think about the dead physicians who very well may have fallen victim to a dark entity that silenced them.

Strangely, pondering the potential dangers in the outside world made her cell feel a little less oppressive.

At least in jail, I am safe.

She should have felt grateful, but thoughts of Lily and Pearl squashed her gratitude. Thinking of them was torturous. Her earlier bravado slipped away as she realized, once again, that she was very much alone.

I have to make it out of here for my girls!

Maryn quit pacing.

My babies. Thomas. My parents. My life. Everything's gone.

The intensity of her agony made her nauseous. Slowly, she crumpled down onto her bed and wound herself into a tight ball. As she rocked back and forth, hot tears slowly trickled from her eyes, then swiftly turned into rivers of pain.

"I have *nothing!*" she cried, "No one! Everything I ever loved has been taken from me. Why God? Why did you let this happen?"

Blessed are those who mourn, for they will be comforted.

The truth penetrated her tears but was tossed aside, as the war of fear and rejection raged within her.

"In *death*, yes! I will be comforted," she sobbed. "I just can't do this, Lord. I am *alone*," she choked, shaking her head woefully. "Please…take the pain away…it's too much…"

The sound of footsteps approaching halted her lamentation. She recognized the clanging noise of the gruff male guard who had been the one to inspect her cell that morning. He carried a set of handcuffs that jostled noisily against his billy club as he walked.

The guy was massive—exaggerated biceps, thick neck, legs like tree-trunks, and a barrel chest that surely made him a force to be reckoned with. Despite his ominous presence, she had dared a glance at the badge on his uniform that morning. The name Mack suited him—whether it was his first name or last, the guy was built like a truck.

Nervous anxiety swiftly eclipsed Maryn's sorrow as she recalled the feeling of his piercing eyes as they observed her every move during breakfast, and again at lunch.

He's coming for me.

Rational or not, the thought caused her adrenaline to kick in. She hastily wiped at her tears and sat up, her back, ramrod-straight.

Sure enough, his footsteps drew closer and stopped at the door of her cell. Her heart raced with the confirmation as her eyes locked on the door's observation window. It was open. Mack's piercing, unreadable gaze was upon her.

Just seconds later, his ominous frame filled the doorway, his expression, a mask of indifference. "Come with me," he barked. "Stay close. Don't try anything, or I will use the cuffs."

Maryn nodded. "Where am I going?" she asked, now petrified.

"You have visitors."

Gavin! Sister Helena!

Greatly relieved, she released the air in her lungs she'd been holding. Still, as Mack led her in the opposite direction of the room she had previously met with Sister Helena and Gavin, anxiety began to creep back in.

Immediately, a conversation she'd overheard at lunch raced through her mind to further intensify her fears. One woman, who looked young enough to still be in high school, mentioned that one of the male guards was a rapist. The woman next to her, whose leathery-skin and missing teeth made it impossible to guess her age, was sitting across from Maryn. While twirling her thin, graying hair she answered with a leering grin, "Well, if it's Mack over there, I sure hope I'm next."

Maryn hadn't laughed with the others, and she definitely wasn't laughing how. Uncertainty made her legs feel heavy, her feet, increasingly leaden with each step. She felt a fight or flight instinct kicking in, and though it was unrealistic to think she could escape from the facility, she began to think of how, if necessary, she could create a loud ruckus.

Nervous energy pulsed through every fiber of her being, as Mack turned down yet another corridor before they stopped. Maryn nearly collapsed with relief as her eyes fell upon the visitor's sign above the doorway.

Mack unlocked the door. Then, taking her forearm, he half pushed, half ushered her in. "You have an hour," he said gruffly, before locking the door behind him.

Maryn's eyes quickly took in the surroundings of the very large room. She never expected to find it empty, nor did she expect the dark navy sofa, matching loveseat, and two red chairs surrounding a marble-top coffee table. Despite the same concrete floor that ran throughout the entire facility, the room was brightly lit and included a wall-mounted television and shelves filled with toys.

The sight of the toys reminded her that her girls would not be allowed to visit her. Still, her pierced heart held out the hope that Sister or Gavin would come soon.

The door slowly opened on the opposite end of the room.

"Mommy!"

The word was screamed in unison, as Lily and Pearl came running into the room. It took just seconds for them to reach her, for Maryn to feel the weight of their two small bodies filling her arms and soothing her soul.

For the girls' sake, Maryn tried hard to be brave and choke back the tidal wave of tears that threatened to capsize the room; but seeing their beautiful, tear-streaked faces made her efforts futile.

For several minutes, she just cried with them. In those moments, she didn't care about the future, the past, the pain of loss, her surroundings, or the hard, cement floor she was sitting on. She simply let her emotions flow and basked in the comfort of feeling their arms woven tightly around her neck and waist.

Maryn inhaled the sweet fragrance of their hair and skin and relished the softness of Pearl's cheek tucked underneath her chin. Lily's cheek was pressed against Maryn's cheek so firmly, that her breath and tears become one with her own. Maryn never wanted to let go, never break the spell. To hold them forever. Still, she knew that they must be frightened and have dozens of questions. Their survival through this trauma would be partly up to her. She had to be brave for them.

God, help me. Give me answers I don't possess. Please, Jesus...be with me now.

"Mommy, how long do you have to stay here?" Lily asked, breaking the silence at last. Her ocean-blue eyes searched her mother's face as she leaned back in Maryn's arms. "Daddy said that you are sick. Are you getting any better?"

"You don't look sick, Mamma," Pearl interjected, her clear green eyes enhanced by unshed tears. "Do you have a tummy ache? Cause you can come home wif us! Me 'n Lily will take good care of you, so ya don't hafta worry one teeny bit! 'Member that icky pink stuff you gived me when my tummy hurt? We still have some and you can have some of it too! I'll help plug your nose if ya want me to."

Despite her stomach feeling like she'd swallowed a brick, Maryn snorted a sad laugh. Her precious angels were trying so hard to be brave. There was nothing in the world more exquisite or charming than the two questioning faces just inches from her own.

She was grateful to Thomas for keeping the truth from them, but it was brutal to see their sweet, sincere expressions mixed with both hope and fear. Neither of them could possibly understand how much she wanted to be with them.

Maryn had rehearsed what she would say to them a hundred times, but in that moment, she couldn't think of a single word that could adequately explain her feelings or why she couldn't come with them.

God help me! she begged silently as she struggled for the right words.

"I am sure that your mommy will start to feel *much* better after a while," a female voice interjected.

Startled, Maryn looked up to see a woman standing off to the side. She was wearing a tailored, black pantsuit and crisp, white shirt. Her short, dark hair was sleek and framed a flawless, fresh face.

Maryn wondered if she was a lawyer and how long she'd been standing there. Before she could even ask, the woman held out her hand and introduced herself.

"Hi Maryn. I'm Lexie from CPS. I've been assigned to your case, so I'll be here with you and the girls when they come for a visit."

Maryn took Lexie's slender hand and shook it woodenly. "CPS? You have to be here during all our visits?" Maryn asked, disbelievingly. "I'm their *mother*."

"Yes, and I can see you're a *good* mother," she answered quickly, giving her head a slight shake, along with a look that begged her not to make an issue in front of the girls.

Despite the woman's amiable presence, Maryn was taken aback by the fact that her children and their visit were being overseen by Child Protective Services. Immediately, the gravity of the situation threatened to steal her joy. She pushed the intimidation aside, making every attempt to ignore the shame she felt sitting there in prison garb. Her maternal instincts kicked into overdrive and helped her to force everything from her mind except her daughters.

"Oh girls," she crooned, smiling into their searching, angelic faces, "Mommy is doing *everything* she can to come back to you. I miss you both so very much, and I know that you are being good girls until I come back, right?"

Both girls nodded, but tears immediately filled Lily's eyes again. "You're not going to die are you?" she asked, her lip quivering.

"No!" Maryn nearly shouted, pulling them close to her once more. With their heads lying, one on each shoulder, she crooned, "Mommy just has to get some things worked out here for a while...my heart is hurting, and it needs to be fixed before I come home."

It wasn't a lie. In that moment, Maryn's heart was broken in pieces. So many pieces, she wondered if it could ever be mended again.

Chapter 18

Sylvie checked her phone for the umpteenth time, silently praying that Gavin would text her soon. She hadn't heard back from him since she'd sent the text about Eduardo Rojas's murder more than two hours ago. It wasn't like Gavin to not answer back, so she was worried sick.

She'd already made the decision to close the office an hour ago, but she couldn't possibly go home until he contacted her.

"Where *are* you?" she grumbled, crossing to the front office door to check the lock again. "I don't even care if he's pissed at me for closing," she declared defiantly and continued pacing.

Despite her tough attitude, she wasn't fooling even herself with her bravado. She had no idea what was keeping her mostly-predictable boss, and that fact was more than scary.

God, please let him be okay.

A professed atheist for much of her adult life, she couldn't bring herself to say the prayer aloud—to do so would have both validated her fear and exposed her hypocrisy at the same time.

Admittedly, her ex had proven her suspicion that God was just a safety net and pleasant dream most latched onto in order to make themselves feel better about the crappy things that happened to them. She also thought of her own deadbeat father and the drug overdose that had killed him. Her poor mother had prayed so hard for him.

Mom spent most of her life praying for something that never happened. Her prayers have been useless, just like my prayers for Andy. I begged God to change his mind about staying with me and the boys, but he walked out anyway.

Sylvie hadn't been in touch with him or God, since.

I wonder where he is these days?

"Probably still smoking weed and collecting unemployment," she muttered, walking into Gavin's office to straighten a slat in the vertical blind.

Her hand froze in mid-air as she came eye to eye with the lens of a drone that was hovering over the only spot in the window that was exposed. With her heart slamming in her chest, she quickly slapped the blind back into place.

Shaken, she rushed from the room and closed the door. She turned around and let out a blood-curdling scream.

"Gee-zus, Sylvie!" Gavin exclaimed, grabbing his chest and backing away from her. Pale and clearly as shaken as she was, he flopped into her chair and took some deep breaths.

"Sorry!" she shouted back, tears of relief pooling in her eyes, "but you scared the *crap* out of me. I didn't hear you come in and I almost ran right into you! Where the *hell* have you been, anyway?"

She didn't give him a chance to answer. "I've been so *frickin* worried! Where the *hell* have you been?"

"You already asked me that," he replied wryly, but not without sympathy. "Give us both a second to calm down and I'll tell you, okay?"

Sylvie nodded and hastily wiped her eyes with the back of her sleeve. "Want something to drink?"

"Yeah, a scotch on the rocks."

"I *meant* water or tea," she answered, reaching into her big, cloth purse. "I brought a couple drinks from home."

Sylvie noticed that his hand shook as he took the tea from her. "Have you eaten anything today?" she asked, again noticing his lack of color.

He nodded. "Sunflower seeds."

She shook her head. "No wonder you're so pale," she began her lecture, but Gavin cut her off.

"Sylvie...I just came from Isabella Sanchez's place. She's *gone.*"

"Well, considering Eduardo's murder, I would imagine there's a lot to do. She's probably with family making funeral arrangements."

"No," he interrupted again, "the place reminds me of a ghost town."

"What do you mean? If she wasn't home, how would you know?" she asked, both skeptically and apprehensively.

Gavin took several long swallows of his tea and then said, "I rang the doorbell and didn't get an answer, so I went around the house and knocked on the back door. There's not a stick of patio furniture back there. No grill. No toys. Nothing. The garage had a window, so I looked in. It was *empty*. I went back around to the front and opened the screen, so I could pound on the door, and it *opened.*"

"You mean it was unlocked or you pounded the door down?" she asked, confused.

"*Unlocked.* The house has been abandoned. The closets are all empty. Scarcely any furniture left. Beds are gone, and there's stuff scattered all over the floors—a toy here, a book there. They took what they could and left."

Sylvie shook her head. "Are you sure you were in the right house? Maybe you had the wrong address."

"I wish that was the case," he answered tiredly, downing the rest of his tea before explaining. "I double-checked it with the county's records. When the address checked out, I called the garage where Isabella's husband, Daniel, works."

"How did you know where her husband works?"

"As a last-ditch effort when she was trying to get me to take her case, Isabella offered his service of my car for life. When I called the number on the card, she gave me before she walked out the door, the guy that answered confirmed that Daniel didn't show up for work this morning. Ironically, they were hoping I knew how to reach him because he wasn't answering their calls—apparently, he's the manager."

"Oh geez...that doesn't sound good. What's going on? What does this all mean?" Sylvie asked, clearly shaken.

"I wish I knew," Gavin answered honestly. "Whatever it means, I don't think it's anything good."

"What are you *saying*? Just *tell* me!" she demanded.

The apprehension in her eyes pained him. Gavin sincerely wished he could keep it all from her, but he couldn't leave her in the dark. For her own good and for her boys, Sylvie needed to know the gravity of the situation.

"I'm trying not to overreact here, but there just *has* to be a connection. Isabella is not returning our phone calls. Meanwhile, her cousin is found murdered and suddenly the entire family flies the coop. I mean, they just picked up and left. There's still milk, eggs, lots of food left in the refrigerator and even food in the pots on the stove. Wherever they were going, they left in a hurry."

Sylvie leaned against the side of the desk and chewed her lip. "Why would they have to leave? I don't get the connection."

"I don't know, exactly," he admitted, "but something's just not right. Isabella's the one who came in here like a mother bear ready to take me down if I didn't help her, but now she won't answer my calls? Doesn't make sense."

"Well *of course* it doesn't make sense, but that doesn't mean Eduardo's murder has anything to do with it."

Gavin shook his head. "I'd like to agree, but my gut says it's all connected. I haven't had a chance to tell you the rest of it."

Her eyes widened. "What do you mean, the *rest* of it?" she asked, her voice trembling slightly.

Gavin could've kicked himself. Sylvie was a tough cookie—certainly no lightweight. She survived life by acting tough and indifferent, but in that moment, she looked like a scared teenager. The fear and uncertainty in her eyes said it all. *I should've kept my mouth shut.*

He no more had formed the thought when she barked, "Tell me, *damnit*! Don't you *dare* leave me in the dark now! First you send me a *scare-the-hell-out-of-me-text*, and then you don't show up for several hours—which you still haven't explained. And now, you say I don't know the *latest*?"

"For your information, I just closed the shades on a *drone* outside your office window, and I'm about ready to jump out of my *own* damn skin, so you are *going* to tell me what you know!"

"Drone?" Gavin blurted, completely ignoring her rant. "What drone...where?"

"I *told* you. When you didn't answer me back, I wigged out a little—you know with Eduardo being murdered and all, and so I closed the office and locked up. While I was waiting for you, I realized that one of the blinds was caught up, so I went to straighten it. That's when I saw the drone hovering outside your window."

"What would be the purpose of looking into an office window?" he interjected.

"I don't know...but feeling creeped out has taken on a whole new dimension for me. I hate those damn things flying all over the place. You just know the pervs are all using them to look in windows and get their jollies..."

Sylvie stared at him for several seconds before he completely shifted directions and said, "Let's get out of here. I know a place where we can talk...and I'm *starving*. I'll fill you in on the way."

Chapter 19

As she sat down with her visitors to sort through the pieces of a seemingly, ever-changing puzzle, Sister Helena was glad she'd asked the other sisters for privacy. Gavin's retelling of the recent events was enthralling. Helena interrupted only briefly to pray for Isabella Sanchez and her family and for the soul of Eduardo Rojas.

The looks of skepticism that crossed both Gavin and Sylvie's countenances, when she prayed for Eduardo, had not escaped her notice. She also noticed Sylvie's curious gaze moving from statue to statue in the beautiful visitor's area.

The room was simple, yet, at the same time, ornate. Mostly, it was peaceful. Sylvie's demeanor suggested to Helena that she was both uncomfortable and completely enthralled by the beauty of it all.

A wall-length picture window gave them a stunning view of the garden area where seasonal herbs, vegetables, flowers, shrubs, and even the birds were lovingly cared for by the Sisters of the Sacred Heart. No matter the time of year, the space was a beautiful sanctuary.

Still, as peaceful as the space was, Helena could sense the nervous energy in the room. She also noticed that neither guest had touched a morsel of the food they'd brought along with them.

"Okay, you two," she clucked, "now open those bags and get started on your meal! You can't help anyone if you pass out, so eat up."

Sylvie smiled at her and obediently reached for her sandwich.

"We don't have *time* to be leisurely here," Gavin barked, arguing with only himself. "We've got two dead men, an entire family missing, a mystery fax, falsified records, and a woman waiting in jail for her kids and two people who didn't show up today."

Helena cringed at his words. "Poor Maryn, she must be beside herself wondering why we didn't come."

"And don't forget about the drone and you being followed," Sylvie interjected before taking a bite of her sub.

"What *drone*?" Helena asked, clearly shocked. "And you never told me you were followed."

Gavin ignored her comment and set to the task of unwrapping his sandwich while Sylvie explained about the drone outside the office window.

"That's *very strange*," Helena answered. "But maybe it was just some teenager's drone. Or...I guess the government uses drones to do surveillance to watch for terrorist activities now..."

"I was followed on the freeway on my way to visit Isabella," Gavin interjected swiftly to give Helena the full picture. "At first, I thought I was imagining it, but now I am sure. Someone was purposefully following me."

"Why? Who would be following you?" she interjected. "What happened? How'd you manage to lose them?"

Gavin appeared to swallow the bite he'd just taken without hardly chewing, and answered, "Would you believe me if I told you it was Divine intervention?" he asked, giving her a sheepish grin.

"Of *course* I would," she answered assuredly. "You're *here*, aren't you? God willed you to get away. I just want to know *how*."

Despite his brief affirmation of faith, Gavin instantly appeared irritated. By now, Sister was used to his quickly-changing moods, and knowing that he was tired and keyed up, she was resolute to stay calm.

"Everything is so black and white with you, isn't it, Sister? So, tell me then, if God wills *everything*, then why is Maryn in jail and why are we sitting here wondering if Towne's death and his new position are somehow related? How is it God's will and equal justice that both a drug dealer and a public servant deserved to die? And what about *David*? Was it just his time too? And tell me this…how is it God's will that Sophia Sanchez is walking around like a vegetable instead of acting like a vibrant little girl? How about you tell me where God's will fits into *all* of this shit."

"C'mon, Gavin, knock it off," Sylvie interjected, embarrassed by his harshness.

"It's okay," Sister Helena quickly answered, "he's got a point. What is happening seems very unfair and downright cruel. I don't profess to have all the answers…but I truly believe God *does*, and I only know that He is *just*.

"We don't look at life and death the way God does. While we don't fully understand death or dying, we have to believe that God works *all* things to the good for those who love Him. The greatest example of this is in His plan for our salvation. No one would have ever believed that Jesus would freely *choose* to die in order to save us, but He did just that. Some of the answers to these tragic circumstances may not ever be revealed until we meet God face to face, but He has made a promise that nothing will remain hidden and that those who trust in Him will be saved. And truly, if we knew the beauty and joy that awaited us in Heaven, we would see things differently here on earth. We *must* focus on all the good things God has already done."

Sylvie remained quiet, but Gavin was anything but ready to concede. "Sorry Sister, but that sounds a little like you're trying to turn B.S. into a bouquet. What is good about beautiful little Sophia's life being ruined?"

"In your eyes, her life is ruined," Helena responded immediately, "but to God, she may look different—maybe even like a savior of sorts, whose sufferings will be used to prevent more suffering. Truth is, Gavin, Jesus could come back for the faithful tomorrow…*today*, and Sophia would live the rest of eternity with Him in perfect health and happiness, and her suffering would be long forgotten."

Gavin stared back, his expression now unreadable.

"And lest you forget," she added, wagging an arthritic finger at him, "miracles *still happen*. We can keep praying and trusting God for her healing…"

"Speaking of healing," he interjected dryly, dismissing the argument completely, "what did you find out from your cousin? You told Sylvie you were hopeful."

"I was wondering when you were going to get around to asking me…oh ye of little faith," she offered with a smirk.

Gavin swallowed the food in his mouth and grumbled, "Just tell us what happened without the corny clichés please."

"Okay, *Cranky*," she answered, exchanging a knowing look with Sylvie before going on. "Cousin Tony told me that a fellow friar has a nephew who might be able to help. Apparently, he's got a really important job and is *really* good with computers."

"That's *it?*" Gavin asked, scowling in disbelief. "Well, my kid, Lucas, is *really* good at computers too, but I don't see how that's going to help."

Helena shook her head, "You *are* in a bad mood today, aren't you? I'm going to assume it's because you're tired and upset so I'll just ignore your bratty behavior and forgive you."

Then, turning to Sylvie, she said, "As I was saying, he works for a company that specializes in credit card fraud. Tony says he can track anything."

She had Gavin's complete attention now. "But you're talking about *tracking*, and what we need is *hacking*—which, last I checked, is against the law."

"I wasn't born yesterday," Helena answered, rolling her eyes before she laughed and added, "I guess *that's* obvious."

She raised her eyebrows at Gavin and said, "Being a drug dealer is against the law too…but *some* are willing to bend the rules—especially if it is for what they believe is a greater good."

His face colored. "So, what are you suggesting?" he asked, completely sidestepping her jab about the defense he provided Eduardo.

She shrugged. "Little David is with God now. He cannot be hurt if we break the confidentiality law, but potentially, other people could be helped. I don't see what harm it would do to at least find out if the autopsy results were altered. If it turns out that they were, the fax is validated and tells us there is someone out there working in our favor."

Still skeptical, Gavin asked, "So, how do you suppose we go about getting this accomplished without getting this guy arrested and us along with him?"

"Well, Tony says all his nephew needs is to know David's date of birth, his parents' name, and address, so he can be sure of who he's checking on."

Gavin shook his head. "Please tell me it's not that easy to hack into the government's system."

Helena chuckled, "I said the exact same thing, but Tony told me his nephew says that state agencies have some of the easiest systems to hack."

"Nice. *Real* comforting," Gavin replied sarcastically, rubbing his eyes tiredly.

Unlike Gavin, Sylvie was full of enthusiasm. "I can't *wait* to hear what he finds out. I hope he can do it soon."

Gavin nodded. "You and everyone else, including Maryn Pearce. Speaking of which, she doesn't know any of this. I wish there was some way to get a message to her. I won't be able to talk to her until tomorrow. I can only imagine what she's thinking."

"I can get a message to her," Helena said confidently.

"How are you going to do that?" he asked doubtfully. "Your time slot is over too."

"You are such a doubting Thomas," Helena answered with a good-natured laugh, and then added wryly, "It would take a pretty cold-hearted person who could say no to an arthritic old nun."

Her expression was priceless. In spite of his foul mood, Gavin couldn't help but chuckle. "And God help whoever tries to tell *you* no," he answered, shaking his head.

Chapter 20

Maryn sat on the edge of her bed with her back ramrod straight. Between Gavin and Sister's no-show and her visit with the girls, a restlessness filled her being that she couldn't shake off.

Seeing her girls was salve for her wounded soul; yet, when they left, it felt like her heart had been ripped from her chest once again. Both girls had valiantly tried not to cry when it was time for them to leave, but eventually, their lips began to tremble. They wrapped their arms around her neck even tighter, wound their legs around her waist like they were clinging to a buoy in the middle of the ocean. Eventually, full-blown tears and screaming ensued. Even now, the sounds of their mournful pleading, pierced her soul.

Initially, after the visit with her girls ended, Maryn's anger became an unexpected ally, making her more determined than ever to endure whatever was necessary to ensure they would not be raised without her. Now, the absence of their sweet essence—their voices, expressive eyes and faces, their warm bodies molded tightly to her own, was like being buried alive. She felt trapped— as if the air was too thick to take in. She didn't think her heart could function with the agonizing memory of seeing them so distraught. The pain was so intense, it was hard to breathe. Hard to think.

Hard to do anything, except die.

Maryn was fully aware that she was battling for her life, her soul. Most importantly, she knew that the only way she could win the battle for her own life was to care more about the lives of her children than her own. Lily and Pearl were gifts from God-two souls entrusted to her on this earth to nurture and love until the day He called them home. It was His will that she gave birth to them, His will that she fight for the truth—the truth she knew she must cling to now. If God willed her to raise her girls to know and love Him, He would somehow have to free her. Sustain her. Carry her.

Despite this conviction, her anguish and loneliness waged a war within her, pressing against her and eclipsing her ability to cope. She teetered between feeling devasted at losing Thomas and her anger at his utter betrayal and rejection.

She would never forget the confused, lost look on Lily's face when she'd said, "Daddy said you did some things that were wrong. Did you do bad things, Mommy?"

Though she was grateful Lily had asked the question, so she could assure her that there was much she didn't understand, hot pain coursed through Maryn's body at the memory. The agony swiftly crossed over to anger, then to emptiness, and finally, to paralyzing fear of losing them forever.

Her emotions became so intense that soon her spirit was perilously close to the breaking point of no return. She was almost there—that broken and desolate place that willed her to close her eyes and pray for death.

The five-minute warning for lights out startled her. It served as yet another reminder that she was powerless. Her life was not her own. Others, who were stronger and more powerful, were calling the shots.

Yet even in those five minutes, she made every attempt to hope for a miracle. It seemed like seconds rather than minutes until the lights slowly dimmed until they were completely out. Maryn turned onto her side in the pitch-dark cell, winding her arms so tightly around her body that her muscles ached with the effort.

In the darkness, the familiar sounds and smells of the facility intensified—the constant clanking, pounding, and loud voices, the musty smell that permeated her bedding.

The gratitude she'd felt at having her girls back in her arms was now as threadbare as her blanket.

She shivered uncontrollably and found herself wondering if she was just imagining the extra activity on the floor, or the over-the-top gruffness in Mack's demeanor when he'd taken her back to her cell earlier.

The challenges she faced seemed insurmountable, her previous hopeful expectations, seemed foolish and implausible. A fresh wave of lonely sadness rose up like a tidal wave to drown her.

With the hope of blotting it all out, Maryn squeezed her eyes shut even tighter, but the faces of her girls instantly appeared. The sorrowful expressions they wore as the social worker took them away, haunted her. She wondered how long it took them before they quit crying after they left. How long it took them to smile again. She wondered what they'd eaten for dinner and if Lily had experienced any episodes with her hives lately.

What if my poor Pearly is crying herself to sleep every night? My sweet Lily will be her only comfort...and who will comfort my precious Lily?

The agony continued to build as she pondered the potential length of time she could be separated from them. The fact that neither of her allies had come to visit, mocked her. She pushed the thought away and refocused.

God, protect Lily and Pearl...please. Help them to feel my love.

Despite her silent prayer, death whispered her name. Slowly, steadily, it called out to her, repeatedly drumming in her ears. The sound reverberated in her heart and mind, causing hot, fat tears to slip from her burning eyes, roll down her cheek, across her nose, and onto her worn, foul-smelling pillow.

"God help me!" she cried out hoarsely, finally breaking into uncontrolled sobbing.

Nearly an hour later, buried by her own sorrows, Maryn lay awake, feeling as heavy as a corpse. Empty. Alone.

Still, her mother's heart resisted defeat, and she willed herself to pray, "Our Father...who art in Heaven, hallowed be thy name. Thy kingdom come, thy will be done..."

Her prayer was suddenly cut short when the light in her cell went on. She sat up quickly, shading her red, swollen eyes with her forearm. Only moments later, she squinted into the harsh light to see the cell door opening.

Mack's portentous form filled the doorway. He stared at her silently for several seconds. Maryn couldn't seem to find her voice either, and was sure that even if she had, the only thing that would have come out was a scream.

"You have a message," he barked, crossing the space between them to hand her a white envelope. "You've got exactly two minutes before the lights go out again."

He turned and walked to the door, but before he left, he looked back and said, "Don't expect this kind of favor again, because it won't happen."

Maryn nodded woodenly. Then, after swiping at her tears with the back of her hand, she tore the envelope open before the door had even fully closed...

Dear Maryn,

I wanted to get word to you to let you know that we are still working on things from this end. Much has happened that you will be interested in.

Do not give up. You are not alone. God's love and Spirit are with you always, along with my love and prayers. Together, we will fight the good fight of faith and win. Things are not as they seem. Do not forget that Jesus was dead for three days before He rose from the tomb. All who knew Him thought they had lost everything, but God had a plan so grand that none of them could even imagine, even though Jesus told them before it happened.

Don't let fear cloud your vision or judgment. Together we are praying that angels surround your daughters during this trial and I wholeheartedly believe that they will overcome all with His grace.

As Saint Padre Pio admonished, we must: Pray, hope, and don't worry. God willing, I will see you tomorrow. Until then, I pray that you feel my love and the Eternal love of Christ embracing you.

In His love,

Sister Helena

Maryn was able to read the note several times before the lights went out again. She crawled under her blanket and hugged the paper against her chest, as if by doing so, the hope infused in Sister's words would somehow saturate her soul.

As she pondered the memory and promise of each word, the peace and hope she needed and longed for, slowly and steadfastly, rocked her to sleep.

*****

Just seconds before his feet slipped off his desktop, Gavin's snoring woke him. Startled, and still half asleep, it took him a while before he could make out the furniture in his office and realize where he was.

He glanced at his watch. It was just after three in the morning. *No wonder I feel like I've been run over by a truck.*

He groaned aloud and massaged the pain in the back of his shins and neck that was caused by his awkward sleep position.

"I guess this is part of the payback for all my screw-ups," he grumbled.

Despite the discomfort, exhaustion won out—it was too late to go home or to a hotel. He repositioned himself more comfortably and shut his eyes, knowing full-well that shutting down his mind would be the greater feat.

It hadn't been his intention to stay at the office. After he'd left the convent and dropped Sylvie off at her car, he ended up searching the net from three different locations, until the only places still open were outright dumps or too cheap to offer wi-fi. It hardly mattered though, because he'd found more than enough to scare the hell out of him and increase his paranoia.

At that point, going to his known address, where anyone could find him, seemed not only risky, but a waste of precious time. There was a mountain of potential evidence to sort through—charts, graphs, data, and statistics analyzing infectious diseases, that he'd never seen before, or even knew existed. The information haunted him now, as he marveled at how such conflicting data was left exposed, and unchallenged.

If the data and the video testimonies from doctors and vaccine-injured victims and their families weren't enough to set him on edge, the cryptic fax, being followed, Eduardo's murder, and Isabella's disappearance, were. Moreover, the timing of Congressman Towne's death left him anxious.

Sure hope it's just a coincidence.

The wishful thought survived for several seconds until the faces of the dead physicians shattered it.

Gavin's eyes flew open and he sat straight up. "How the *hell* could it all be a coincidence?" he barked into the darkness.

The revelation was as shocking to his senses as getting hit with a bucket of cold water. Sleep suddenly became the last thing on his mind—getting to the truth, the first. It was the only way to prove negligence.

He turned on the lights and put on a pot of coffee before settling himself at the conference table in his office. Flipping through his notes reminded him of the evidence indicating that the present vaccine schedule had gradually increased over the years, notably since 1986. Yet, one of most puzzling and explosive revelations was that the rate of death for many of the common viruses on the schedule had gone down drastically before vaccinations were ever introduced to the public.

Gavin stared at the numbers he had scribbled down from the charts he'd found on the net.

Measles associated death dropped 98% before the vaccine was ever given, so what was the rush?

From what he'd been able to gather from physician testimonies, improved sanitation, better nutrition, and overall advancements in healthcare had made the childhood viruses not much more than a nuisance, like most any other bug.

If the Lunavirus and other viruses are mostly mild, especially in otherwise healthy children, why take the chance on the side effects?

Equally disturbing was the reminder of what Maryn had previously mentioned—live viruses in some vaccines can actually spread the virus.

This all can be found on the internet and on the vaccine inserts, so where's the public outcry?

"I guess self-preservation, fear, and the concept of being disease-free is just too enticing a prospect for most. It sure has kept people coming back for more," he murmured. "The pharms and government entities must be laughing their asses off…the truth is hidden in plain sight."

Plain sight.

The concept was deep and intriguing. *What else is hidden in plain sight,"* he wondered as he got up to pour himself a much-needed cup of coffee.

He plodded back to the conference table. "Speaking of hidden…I wonder who sent me that fax," he pondered aloud before taking a sip.

The coffee wasn't the best, but he hardly noticed. His focus was on making his mind and the facts come alive.

"Who is working on our side?" he asked the pages of notes staring up at him. The physicians' names and details of their deaths seemed to jump off the page. Some of the deaths seemed plausible; some of them had occurred in mob-like style, including Eduardo Rojas' assassination. Though Rojas was certainly no innocent, his death opened up a whole different basket of questions.

Our anonymous ally is probably a physician or nurse who's scared shitless they'll disappear if they speak out.

"Who killed them and *why*?" he whispered.

The pharmaceutical companies are already making bank and protected by the government against vaccine liability, so why would they go to such great lengths to kill the natural docs over the potential side effects? That doesn't really make sense. There has to be more. Where is Isabella and her family? Have they fled because of this vaccine issue or because of Eduardo's involvement? Is there any connection here? Will I ever hear from her again, or is she and her family dead now too?

"Dammit! I need answers!" he growled. "Isabella, where *are* you? Your testimony would have weighed heavily in Maryn's favor."

Favor. The word stuck in his throat, reminding him of yet another unanswered question.

Could it be that Eduardo is the one who sent me the fax? Did he pull some strings as a favor to Isabella? They were obviously a close family. He knew about Sophia's issues, and surely Isabella told him of our meeting. He would have had my fax number...but how would he have known details about the case against Maryn?

"I guess as his crooked lawyer, I should know he had connections with people who know how to get information," he scoffed, intrigued and ashamed of his association at the same time.

Is it possible that whoever is killing the doctors to keep them quiet discovered that Eduardo hacked into the system?

The thought snapped his head up. "Oh my *God*...if Sister Helena's guy isn't careful, he could be next."

Gavin's phone suddenly buzzed, startling him. He swore loudly in protest. *Who in the hell is texting me at this hour? It can't be good...*

With a shaking hand, he reached for the phone and swiped his thumb over the security bar. In the next instant, he was reading the text:

Frank's Place. 6:45 a.m. tomorrow. Just you.

Despite his relief that the text wasn't from either of his kids, Gavin's heart slammed against his chest. The message was from an unknown number. Whoever sent it was smart enough to phrase the message in a way that would not send up red flags to anyone watching for key words.

He took a deep breath and shook his head to clear it before irrational fear took hold of him.

Sister Helena doesn't have texting, so this has to be from Fr. Tony's guy. Either that, or it's from whoever sent the first fax, which would be great to confirm that we still have an ally who hasn't been silenced.

Though the possibilities were mostly positive, the element of mystery surrounding the message made him tense and uncertain.

I've got just enough time to go home, shower and get to Frank's in time to meet my mystery man...or woman, I guess.

"I suppose it's probably too much to hope that the text is from Isabella," he declared aloud.

He slipped on his overcoat and then shoved his notes into his briefcase.

With his collar up, his heart beating wildly, Gavin almost sprinted through the parking garage. After pushing the auto-start on the fob, the headlights on his BMW welcomed him like a lighthouse amidst a storm.

Once he was safe inside, he was never more anxious in his life to pull away from the office and head home. His relief was short-lived, however, as memories of the car that had tailed him earlier surfaced.

"C'mon Gavin," he whispered, "keep your act together. The streets are pretty empty."

A fine mist forced him to use his wipers; but even their quiet, hypnotic swiping did little to calm him. His eyes constantly shifted to his rearview mirror.

Stopping at a red light just blocks from his apartment made him downright anxious. The area was lit just enough to make him feel like a sitting duck, the wipers' steady motion, reminding him of the ticking of a time bomb.

"C'mon!" he growled, pounding the steering wheel impatiently with the palm of his hand, seriously wondering how much time he had until something exploded or until some maniac came after him. "There's not another nicotine-addicted, sleep-deprived, alcoholic dumbass besides me on the road!"

He forced out a nervous laugh and added, "Except for the cop that will appear out of nowhere to pull me over if I decide to run this damn light."

His eyes canvassed the area. Nothing seemed amiss. When the light finally turned green, the dark seemed less ominous.

Just minutes later, Gavin pulled into his private garage and eagerly reached over to grab his briefcase while the door enclosed him in safety.

Upon lifting his briefcase, all motion stopped as his eyes fell upon a standard white envelope on the passenger seat.

How did I not see this when I got in the car? How did it get there?

The blood rushed to his head so fast, he felt like he was going to black out. Thankfully, his survival instinct kicked in first, prompting him to look around the garage to make sure he was alone.

As far as he could see, the space was empty. He dared a glance in the rearview, nearly convinced that a face would materialize as quickly as the envelope had.

"There's no one here," he reassured himself, his shallow breaths slowing a bit.

Reaching for the envelope, he wasted no time in ripping it open and retrieving the single piece of paper inside.

You need to trust that the records were altered. Whoever hacked the records today was detected. Follow directions and wait for further instruction. No cops.

Adrenaline pulsed through Gavin's veins as he shoved the paper and envelope into his briefcase and exited the car. Grabbing a tire iron from his trunk, he headed into the elevator and up to his apartment.

A quick glance at the security system indicated that all was well, but, at that point, it meant nothing to him. Security systems deterred thieves, not assassins.

Once inside, he headed straight for the bedroom closet. Kneeling down, he retrieved the worn, but sturdy, shoe-shine box his father had used all his life. After tossing the contents on the floor to uncover a metal security box, Gavin quickly worked the combination.

He pulled a nine-millimeter Beretta from the box and loaded the magazine next to it.

With a steadiness in his hands he wasn't feeling, Gavin shoved everything back into the box, then left the apartment as if the devil himself was after him.

Chapter 21

At 6:29 a.m. Gavin swung his car into a parking space in front of Frank's Place—a hole-in-the-wall diner that stayed open until two in the morning and was reopened by the diner's eighty-two-year-old owner every day at six-thirty a.m. sharp.

Sinatra memorabilia covered the walls of Leroy Frank's small establishment. Preserved in the classic style of Sinatra's era, black and white booths lined the wall of windows, classic mushroom-shaped steel stools surrounded the bar around the grill and kitchen counter. No matter the time of day, the crooner's tunes played in the background.

The food was a little greasy, but tasty and reasonably priced, so the place was usually packed, especially the pick-up window just before rush hour. Today was no different.

Most of the patrons looked completely out of place in their business suits. Their zombie-like focus on their phones made them wholly oblivious to everyone around them. Ironically, the disconnect helped him feel a little less conspicuous.

A contradiction of eras to be sure, he mused.

His own presence was no different, he realized, as he shuffled along with the crowd of patrons through the open door, trying to maintain a cool, indifferent persona.

Gavin slid into one of the open booths and checked his watch out of sheer nervousness. He was early, but he already knew that. Admittedly, he could smell his own sweat and wished he would have checked into a hotel room and grabbed a shower, rather than choosing to park in front of a Lutheran church across town, until it was time to meet the mystery texter.

The black Lexus still haunted him. So much so, he'd been afraid to drive around and reluctant to call anyone, especially his family. Even knowing his father's gun was tucked into his trench coat pocket did little to assuage his nerves. In fact, it wouldn't surprise him at all if the cops were to show up at any minute and arrest him for possession of a firearm.

Since the complete ban and recent state-wide confiscation, a zero-tolerance policy had proven to be more than effective in boosting added fine revenues and the price of black-market weapons. Moreover, it was highly profitable for the thugs who always managed to get their hands on an unlimited supply. They found it much easier to rob and terrorize knowing that law-abiding citizens weren't armed.

Inwardly, Gavin scoffed. *Yeah, we're all much safer now that the bad guys are the only ones with guns.*

From his perspective, the ban was a non-issue—there was no way in hell he would have given up such an important piece of his old man's legacy; and in that moment, getting arrested was the least of his problems.

He wondered if it was the lack of sleep or nicotine withdrawal that made him feel like he was teetering between mind-numbing terror and awakening from a nightmare similar to a cheesy, predictable film with a mobster plot. In reality, the moment was anything but predictable. He was certain of nothing. His goal was to survive the moment.

With absolutely no idea as to who would meet him there, Gavin wasn't completely sure he even wanted someone to show up. Regardless, he had nowhere else to go. No one to turn to for help or even advice. His only comfort was in knowing that soon the events of the day would play out. Anything was better than waiting around like a sitting duck.

As if on cue, a tall, dark-complexioned man dressed in an expensive business suit caught his attention and nodded his head. Gavin nodded back and waited for him to approach.

The hammering of Gavin's heart was much faster than the tempo of Sinatra's "Strangers in the Night," and he wondered if the sound was loud enough to be heard by the other patrons. If he wasn't scared enough to wet himself, he would have laughed at the irony of it all.

Gavin held his breath and waited. The man drew nearer and then walked right past him. Exhaling shakily, he fought the urge to turn and see where he'd gone or to whom he'd been nodding, but a blonde waitress, dressed in an aproned uniform from the era, materialized out of nowhere and redirected his focus.

Her smile was even thinner than her frame. Immediately, he thought of Sylvie and her humiliating Sub-n-Salad uniform and offered her what he hoped was a genuine smile.

"Coffee with cream," he blurted nervously, before she even asked him.

"Uh, yeah...sure," she answered. "That's *it*?"

"And sugar—a couple packets."

"You know there's a health tax on the sugar and cream, right?"

Gavin sighed. "Yes."

"Okay. I always have to ask. I'll be back with your coffee in a few minutes. Oh yeah...and Frank told me that this goes to you," she added, tossing a white business envelope onto the table in front of him before she walked away.

Gavin stared at it for a split second before sliding it from the battered table top, trapping it between his thigh and the booth's padded bench. Despite its thinness, the envelope felt as conspicuous as an elephant hiding under his leg. His mind raced, wondering who saw the exchange.

Should I open it here? Leave? Do nothing and wait? Maybe this has nothing to do with the mystery text. Then again, why would Frank give me an envelope? He couldn't possibly be involved in any of this.

Gavin used every ounce of self-control he possessed to resist the urge to turn around and look for Frank or anyone else approaching.

The temptation to run was fierce. He could leave the whole nightmare behind him and never look back. For now, he'd be satisfied just to walk out the door without getting a bullet to the back of his head.

I know I'm probably exaggerating the danger here, but it's not even seven o'clock and I've had enough excitement to last me a lifetime.

He started to rise, but a firm hand clamped down on his shoulder from behind, pressing him back down into the booth. Gavin's hand automatically reached into his pocket for the gun, just as Frank slid into the booth across from him.

Despite his advanced years, Leroy Frank's large frame filled the space in a way that was both formidable and relaxed at the same time. The grin that spread from one giant earlobe to the next, lifted the Shar Pei-like folds on his cheeks so thoroughly that Gavin immediately sensed he could relax.

"You look even whiter than usual today, Superman," the old man teased with a laugh.

Gavin settled back down into the booth. "And you still look like a gangster who's about a pint low," Gavin countered, giving it right back to him.

Frank threw his head back, chuckled, and said, "Well, it's no wonder! Eighty-two years of trying to stay ahead of the rat race'll definitely suck the life-blood right outta ya."

"Now there's a true statement," Gavin answered with a nod.

Frank raised one eyebrow and answered, "Well…looks to me like you at least have *something* to keep your motor going these days…who's the pretty lady who left the envelope for you?"

Gavin tried not to act surprised. "It was a woman?"

"Yeah. Said she couldn't stay."

"What'd she look like?"

"Hispanic."

Isabella!

"Was she petite and very pretty?" Gavin asked, eager to confirm it.

Frank shrugged. "Attractive, yes, but she was more tall than short and a little stocky…wait, how come I know more about who you were meeting than *you* do?" he asked with a chuckle, just before his expression turned serious. "Aww…for cryin' out loud," he groaned, "you're not trying to meet women on the *internet,* are you? Don't you know…"

"I wasn't meeting *anyone* here," Gavin quickly retorted, cutting off the lecture he knew was coming. "I just came in for a cup of coffee," he explained nonchalantly, hoping the old man missed the slight hesitation and tremble in his voice.

"Oh *really?* Well that'd be the first time you came to see ol' Frank when you're sober—and for just coffee. You're not hittin' the sauce again are you?" he asked, eyeing him suspiciously.

Relieved he had dropped the subject of the woman and the envelope, Gavin gave Frank a tired grin and answered honestly, "Not yesterday, and not so far today…but it's *early.*"

Frank smiled. "Atta boy. I'll send you over a plate of some good grub to help you resist. You're lookin' a little pale and skinny to me."

"Gee Frank…for a minute there, I thought you *cared*," Gavin teased. "The health tax on the food you serve here is enough to break even a lawyer's bank account."

Frank chuckled. "Yeah, the government don't wantcha eating it—that's how you know it's *good*," he answered with a wink and headed back to the kitchen.

The minute the old man walked away, Gavin exhaled the breath he hadn't realized he was holding. The ominous envelope beneath his thigh couldn't have weighed more than a few ounces, but its presence seemed more like a massive anchor, pulling him further down into the murky depths of uncharted waters.

Once again, the urge to bolt and escape the danger and Frank's watchful eye was powerful. The decision to stay put came just seconds later with the arrival of a steaming cup of freshly-brewed coffee, a plate piled high with scrambled eggs, crispy-brown potato wedges, linked sausages and three strips of bacon. The waitress he'd talked to earlier handed him a fresh napkin and silverware and said, "Frank said to tell you, this one's on him."

She was gone before he could object.

In the end, the savory aroma proved to be too great to resist. Gavin wolfed down almost all the food on the plate.

Then, thinking of the waitress, he dropped a pair of twenties on the table and headed out to face another day of unknowns.

*****

Gavin waited impatiently in the visitor's room for Sister Helena to join him. The sealed envelope stared up from the table to mock him, making him feel even more like a coward than ever before.

Having decided to drive straight from Frank's Place to the convent, he waited to open it. It was easier to tell himself that he needed to touch base with Sister, to see if she'd heard anything from the friendly neighborhood hacker they'd enlisted, than to admit he was scared.

He felt pathetic as he sat there—like a lost boy running to his mother to be saved from the boogie-man. It was humiliating and painful to admit the truth—he had nowhere else to go.

His eyes searched the room. A giant crucifix on the wall served as the centerpiece, statues of the Blessed Virgin Mary and Saint Joseph graced each side. On the adjoining wall, framed images of St. Padre Pio and St. Mother Teresa seemed to smile at him, their soulful eyes making him feel as though they understood the difficulties he was facing. It seemed stupid and unreasonable, but somehow, he felt comforted.

At every opportunity possible, Sister Helena never failed to speak to him about his need to grow in holiness. To Gavin, the idea seemed as likely as becoming a transgender. But, like the images surrounding him, there was something about Sister and her words that reset his emotions and calmed him down. She chastised him just enough to make him mad but also ignite a spark of truth within him to push him forward.

As she came rushing through the door, her face held an expression that undeniably assured him she knew something. He almost smiled.

"I heard from Tony!" she blurted as soon as the door closed behind her.

"I hope it was a private message," he answered, inwardly cringing.

"Yes, yes...it was," she assured. "He confirmed that the autopsy findings *had* been changed."

"I *know*. Our informant's legit."

She raised her eyebrows. "What do you mean, you *know*? What's going on? Why are you here?"

Gavin managed a weak smile. "Because I need you to keep me from running away from home," he answered honestly.

"What's the matter? Tell me?" she crooned sympathetically, slipping into the chair across from him. She pushed up her glasses and asked, "Have you eaten? Are you hungry?"

Gavin shook his head wearily, but she wasn't convinced. "You look pale. Are you coming down with something?"

Gavin chuckled. "See...that's why you calm me down—you're a typical mother hen. Yes, I've eaten, and I look like crap because I've been awake most the night and need a shower. Sorry for the smell. Anyway, I want you to contact your cousin Tony and let him know that his friend's nephew should lay low for a while. Tell him to stay off his computer and watch his back."

"Gracious God! Do you really think we've put him in jeopardy?" she asked worriedly.

"I wish I didn't have to say yes, but it's possible. I received this note that was in my *locked* car," he declared, putting the paper up on the table in front of her, "And also received this text," he added, placing his phone next to it.

The color drained from her as she glanced from the note to the text. Immediately, Gavin felt guilty for having told her. So much so, that he casually covered the envelope on the table with his elbow and swiftly brushed it off the edge and onto the floor.

She leveled her gaze toward him. "So then, who did you meet with and what's in the envelope?" she asked, looking at him with razor-sharp eyes over the top of her glasses. "It won't do either of us a bit of good if you keep it from me, so *spill it*. What happened and what are you afraid is in the envelope?"

Gavin exhaled and leaned over to pick the envelope off the floor. "I didn't meet *anyone*. A woman left this for me at Frank's. I didn't get to see who it was, and I shouldn't have brought it here. I just...well, I'm a coward who couldn't bear to open it. I didn't know where else to go."

Sister Helena's face literally melted with sympathy. The sight made him feel even worse. There was nothing he could do to change what either of them was feeling, except buck up.

He mustered all the courage he could scrape up and said, "Sister, I'm going to leave here now and do whatever I can to put together an air-tight case, so I can file a motion to present what I have to Judge Burton. Hopefully, it will be enough to get Maryn released on bail, and maybe even cause a grand jury investigation to be launched, but I can't do it if I'm worried about you too. I need you to be *extra* careful and on your toes. Don't trust anyone and don't talk to anyone."

"I will...don't worry," she answered quickly, reaching over and patting his hand.

Her assurance did little to stop his apprehension. "I would imagine that you can get away with visiting Maryn because that's your job as part of the prison ministry, but someone is out there watching me. They've got my number. They know my car. They've got..."

"For crying out loud, just open the envelope!" she exclaimed. "There might be something in there we need to know about right away!"

Gavin's gaze locked with hers. He had hoped the overwhelming fear he was feeling wasn't obvious, but, somehow, she always knew what he was trying his best to bury.

"Gavin," Helena began again, this time much more gently, "*none* of this is your fault. I *asked* you to get involved. *I am* involved and wouldn't want it any other way. What good are our lives if we don't live them for others? What will we leave to this world if we can't offer our help and hope for the good? We have a chance to help so many...Maryn, her *children*, Isabella and *her* children, and ultimately, potentially, the *entire world* by getting to the truth!"

"And what if the truth gets us *killed*?" he asked quietly but firmly, his eyes searching her face. "And what if that poor sap who hacked the system to help us is lying in a pool of his own blood as we speak?"

Gavin could tell by the look on her face that his words hit home. Still, she was undeterred. She squared her shoulders, lifted her chin, and answered confidently, "If that's the tragic truth, then he's in the arms of Mercy, itself. I've prayed for Fr. Tony's friend as I've prayed for your safety, and for Maryn...and for all. I believe that we are on a mission for good and that God is watching out for each of us. But even if we die doing His will, then Heaven will be our reward. On the other hand, if we live out our lives doing nothing to help mankind, we are already in Hell."

Gavin stared at her for several moments. He could relate to her words. Many times, during the divorce and when he was sobering up, he felt like he was experiencing glimpses of what Hell might be like—burning, suffering, wanting what is good, being able to see it, but having it all just outside his reach.

"Truth is our only hope, Gavin," she reiterated, reaching for the envelope and holding it out to him. "Without truth, there is only darkness that awaits. Evil flourishes in shades of gray, secrets, and half-truths. Love, joy, and *real* mercy flourish in light and truth. If we want God's best outcome, we must be willing to embrace His truth."

Gavin waited several more seconds as he pondered the wisdom in all she'd just said. Finally, he took the envelope from her and used his finger to break the seal.

Simultaneously, they held their breath while he unfolded the single piece of paper inside.

"Oh my *God*!" Gavin blurted.

"Isn't that Eduardo Rojas?" Helena asked, looking back and forth from the picture to his shocked expression. "I saw his picture on the news."

"Yes," Gavin confirmed, his hands now shaking.

"Who is the man with him? He looks a little familiar..."

"That's because he's a former congressman," Gavin replied woodenly. "His name is Roger Townes. He was appointed by the new president to oversee vaccination safety. He is the *founder* of the VSIPC."

"Isn't that the vaccine safety council?" she asked, looking up so quickly that her glasses slid to the tip of her nose.

Gavin nodded woodenly.

"Oh my *God!*" he repeated disbelievingly.

"Gavin *Steele*," Helena scolded, "unless you are praying, you better stop using God's name in vain…"

He cut her off. "Sister, we *both* better start praying. According to the date on this picture, Eduardo was found murdered just three days after it was taken."

"Lord Jesus, have mercy," Helena whispered, crossing herself. "Are you *sure*?"

"Yes. A hundred percent sure."

"Then we need to contact this Roger Townes—maybe *he's* the one helping us!" Helena exclaimed. "Or…gosh…could he be in on the coverup?"

Gavin shook his head. "No…he can't be…because he's dead now too."

Helena gasped. "Oh no!"

Gavin rubbed his eyes to buy himself time, while he fought back a myriad of emotions. He finally looked up at her and explained, "I heard it yesterday on the news—an apparent heart attack. But considering all these mysterious deaths, what do you think are the chances of that report being the actual cause of death?"

Helena adjusted her glasses and stared at the slightly grainy picture of the two men sitting together on a park bench. Silently, she absorbed the implications of what he'd just told her.

"Holy Lord in Heaven," she prayed sadly, "have mercy on us all.

Chapter 22

Maryn startled at the sound of her wedding band hitting the worn, concrete floor. Allowed only a single piece of jewelry, she'd chosen to keep her band and leave her engagement ring behind. As foolish as it seemed, and despite all that had occurred, she was determined to wear it, no matter how often it slipped from her thin, often cold, hand. Her vows meant something to her. Unlike Thomas, she would not so easily cast them aside.

Still, there was no doubt that his betrayal had done damage— possibly, indelible damage. She hadn't felt completely safe or content since the arrest—jumping at every sound, always wondering what ill-fated incident awaited her next. Now, because it was almost visitation time, every noise, big or small, caused her heart to pound. Most of the time, the pounding was out of fear and anxiety. Sometimes though, her heart pounded with the hope of hearing the heavy, metal, electronic locks on her cell door disengaging, indicating that someone, anyone, was coming to see her. During these rare moments of hope or delusion—at times she wasn't sure which—she waited for the moment she would be set free and could return to her girls.

Second only to that heart-pounding wish, was the seemingly futile hope that Thomas would finally walk through the door and take her in his arms. Every night she dreamed he would fall to his knees crying and express his deep sorrow for all the pain he had caused her.

Often, she woke to find fresh tears on her cheeks from the intensity of re-living the seemingly real-like experience of rushing into his arms and all was made well again.

Last night had been no different. Between seeing the girls and wondering where her attorney had disappeared to, her emotions were all over the map. Thankfully, wrapped in the comfort and warmth of Sister Helena's letter, she was able to sleep—initially, anyway. The dream came back in the middle of the night. Like usual, she woke up hopeful, only to realize that she was still alone, on a dirty cot, in a dreary prison cell.

The beautiful memories disappeared quickly, washed away by her tears, much like the destruction of a sand castle with the force of a powerful ocean wave. Afterward, her tormented mind was simply unable to rest.

After retrieving her ring from beneath the cot, Maryn stood up and caught her reflection in the mirror. Her red, swollen eyes stood out in her pale, lifeless face. She felt like a zombie—alive, but dead inside.

Reaching up, she used her fingers to smooth her tangled hair, before it even occurred to her to use her brush. In truth, the most familiar tasks had become foreign and unimportant. Her focus often vacillated from surviving life to surviving death.

Suddenly, she remembered lying with her back against Thomas' chest and how it felt to have him run his fingers over her scalp and through her hair. Many times, she would wake to find him lightly scratching her back—something she could never get enough of. Each time she turned to thank him, he would smile and say, "I've *always* got your back, Mare," and she would answer, "You're my knight in shining badge, Sir Thomas," before the lovemaking began.

Those were the times Maryn felt absolutely cherished by Thomas—the times that carried her through the long days and nights waiting for him to come home after the late-night shift. The times that carried her through his sometimes somber and pessimistic moods.

Occasionally, especially when they worked opposite shifts, Thomas went for weeks without talking much to her at all, except for what was necessary—schedules, finances, the girls and their safety. But, there were also times when it was as if the cloud lifted and the man who proposed to her on the beach was back with his winning smile, a bouquet of flowers, a bottle of wine, and a passionate embrace.

She'd gotten used to holding on, waiting patiently for those breaks to come. Admittedly, the oasis moments, as she had come to think of them, had become much less frequent the past couple of years. Maryn was well-aware that the pressures of his job and the welfare of their girls was a great concern for him. She had mistakenly believed that she was as well.

How could I have missed so much? Thomas had been moodier than ever during the months before I was arrested. Why didn't I see this coming?

Maryn recalled how he was always so exhausted after his shifts, admitting more than once that it was getting more and more difficult to shut out the memories of the horrific things, he witnessed every day while on duty.

His job was always hard, but we both knew that going in. What changed? What could have turned his heart so against me? He knew my concern about the vaccines. He never acted really sure of them either, so where is this hatred coming from, this complete unforgiveness?

Her mind began to race with the possibilities. Like always, the voice of destruction whispered horrific scenarios that pierced her heart in so many places that she wondered if it would stop beating altogether.

One of the hardest worries to push away was the recent discovery that Thomas had been withdrawing money from their savings account.

Since he took care of all the finances, she would have never even noticed the withdrawals if the bank hadn't called and left a message that there might be potential fraudulent or unauthorized use of their account.

When she called Thomas to tell him about it, he told her he would call the bank and take care of it. Later, when she asked him about it, he explained that he was investing money in secure commodities. Having grown up in a family that struggled to put food on the table had made Thomas extra cautious with their money.

Now, Maryn marveled at how much trust she'd given him. Her confidence in allowing him to handle all their finances would be considered just plain foolish to most, and presently, she wholeheartedly agreed. She sincerely hoped her foolishness wouldn't be responsible for the squandering of the inheritance her parents had left her. She and Thomas had always agreed it would go to Lily and Pearl someday.

I wonder how much money is left in our accounts? If I spend the rest of my life in here, I will never know how much was taken.

Another devastating possibility that haunted her was another woman. There were several attractive women on the force that served with him, but Maryn liked and respected them all—so much so, that the notion would have seemed impossible prior to her arrest. Still, she was immediately reminded that people who work in stressful situations often form a tight bond.

The memory of a piece of paper she found in the pants pocket of Thomas' uniform rose up to haunt her. It was a woman's name, written in his handwriting. When she questioned him about it, he explained that she was a stock broker he was using.

Why didn't I look that woman's name up? I can't even remember it now. Suzanne...something.

Immediately, she wondered what Suzanne looked like and whether she was reading Lily and Pearl bedtime stories and making them their favorite snacks. The very thought landed a punch to her stomach so hard Maryn nearly doubled over in pain.

She lifted her head and gazed into the mirror, staring long and hard at the near-stranger looking back at her. Without a stitch of makeup, her puffy eyes and gaunt cheeks made her look old and worn out. Truth was, lots of other adjectives came to mind, but attractive wasn't one of them.

Maryn cringed at the realization that she couldn't even remember how many weeks it had been since she and Thomas had made love. Often, when the days had stretched into weeks, she prided herself on being patient and supportive, content to wrap her arms around him and hold him close, rather than making love.

He was tired because he'd already made love to someone else.

With the imagination came a hailstorm of negative feelings and memories—every cross word spoken, each moment of anger, and every disagreement they had ever had.

Also distressing was the memory of the times she'd been too tired to make love when he reached for her—times she'd worked a double-shift, or helped at gymnastics, or had playmates over all weekend. She couldn't deny that she'd gone through hormone swings on occasion that made her less than pleasant and anything but in the mood.

The reality pummeled at her weary heart and mind. Maryn turned away from the mirror and pressed her hands to her ears, as if the effort would stop the accusations her conscience shouted at her.

She just couldn't go there. Not now.

If she wanted to survive and get her girls back, she *had* to push out the pain and fear.

Focus on the good—only the good.

In the early years of their marriage, she and Thomas had prayed together. With God's grace, they had been blessed in many ways. Together, they'd enjoyed many good times and the greatest gifts they could ever have been given—the girls. They were more than enough to fight for, to love. To live and to die for, if necessary. Even if it was without Thomas.

Maryn fell to her knees and prayed for strength. She prayed for Lily and Pearl. Then, especially for the girls' sake, she prayed for Thomas. He'd become unrecognizable. If any of her suspicions regarding his behavior turned out to be true, she figured he was in a worse kind of hell than she was.

With Sister Helena's safety in mind, and fully convinced that he had both an ally and an enemy watching him, Gavin left the convent and headed straight to the office. His plan was to enlist Sylvie's help in sorting through and organizing all the information he had so far.

Now, more than ever, even a successful outcome scared the hell out of him. No matter when, or how, he exposed what he knew, doing so could put any or all of them in immediate danger.

I've got to make my argument airtight. The circumstantial evidence, along with the horrendous, undisputed facts have got to stick in Burton's craw, to the point that the only words he can utter are, "Get me the Attorney General on one line and the President on the other."

As he pondered Sister's resolute confidence that everything was going to turn out all right, he sincerely hoped that an elderly nun visiting the prison was not considered a threat to the thugs. On the other hand, he knew his discovery would be a threat, so he focused his attention on his rearview mirror.

So far so good.

Relieved, he dialed Annie's number. It'd been months since he'd talked to her, and he just wanted to hear her voice. For the millionth time, he wondered if he would ever get over missing her.

Her voicemail picked up. Knowing that she kept her phone close by because of the kids, he immediately felt angry and rejected. Still, he reasoned that she could have a hundred reasons why she didn't answer, so his better-self went ahead and left her a message.

"Hi Annie, I just wanted to call and see how everything's going. I know graduation will be here before we know it, so I was just checking to see if you needed anything. I haven't talked much to the kids…"

"Gavin…I'm here," Annie answered suddenly. "I'm glad you called."

"Annie!" Gavin exclaimed, more exuberantly than he'd intended. "I was just leaving you a message…wait…you're glad I called? What's wrong? Are the kids okay?"

The sound of her chuckling at his half joking, half serious questions made him relax a bit.

God, I miss her.

He could picture her holding her cell phone a safe distance from her mouth, twisting one strand of her deep-chestnut hair and then letting it unwind. Just hearing her voice made his heart feel tight.

"Probably nothing," she finally answered, "and more annoying than anything. I just needed to ask...did you make a contribution to the University of California-Berkley recently?"

"Of *course* not," he scoffed. "Berkley is one of the most liberal schools in the state. Why do you ask?"

Even before she answered, alarm bells caused his heart to thump in his chest.

"I *knew* you wouldn't have changed your mind about that school!" she exclaimed. "Yesterday I got a call from an unknown number asking to verify our address, so they could send me a receipt for my donation to Berkley."

"What did you tell them?" he asked, now officially worried.

"That I didn't make a donation."

"Then what?" he asked, his voice slightly trembling now.

"He asked me if I was Mrs. Gavin Steele, and well, I didn't really want to explain that we were divorced, so I just said yes. Then he said, 'Oh, the donation must have come from your husband,' and asked me to verify the address again."

"Did you?" he asked, praying she didn't.

"No. I ended up hanging up on him because I figured it was some sort of scam. Later, the whole conversation just didn't sit right with me. Do you think I should report it to the University, so they are aware someone is using their name for some sort of scam?"

"Yes...well...wait...let me think..."

"You sound worried. Are you okay?"

"No," he admitted, before he could even stop himself. He was sweating profusely and swore under his breath.

"Gavin, what's wrong?" she asked, "You're scaring me. Have you been drinking? It's not even eight..."

"No, no. I'm dead sober, *believe* me," he answered, secretly wishing he could drink himself into the next county.

"I'm sorry, Annie," he continued, "but I need you to do something for me—something that won't make sense, but I need you to do it anyway."

"What's this all about?" she interrupted sharply. "Tell me or this conversation's over. I don't want to play games."

Gavin's heart was pounding so hard, he wondered if she was suspicious because she could hear it through the phone connection. "Annie, *please*, just listen. I am *so sorry* for everything I've ever done to hurt you and the kids…"

It's all my fault that she's alone.

He swallowed hard to keep his emotions in check. "Oh God, Annie…I'm *begging* you. If I've ever done even one thing in my whole life that you consider good, do this for me, *please*. I need you to go to a public phone somewhere and call my office, not my cell…"

The line went dead.

Gavin stared at the phone in his hand for several seconds. Fear raced down his back. For a split second, he wondered if she hung up on him because something terrible happened. His imagination was running wild with the possibilities, just as a text came through.

I'm not going to play this attention-getting game.
Call me when you sober up.

Her text both relieved and saddened him. He knew he deserved every ounce of her suspicion and anger, but her words felt like a sucker punch to the gut, much like when the divorce just happened.

Still, he had absolutely no time to feel sorry for himself. Desperate to protect her and the kids, and without a clue as to how to accomplish it, he pushed the speed limit to get to the office, as his mind raced faster still.

Between weaving in and out of traffic and watching his rearview for cops or someone following, he felt like he was on the brink of full-blown panic. Thankfully, Sister Helena's words about God being with him pushed through the fog.

Though it was completely foreign to his nature to do so, Gavin gave in and prayed, "God…I'm *begging* you to take care of Annie and the kids. She's been hurt by me many times. Please don't let her get hurt again just because she married me in the first place. She doesn't deserve it and either does my kids.

"For the first time in a long time, I'm trying to do the right thing. I've been warned to keep the cops out, and I have, especially because Maryn's husband's a cop, but I've got no one who can help them if you won't. Please protect them…protect us *all…please.*"

Chapter 23

It was almost nine when Gavin pulled into the parking garage. The heavy traffic and all that had transpired set him back in more ways than just time. He was exhausted—physically, mentally, and emotionally. On complete overload, his mind sifted through every possibility and course of action he could take, to the point that nervous sweat rolled down his brow even before he exited his car.

Feeling vulnerable, he frantically searched the glove compartment and retrieved the Bluetooth smartwatch Lucas had given to him several years ago on Father's Day. Lucas had been so excited to have him try it, but Gavin abhorred useless gadgets and overrated technology. Now, he was happy to find it was still there. A twinge of guilt for never using it crept into his mind, but with no time to even go there, he set to the task at hand.

The technology had been replaced and upgraded by now, so he had to search the internet for instructions on how to sync it to his phone. Eventually, remembering why he hated technology, he gave up and simply secured the device to his wrist.

With his phone in his pocket and 9-1-1 on speed dial, he opened the door and proceeded to carry on a phony conversation with his wrist while he walked. His hope was that anyone observing would believe that an attack on him would be heard immediately and could be tracked.

Sheer adrenaline kept him moving at a near-jogging pace through the open garage—a space which suddenly seemed to possess many obscure areas he hadn't noticed before.

The interior of the professional building welcomed him in a way he could have never imagined; the normalcy of the activity helped him relax a little as he touched the sensor on the elevator and waited for the doors to open.

I'm sure Sylvie's wondering where the hell I am. She probably thinks I'm dead.

She'd tried to call him several times, but he was so rattled, he didn't want to talk to her until he was sure their conversation would be private. Admittedly, he felt a little guilty for leaving her hanging, but it couldn't be helped. There was just too much at stake to take chances.

Remembering that Eduardo and Townes were both dead caused him to squeeze the handle of his briefcase containing the fax and picture even tighter. His other hand was buried deep in the pocket of his overcoat, wrapped firmly around the handle of his father's gun.

The elevator doors opened to reveal a lesbian couple sharing a kiss before they exited. As usual, Gavin kept his eyes averted so as to not give them any reason to file a discrimination complaint.

As much as he wholeheartedly disagreed with the new zero-tolerance laws against sexual orientation discrimination, he wasn't about to be caught in the trap. The fine he would have to pay if he was ticketed was the least of his worries—the real cost would be the waste of valuable time it would take to appear in court and attend the required anti-discrimination program.

With his head down, he moved into the elevator. Before he turned to face the closing doors, he felt a hand grasp his shoulder. Sheer panic made him swing his arm around and use his briefcase to knock the perpetrator to the floor. In a split second, he grabbed the Barretta and took aim.

"Geezus!" he exclaimed, immediately lowering the pistol.

He bent over and placed his forearms onto his thighs and sucked in some deep breaths to calm his racing heart.

"Geez, Sylvie…I'm sorry…*so sorry*," he exclaimed hoarsely, as she stared at him in disbelief.

"What is *wrong* with you?" Sylvie gasped, her eyes wide with fear.

Several seconds passed before Gavin straightened. With a shaking hand, he put the safety on, shoved the gun back into his pocket, and reached out a hand to help her up.

Though the threat of danger was over, a different kind of dread washed over him.

I'm losing it. Fear is winning this game.

As the elevator slowly climbed, for the first time ever, he wished that his office was higher than the tenth floor. He was in no hurry to leave the safety of the small, confined space. No hurry to face what lay ahead. He had no real plan and was trembling like a leaf. He felt small and powerless, like a lowly pawn in a game of chess. The only thing that kept him from crumbling like a discarded rag was not wanting to scare Sylvie even more.

Despite having just been knocked to the ground and a gun pointed at her, Sylvie worriedly searched his faced and asked, "Are you *okay?*"

He nodded mechanically. "Are *you?* I am *really sorry,* Sylvie…I felt your hand and panicked."

"It's okay," she offered quickly, "I shouldn't have grabbed your shoulder. I was just catching my breath and thankful that I'd caught the elevator…and that you were *alive!* Do you *realize* that I've been *crapping* myself wondering where you've been? Why didn't you answer your phone? I have *so* much to tell you!"

Gavin stared at her for several seconds. She was blissfully unaware of all that had transpired—the very real, potential danger to which they were exposed. Young and ambitious, she had her whole life ahead of her and he had no way to guarantee her safety—or anyone's for that matter. Old enough to be her father, he should be protecting her with his wisdom and experience. He had a thriving practice and enough money and holdings accumulated to leave California and never look back; but in that moment, he felt like the biggest failure alive. Completely inadequate. The realization made him want to drink himself into a coma.

The elevator doors opened. Still quiet, Gavin picked up his briefcase and followed Sylvie out and down the hallway to his office. He sensed that his silence was alarming her but didn't dare say another word until he was sure their conversation would remain private. The risks were too high. Already, it occurred to him that the camera in the elevator would have caught the entire incident. If anyone requested the footage, he could be charged with multiple counts, including possession of a loaded firearm and public endangerment for starters.

He unlocked the door and waited for her to pass through before he closed and locked it again.

"Are we…" Sylvie began, before he put a finger to his lips and shook his head.

Immediately grasping his intent, she nodded and then waited in silence as she watched him go through the rooms, examining the light fixtures, the dinosaur, the fax and copy machines. He looked behind every door, under every chair, his desk, the conference table, the breakroom counter, even the back of the toilet and under the sink.

Finally, when he felt satisfied, he turned to her and said, "Okay…I think we're good."

"So, we're closed for the day?"

"Yes." *Maybe permanently,* he wanted to add.

"Well, that's good because I have something *big* to tell you."

He wanted to laugh. She had no idea what big really was—no inkling of the ominous dark cloud that was hanging over their heads.

"…So, I called her and asked her and her son to come play with my boys."

"Wait…what? I'm sorry, I wasn't listening."

"Damnit Gavin! I know you're stressed out, but so am I! I'm *trying* to tell you something important, so would you do me a favor and just freakin' *listen*?!"

She didn't wait for him to answer. "Okay…so there's this kid in Kade's class—Ricky Martinez. Kade's been wanting to have him over, so last night he came over with his mom, Chelsey—she's a single mother too. She's got Ricky and Clare, but I really never got to meet Clare because she stayed sleeping in her carrier. Anyway, after the three boys ran off to play, Chelsey mentioned how hard it is to find daycare and asked who I used. When I explained to her that my mom cares for my boys, she started crying—I mean, just *wailing*."

"Sylvie…why are you telling me this? Can it wait until another time? I need to let you know what's going on."

"No! It can't wait because it's *about* what going on! It's important! Just *listen* a minute and trust me. I wouldn't be wasting your time right now. Geez, give me a little credit, would you?!"

Gavin sighed and ran his hands back through his hair and then down his face. "Okay. Go ahead and finish."

"So, like I said, she was bawling like someone just died, and when I finally got her to calm down, she asked me if I could keep a secret."

Gavin's head lifted. "What *kind* of secret?"

"She told me that her daughter, who just turned two, has been having weird symptoms."

"Go on."

"She told me that ever since her daughter, Clare, got her eighteen-month-old vaccinations, her eyes won't focus like they should."

"Well, well…what a surprise!" Gavin blurted sarcastically, his earlier fog now replaced with rising indignation.

"*Yeah*. Scary, huh? And there's *more*. She goes on to say that the reason she was crying is that there are no daycares who will take Clare without her being fully vaccinated, but she doesn't want to take the chance that Clare's symptoms will get worse."

"Has she tried to get an exemption?"

"Yes. She got one. But the daycare providers and the parents of the kids attending are all scared that her kid is going to spread diseases if she doesn't get vaccinated."

"Well, that's ridiculous. If their kids are vaccinated, they shouldn't get sick. And anyway, the daycares don't get to decide. As long as there is a medical exemption, they *have* to take Clare, or they could be sued."

"I *know* that, but the parents also know that there's a bill up for consideration that would do away with all exemptions. This makes them think that the government knows the diseases are getting worse and that everyone needs to be vaccinated."

"Okay—I *get* it. But for now, the daycares *have* to take Clare, or face a lawsuit."

Sylvie rolled her eyes, frustratingly. "They don't *tell* Chelsey the vaccines are the reason they won't take Clare, they make *excuses*—like they're full, or a current family is having another child and has first priority."

Gavin stared at her. He was so tired that he could hardly think straight. "Sylvie, I know you're trying to help me out by reiterating the dangers of vaccines here, but…"

"Hold *on*!" she exclaimed. "I *told* you what I had to say was important!"

"Then get to the part where I'm going to be impressed, because what you're telling me here is nothing I don't already know!" he bellowed.

Sylvie stared back at him with fire in her eyes for several seconds before the fire transformed into what looked to be fear.

"Gavin…*listen to me*," she pleaded. "Chelsey told me that Clare had a strange lump on her head at the same time her symptoms started."

"Are you frickin' *kidding* me?" Gavin exclaimed, now all ears. "Did you ask her what shots her kid got?"

"Of *course*! Lunatia was one of them."

"Now we're on to something! Did she take her in and report any of this?"

Sylvie nodded. "Yes. They told her it was nothing to worry about and sent her to a clinic across town where a surgeon drained the lump."

"What was the diagnosis?" he asked, now writing furiously on his legal pad.

"They told Chelsey that Clare must have fallen and hit her head. They called it a hematoma."

"Did she fall?"

"Not according to Chelsey. She said the lump was small, like the size of an almond, and hard—not like the kind of bump you get that's swollen from getting hit."

Gavin nodded. "Did you notice any odd symptoms in Clare?"

"No. She stayed sleeping the whole time. Chelsey said that she'd been up all night—maybe teething, so she was glad for the break."

"Too bad. I would have liked you to describe her eye movements to me. Maybe next time. For now, I need you to figure out a way to ask Chelsey what clinic she used and get the name of the surgeon out of her. Do you think you can do that without her being suspicious of your questions?"

"Yeah, I think so. I told her I would talk to my mom about maybe taking Clare for a while at least—she gets a little break from my boys while they're in school."

"Tell your mom I'll pay her double what the daycare charges if she'll take Clare," he blurted without looking up.

"Are you *serious*?"

"Yes. And with any luck at all, if we blow this whole thing wide open, Chelsey could be awarded enough money to afford private daycare—and then some."

"That would be so amazingly *awesome*," Sylvie exclaimed happily.

"Well don't get too excited yet. We've got a crapload of work to do and we're going to have to watch our backs like we've got the Gestapo watching us. Now, how about you put on a pot of coffee so we can get to work."

"Who's the Gestapo? I guess I've heard of Gazpacho..."

Gavin shook his head and chuckled. "Never mind."

Chapter 24

The familiar clicking of the cell locks brought a surge of hope to Maryn's heart so fast that her eyes immediately filled with tears of joy.

Someone's coming. Someone cares!

Just moments later, hope did not disappoint. She was pulled into the strong, but cushiony, embrace of Sister Helena's arms. The older woman held her tightly while she wept. She didn't ask questions, she didn't try and make small talk. She simply held her and let the emotions that sprang from an unimaginable trial and pain pour out, until Maryn felt spent at last.

Helena pulled several fresh tissues from her big black purse and handed them to her. "God is aware of every single tear you cry, honey. He *knows*. He's working things out that we can't see, and I'm here to tell about the things he's moving that we *can* see."

"Are you staying here or going to the conference room?" Mack interrupted, with his usual lack of emotion.

"The conference room," Sister answered quickly.

Mack didn't wait for confirmation, but immediately ushered them to the tiny room that had now become familiar to them.

When the door locked into place behind him, Sister Helena urged Maryn to sit. Then, trying not to be too obvious, she went through the same routine she'd watched Gavin perform—reaching for her purse on the floor so she could look underneath the table and chairs.

When she was satisfied that there was nothing new or suspicious in the room, she positioned her chair across from Maryn. After bowing her head, she made the sign of the cross and then reached over and took Maryn's hands to pray, "God, make this time together fruitful. Uncover all that needs to be revealed. Protect Gavin and all involved, especially Lily and Pearl. Change Thomas' heart and give Maryn the strength and peace she needs to endure this trial, that Your perfect and holy will may be accomplished in and through her and through us all. In Jesus' Name."

"Amen," they declared in unison.

"Maryn," Sister Helena began without pause, "I've got so much to tell you. I promised Gavin I would fill you in on what's going on and try to answer any questions you might have or want me to ask him. He's tied up again today and couldn't be here."

Maryn's face fell. "Again? I mean…are you sure? I'm beginning to wonder if he's willing to continue with this. I'm not trying to seem ungrateful, but I'm in *real trouble*! I just hope he's not going to drop my case."

Helena shook her head so hard that she wondered if her neck would be sore in the morning. "No! No! No! He's working on it! *Believe* me!"

Fresh tears filled Maryn's eyes. "I'm sorry…I am just so worried about my girls and our future…"

"Hush now! You don't have to apologize or explain why you're worried. You have every reason to be concerned, but not about what you think."

Helena then proceeded to fill Maryn in on the incidents, one by one, including the fax and the envelope left in Gavin's car.

This time, Maryn's tears were joyful, especially in hearing the news that David's death was completely unrelated to the Lunavirus.

"Oh Sister, how can I be so filled with happiness and sorrow at the same time?" she asked, dabbing at her tears. "I am so relieved to know the truth, and yet, poor little David is still gone forever. Why did that happen to him and why is this happening to *me*? Who is behind all this?!"

Helena shook her head. "We just don't know yet. I am also thankful for this information, but it means that there is someone working hard to pin David's death on you."

"That's true," Maryn answered soberly.

"And I'm sorry to have to admit that I have more bad news," Helena continued, "but thankfully, at least no one can blame you for it."

Maryn seemed to be in shock after Sister had filled her in on the mysterious picture of Eduardo Rojas and Congressmen Townes and the fact that both men were now dead. Finding out about the commission Townes had recently created made the hair on the back of her neck stand up. It took her several moments to absorb and process the implications of all she'd been told.

"I don't even know where to begin to sort this out," she finally declared, looking intently at Helena. "There just *has* to be a connection! What are the chances of Townes dying and Eduardo being murdered just days later? Eduardo *knew* about Isabella's predicament with Sophia, right?"

Helena nodded. "Yes, from what I understand, he was the one who initially contacted Gavin's office to set up the meeting with her."

"So, what does Isabella think of all this? Poor thing...she is sick with worry about her children and now she has is mourning too."

Helena nodded woefully and admitted, "Maryn, I hate to tell you the worrisome truth...but we haven't heard anything from Isabella since our last meeting. Gavin even drove to her place to talk to her, but the house has been completely abandoned."

Maryn shook her head disbelievingly. "Sister...this is *unreal!* Almost too much to take in! Do you think she's on the run?"

Helena shrugged. "We just don't know, dear," she offered truthfully. "I am praying she will contact us at some point."

"Dear God, you don't think she's *dead* do you?" Maryn blurted, suddenly realizing the grave danger Isabella may be in due to her connection to Eduardo.

"We can always hope that she's just in hiding somewhere," Helena offered. "Remember, Eduardo was no choir boy. He was heavily involved in selling and producing illegal drugs. It's possible that he could have been murdered by the drug cartel, and she and her family have fled to protect themselves from them as well. On the other hand, Isabella did tell Gavin that those who spoke out against the Lunatia were turning up dead. So now, we have every reason to speculate the possibility that Eduardo and Townes could be two new victims."

Maryn stood and began pacing. "This is just horrible."

Helena sat helpless, unable to do anything but nod and watch the full impact of what she'd learned hit home.

Suddenly, Maryn stopped and blurted, "Then we're *all* in danger."

Helena nodded. "Possibly...yes."

"Oh my gosh, Sister! I've put you in potential danger...and Gavin too!"

"You did no such thing!" Helena interjected. "You didn't *tell* me to show up here. You didn't *ask* for Gavin's counsel. *I did*, remember?"

Despite Helena's argument, Maryn's distraught expression was heartbreaking to see, clearly indicating that she was not convinced.

"You *cannot* blame yourself for the evil that is going on in the world!" Helena continued firmly. "You didn't start it! All you did was to try and stop it, the rest is *God's* business."

Maryn blinked and fresh tears spilled from her eyes. "I can't *bear* the thought of what could happen to you or Gavin!"

"Nothing's going to happen to us!"

"But you don't know that! And if they've gotten away with murder, they'll get away with imprisoning me for life. What will happen to my babies..."

Helena shook her head stubbornly. "*Nothing!*" she exclaimed confidently in a near shout. "Don't you even *go* there!"

She placed her hands on Maryn's shoulders and spoke to her with conviction. "Maryn... please, do *not* disappoint our Lord by acting as if you don't trust Him to work things out. Remember, He went to great lengths to warn you to protect your children! His *trust* in *you* is the reason you were given the knowledge of the dangers of Lunatia in the first place!"

Maryn paused for several seconds before she nodded wearily and brushed the tears away with the back of her hand.

"God is in on *all* of this," Helena continued, handing Maryn a tissue from her purse. "It is *impossible* that all of this is coming together without His help! He even provided us with confirmation that the fax about David was correct."

Maryn nodded. "So true. I can never be thankful enough for that. But did you ever find out who sent the fax...who sent the picture?"

"No," Helena admitted, "but I can tell you, he or she is in my constant prayers, and I know that God is with whoever is helping us. I *know* it!"

Maryn looked into Sister Helena's eyes—sage green with tiny brown flecks. Their beauty had not faded at all. There was such hope and confidence in them that she couldn't help but feel it catch fire in her own heart.

"You're right, Sister," she agreed at last. "God is answering my prayers...one by one. Do you want to hear about my visit with my girls?"

"What?!"

Maryn nodded happily. "Yesterday. I got to *hold* them! It was pure Heaven to feel them in my arms again."

To see the transformation in Maryn's entire being caused Helena's eyes to fill with tears. "I want to hear every detail!" she exclaimed enthusiastically, "but before I forget, I must warn you again...from Gavin...don't speak a word of what you know to anyone. Trust *no one*. We just can't afford to take any chances, okay?"

"You don't have to tell me twice," Maryn declared firmly. "My goal is to make it out of here alive and healthy, so I can be a mother to my girls again. I would never take any foolish chances that would jeopardize that. Besides, I don't really talk to anyone here."

"Perfect! Now tell me all about the visit with your babies, and don't leave out a single detail!"

*****

Sister Helena left the correctional facility with a spring in her step, feeling the most hopeful she had in days. To witness Maryn's sheer joy as she related the details of her daughters' visit had been a sight to behold.

If she wasn't already confident of God's will to reunite them, she certainly would have been after what she'd just witnessed. Maryn absolutely glowed with mother's love as she spoke of her daughters. It was a powerful confirmation of God's grace, helping to squelch the unspoken worries that sometimes surfaced within her.

Until everything played out, Helena was adamant that neither Maryn nor Gavin see the fear that she fought to suppress at times. Though she was confident that eventually God's will would be done, she was well-aware that unpleasant and downright awful suffering sometimes occurred before the ultimate victory.

As she walked through the parking lot toward her car, Helena was so happy she almost forgot about the potential danger they were in. The realization caught her off guard, but she immediately snapped her head to the right and left, taking in every aspect of her surroundings, as she walked the remaining distance to her car.

Nervously, she fished around in her purse for the key fob to the convent's 2015 Taurus, but by the time she slipped inside and locked the doors, she was almost giggling at her foolish apprehension.

Okay...so now I know how skittish Gavin must feel.

Even the jitters couldn't squelch her mood, though. As she merged onto the freeway, she pushed play on the CD player and joined in singing, "How Great Thou Art," with gusto.

*****

Mack walked casually down the corridor and into the locker-room bathroom. Glad to find it empty, he entered the last stall and went through the motions of unbuckling his belt and settling himself onto the stool.

Reaching into the pocket of his uniform pants, he retrieved a phone and quickly texted:

Mission accomplished.
Subject unaware. Stand by.

As soon as the text went through, Mack deleted it. As instructed, he popped off the back of the phone. With the file from a pair of nail clippers, he vigorously scratched the panel inside. Then, after sliding the disposable phone back into the pocket of his pants, he exited the stall.

He yawned tiredly, as he leisurely washed his hands at the sink, taking care to dry them with a generous amount of paper towels. Then, carefully positioning himself so the surveillance camera was behind him, he walked to the trash receptacle, and with one swift motion, rolled the phone up in the towels and dumped it all into the trash can.

Knowing that the janitorial services would not be completed for several days, Mack felt certain that the phone would soon be concealed under a mound of trash and then carted away, never to be seen again.

More and more people were using burner phones to avoid invasion of their privacy, and law enforcement was more aware of the infringement than most, so even if it was spotted, it would probably be ignored.

Satisfied, his low whistle became a carefree tune. Whistling all the way down the cell block, he went back to his duties.

*****

An overwhelming sense of awe and gratitude welled up in Sister Helena's eyes as she hit the final note of How Great Thou Art. God was in control. She could feel it in every cell of her being. The crucifix that hung from her rearview mirror was a reminder of God's power to overcome all obstacles.

"He rose from the dead, just as He promised," she affirmed aloud just before a car behind her laid on the horn and sped past her. The driver gave her the finger.

A quick glance at her speedometer told her she was driving just under the speed limit, so she sped up just a little. Despite the crude gesture, Helena chuckled. For the first time in a long time she wasn't putting St. Christopher to the test with her lead-footed driving.

She looked up at the medal depicting the great saint that was clipped to the sun visor and said, "Even though I'm anxious to spend eternity with God, I do thank you for your prayers to keep me safe on all my journeys as I travel these busy highways."

Helena didn't get a chance to say, Amen.

A thundering boom exploded in her ears. She fought to control the steering wheel, but the vehicle was spinning, then rolling, before it finally landed upside-down.

The distinct smell of gasoline flooded the interior as quickly as confusion filled her aching head.

"Jesus, I trust in You," was the last thing Helena whispered before darkness enveloped her.

Chapter 25

After using the dinosaur to leave a message on Annie's home phone, Gavin felt slightly more in control of an out of control situation. In essence, he asked her to be extra cautious of strangers and to call him at the office if she wanted more information. Now, all he could do was hope she believed his sincerity and eventually contact him. In the meantime, he had little choice but to keep pressing forward.

Side by side, he and Sylvie worked furiously to sort through and compile the mounting evidence he would present to Judge Burton.

"Getting that stubborn mule to listen is going to be tricky, Sylvie," Gavin confirmed aloud. "We have to put *powerful, key* elements into his hands that will get his attention right away—hopefully, before I'm thrown out of his chambers. I'm already treading on thin ice with him."

Sylvie nodded. "You're not telling me anything I don't know. I'm the one who takes his calls for you, remember?"

Gavin didn't respond.

"Want another cup of coffee?" she asked, getting up to get one for herself.

When he still didn't answer, she took his cup and filled it anyway. Despite his enthusiasm, he looked rough.

"Thanks," he mumbled, taking the cup from her without looking up. "I'm confident we are on the verge of breaking a scandal of epic proportions, but everything we have so far is circumstantial. We just don't have *proof* without a witness. I need something *credible* to prove there is a conspiracy going on."

Preferably, before we are all picked off one by one.

As tired as he was, Gavin hoped he hadn't spoken his fear out loud. He chanced a glance at Sylvie to see if he had. She seemed unaffected, but watching her work still gave him a heavy heart.

She's so young. She's got two sons who need her. What have I gotten her into?

"What I wouldn't give to have Isabella Sanchez walk through that door right now," she declared suddenly, putting an end to his remorseful thoughts.

Gavin quickly agreed. "Hell, I'd be thrilled with a phone call— even a *text!*"

Sylvie's phone vibrated loudly on the table, causing them both to jump.

"Oh…that would be too good to be true." Gavin exclaimed, with a nervous laugh. "And if it's from Isabella, I'm going to make it my ultimate lifetime goal to make sure that Sister Helena gets canonized after her death. Her prayers are *powerful*."

Sylvie shook her head. "No such luck. It's from Chelsey. She sent me the name of the clinic and the doctor who removed the lump from Clare's head. Hopefully this will lead to some proof."

Gavin wasn't near as enthusiastic. "Possibly, but only if we can get the doc to discuss his findings. Confidentiality will restrict most of what he is able to discuss with us. Not to mention, I don't imagine most physicians are very anxious to get involved in anything this controversial, especially if they are fully aware of what's been happening with the natural medicine professionals. Document his name and phone number. The poor sap may not have a choice in the matter if we have to subpoena him."

Sylvie nodded. "Consider it done…"

The ringing of the office phone cut her reply short. She glanced at the caller ID. It was a number she didn't recognize, and the caller came in as "Unknown."

Gavin didn't miss the hesitation and trepidation that crossed Sylvie's face. To spare her from the stress, he reached across her and grabbed it before she could. Somewhere, buried under his anxiousness, was a flicker of hope that it was Annie calling.

"Gavin Steele's office."

The line was silent.

"Gavin Steele's office," he barked into the receiver, his hope that it was Annie now dashed.

"Uh…Mr. Steele?"

The voice on the end of the line was soft and timid.

"Yes," he answered more civilly. "Who is this?"

"It's Sister Joanna from the Sisters of the Sacred Heart convent. I'm afraid there's been a terrible accident, and I need your help."

Gavin's heart tightened in his chest as dread coursed through his being. Something inside him screamed the truth before she even said the words. He punched the speaker button, so Sylvie could hear, and asked, "What has happened to Sister Helena? Where is she?"

"St. Rose of Lima hospital, in Hayward. I was sure you'd want to know. She was driving the only car we have, and it's completely totaled. Can you please pick me up and take me to her?"

Gavin was already halfway out the door when he turned and said to Sylvie, "Tell her I'll be there as soon as I can. Don't go *anywhere* until I find out what happened. I *mean* it, Sylvie. Stay put until I know more."

Sylvie nodded stiffly and then, with a shaking hand, locked the office door behind him.

******

Gavin stood helplessly by as Sister Joanna lifted Helena's soft, lifeless hand into her own. Her lips moved in silent prayer.

Earlier, the attending physician had explained that, though Helena suffered no broken bones, her head had received the worst of the trauma. Because of extensive bleeding and swelling of her brain, she was placed in a medically-induced coma to give her brain a greater chance to heal. The physician also made it clear that her prognosis was grave.

Tightly-wound bandages now replaced the habit veil Gavin was so accustomed to seeing Helena in. It was brutally hard for him to see the woman who had always been so strong, so larger than life, lying there, pale and lifeless. Without the animation of her smile, her expressive brows, her enthusiastic spirit, she looked old to him for the first time. The reality was devastating.

She had come into his life at a time he needed her most. The loss of his father had been hard enough, but his mother's dying left him with a hole in his heart that dramatically increased when Annie threw him out. When Sister Helena scraped his sorry butt off the ground that fateful morning, she put herself in the path of a selfish, bitter, alcoholic, and adulterer; yet, she never gave up. She always spoke her mind without apology, never failing to set him straight, especially when he was being an ass.

In that moment, Gavin would've given almost anything for her to give him the "look" that said: "Get your act together, Steele."

Tears stung his eyes at the thought. He swallowed hard to fight them back, but with each gulp, his bitterness increased, until he was all-out, good and mad.

He looked over at Sister Joanna. Her mouth was still moving in fervent prayer and his anger intensified.

Sister Helena put all her faith in God's ability to protect her, he seethed silently.

The bitter acid of disillusionment rolled up Gavin's chest until it burned the back of his throat and slowly filled his entire being.

She gave You her whole life in service and this is how You repay her? Why did you let those bastards hurt her? What kind of God are You, anyway?

Rachel, the ICU nurse who had earlier introduced herself, interrupted his tirade when she came in to start another bag of IV fluids. Before she left the room, she turned to them and said, "Just five more minutes, please. She needs her rest."

Gavin didn't so much as grunt in response.

She's unconscious. How is that not resting?

Sister Joanna thanked Rachel and then resumed praying, this time, aloud. "Lord Jesus, we thank you for looking out for Helena and for providing a safe place to give her the special care she needs. Thank you for sending your angels to minister to her until the ambulance arrived. Oh Lord, we ask that you heal her completely, that she may continue to be your servant on earth. May your perfect and holy will be done, Amen."

Gavin remained silent. Boiling with anger at each word she'd prayed until his emotions and fatigue finally got the best of him.

He looked over at Sister Joanna like she'd grown horns and a tail and said, "How can you *thank* God for *protecting* her?" he growled. "*Look* at her! She's in a *coma* for crissakes! How do you *know* the angels cared for her? C'mon! If angels exist, then why'd the accident happen? Why'd she get hurt at *all*? If they were with her when it happened, then they must really *suck* at their job!" he spat.

Sister Joanna stared at him for several seconds blinking back tears. In that moment, Gavin was sorry he'd yelled, but only because Sister Joanna didn't deserve it.

But God did.

He was about to muster an apology to her when Rachel reappeared. After adjusting the drip on one of the IV's, she crossed to the cupboard and retrieved Helena's purse.

"We cannot keep anything of value here at the hospital, so would either of you be willing to sign for her purse and make sure it gets back to her residence?" she asked.

Sister Joanna nodded and said quietly, "We'll take it. I live at the convent with her."

"Great!" Rachel answered, so cheerfully that she could have been talking about getting to have dessert. "Boy, whatever she's got in here is *heavy!*" she added with a laugh, handing the purse to Gavin and the clipboard to Joanna.

Any other time, Gavin would have gotten a kick out of the fact that Sister's purse felt more like a weapon, but his dark mood wouldn't allow it.

"I'm sure it's filled with canned goods and bottled water," Sister Joanna explained, as she signed and handed the pen back to the nurse. "She always kept some with her to give to the homeless on her outings."

Feeling the weightiness of the purse and hearing the explanation brought tears back to Gavin's eyes. The thought of not having Sister in his life was inconceivable, much more than he could handle now.

He felt almost dizzy with fear and disappointment. Worse than feeling plagued with worry for Sister's welfare was the knowledge that she would expect him to pray. She'd want him to be filled with hope, but he was just plain out of hope. Without her there to help him, he wouldn't make it. It was all too much.

Sister Joanna said that her car had burst into flames.

The thought came to him out of the blue. He highly suspected that Helena's car had been tampered with but raising too many questions could potentially put them all in greater danger. He would just have to wait for the police report.

How can I possibly leave her here? What if someone comes in here to finish the job?

The world around him was crumbling, and he felt powerless to stop it.

"Gavin...are you okay?"

It took several moments for it to register that Sister Joanna was speaking to him. The nurse had left the room again, leaving behind an eerie quiet, except for the sound of the heart monitor.

"Sorry, what did you say?" he asked.

She reached out and placed her small, frail hand on his forearm. "You asked me how I can thank and trust God in such terrible circumstances...and how I *know* that the angels were there with her."

Gavin's throat was so tight it prevented him from uttering a single word. He couldn't even muster a nod.

Sister Joanna explained anyway. "I *thanked* God because I *know* Him. Gavin...our God is so *good*. I know that even if something bad was allowed to happen, He will bring a greater good from it. I *believe* this with my whole heart. Secondly, the policeman told me that Helena's car had rolled and that the fuel tank exploded. The car was in flames before they ever got to the scene...yet Helena was not in the car, she was in the ditch, unconscious."

"She must have been thrown," he quickly interjected.

Joanna shrugged. "Possibly…but just look at her. Does she look like she was thrown? Besides her head injury, she doesn't have a bruise on her anywhere. So, tell me…how did an almost eighty-year-old woman escape a rolling, burning car?"

Gavin didn't have an answer to give her. Sister Joanna had no way of knowing why he was so angry. No way of understanding his plight or the fear and worry he was carrying with him that was even weightier than Sister Helena's purse. He swallowed hard to keep his emotions in check.

Several moments ticked by in silence before Joanna handed him a copy of the security release. "Could you please put this in her purse? I'd like to say goodbye before we go."

As Sister Joanna took Helena's hand and whispered a teary, but hopeful goodbye, Gavin opened the purse and slipped the paper inside. Sure enough, there were several cans of processed meat and bottled water at the bottom. His heart squeezed at the sight.

As he zipped the purse shut, his eyes caught sight of a tiny black circle at the base of the handle. Smaller than a dime, it nearly blended into the black handle perfectly. If noticed, most would have overlooked or dismissed it as an embellishment or snap of some kind. Gavin knew better. He pulled it off and examined it carefully to make sure.

She was bugged!

His heart pounded furiously as he realized the implications. He wondered how long it had been there. Immediately, his mind did a quick rewind to recall anything he may have said that could have been picked up.

He relaxed a little upon realizing that she hadn't had her purse with her the last time they were together at the convent, and his conversation with Joanna would have been completely insignificant—she didn't know anything, and he never would have talked about the case or the danger with her, anyway. The purse had been in the closet, so more than likely, the sound would have been muffled.

Still, the questions remained.

Who planted this bug and at what point? Sister Joanna said Sister Helena had gone to do her prison ministry, but how would the planting of the bug be possible at the prison...and for what purpose? Surely, no one planted it here in the hospital. If they had, they would have known it would have ended up back at the convent.

His mind raced with the possibilities.

The security check! Sister would have had to turn over her purse for the scan at the correctional facility, but who could have pulled the strings with security?

Instantly, Thomas Pearce's statement surfaced.

Is it possible that he enlisted someone's help in bugging his wife's conversations? Is there something even darker about him I'm missing?

Either possibility sounded like a longshot, even to himself. Then again, he'd seen every behavior under the sun during domestic issues. Divorce settlements seemed to bring out the very worst in people.

Who's the guilty party here? The scumbags behind the Lunatia cover-up? Are they trying to see how much Maryn knows? How much I know?

He shook his head.

Not likely. Maryn's credibility and reputation are already trashed, and my guess is that there'll be big money offered under the table to keep the coverage of this case minimal. It's got to be that bum she's married to. He's playing some sort of role in all of this. I can just feel it.

He wanted to throw the transmitter to the ground and crush it to smithereens; while at the same time, he wondered how he could use it to his advantage.

The possibilities raced through his weary mind but were soon interrupted when Sister Joanna touched his shoulder. He quickly closed his fist around the transmitter to muffle its effectiveness and stuffed his hand into his pants pocket.

"I'm ready to go now, Gavin. We'll leave Sister Helena in God's gracious care," Joanna offered sympathetically.

Gavin couldn't think straight. Fully aware that he must be freaking Sister Joanna out with his erratic behavior, he fought to erase any signs of terror from his expression and said, "If you don't mind, I need to use the restroom first."

"Of course not. Take your time."

Gavin locked the bathroom door and turned on the fan to cover any noise. He pulled out the transmitter and rolled it several times in a long strip of toilet paper. He then stuffed the wad in between a stack of bills and shoved his wallet into his back pocket. As he he walked out, he sincerely hoped that Sister Joanna hadn't noticed that he never flushed the toilet.

Without a word, he crossed the room and leaned down to kiss Sister Helena's cheek. "I wouldn't blame you if you checked out of this hell we call *life*," he whispered, "but I am asking you to hold on...*please*. I need you..."

A sound from the doorway made his head snap upright in time to see a physician glance into the room and then walk off. Gavin didn't waste a moment's time but hurried to catch him.

By the time he reached him, he was halfway down the corridor. "Are you one of Sister Helena's doctors?" Gavin blurted, his voice sounding strained, even to himself.

The man turned and said, "Yes. Sorry to interrupt your visit back there. I was looking for one of the nurses."

"It's okay," Gavin answered quickly, as his eyes zeroed in on his nametag.

"Henry Pelman, MD—Neurologist," he read aloud. "*Perfect*! I'm glad I caught you. What can you tell me about Sister Helena Brandt's condition? I am her closest friend and attorney," he added, flashing one of his business cards and then handing it to him.

Dr. Pelman eyed the card briefly and replied, "Well, even though ICU allowed you into her room, I don't have any authority to discuss her condition with you. There was only one name on her privacy disclosure, and it wasn't yours."

Gavin gave his shoulders a shrug. "Okay...but that was an oversight. Can you tell me *anything*? The doc who was in earlier said she has bleeding and swelling of the brain. Is there any hope?"

Pelman hesitated for several seconds and then said, "We don't always know how a brain injury will pan out. Her age is a factor, but her general health appears to be good, so that's positive."

"What about her brain—is the damage bad?"

"As you were told, she has bleeding and swelling. Only time will tell. We will do everything we can to help her recover, but there is only so much we can do for her at this point."

Gavin's face fell. He recognized the sound of carefully chosen words when he heard them. She was dying. He was sure of it.

In that moment, he wanted to run out of there, away from her death as fast as he could. Without another word, he turned back so he could do just that.

"Mr. Steele..."

Gavin stopped walking, wiped at his eyes, and turned around to face Pelman. "Yes?"

"Sister Helena's brain was otherwise healthy. In fact, we don't see many brains like hers these days—very few lesions. If the swelling and bleeding stops, there's a chance she may make a full recovery, but we just don't know."

Brain lesions. Gavin had come across the term while he was researching the documentation on a possible link between vaccinations, their adjuvants, and neurological damage.

"Since you're a neurologist," Gavin began quickly before he walked away, "I want to ask you...what do you think causes brain lesions in most people?"

Pelman's expression appeared tired. He seemed to be searching for the perfect, professional answer. Finally, he looked at Gavin and said, "There are multiple factors that can cause lesions. Some hereditary, some from outside or environmental factors."

"Do you believe that vaccinations can cause brain lesions?" Gavin blurted, completely interrupting his answer.

Pelman paused and took a deep breath. "There are many potential causes—diseases and otherwise, but I am sorry, I don't have time to explain them all...and sometimes, we really don't know what causes them."

"I am asking you if it is *possible*," Gavin pressed.

"Why? Did Sister Helena receive an immunization recently?" he asked with renewed interest.

"No. I'm asking on *my* behalf," he lied. "Trying to decide whether or not to get the flu shot—even though it sounds like none of us will have a choice before long."

Dr. Pelman hesitated briefly and then chuckled wryly. "You are an *attorney*, Mr. Steele. If you think, for one minute, I'm going to answer that question, you're *crazy*. I really don't care to have everything I say used against me at some point in the future. California Law is already camped outside on the hospital lawn watching every move we make, so I think I'll just plead the fifth."

"So, the answer is, yes—you do think it's possible that immunizations can cause, or contribute to, brain damage."

He shook his head. "I gave you my answer. Now, if you'll excuse me, I've got patients to see."

"Okay. I understand...but if I was to look into this matter, where would I find the most accurate and reliable sources of information? The CDC? The FDA?" Gavin pressed.

Henry Pelman stared at him intensely for several seconds before he turned to leave. He stopped suddenly, turned back to face Gavin, and said, "My father once told me that, while serving in the military, he was ordered to submit to a series of three anthrax vaccinations under the threat of court martial and dishonorable discharge."

"Are you *serious*? How did they ever get away with that?" Gavin gasped. "I had no idea...that's unconstitutional! When would this have happened?"

Dr. Pelman shrugged. "In 1997 and '98. Apparently, according to the policies of the U.S. Military, it's not unconstitutional. After receiving the third shot, my father experienced burning under his skin, which he described as hot beetles crawling around inside of him. Within just weeks, he began to suffer with rheumatoid arthritis symptoms—to this day, he still suffers from the symptoms, but tests negative for it."

Gavin shook his head and swore under his breath.

"So, to answer your question," Pelman continued, "I don't take anything for granted, or fully trust *any* institution. In a nutshell, I'm much more apt to trust those who have nothing to gain and everything to lose if they tell the truth."

Before Gavin could respond, Pelman turned and walked swiftly down the corridor and disappeared into the elevator.

Chapter 26

After dropping Sister Joanna off at the convent, Gavin drove back to the office, functioning on sheer adrenaline. Dr. Pelman's remarks had fired him up but finding the bug on Sister Helena's purse had further set him on edge. He kept his eyes on the rearview for any sign of the Lexus and one hand on his gun.

As he walked through the parking garage and up to his office, he gave no thought to the illegal possession of a firearm. At that point, he didn't give a flying fig if he was caught—he had no other choice. Too much had happened. Too many people were in harm's way. He needed to be able to defend himself.

Though she was in a coma, he somehow knew that Sister Helena was still praying, willing him to push forward and do all he could.

Knowing her, she's probably arguing with God about what she wants to accomplish before she agrees to go with Him.

The thought almost made him smile, but he just couldn't muster it. "I hope I don't let her down...and everyone else too," he whispered woefully, as he pressed his finger onto the auto-lock pad.

Sylvie sprung from her chair and rushed to meet him.

"What's going on? How is Sister?" she blurted as he locked the door behind him. "Why didn't you answer your phone or text me back? I've been sick with worry and stuck here, scared to death!"

Gavin shrugged his shoulders slightly before pulling his gun from his coat and laying it on the coffee table next to him.

The sight of it caused Sylvie to come unhinged. "Why won't you answer me, and why are you still slinging that gun around?" she shrieked. "You are going to get us both arrested—or *killed!* Do you even know how to *use* it?"

Gavin mustered a small chuckle. She'd gone from outraged to curious without missing a beat.

"Yes. Don't worry, it was my Dad's and it's just for added protection."

Sylvie simply sighed and changed directions. "Gavin, please tell me...is Sister Helena okay?"

"Please tell me that Isabella Sanchez called," he answered.

"No!" she answered in a near shout. "I would have *texted* you. Why won't you tell me how Sister is doing?"

"Because I don't really know...she's in a coma," he answered without emotion, the sadness in his eyes saying what he couldn't say. "She's suffered a bad head injury...I don't think she's going to make it."

"Oh geez, Gavin...I'm sorry. No wonder you're acting so weird. Are you okay?"

"No. We've got some work to do. Do you know anyone you can trust at Sub 'n' Salad?"

"No. I haven't worked there for years...why?"

"If I can't smoke, drink booze, or take drugs, I'm at least going to overindulge my burning stomach."

"Okayyy..." she answered with both eyebrows raised. "So are you going to fill me in as to why we need to *know* someone in order to get food?"

He put his finger to his lips to silence her, and then took out his wallet and unrolled the tiny receiver. With his finger still to his lips, he grabbed a notepad and scribbled:

Sister Helena was bugged.

This transmitter was attached to her purse.

As the full impact hit her, Sylvie's eyes widened. She covered her mouth to prevent her gasp from being heard.

Gavin nodded and then carefully rolled the bug back up inside the tissue. He then placed it into his wallet between the cash, pulled out a credit card, and closed the wallet.

Once the billfold was securely locked into the safe under his desk, Gavin closed the door and came back into the reception area and said, "Okay...so now you know why I don't trust anyone."

"Who...why...I don't understand!" Sylvie stammered.

He unbuttoned his coat, loosened his tie, and said, "I don't know if Sister's accident was an *accident*. At first, I thought I was being ridiculous for wondering, but after finding that bug on her purse, we have to be on our toes to suspect *anything*."

"Geez Gavin, this is really freaking me out. Why Sister Helena? Who would want to hear her conversation?"

"You tell me," he answered tiredly, sinking down into one of the plush visitor's chairs before thoroughly rubbing his eyes. "Sylvie, we need an ally we can trust to help expose what we've discovered. If we fully expose the deception and our evidence is credible enough to bring down indictments, the killing will stop. We can't go to the police, so the only one I can think of is Judge Burton. He will have to recuse himself afterward, of course, but we've got to uncover something significant to convince him that we aren't just trying to get Maryn off the hook, but that something much more destructive is playing out."

"And if we can't convince him, then what? You're basically telling me that we're all in danger! How will we protect ourselves in the meantime? What about my *boys*...my *mother*?"

He shook his head sadly and said, "I'm *sorry*, Sylvie...I really am. I wish I could tell you everything's fine, but I honestly don't know. Sister Helena's car was pretty much burnt to the ground. It's really crazy that she made it out alive..."

She gasped. "She was *burned*?"

"Nope," he answered, disbelievingly. "I guess she was thrown from the car. She didn't give off even a whiff of smoke...smelled like ivory soap and arthritis cream, just like always."

His voice cracked. He turned his head and swallowed the lump of emotion that nearly choked him.

"You are so tired," Sylvie offered like a mother would, putting aside her own anxieties. "I know the delivery guy from Lennie's Pizza pretty well—we eat pizza a lot at our house," she added with a grin. "I'll ask for him. What kind do you want?"

By the time the pizza arrived, Gavin was sound asleep, his chin resting on his chest.

Knowing he needed rest more than food, Sylvie didn't wake him. She wondered how much longer he could go without going crazy. Truth was, something needed to give—for everyone's sake.

She thought of Kade and Jack as she bit into a slice of BBQ chicken and smoked cheddar pizza. Hands down, it was their favorite. In the next instant, Maryn was on her mind. She wondered what it would feel like to be away from her boys for such a long time.

Worse than being apart would be knowing they thought I'd done something terrible.

The thought dampened her appetite.

Gavin's right, we need an ally in Judge Burton. What's the one thing we could show him that would convince him?

Sylvie set her pizza down and picked up her water. Mindlessly twisting it, she stared through the clear plastic bottle and noticed that looking through it distorted everything behind it.

It's just like the Lunatia vaccine...whether it's a life-saver or potentially destructive depends on the perspective through which it's viewed. There has to be a way to get a clearer perspective—something we could refer to.

"Think!" she whispered passionately.

It was in moments like these that she wished she would have read more, paid more attention to what her mom talked about, and less attention to social media and which celebrity got knocked up or was caught cheating.

In truth, she had lots of regrets—and putting all her energies into guys and partying in her younger days was at the top of the list. At the same time, she acknowledged that her own boys were the best thing about her life. She couldn't imagine living without them.

Again, she wondered how Maryn could stand it. She thought of Chelsey and Clare and wondered what would happen to her if she was forced to endure another vaccination.

She thought of Isabella.

How awful it must be for her to know that Sophia's condition could have been prevented and to wonder if her son will meet the same fate. And...where are they now?

The countless testimonies she'd read or watched came to mind. Parents lamenting everything from chronic constipation from the Rotavirus vaccine, to a high school age girl so physically tormented after a Human Papilloma Virus vaccine that she finally ended her life.

All of it was scary. More so, because she had no idea how she would handle the future vaccinations her boys would need for school. With all the research she had done, she was now convinced that some kids would inevitably be injured by them, and the numbers were increasing.

Vaccinations should never be mandated. Parents should be made aware of the risks and make their own decisions. All the literature or experts in the world professing vaccine safety doesn't mean jack-crap when it's your kid that's injured, like Sophia or Clare.

Immediately, she recalled a video she watched on a forum featuring the parents of a vaccine-injured son. She had fished through dozens of internet pages before stumbling onto it. After she'd watched it, her tears came like a tsunami. The raw pain of the parents made it all real.

Sylvie felt she deserved the grief she was feeling for them. Too many times she had embraced the "that stuff happens to other people," and "anti-vaxxers are morons," attitude.

In that moment, she wished she could watch the video again to see if there was something she missed, something that could be used to sway the judge. She didn't dare search for it though. Gavin had warned her not to do anything at the office that would give off any red flags to those who may be tracking their searches.

Hoping to recall as many relevant details of the story as possible, Sylvie lay her head back against the headrest and closed her eyes. She vividly remembered the footage of the couple's darling baby boy as he playfully stacked blocks. Often, he would look up and grin at his mamma and clap at his success or say simple words and short phrases like, "Mamma...block, uh-oh, fall-down."

Just six weeks later, after his immunizations, the stark contrast was staggering. The poor little toddler wouldn't smile. Wouldn't talk. Wouldn't play. He just stared into space as his mother talked to him, hugged, caressed, and kissed him.

At one point, when she handed him a toy, he put his hand on it, and then suddenly started crying and banging his head on the ground with such force that the father dropped the camera to go to help his distraught wife and son.

Sylvie would never forget the face of the little boy or his violent actions. Though the parents had already sought the help of their pediatrician because of his high fever and sudden inability to focus, the onslaught of the head-banging forced them to rush him back in for help. Unfortunately, instead of having their questions answered with caring concern, they were reported to the authorities for child-abuse.

The charge was shaken-baby syndrome. The only evidence that weighed heavily in their favor, ultimately saving them from prosecution and having their son taken from them, was their home videos. But, the ordeal lasted for months and cost them dearly—emotionally and financially. The stress they were under almost caused them to split. The father lost his job because of his lack of focus. This, along with the medical and legal fees, resulted in the couple's inability to pay their mortgage. Eventually, they lost their home.

Sylvie shook her head sadly. She sat up straight and looked over at Gavin, who was now sleeping so hard he was drooling. She would have laughed if she wasn't on the verge of tears.

Parents should be warned of the risks—no matter how small or great. When we get through this mess—if we get through this mess, Gavin needs to get on some sort of legal committee and help keep the government from forcing us to inject what could be harmful into our bodies.

"Now I know why mom constantly says, 'It's always about the money,'" she grumbled.

She jotted down a reminder to tell Gavin about the family she was just thinking about. *Their testimony was powerful. Maybe Judge Burton would watch the video if I can pull it up again.*

Feeling a glimmer of hope, she reached down and picked up her pizza for another bite. She stared into space as she slowly chewed, thinking about how the boy ended up having to wear a helmet regularly, and how his daddy had looked into the camera, his eyes shiny with tears, and said, "Our heads were just not made to take that kind of punishment."

Our heads were not made to take that kind of punishment.

The statement rolled over and over in her mind until she stopped and stared at her water. She picked it up and brought it to eye level.

If you look at something from one angle, it can be clearly seen, but if you look at it from the wrong angle, what's beneath can be distorted or hidden.

"That's it!" she exclaimed exuberantly, completely forgetting that Gavin was asleep.

Startled, he looked around the office and then stared at her, obviously trying to figure out where he was. "What? What's wrong? What time is it?"

She couldn't suppress a smile. "Sorry I woke you," she said with sincerity, "but I think I might have just figured out a way to get Burton to hear us out and take some action."

She popped the lid open on the box that contained his supreme pizza. Handing him a slice, she declared triumphantly, "The truth just costs too much."

*****

Rachel stared at the computer screen and took a sip of cold coffee before she typed her observation notes. It was the second of three, twelve-hour shifts she worked each week, and she already felt exhausted.

"It's going to seem like an eternity before my shift's over," she murmured as she tucked a wayward strand of hair behind her ear and yawned.

She glanced over at Sister Helena Brandt's monitor. *Hmmm...her pulse and blood pressure are up a little.*

Her eyes shifted to the monitor of her only other male patient. "All's well with you, big fella," she murmured, before looking back at Sister's monitor.

Rachel scooted the stool out from underneath her and said to her co-worker, "Keep an eye on my guy in 309 while I go see what's up with 307's pulse and pressure, okay?"

After just a few long strides, Rachel walked through the doorway of Helena's room. After a quick check of her IV's, she then turned toward her patient.

While watching the monitor closely, Rachel took Helena's hand. "What's wrong, Sister," she asked tenderly. "Don't worry," she soothed, gently stroking her soft hand with her thumb. "I'm here. You're not alone…"

Abruptly, Rachel's hand went still. The hair on the back of her neck stood up. Instinctively, she turned around just in time to see a man dressed in dark clothing rushing out the door.

"Wait!" she called out, swiftly laying Helena's hand back down so she could go after him, but the high-pitched beeping of the monitor stopped her flight. Helena's heartbeat had flatlined.

Just seconds later, a fellow nurse rushed in and declared, "She's a DNR!"

"She was doing so well up until a few minutes ago. Check the IV lines again!" Rachel commanded, lifting Helena's wrist to check her pulse. "And test the monitor connection," she added, her eyes fixed on Helena's chest for any sign of movement.

"It's okay, Sister…I'm here," she crooned, "You're not alone."

Rachel couldn't feel a pulse. She stared at the monitor, silently willing the line to spring back to life, as she prayed, "Lord, have mercy! Hail Mary, full of grace…the Lord is with thee…pray for Helena now, and at the hour of her death, Amen."

Chapter 27

"Okay, you've got my full attention," Gavin announced around a mouth full of pizza.

Sylvie wanted to laugh. For a boss who was always impeccably dressed for the office and court, he looked more like an overgrown frat-boy after a night of partying. His hair was sticking straight up in the back, and the wrinkles in his pants and coat confirmed he'd slept in them. His tie was undone and hung down past his belt. With his stocking feet crossed and resting on the chair across from him, he was devouring his pizza like he had the munchies.

"Wow, you're really hungry," she said, handing him a bottle of water.

He shook his head. "Not really. I'm trying to wake up and eat myself out of the urge for a beer...scotch...wine...a cigarette...all the aforementioned. Hand me my phone, would you?"

She nodded, sliding his phone across the conference table.

After swiping his thumb across the top, he shook his head. "No word from the hospital. I wonder how Sister's doing."

"Probably fine," she answered sympathetically. "I'm sure Sister Joanna will let you know if something happens."

He nodded. "Yeah that's true. So...now, tell me what's on your mind."

"Okay, there's a couple of things. Now don't go lawyer on me and interrupt a million times—*hear me out*."

"Then spit it out and I won't have to," he replied without missing a beat.

"Okay...first of all, did you know that that there are peer-reviewed studies from 2016 and 2017 that unequivocally declare that aluminum is causing Alzheimer's disease and Autism—and that most every vaccine contains aluminum?"

Gavin stopped chewing and stared at her before he finally swallowed and asked, "Do you have access to these studies?"

"Yes. I found the information on the net at home." Sylvie grabbed her notebook for reference. "Now I know that's been a while ago, but I went to the CDC's website and looked up the vaccine ingredients and sure enough, most of them contain aluminum. And so far, I can't find *anything* to refute these studies reporting that children receive a whopping 5,000 mcg of aluminum in vaccines by the age of 18 months and up to 5,250 additional mcg if all recommended boosters, HPV and meningitis vaccines are administered—and that was *then*...our kids get even more immunizations now."

"Yes, they do, but those numbers don't mean anything to me. I know that there's been talk about aluminum causing Alzheimer's for a long time. There for a while, everyone was scared to use deodorants that contain it and were trying to avoid cooking with it, but what is the amount of aluminum that would be considered *normal* in any given person's body?"

"That depends on a person's weight, but no amount of aluminum is really considered safe, so to speak, but the EPA says 5mcg per 5kg of body weight is acceptable. But that means that an eleven-pound baby can have 25mcg, but newborns, who usually weigh substantially less than that are given the Hepatitis B vaccination within 24 hours of birth and it contains 250mcg of aluminum!"

Gavin whistled and then asked, "How is this type of Hepatitis spread?"

"That's just the infuriating part—it's spread by the exchange of bodily fluid—which is primarily through vaginal or anal sex."

He pulled a face and said, "Then why the hell are they giving *newborns* this vaccination? Why not just test the mother?"

"Exactly!" she exclaimed and then stood up to pace the floor. "And why the *hell* hasn't anyone ever told *me*—a mother of two, about the aluminum adjuvant in vaccines? This makes me furious! This is *huge*, Gavin. We are told our children will *die* without them! That's just plain damn *scare* tactics, bullying…downright *fraud*, if you ask me. It should be used in your report to Judge Burton."

"I agree. He's at the age where Alzheimer's is a scary possibility, so he just might be intrigued."

He grabbed another slice of pizza and said, "You said a couple of things…what else do you have for me?"

"Just a big ol' slam dunk on medical coverups *ever*!" She answered confidently, grinning smugly.

He couldn't help but chuckle at her enthusiasm. He swallowed the bite he'd taken and said, "Okay, Sherlock—let's hear it."

"Who's Sherlock?"

"Holmes…never mind, just tell me," he answered eagerly.

"Okay…do you remember some kind of announcement coming out about football concussions a while back? It would have been like ten or fifteen years ago—too young for me to remember, but you might remember it. A forensic pathologist figured out that some football players were suffering brain damage from their repeated head injuries. It's called CTE…Chronic Traumatic Encephalopathy."

Gavin took several swigs of water and said, "Yeah. I remember it. I read about it after the settlement. I guess the injuries were causing some players terrible pain. Some were hearing voices and even became violent or suicidal. I don't recall the man's name, but this doc stuck his neck out to find and prove the damage was happening. I guess that even an MRI didn't show any evidence of a problem, but this doc persisted. It was a great discovery, but how is this relevant to vaccine injury?"

"Because! When this doctor tried to expose the dangers to the NFL and those associated with football—at all levels, his life became living *hell*. His research was *squashed*. They laughed at him, fired him, and fired his boss. His wife even felt threatened. It was *years* before his findings were accepted."

Gavin stared at her. "I *know* all this, but why are you telling *me* this? Relevancy, please."

Sylvie rolled her eyes. "You know…for a successful lawyer, you're really slow sometimes."

"Humor me and get on with it. I've got my own brain damage to work with, so I can't worry about anyone else's problems right now," he answered crankily.

"So, tell me," she continued, ignoring his comment, "why did they want to squelch his findings? Wouldn't the powers that be want their players to be healthy and their fans happy?"

"The game is worth protecting, but at the root of it all is the money, of course" he answered confidently. "Do you have any idea how much money is generated in pro-sports?"

"Helloooo? C'mon Gavin! Wake up! Or do you have to eat the whole pizza before you figure out where I'm going with this?"

Gavin slowed his chewing a bit and narrowed his eyes.

"It's so *obvious*!" she exclaimed, throwing her hands in the air. "Football is *huge*! It's *America*! It's a *favorite*. Some people *live* for it and schedule their whole lives around it. Can you *imagine* the loss of revenue if most or even *some* of the players quit because of the potential injury to their brains?"

"Okay. I'm following…"

"Finally!" she exclaimed, throwing her hands up in the air. "I mean, think about how it would change the entire country—kids wouldn't play football in school. There'd be no Superbowl Sunday…no Monday night football and its revenues…you see where I'm going with this…right?!"

Gavin nodded. "Go on…"

"So…c'mon! Is it *that* far of a stretch to imagine this type of rejection of truth or even manipulation of evidence could happen again to protect the status quo?"

Gavin was still staring.

"Of *course* it could!" she cried, coming out of her chair to stand before him. "*This* concussion case is enough to remind the judge that money can sometimes get in the way of objectivity and can absolutely drive medical coverups."

"I agree with you, Sylvie, but even as big as pro-football is, the numbers who play it are miniscule compared to those who are vaccinated."

"Yes! But that's all the more reason they don't want anyone to know about a coverup in the vaccine industry. Can you imagine the outcry? The panic? The loss of trust? It's *definitely* something to compare our case to!"

"It is," he agreed, "but because the numbers are so astronomical—remember, the entire world believes they've been saved by vaccinations, it will make it almost impossible to convince them."

"Well, *I'm* convinced. It didn't take me long."

"Good point. So…what else have you got," he asked with a small grin.

"Okay…so what about this…these days, most families are two-income households. Imagine the loss of productivity if parents had to miss work to stay home with their kids because of measles or chicken pox…uh…just picture your mood if I was calling in and needing several days off so I could stay home for each of these illnesses."

Gavin nodded. "Point made. Go on."

"Okay, so besides that, there's the potential hiring disadvantage the childhood illnesses could give women in comparison to men, who generally still don't play an equal role in caring for their children."

"Good point," Gavin answered. "But let's keep focused on the hidden motivations that would be big enough to create a coverup of monumental proportions."

"Right," Sylvie answered, nodding. "So, as a society, we're given every reason to vaccinate our children—I mean, we parents are told that we are irresponsible and that our children's lives are in danger if we don't vaccinate. So much so, that we have passively accepted the medical community and government's word that they are necessary and *safe*—just like the football players believed their helmets were supposed to protect their heads. But imagine…just for a moment…what would happen if the number of injured football players were to ever reach even a fraction of the number of vaccine-injured children. There would be an outcry of epic proportions! Even the biased news media couldn't resist covering it!" she added, triumphantly.

"True...true. Not to mention," Gavin began, his mind now fully-absorbed with the parallels, "that despite the clear evidence which finally legitimized CTE, hardly anyone talks about what was proven and the potential for injury that still exists. It's as if it doesn't exist and the whole thing never happened. This is the result of a public that is willing to overlook the risks to get what they want—football."

"Exactly! Most people want to be illness-free so badly, they are willing to do whatever is necessary. But then there are others who just don't know the risks, because they aren't *told* the risks. They want to do what's best for their children and are scared to death that if they don't vaccinate, they will be destroying their own children!"

Her statement rose in the air like a dense fog for several seconds before Gavin affirmed, "*Imagine* the impact on our country if the public was bombarded with the facts and figures we've come across like they are bombarded with the pro-vaccination propaganda. I mean...we've got multiple generations affected now—it seems that the effect is cumulative. They might start to question *everything* the government has told us, and *everything* put out by the medical industry and pharmaceutical companies...like the use of chemotherapy and other treatments..."

"And maybe they *should!*" Sylvie blurted angrily.

"I agree," Gavin answered soberly. "But it's like with the football risk...it's much easier to look the other way and get what you want and to avoid what you fear most. People want a magic pill for everything, but there is just no such thing.

"Our concern right now needs to be focused on the fact that people are getting hurt, sometimes *dying*, because of a faulty product, possibly an erred medical model. If we know this, we have a responsibility to help those who *know* about the dangers and want the right to refuse what they don't believe in."

Sylvie nodded. "Yep...and if you're this convinced now, wait until you see the video footage of a vaccine-injured kid I found. We have *got* to show it to Burton."

Gavin shook his head. "He's not going to want to take the time to watch some home video—trust me. He's going to want *hardcore* evidence."

"This *is* hardcore evidence! And I'd bet my *life* you will argue and pressure Burton to watch it once you see it. Don't say no...just *trust* me. I wouldn't waste your time. If he won't watch the video, we can take still-shots of this poor little boy before and after his vaccination injury." she added with enthusiasm.

Gavin blew out a sigh. He didn't want to quell her enthusiasm, but there was so much work to do.

"I've seen lots of videos of the vaccine injured," he finally said.

"Yeah, but you haven't seen *this* one. This video was used as evidence in court once already. The testimony is *compelling*."

Now curious and sure she wouldn't give up until he watched it, he asked tiredly, "Can you pull it up on your phone?"

"Yes, but I'll have to search for it again. It's buried on the net—but you know, that actually worked in our favor too. It's how I found the concussion story. I had to weed through so many pages of posts about brain injuries that I just ended up clicking on it. It's actually kind of crazy how it all came together—like it was meant to be."

"Okay, so there has to be more," he stated flatly, ignoring her slight insinuation that her discovery seemed supernatural. After what had happened to Sister Helena, he wasn't about to give God credit for it.

"What do you mean?" she asked. "More of *what*?"

"More incidences of crucial medical evidence being suppressed. There's got to be more out there—the tobacco companies, pharmaceutical companies. Everything *we* have is circumstantial at this point. Unless we can find Isabella, our only credible witness is in jail."

"I know, but..."

"You've done great work, Sylvie. It's a start, but not enough. Until we figure out who's working for us and against us, we've got to keep digging. If we can get Burton to take notice, then we have a chance that whoever's killing the natural doctors will be festered out. And if we are so lucky as to ever hear from Isabella, we might uncover what, if any, connection there is between Eduardo's murder and Roger Townes' untimely death."

Sylvie rolled her eyes. "There's a connection...surely you believe that."

Gavin nodded. "I do. Townes' meeting with Eduardo and heading up the VSIPC position makes me more certain by the minute, but I have to stay objective. If there is a connection, it's a sign the heat's being turned up by someone—maybe even the anti-vax movement, but we need evidence. For now, we'll compile what we can—go ahead and find that video for me."

"You're not worried about me searching from my phone?"

"Here...use this," he answered, sliding Lucas' laptop across the table to her.

She grinned. "Perfect...now sit back and watch a genius law clerk in action."

*****

After watching the video, Gavin and Sylvie sat in silence for several moments as the reality of what they'd just witnessed sank in.

"It was worse watching this time," Sylvie finally declared. "I felt like I knew them...and now...it feels *personal*."

"Personal and *real*," Gavin admitted.

Real enough that I'm scared shitless.

He sincerely hoped that his face didn't give away what he was thinking. But as Sylvie stared back at him with fierce determination in her dark blue eyes, he wondered which one of them was the responsible one—the elder, the one who should have the answers.

When did she become so wise? So mature?

He stared at her for several seconds. Her sable-brown hair was short—one side tucked behind her ear, bangs to the side, framing her heart-shaped face and expressive eyes.

When did she quit dying strips of her hair purple? When did she start wearing such professional clothes?

As he looked over at the competent woman before him, he realized, yet again, how out of touch with everything he'd been the past several years.

"What?" she asked nervously. "Why are you staring at me...do you have some sort of plan?"

Inwardly, he shook his head, fighting off temptation to scream, No*! I don't have a plan. I've been screwing up for so long that I don't know how to do anything else!*

Gavin fought valiantly to keep from saying the words. Sylvie needed him to be strong. A lot of people needed him to be strong, and Sister Helena was counting on him.

If this kind of evidence has been presented in court and yet mandating vaccines is still being considered, there's something big and powerful behind it. What am I missing?

After swallowing hard to keep the emotion from his voice, he said, "I wish I could tell you I had something more than just going to Burton with this, but I don't...but it will come to me, eventually. You've done great work here, Sylvie. I'm impressed."

"Well, thanks—two compliments in a row," she answered with a grin, "but right now, I just want the truth to come out. I'll sure feel better when we can get this information in front of the judge...so what do you want me to do now?"

He didn't answer.

"Gavin...is there something you want me to do next?" she asked again.

"Yes," he finally answered. "Go home."

"But...I don't understand..." she stammered. "Why?"

"I want you to go home to your boys, Sylvie. Spend some time with them and with your mom too."

"But I want to help!" she insisted.

"Sylvie, *listen* to me. I *know* you want to help, but I've got to come up with a *plan*...I *have* to do this *right*. I don't want to even go to Judge Burton until I figure out a way to ensure that he listens."

"He will! He just *has* to!" she interjected.

"No," he said tiredly, "he *doesn't*. He's a judge. He could throw me out after listening to me for fifteen seconds."

"I can't believe he would..."

"And if he *does*...what then?"

Sylvie's eyes welled up. To see her so upset strengthened his resolve to protect her as much as possible. She had her whole life ahead of her, and her boys needed her.

"Look," he began again, "if he dismisses my claims and throws me out, we're exposed—all of us. I *know* him. Even if he doesn't believe me, he'll start asking questions, probing around...these judges all have connections. They all know more than they let on."

"But I want to *help*."

Gavin forced a smile he wasn't feeling. "You can help me by going *home*. I'm going to check into a motel room and shower, anyway. I want to go back up to the hospital to see Sister Helena at some point, but we both could use a break right now. In the meantime, I'll take everything we've found so far along with me, so I can brainstorm and figure out the best way to get through to Burton. When I take the opportunity to blow this wide open, I have to do it in a way that won't set off any alarms until the eruptions so big, there won't be any way to cap it off."

She was clearly disappointed, but finally agreed. "Okay...but will you let me know if you hear anything about Sister?"

"Of course. And you can text me if you think of something else, but..."

"I know, I *know*...I won't text anything revealing."

"Okay, good. Now get going...and text me when you get home."

After Sylvie left, Gavin locked the door behind her and set out to do as promised. He gathered up his notes, along with the bullet points and neatly organized websites, charts, and data she had printed out, and shoved them into his briefcase.

He shook his head. It was mind-boggling to realize how much of the information they'd garnered was out on the web for anyone to find. "If you're looking for it, anyway," he grumbled.

After robotically shoving his arms into his coat, he lifted his gun from the table and buried it in his pocket.

Feeling guilty for wanting to take a shower before going back up to the hospital, his mind raced worriedly, as he wondered if he would ever see Sister alive again.

He sincerely wanted to do her proud by hoping and praying for the best, but there were just too many unanswered questions. He never even got to hear how her visit with Maryn had gone.

I wanted her to hold on...but I should have told her goodbye.

He quickly pushed the thought from his mind. It was too painful to think of, so he replaced it with wondering who had secured the bug to her purse and if her car had been tampered with.

The pondering made him realize he'd almost forgotten to bring the transmitter with him. If, for some reason, an emergency arose, and he had to meet with Judge Burton at some ungodly hour, he wanted it as proof.

After retrieving it, he put it back into his wallet and secured it in the inner pocket of his overcoat.

His phone went off, startling him so badly, he jumped. With his heart pounding, he swiped the screen and then sighed with relief to read that Sylvie was home safely.

"Well, that's one less person I have to worry about now," he murmured.

I wonder if there will ever come a time when I won't jump at the sound of my phone buzzing.

As he turned to leave, he stopped and walked back to Sylvie's desk. He picked up the receiver and punched in Annie's number. As he expected, her voicemail answered on the second ring.

He wasn't too proud to grovel.

"Annie, I wasn't drinking earlier today, and I'm not drinking now. I can't explain everything to you over the phone, but I just really think it would be a good time for you to take a trip or go visit your parents. I'm not playing games. If you want to call me back here at the office, I'll wait here for a few more minutes. If not, just text me when you get this, and I'll get back to you. I…"

His message was cut short by a prolonged beep, but he figured that might be a good thing. She would surely think he was drunk if he told her he loved her, especially after so much time had passed. After all the pain, all the betrayal and disappointments.

Thinking about what his past behavior had cost them and their family threatened to pull him under. But if he was going to survive, he just couldn't go there. He decided to give Annie five minutes and then carry on.

It was only a little after 5:00, but his body was screaming midnight. He wanted a shower in the worst way. He wanted a cigarette even more, and a bottle of scotch was a close second to Heaven.

The thought of Heaven gave him pause. In truth, he didn't really doubt what his parents had taught him about Heaven and Hell. Everything Sister Helena had preached to him made sense too. What he couldn't believe in was himself.

His rejection of God was always rooted in anger and fear of his own weaknesses, which made him part of the problem rather than the solution. Most times, he was tempted to let the booze help him escape; sometimes the temptations plagued him every single minute.

The gnawing unrest within him increased with the realization that the five-minute window he'd allotted for Annie's call had expired.

As he closed the office door behind him, he mustered a silent prayer. *God, if you're listening, please help me stay sober. Protect us all and help me figure out a way to bring about justice... Amen.*

Anxious to get on with his plan to shower and get back up to the hospital, Gavin wasted no time covering the distance to the elevators.

The wait felt longer than usual—especially because he still fought with the idea that he could have sworn he heard the office phone ringing after he was halfway down the corridor.

"Yeah right," he grumbled, as he stepped through the open doors. "I'm sure Annie will ring the phone off the wall trying to get ahold of me," he added sarcastically as the doors closed.

*****

Sister Joanna let the phone ring for what seemed an eternity before she finally hung up. Knowing she had no other way to contact Gavin Steele only added to her sorrow and fatigue.

That poor man seemed on the verge of a complete breakdown earlier. I would hate to think of him getting this kind of news when he arrives at the hospital by himself.

Her heart squeezed at the thought. Still, there was nothing more she could do but try back later and head to the chapel to pray.

Chapter 28

Gavin was watching his rearview so intently, that at one point, his neck and shoulder muscles felt like they would snap in two.

He had never heard of the Newbury Suites in Menlo Park, but that suited him just fine. He wanted to disappear. In fact, if he hadn't planned on going back to the hospital, he would have chosen a hotel even farther from his office, his penthouse, and his worries.

Now, as he lay soaking in the jetted-tub of the only room available, he tried to relax. The high-rate he'd paid for the privilege seemed worth every penny, but not even the luxury of the hot water massage could quell the unrest within him. Moreover, considering everything he was going through, his money felt almost as worthless as his wedding vows.

He lay there with his eyes closed, his weary spirit drained. The rest he'd hoped to find wouldn't come. He felt void of hope and confidence and found him wishing, of all things, he could talk to his mother just once more.

He could almost hear his mother's voice as she spoke in a near-whisper to him just before she took her last breath…

"'I am the vine; you are the branches. If you remain in me and I in you, you will bear much fruit; apart from me you can do nothing.' Remember my sweet boy…without God, nothing is of value and nothing will last."

The vivid recollection of the memory caused him to open his eyes.

I'm still alone, Mom. No one knows where I am. Annie, the kids—none of them care. Annie didn't answer me back.

Suddenly feeling like a lost little boy, he squeezed his eyes tightly against the pain. In that moment, he really wished that he could just join his mother. Her love had been powerful. He'd give anything to feel her embrace and to bask in her unconditional love that was always so evident in her clear blue eyes, which mirrored his own.

His father's eyes were brown—dirt-brown as he called them. Any other time Gavin would have smiled at the memory of his Dad's unabashed admiration and love whenever he complimented his beloved Sarah on her "gorgeous baby-blues," but the memory was bittersweet; those times were gone for good. He had ruined his only chance at having that kind of love with Annie. The pain burned so badly within him, that it was as if the water in the tub was boiling. The longing for release became so intense that he forced himself to open his eyes.

Breathe. Just breathe.

He looked around the bathroom that was bigger than the bedroom he grew up in. The marble floor, brass fixtures, luxurious towels—all were meant to give comfort to the wealthy. They were a reminder of how out of touch he'd become. A reminder of everything he'd worked so hard to achieve, but now, would gladly give up for one more chance to get it right.

Why are the wealthy more deserving of comfort than the poor?

"Without God, nothing is of value and nothing will last."

His mother's advice came to him, yet again. This time, he wondered why. Of all the things that she, his father, and Sister Helena had taught him, he was puzzled that this phrase had come to mind, not once, but twice.

Mom was always there to comfort me, so why were those her last words, and why are they haunting me now?

"I *know* nothing lasts!" he cried aloud into the empty room.

My marriage didn't last. My relationship with my kids is weak at best. My sobriety hasn't lasted.

The urge for a drink to combat the loneliness, the helplessness, the fear, was irrepressible.

"The only thing that has lasted for me is my nothingness. I live in it *every, single* day," he whispered woefully.

Squeezing his eyes shut, he lowered himself deeper into the water until it covered his head. The water quickly rushed into his ears, as did the muffled swishing of the water's movement around him, along with the rhythmic sound of his beating heart.

The effect was pleasant, peaceful. He forced himself to relax and pretend that he could hold his breath long enough to simply drift away. He wondered how long it would take to test his body's fortitude. But just as he knew it would, his chest tightened. His adrenal glands shifted into high gear, forcing him to lift his head from the water and gasp for air.

I am the vine, you are the branches. Apart from me you can do nothing.

Gavin sobbed at the reminder. His wish to escape the pain was not of God.

Without God, nothing is of value and nothing will last.

Gavin sat straight up and looked around. He eyes saw nothing amiss. His ears were met with silence, yet the energy in the room was palpable.

Without God, nothing is of value and nothing will last.

His heart hammered in his chest. Faster. Louder.

"That's it." he murmured disbelievingly.

"That's *it!*" he exclaimed again, reaching for a towel and exiting the tub.

He made a futile attempt to dry himself but gave up quickly and thrust his arms into one of the plush robes, hardly noticing its elegance. All his focus was on getting to his phone.

When he reached it, he texted Sylvie:

I know I gave you the night off
but I need you to meet me at the office.
If you can't come, please let me know.

The instant he sent the message, the robe hit the ground. He dressed in a pair of jeans, a charcoal-colored turtleneck sweater, and a pair of boots he'd bought in law school.

As he pulled on the well-worn boots, he wondered if he'd grabbed them in an attempt to bring something familiar with him. Maybe it was because he'd recently cleaned and conditioned them. The bigger truth was, they reminded him of Annie. He'd worn them on their first date—the very date he'd secretly vowed to marry her. They were a part of his wardrobe long after they got married and even through the birth of both kids.

He smiled as he remembered Annie once saying, "I think there's more smell holding those boots together than leather."

At the time, it had made him laugh, but now, the memory punched him in the stomach.

"Annie, you threw me away like a dirty, useless pair of boots," he whispered, "when what I needed was for you to help me shine again."

It was tempting to give in to the self-pity, but something bigger called him to face the reality and hold onto the revelation he'd just been given.

"Who are you trying to fool, Steele? She tried to help you shine too many times. You're the one who insisted on spending your life wading in the mire."

He grabbed his coat and stuffed his gun into the right pocket. As he reached for the door, he affirmed, "I let my family down once, but I'd rather die trying than to fail them again."

*****

When Gavin pulled into the parking garage, he was relieved to see Sylvie's car there. Strangely, he couldn't deny that he felt comforted by her presence. He supposed it was because she was one of the few "normal" facets of his life.

Neither spoke a word as they walked through the near empty space, making their way through the lobby area and into the elevator. It wasn't until the door was locked behind them and Gavin had done his best to scour the rooms for bugging devices, that Sylvie blurted, "What's going *on*? Has something happened to Sister? Did someone try to kill her?"

Gavin shook his head vigorously. "No, no...well, not that I know of, anyway. I called the hospital on the way here to check on her but the dictator who answered the call wouldn't tell me anything about her condition. I really hoped to get up there tonight, but this is more important."

Sylvie looked at him skeptically. "*What* is more important? Why am I here?"

"I've got a plan to draw out whoever's involved in this whole thing...but the only way it will work is if you and I are good at playing pretend."

Sylvie rolled her eyes. "Gavin...*please*...I left my boys with my Mom *again*. She will be the one tucking them in bed instead of me, so would you just cut the mysterious jargon and tell me why I'm here? I'm all out of humor at the moment."

He sighed. "I know...I'm *sorry*, but I need you to make this seem legit."

"What?" she asked again.

"Whoever put the bug on Sister's purse wanted to know what Sister knew—and more than likely, what Maryn knows, or even what I know if they've gotten wind that I'm her new counsel."

"Okay, I'm following. So, what's that got to do with me?"

"By now, whoever planted it may or may not know that Sister has had an accident. If we pretend that it's still attached to Sister's purse, we can manipulate them with our conversation."

"How?" Sylvie asked, pulling a face. "Even if we fool them, how will this make Judge Burton listen? I don't get it...not to mention, I have serious doubts as to whether either of us could act natural when we know that someone dangerous is listening. That's just freakin' *scary*, if you ask me."

He nodded. "I know. All we can do is rehearse the main points and hope we make it convincing."

When she still looked doubtful, Gavin confided, "Sylvie, I realized tonight that those who are trying to keep the vaccine scandal quiet are getting bolder and bolder. They've killed more than twenty people in the past year alone—that we know of, and God only knows how many altogether. If these thugs went to such lengths to find out what Maryn knows, there's a chance they might try and get to her at the correctional facility."

"What do you mean…*kill* her? How could they do *anything* to her under such a close watch?"

He shrugged. "When crooks are determined, they find a way. But at some point, their boldness is going to cause them to slip up. Someone out there is on to them besides us, but whoever it is, is also trying to exterminate and silence anyone or anything that will expose the Lunatia vaccination…and maybe more."

She stared at him for several moments while fear and indecision waged a war with courage and conviction. Finally, she blew out a gust of air and said the words he hoped to hear.

"Okay, so what's the plan?"

Chapter 29

Maryn finished her prayers and slowly crawled into bed. Emotionally and physically spent, she hoped she would be able to fall asleep early and stay asleep until morning. The waiting for sleep to come was the hardest—even worse than waiting and hoping for visitors. It intensified her pain.

Besides prayer, sleep was the only escape she could count on, and at times, even sleep betrayed her. The realization prompted her to say a prayer that the dreams about Thomas would stay away. Waking up and having to acknowledge the reality of her circumstances always intensified the pain. She also prayed she wouldn't have to endure the tormenting nightmare of hearing Lily and Pearl calling her name but was unable to reach them because she was in shackles.

As she lay there trapped with the thoughts of all the obstacles, she could only hope that her trial would come soon, and that she would be exonerated before she was done in by her fellow inmates. The atmosphere in the lunchroom and during chore time had soured considerably the past couple of days. The word was out that she was the "kid-killer who thinks she knows better than doctors about what's good for our kids."

The hostility was universal, coming from women of every age. Ironically, two of the most antagonistic inmates admitted they didn't have children because they'd had abortions. Still, they called her a monster for not giving "innocent kids their shots."

Immediately, the memory of the beating she'd received from the two caused her to reach up and check the bandage on her forehead. Her right eye, which was swollen shut, throbbed almost as painfully as the deep cut beneath the bandage.

The confrontation had taken place in the laundry room. Several inmates blocked the doorway while the pair were quick to do as much damage as possible before the guard pulled them off her.

A single salty tear escaped her swollen eye, trailed down her temple, and pooled in her ear. She ignored it like she tried to ignore the pain of her injuries, including her ribs, which had been kicked repeatedly.

It was painful to remember the accusations and names they called her. The days she'd worked so hard in the clinic, thinking she was doing the right thing, now haunted her. She wished she could forget the terror she felt each time she'd placed herself between the unsuspecting parent and the patient.

"Now everyone look at Mr. Healthy Bear!" she'd exclaimed, urging them to look at the smiling bear picture on the wall so she could give them just a tiny poke before emptying the syringe into the wad of cotton cupped inside her hand.

She'd even gone so far as to sew a plastic pocket on the inside of her scrubs, so she could transfer the cotton there until she disposed of it later.

Often, she felt like a criminal, much the same as she did now.

In the darkness of her cell, the demons told her that her assailants were justified.

Maybe I deserved this beating...this jail cell. Thomas begged me to just do my job and wait the Lunatia out with the girls. Why did I have to try and play the hero?

At times she felt like a two-headed monster of sorts—one minute, filled with conviction and hope, the next, filled with resentment, anger, and fear. Another tear trailed slowly down her neck. *Maybe I did think I was smarter than the doctors...my supervisor...*

Why do you profane what I have made perfect?

Maryn choked back a sob at the memory of God's voice that had come to her in the dream. It had all seemed so real at the time. It made sense, then. Now, the darkness surrounded her like a shroud. Nothing made sense. Despite the encouraging news from Sister Helena, the visit from the girls, and even the prayers she'd just said, God felt distant. Obscure. Unreachable.

Just like Thomas.

In that moment, she felt her husband's anger and rejection. She pictured him lying in bed each night, filled with resentment and fury, or worse, assuaging his anger in the arms of another woman.

Her stomach rolled. It was all too much. So unfair.

Why me, Lord? Why me? Dear God, why did it have to be me? I've tried so hard! I've come so far. Why me?

I'm holding on. I'm clinging to Your promises—the Word of Truth. But though I try with all my heart, doubts remain. Nothing seems right. I'm swimming in self-pity, and I just can't understand why life's become so hard. Why can't I feel Your loving hand?

Rescue me!

"Please God, rescue me!" she whispered woefully.

In an attempt to erase the painful torment, Maryn gingerly repositioned her battered body and pulled the lone blanket up over her head. Never would she have guessed she would desire even more darkness, but she wanted to shut out all thoughts, all memories. Everything. She couldn't bear to think or feel anything. She wanted to be released. To slip into obscurity where there would be no more pain or sorrow.

But behind her closed eyes, a vision of Jesus' crucified body came to her. His eyes, also bruised and swollen, beckoned her from the cross. The drops of blood that rolled down his face from the crown of thorns were mixed with his tears. His breathing was raspy, agonizing, as he fought to bring air into lungs which couldn't properly function in the position he was hanging. His entire body was covered in lacerations too numerous to count. In his agony, he cried out, "My God...my God, why have you abandoned me?"

Maryn's eyes flew open.

Why him? Why him? Oh, Dear God, why did we crucify him? He tried so hard. He was all good.

It was for me…
He died for me!

"Why me?" Maryn whispered into the dark cell.

In that moment, she connected with the truth that had long been buried.

"If any want to become my followers, let them deny themselves and take up their cross daily and follow me. For those who want to save their life will lose it, and those who lose their life for my sake will find it."

The realization that she had also chosen to carry a cross to save others became her strength. The Father had not forsaken Jesus. He had not forsaken her.

"Oh Jesus," she choked, "I will carry this cross you've given me, but I am not strong enough to carry it without you. Be with me. Help me to endure it, so that my suffering will be turned into good…no matter what comes. Have mercy on my girls, Lord. They are so innocent."

Like the innocents you were trying to save.

"Yes!" she cried with tearful exuberance, as the clarity of the admission fully impacted her.

Just seconds later, she startled at the pounding on her cell door, before an overly-bright light filled her room.

She wouldn't have needed the lights on to see that it was Mack's face watching her through the observation window. His intense, watchful stare was ever-present when he was on duty.

Without meeting his gaze, Maryn carefully curled her body toward the wall, pulled up her blanket, and squeezed her eyes shut until the red light behind her eyes faded to black.

The confirmation she'd been given was solace enough to rock her battered body and weary soul to sleep.

Chapter 30

"Thanks for bringing me some food. It smells delicious."

"Sure...no problem," Sylvie replied. "I was out anyway, and I knew you'd still be working and probably hadn't eaten yet."

She stared intensely at the paper before her and added, "By the way, all the movies at the theater *suck* right now."

"Oh yeah? What'd you see?" Gavin asked.

"The latest Bond sequel. Only—get this—Bond's a *woman* in this one."

"What? A *woman*?"

"No. Well, technically, yes...but...well...in this one, Bond's a guy who became a transgender woman. I couldn't really get into it. Bond kept having flashbacks of when he...*she* was a guy, and I just kept getting confused as to who was seducing who. It just didn't work for me."

Gavin offered a genuine chuckle. "Sounds...uh...*interesting*."

"No. It really *wasn't*," she answered truthfully, recalling how lame the entire concept was. "And speaking of men becoming women...I see you have a purse there. Is there something you've been meaning to tell me?"

"Hardly," he answered quickly with a laugh, hoping his voice didn't sound as shaky as his insides were. "It's Sister Helena's."

Sylvie was playing her part like a pro. "What are you doing with her purse?" she asked.

"Sister Joanna brought it from the hospital but forgot to take it with her when I dropped her off. I brought it up, so I could look through it to see if she took any notes when she met with Maryn last. I've uncovered some new information that could blow this case wide open. If I can confirm it, Judge Burton will be forced to turn over what he knows to the feds. Once they open an investigation, Maryn's bail will have to be reconsidered.

"Holy crap!" Sylvie exclaimed, "That sounds intriguing, but also scarier than hell, so I really would rather not know anything about it."

Gavin almost wanted to laugh and cringe at the same time. He knew that she was both acting and partly speaking truth. He had to play on.

"Why would you say that? What's got you so scared of this case?" he asked.

"Well, I'm just a little worried about the repercussions of Maryn's actions, and I'm not the only one. The school board called a meeting for all parents to discuss the development of a protocol to be followed for testing our children for immunity—you know, so they can be sure whether or not they had been given all their shots."

"That's understandable, but surely that would only apply to those who went to the clinic where Maryn worked."

"Normally, yes, but I guess the parents are all concerned that if it happened at one clinic, it's possible that it's going on at others."

"I guess that makes sense too," he replied. "Everyone worries about the health of their kids...but that hardly seems enough to scare you."

"You're right. It's what the parents were talking about afterward that creeps me out."

"And that would be?"

"Several of them mentioned they heard that there's been a bunch of natural doctors who have died suddenly...like twenty or so just in the past year. I had never heard such a thing, but it kind of spooked me. But...get this...I looked it up, and it's *true*."

Just as they had rehearsed, Gavin paused and then answered, "Well Sylvie, that just confirms my decision to keep you in the dark regarding the details. I've set up a meeting with Judge Burton for tomorrow morning. I'll present the new evidence to him. It's pretty airtight, so I'm just going to go for it."

"Wow! Where'd you get it? What *kind* of evidence?" She fired off the question, convincingly.

"You just *said*, you didn't want to know," he countered with a chuckle, "and I'm *not* going to tell you. Except the informant who contacted me, I'm the only one who knows what's really going on, and I want to keep it that way. I'm not sure when I'll get out of here tonight—I'm going to tighten up my notes. In fact, I may just leave from here if I have to."

"Wowww!" Sylvie exclaimed again, in perfect imitation of an airhead. "Aren't you creeped out to know all this stuff? Aren't you a little scared to stay here by yourself?"

"Well, I'd be a liar if I didn't admit that it's a little daunting, but overall, I feel pretty safe," he replied, forcing himself to say it with conviction. "The meeting with Judge Burton isn't until nine. By then, there'll be plenty of people milling about, and besides, there are security cameras everywhere in this building and in the parking lot. They keep them well hidden, but you can't even fart without the smoke being seen and the sound being picked up by one of them."

Sylvie chuckled. The part about the fart was improvised. Gavin grinned and then nodded for her to continue.

"Okay...just be careful," she said, meaning it.

"Don't worry, I will. The more I think about it, I'll probably just stay here and work through the night."

"Okay, but before I head out, I'll take a look in Sister's purse for you," she offered.

Sylvie then went through the motions of stirring the contents of the purse around and then said, "Only paper in here is this...nothing but an address on it."

"What's the address?" he asked.

"6402 Wildorn Drive."

"Hmmm...doesn't ring a bell. Knowing Sister, it's probably some homeless shelter," he said with a chuckle.

"I don't think so. It has a doctor's name on the back...Dr. Benjamin."

"No last name?" Gavin asked, deliberately trying to sound a little nervous.

"Nope...unless Benjamin is the doc's last name."

"Could be. Can I see it?"

"Sure."

Gavin paused before saying, "Probably just the name of one of her doctors. Nothing to worry about, I guess. Enjoy the rest of your night."

"Yeah, you too...do you want me to drop the purse off at the convent on my way home?" Sylvie asked.

"Nah. I'll just lock it in my safe and take it to the convent the next time I'm headed that direction."

"Okay...goodnight."

"Goodnight. I'll be in touch after I meet with Burton. Send me a text when you get home, would you?" he asked with concern.

"Sure. You sound like the dad I never had," she answered.

Neither Gavin's request nor Sylvie's answer were part of the script, but Sylvie's eyes were glossy with tears when she gave Gavin a silent hug and mouthed the words, "Be careful," before she walked out the door.

*****

After hearing the slamming of what was probably the safe in Gavin Steele's office, silence ensued.

Rivera stopped the recording, stretched his neck, and declared, "And that's a wrap."

The night had been painfully quiet up until a series of loud bumping and scratching sounds registered in his headset. He'd been playing Candy Smash on his phone for almost two hours, so the transmission he picked up was more than welcome, it was exciting.

The signal had been weak at times, but before he even looked up at the control panel to pinpoint the location, he knew that the device from the nun's purse was finally about to produce some action.

He'd been right. Now, with something tangible in hand, he sent a text:

Device status: Intact
Information: Pertinent
Action: Immediate

*****

The second the purse was locked safely away, Gavin exhaled a tremendous sigh of relief.

The dialogue between him and Sylvie couldn't have gone better. He certainly hoped they had accomplished all he'd hoped for—to buy him some time, and with the assurance that he was the only one with the pertinent information, to back the wolves off Sylvie, Sister Helena, and his family. Lastly, he hoped to provide Judge Burton with a powerful piece of evidence to prove that an unknown entity had a huge stake in the game.

With that in mind, he packed up his notes and photocopies of graphs, schedules, and video screenshots, placing each folder in his briefcase alongside the envelope containing the faxed messages and the picture of the Eduardo and Townes meeting.

He spent some time typing a summary of the information he'd gathered and the reason for the compilation of evidence. After printing multiple copies, he penned a note he was sure would be analyzed for authenticity, copied it, and included it with duplicate copies of everything into five different envelopes and addressed each one. The lot of these went into a larger, prepaid envelope that he sealed, addressed, and added to his open briefcase.

"If my body ends up atop the mounting heap of victims, at least I have the hope of getting this much information exposed," he declared aloud.

The slight trembling of his hands as he closed each latch didn't go unnoticed by him. The outward display of nerves made him want a drink in the worst way. Ironically, drowning his troubles until he passed out was both appealing and terrifying at the same time.

But since part of the plan was to buy some time by sending the enemy on a wild goose-chase looking for a fictitious address and doctor, there wasn't time for self-medicating. There wasn't time for anything except action.

Gavin glanced at his phone several times, willing it to buzz with an incoming text from Sylvie. Just thinking about the possibility of her not getting home safely made him break into a cold sweat that increased with the rising doubts his plan would work.

I'm the one with the information to turn over to Judge Burton. Surely, whoever was listening wouldn't take the chance of hurting Sylvie when I'm the bigger fish to fry.

The thought calmed him a bit, but not enough to stop the trembling deep within. He found himself questioning his every move, every thought.

His reflections shifted to Sister Helena. He wondered how she was doing—whether she'd improved at all, or whether she'd taken a turn for the worse. Suddenly, he realized he hadn't checked the caller ID since he'd gotten there. He crossed over to the dinosaur and punched the arrow that displayed the names and numbers.

"C'mon...c'mon..."

He listened to his messages—a hang up and yet another drug dealer needing a lawyer. "Not available," he barked, just as his phone buzzed. It was a text from Sylvie:

Home now. Turn on the news!
It's coming up—Clare's surgeon.
Call my mom's phone when you can talk.
Praying.

Clare? Who is...

"Chelsey's daughter," he murmured, his heart immediately increasing its tempo when the answer dawned on him.

More unsettling was the fact that he had never heard Sylvie mention prayer. If she was praying, it meant one of two things—someone other than Sylvie sent the text, or that she was trying to convey to him that something very serious was happening.

Just seconds after swiping his finger across his phone screen, he was connected to a local news outlet and watching the coverage of a crime scene:

"Dr. Andrew Long, a respected Pediatric surgeon, along with his wife, Susan, were found slain in their home. Police estimate the murders took place sometime between yesterday evening and six p.m. this evening.

"The Long's son, who'd been unable to reach either parent all day, discovered the fatal crime when he came to check on them. Both victims were shot in the back of the head. A motive of robbery is a possibility. The slain couple leave behind three children and four grandchildren. Stay tuned to KRCA-channel 7 for updates."

The smiling faces of Andrew and Susan Long flashed on the screen, causing Gavin's stomach to churn and his mind to race as he listened.

He quickly crossed to Sylvie's desk and dialed her mother's landline phone. Sylvie picked it up on the first ring. "They're dead, Gavin. Two more victims."

"Wait...wait...I know it looks like it's all connected..."

"It *is* connected!" she exclaimed. "How could this possibly be a coincidence?"

"Well, I admit it's curious, but Dr. Long wasn't a natural medicine doctor, he was a surgeon, so maybe just this once..."

Sylvie cut him off. "He was the *surgeon* who operated on the *lump* on Clare's head—the same mysterious symptom that Maryn found on her patients!"

"Well...yeah...I'm just trying to think this through before I jump to conclusions. It's my job to look at all angles. I don't want to do a computer search on the doc's name on my phone or from the office, but could you get to the library early tomorrow and see what you can find?"

"Sure, but I'm pretty sure there will be a lot of searches popping up because of the murder, so I think it would be okay for me to search from here. I'll let you know what I find. You've got enough going on."

"Good point about the searches. Okay, but be extra cautious if you go out, Sylvie and don't talk about this to *anyone*. And make sure you lock the doors!"

"Don't worry...I'm scared shitless. I can't stop shaking."

Her admission tore him up. Once again, he felt responsible for her fear. "I'm sorry, Sylvie. I hate that you've been pulled into this..."

"You're not responsible, Gavin," she interrupted, "someone evil is. I meant it when I said I'm praying. Sister Helena would be praying, and at this point, I'd say we better do everything we can. Be careful, okay? I'm scared for *you*."

That makes two of us, he wanted to say.

"I'll be okay. Just take care of your family and lay low."

After he hung up the receiver, Gavin's head fell to his chest. His throat was so tight he wondered if he could even utter a word.

"God," he choked, falling to his knees, "I'm so out of my league I can hear the devil laughing all the way from hell. This plan I've come up with is about as solid as my sobriety."

At the truth of his words, he paused and sadly shook his head. "I've got zero reasons to believe I can pull this off...so right now, I am all-out *begging* you to protect Sylvie and her boys and mother. I'm *begging* you to protect Annie, Lucas, and Brenna."

His voice cracked. He swallowed hard to continue. "Whoever's at the center of this coverup seems to be killing everyone who gets in the way. Please protect Isabella Sanchez and her family...wherever they may be...and especially *Maryn*. That woman's been through enough."

Thinking of her made him realize how thankful he was that she was safe behind iron bars.

If this is as big as I think it is, Maryn may just be better off staying put until the trial.

Completely overwhelmed by the entire predicament, but filled with the urgency to act, he finally stood. His feet felt leaden as he picked up his briefcase and walked to the door.

Before he opened it, Gavin uttered one last prayer, "And God, please keep Sister Helena safe and heal her. Don't take her from me...please. Don't let the bastards win."

Chapter 31

Not a single soul could be found in the entryway of the office building when Gavin shoved the thick envelope into the mail receptacle.

He was greatly relieved to make it to his car without incident—even more grateful that he wasn't blown to smithereens when he started the engine.

His good fortune continued when no one seemed to be following him as he drove down odd streets, weaving his way across town to the rental agency. Neither was he followed on the twenty-minute drive to the courthouse to survey the area where he hoped to expose the actions and those involved.

Ironically, though the Almeda County courthouse served as the hub of justice, he would have never considered venturing into most areas of the county after dark. It was well-known that the gang violence was so out of control that the police wouldn't even patrol certain areas after sundown. Even a 911 call was ignored until morning.

The number of drones covering the area had also been cut way back because the thugs, who weren't supposed to have guns because of the ban, were shooting them down. In the end, it was determined that the cost to replace the drones greatly outweighed the benefit. A self-imposed curfew seemed to be the only way for the residents to increase their chances for safety after dark.

Gavin never would have guessed he'd be comforted to know he was basically on his own, with no police protection; but presently, the lack of protection worked in his favor. The last thing he needed was to be stopped and searched or to have a drone spying on his every move.

Still, parked on a residential street, just blocks from the courthouse, his feelings of relief turned anxious. It was puzzling how smoothly everything had gone. Considering the fact that so much hinged on his thrown-together plan, things seemed a little too quiet for his liking.

I've got to remember that there's a good chance no one even picked up our conversation. The transmitter had been inactive since it was removed from Sister Helena's room, so whoever planted it could have assumed it had been discovered or disengaged. There's also the possibility that whoever was listening could tell we were bullshitting the whole conversation.

The unknowns gnawed at his stomach, which had been empty for longer than he wanted to think about.

Ignoring the hunger pains, he focused on all that had gone right, including the fact that he'd found the perfect spot across from the courthouse parking lot to conduct his surveillance. A new office building under construction made him sure he would blend right in with the heavy equipment and trucks there.

He also felt good about his choice to rent a charcoal-gray minivan. Every soccer mom in the state drove something similar. Moreover, it was nothing a California lawyer would ever be caught dead in.

If his spot behind the construction equipment fell through, he planned to park in one of the corners of the courthouse's parking lot. By the time nine o'clock rolled around, it would be full, and he'd blend right in with all the rest.

His plan was to take pictures of every incoming vehicle and license plates, with the ultimate goal of spotting the black Lexus and getting pictures of the plate and passengers.

I guess it's also conceivable that the big, bad, Lex-asses will come early and position themselves in the parking lot like I plan to.

"That would be interesting," he whispered.

The thought was more than a little unsettling—even more so, as he pondered the possibility of would-be assassins being strategically placed inside the courthouse.

His heart hammered a little faster as he pictured himself walking down the hall to Judge Burton's chambers only to take a bullet in the back of the head.

No...they'd have to be more creative than that. They'd probably bump into me and inject me with poison or some other less conspicuous method. And I'm sure the report would say my heart gave out on me...or my liver was shot because of my alcoholism.

"Hell, they've jacked with at least one autopsy, what's one more?" he grumbled, sickened by the reality.

Gavin's stomach twisted tighter still at the thought of what his kids and Annie would think. In some ways, the thought of their disappointment was worse than the thought of dying. He quickly pushed both possibilities from his mind. It was imperative that he stay focused, driven.

Either way, I'm going to Burton with my findings. I have nowhere else to go. I've been warned against going to the police, so I guess I'll cross whatever bridge I need to after I talk to the judge. Maybe he'll know what to do.

His phone buzzed, startling him so much that he bumped his head on the roof of the van.

It was a text from Sylvie:

Connection: The wife was a fruit and nut.

He stared at the simple phrase for several seconds before the meaning became clear.

She's telling me that Dr. Long's wife, Susan, was a health enthusiast. Sylvie must've found enough on the net to make her believe that the doc and his wife were killed because of what they knew.

Despite the fact that the van was still warm, sweat beaded up on his forehead. As the victims' faces flashed before his eyes, fear settled into his bones.

Their son found them murdered in the home he'd grown up in. What kind of monsters commit such heinous acts?

The thought sent chills down his spine.

Who are they? What are they trying to cover up?

His insides began to tremble as he imagined Lucas or Brenna coming home to find Annie in a pool of her own blood.

The vision caused his hand to immediately reach into his coat pocket and grab hold of his gun, but the heavy metal form did little to comfort him.

Who am I trying to kid? I'm dealing with pros here. What the hell do I think I can really do about all this?

"Trying to play cop like my old man?"

The question spoken aloud seemed to echo through the van's interior. The ensuing silence was deafening as the unanswered question mocked him. He let out a derisive laugh that quickly changed into emotion that clouded his eyes.

The voice of destruction reminded him that he would never even come close to being as good a man as Joseph Steele.

Gavin wholeheartedly agreed.

A familiar yearning beckoned him. He started the car's engine and pulled away from the curb.

The liquor store wasn't far. In less than half an hour, Gavin was parked on a different block in the same neighborhood.

As he tipped the bottle of scotch and took his first drink, the warmth that spread through his body felt like an embrace from an old friend. He took another. The trembling he'd felt earlier seemed to lessen.

As the time passed, he wondered if he had let his imagination get the best of him.

Maybe I should have gone back to the hotel for the night. If the bad guys didn't follow me from the office, there's a good chance they aren't aware of where I was staying.

After several more swigs, Gavin was feeling completely relaxed, more confident.

No one followed me. Whoever put the bug on Sister's purse probably wasn't even listening. Then again, maybe they were. I suppose it's remotely possible that my plan worked to keep them busy long enough to help me get away from the office unnoticed.

The thought made him laugh out loud. "Yeah *right!* And I'll bet they're *scared* of you too, *Big Guy!*"

He lifted the bottle and took another drink. "I'll worry about getting shit-faced later," he mumbled with a chuckle. "Right now, this is called *survival.*"

He started the engine again and ran the heater until he was warm. After he shut it off, he glanced at his watch. *Three o'clock.*

"In a few more hours I'll be watching for the big badass wolves," he declared, chuckling at his cleverness.

Still, something about the time sobered him. Before long, his heart squeezed at the memory of a lecture Sister Helena had once given him. In the weeks and months after he'd hit rock bottom, she visited him on a regular basis, always full of advice he wasn't sure he wanted, but was scared to death to ignore:

"When you're having trouble sleeping, pray. If you wake up in the night and can't get back to sleep, pray—especially if you wake up at three o'clock. That's the Divine Hour of Mercy—chances are, somebody needs your prayers."

"It's three o'clock, Sister," he mumbled, "and *somebody* needs your prayers...*me!*" he shouted, slapping his chest.

Shame filled his being as he pictured her lying helpless in a hospital bed. She would be so disappointed to know he was drinking again.

"For all I know, she's *dead,*" he whined defiantly, sounding like a spoiled brat.

Still, his eyes filled with tears as the devastating possibility penetrated his false bravado. He'd failed her. He was failing them all.

The bitterness in his heart now matched the bitter cold that had penetrated the vehicle.

"God, where are you? Why can't I ever get anything right?" Gavin cried out in anguish.

He reached into his pocket and removed the gun from its holster. With tear-filled eyes, he stared down the barrel. His finger hovered over the trigger.

The world needs each one of us to do our part, Son.

His father's familiar instruction only added to his shame.

"Oh Dad, I am so worthless!" he cried. "I'm not like you. I'm wasted when they all need me. So many innocent people are counting on me, and I am failing!"

Oh God, please help me!

He tossed the gun on the seat, opened the car door, and vomited onto the pavement. Afterward, his head dropped to his chest and he sobbed so hard that he didn't know whether it was tears or his nose running down his chin.

He reached for the gun again. This time, he clicked the safety on and shoved it back into his pocket. His hand brushed against something. He knew what it was even before it lay in his open hand. It felt as light as a feather and as heavy as an anvil at the same time.

Gavin started the van and unrolled the window. The frigid air rushed at his face, and instantly, he felt more alert. After emptying the remainder of the scotch into the street, he closed the window and ran the back of his sleeve over his face.

His used his phone to illuminate the card in his shaking hand. The image of the angel warrior, St. Michael, stared up at him. With sword in hand, his foot crushing the head of the devil, the angel's visage stirred something deep within his soul.

Somehow, in that moment, he knew God was telling him that it was his time to fight like a warrior. His time to do everything he could to crush the devil or die trying—just like Sergeant Joseph Steele fought up until the moment he was killed. Just like Sister Helena had fought for him and for so many, every single day.

"Saint Michael, the Archangel," he began, first quietly, and then steadily stronger. "Defend us in battle. Be our defense against the wickedness and snares of the devil. May God rebuke him, I humbly pray, and do thou, oh Prince of the Heavenly host, by the power of God, cast into hell, Satan, and all the evil spirits who prowl about the world seeking the ruin of souls…Amen."

*****

Maryn sensed his presence at the side of her bed. Despite how sleepy she felt, she smiled into the darkness at the thought of Thomas there beside her. She could feel his weight as it pressed the bed down next to her. She reached out her arms and waited for his embrace.

Her heart leapt at the sound of his voice as he called her name. Thomas had come at last.

I'm going to give you something for the pain," he whispered.

She felt the sharp sting of a needle prick on her thigh. Maryn's eye flew open, quickly shattering her dream. She would have screamed, but it was too late.

Mack's large face loomed overhead, but it began to spin and fade away immediately.

God help me!

"Help...my...babies!"

Chapter 32

Weight as heavy as snow from an avalanche pressed down on Gavin's body, encompassing him from all sides. Despite being rendered powerless, in a strange way, he felt protected, safe. There was nowhere to go. No one could get to him or expect anything from him. For a change, it would be nice to just sleep until the sun came out again, but the ringing of his phone kept him from the escape he longed for. His hands were so cold, he couldn't move them to find it, much less answer it. He wondered if they would ever move again.

The persistent sound of his phone roused Gavin from his drunken slumber. His hands felt like blocks of ice. At some point, he'd shut off the van's engine, and the cold had settled into his bones. Stiff all over and still a little soused, confusion clouded his sense of reality.

Clumsily, he reached for the phone just as it stopped ringing. The missed number was unknown to him.

He groaned loudly and glanced at the time.

Who would be calling me at six-thirty in the morning?

He shrugged and lifted his foot, which felt more like a block of cement, and placed it on the brake. After pushing the start button with a pale, trembling finger, the engine turned over. He gasped as a blast of cold air blew directly into his face, before he managed to turn the fan off. As he shivered, his teeth clapped together so violently that he wondered if he would chip a few. His misery was enhanced by a strong urge to vomit.

After dry-heaving onto the curb for several minutes, Gavin closed the door and laid his head against the seat until the nausea passed.

In time, much like the warmth that gradually spread into the leather seat beneath him, his senses slowly awakened. With the increased alertness, he became grateful that the sun wasn't fully up in the eastern sky, so he could make his move early enough to position himself in just the right spot amidst the construction. Remaining obscure was crucial to watching the activity and identifying the vile persons that could show up with the intent to kill him.

Thinking of the very real dangerous possibilities caused him to sober quicker than usual. Moreover, knowing he had nearly slept through his own plan was more than humbling, it was disheartening.

He looked up and caught his image in the rearview mirror. His disheveled appearance and expression said everything his conscience was feeling. *You're a loser.*

Still, there wasn't time for self-pity or second guessing himself. There was no doubt that the day would change the rest of his life. Whether for the good or bad, there was no turning back now. If he didn't press forward, someone else would die—of this, he was certain.

After running an unsteady hand back through his hair, he turned the fan up to high. In no time, his body began to thaw. Adrenaline pulsed through his veins.

Clicking his seatbelt into place, he put the van in gear and slowly pulled away from the curb.

*****

As expected, the courthouse parking lot sprung to life just before 8:00 a.m. A refuse truck that disappeared around the back was the first of many vehicles that slowly made their way into the vast parking space.

Parked on the corner adjacent to the construction, Gavin slouched way down in one of the third-row seats and used his phone's high-tech zoom lens to snap pictures of the plates on every vehicle that arrived. Often, he was able to get pictures of the drivers as well. As the minutes passed by, however, he had a hunch that all he'd taken so far was a bunch of useless pictures of inconsequential bystanders. The nefarious Lexus had yet to appear.

They all look too normal—even the refuse workers.

At that point, he didn't know what was worse—coming face to face with murdering thugs or coming up empty-handed.

By 8:30, he was so completely on edge that his jaw ached from clenching it. To further distress him, his stomach burned like he'd swallowed lighter fluid. Unfortunately, all he had to put out the fire was bottled water, a pack of sunflower seeds, and a half-empty bottle of antacids.

He chased a handful of antacids down with a swig or two of water but didn't dare take the chance of being distracted with the seeds. His window of opportunity would pass by quickly and he couldn't afford to miss it.

He glanced at the time on his phone and then snapped a picture of an attractive woman exiting a black Mercedes. He realized he knew her, but for the life of him, he couldn't remember her name. She used to work in the same office building and had faced him at trial a time or two.

"Well, that was a waste of time," he grumbled. "She's no more an assassin than I am."

Sure wish I knew what the hell was really going on and who it is I am supposed to be looking for. It also would be nice to know who it is who seems to know everything that's going on yet chooses to stay hidden in the shadows.

The irony struck a nerve. "Where's my mysterious informant when I need him?" he spat, before he snapped a shot of the plates on a white Camry. Just seconds later, a plump, middle-aged woman and what looked to be her belligerent teen, exited.

"Oh man...wrong number," he whispered wryly.

As he changed positions to alleviate his near-numb elbow, his comment struck a chord.

Wrong number.

I never checked to see if the missed caller left a voicemail this morning.

He reached for his phone and ran his thumb over the screen. Sure enough, the voicemail light was flashing.

The sight caused his stomach to drop.

Sister Helena.

He wanted to listen to the message but wanted to ignore it more. It scared the hell out of him to think about what he would do if he found out she'd passed away. He couldn't handle it at that point.

I need to stay focused.

The minutes ticked by as he continued taking pictures, still sensing that something had gone awry.

I'm missing something.

Gavin still didn't want to listen to the voicemail, but his gut seemed to be screaming at him to buck up and do it anyway.

I'm running out of time. I was supposedly meeting with Judge Burton in just fifteen minutes. There's no one suspicious here. My plan is a bust.

He groaned. "I've been sweating all this out for nothing."

After sitting in silence for several more minutes, he finally climbed over the middle row of seats and settled himself behind the steering wheel.

I've got no other choice but to carry through with my plans. I guess I'll go in and see if I can either catch him before court or set up an appointment with his assistant.

He reached forward to push the starter, just as a flash of black and the pounding of a fist on the driver's side window jolted his senses. The shock made him feel like his heart would stop beating any second.

The glint of a badge penetrated the blinding heat of his terror. He didn't know whether to be relieved or terrified that it was the police.

Gavin quickly used his knee to scoot his gun off the seat, kick it underneath, start the engine in one fluid motion. Silently, he begged God to keep the gun hidden.

The window came down to reveal a uniformed police officer with a cold expression and a hard, piercing gaze. Unlike his recent encounter with law enforcement, this cop was no rookie.

"Is there a problem officer?" Gavin asked, trying to make his voice sound like anything other than what he was feeling.

"You're parked in a construction zone," he stated flatly, leaning down into the window to look around the van. "I'll need to scan your license ID and registration."

No smile. No appearance of friendly public servant here. Play it cool.

"Oh…I didn't realize that. I'll move—no problem."

"What are you doing here?" he demanded, ignoring Gavin's offer completely.

"Just making some phone calls," Gavin answered. His voice sounded strained, even to him. He handed his license to the officer and said, "This van's a rental. Here's the paperwork."

Officer Phillips took the paperwork and license and gave it a brief glance over. "Really? You must have a lot of calls to make. According to my source, you've been parked here for quite a while…why?"

Gavin paused and shifted his weight in the seat. The sheepish look he gave the officer was real. He felt like an idiot for staying put in one place for so long. "Well, if you really want to know…" he began, trying to buy himself time to come up with a good excuse.

"Yeah…I do," Phillips said with great sarcasm.

"I rented this van because I was worried my girlfriend was cheating on me. As it turns out, I feel pretty stupid now…she showed up here alone a few minutes ago. And like I said, I was just making a few calls before I get on the road."

"What's your girlfriend's name?"

Gavin swallowed nervously. *Here's where I get cuffed…*

"Lynnette Blakewood," he swiftly answered, surprising even himself. Her name rolled off his tongue like he'd been saying it every day of his life. "She drives the black Mercedes parked in the second to the last row across the street," he added, to cement his story.

Officer Phillip's expression clearly indicated he was not fully convinced. "Stay in the car. I'm going to scan your license and run her tags."

The second he walked away, Gavin let out a shuddering sigh of relief. *How in the world did I come up with that name, when just minutes ago, I couldn't remember it if my life depended on it?*

"I guess my life depended on it," he whispered.

The clock on the dash showed the time to be 8:56.

Immediately, he wondered if he'd missed the car he'd been waiting on all morning. Still, his concern would be a moot point if the officer made him get out of the car to search it. If he found the gun it would all be over.

God, I just can't get arrested right now!

He no more had formed the thought when Officer Phillips was back at his window. *He's back too soon. This is it...*

Reluctantly, Gavin hit the button that lowered the window, bringing him eye to eye with Phillips. The officer gave him a hard look that was undiscernible.

"I'm going to let you go *this* time," he finally said. "I suggest you pay more attention to zoning laws the next time you decide to play detective...and I better not find you here again today."

Before Gavin could grasp what was happening, his license was back in his hand, and Phillips was walking back to his squad car. Another traffic stop that had gone smoothly for him. That was simply unheard of—and he'd been stopped plenty of times. Fortunately, the only serious charge he'd ever received was a DUI, but it was wiped from his record because he'd paid a good chunk of money for a diversion.

Still, he didn't waste another moment wondering the reason for his good fortune. He fastened his seatbelt, signaled properly, and pulled away from the curb.

Chapter 33

Gavin's concentration was intense as he drove away from the courthouse—like he was on a mission. In reality, he had absolutely no idea where he was going or what he would do next. His focus was ever-changing from minute to minute, as he made every attempt to keep his emotions in check. Robotically, he merged into the morning traffic on the freeway, quickly blending in with thousands of others who also had a supposed purpose in life, yet he was slowly dying within.

As the gravity of the situation began to sink in, so did the tremors. He marveled at how he'd managed to stay so calm while talking to the officer, but now, his entire being quivered with anxiety as he pondered what could have occurred, not to mention the danger still looming.

His plan had failed. Miserably. The only bright side he could see was that he was still a free man. He couldn't have done anyone any good if he'd been forced to hire his own lawyer from a jail cell.

The thought rattled him even more. Though he was now miles from the courthouse, his hands shook so badly, he had to use them both to steady the steering wheel. His stomach was on fire. The single bottle of water he drank that morning hadn't been enough to alleviate his cotton-mouth or his hunger. Despite the plethora of eateries that tempted him to stop and refuel, the urge to drive as fast and far as he could, was greater.

What he needed was food and water, but what he desperately wanted was a smoke—valium—something—*anything* to help him calm down. Pathetically, if he wasn't still so sick from the night before, the liquor store would have most likely been the only prospect alluring enough to stop for.

He hated the way he was feeling. Hated the truth of his addictive nature.

It's a damn good thing smoking weed wasn't legal when I was young. I'd probably be under a bridge somewhere, laying in my trusty old box, singing Kumbaya. Either that or I'd be dead.

He let out a woeful grunt. "Neither prospect sounds that terrible right now," he admitted, reluctantly taking the off-ramp.

He had no choice but to stop. His bladder was screaming for relief, and he wondered if part of his shaking might be caused by low blood sugar.

At least if they kill me, I'll die with a full stomach and won't be soaked in urine.

He chose the nearest McDonald's, not because of the food, but because he figured the average patron would look different from those who might want to exterminate him.

A modicum of relief washed over him to see that the crowd of patrons was light. There was only just a kid in the restroom and the stalls were empty, so he chose the one closest to the door and set the latch behind him.

As soon as his butt hit the seat, he blew out a gusty breath to calm his wildly beating heart. Still, his hands trembled slightly as he texted Sylvie.

No show.
I'll be in touch ASAP.
Stay home until further notice.
Any word on our patient?

After Gavin sent the text, the reminder that he had a voicemail nagged him. He tapped the screen and stared at the phone number once more. He searched the number. It was unlisted.

Every cell in his body was tired. He was sick of the dead ends, the chase, the unknown. In the worst way imaginable, he wanted to forget all about going to the judge with what he knew. Mostly, because he didn't know if he could take the stress, live with the consequences, survive the day.

By the time he walked out the door with his breakfast sandwich and coffee, Sylvie texted back:

Nothing new.
Don't worry, we're hunkered down at home.
Praying. Keep in touch.

Reading her words stirred a deep emotion within him. Sylvie was a lot of things, but phony wasn't one of them. She would never say she was praying if she wasn't—even to comfort him.

She's scared.

The truth was painful, especially because she was counting on him. Especially because he just might be more scared than she was.

He scanned the parking lot for anyone suspicious-looking before he crossed to the van, got inside, and locked the doors.

Normally, he would have woofed down his food and headed back to work, but the recent murders of the surgeon and his wife had taken away both his appetite and his conviction to go to the judge.

"The bad boys are playing for keeps," he murmured, forcing himself to take a bite to quell his burning gut.

I've got to make sure I'm doing everything I can to stay in the game and win.

He chased down his mouthful with a swig of coffee hot enough to scald his tongue, but he hardly noticed. Preoccupied by the what-if's, he also wondered how Sister Helena was doing. He wanted to talk to her in the worst way.

She always seems to know what to do and how to calm me down, so I can think straight.

Gavin wadded the paper wrapping and stuffed it into the sack. He grabbed his phone to search for the hospital's phone number, when it occurred to him that maybe the phone message was from Sister Joanna.

That would make sense! Who but the nuns are up that early?

Sure that he was on to something, the battle against fear raged on.

She could have bad news to tell me, but I have to face it sooner or later. Good or bad, I need to know.

Eventually, he braced himself and pressed the circle to play the recording.

"Steele!"

The sound of Judge Burton's voice caused both relief and unease at the same time. Never had Burton called him on his cell. Gavin was surprised he even had his number. His calls were always to the office.

"I need to see you in my chambers at 9:00 a.m. *sharp*. I received some information from an anonymous source regarding Maryn Pearce's case that we need to discuss, *privately*. And if I find out you've breathed a word about this to anyone, I'll make it my life's mission to make sure she gets the death penalty and you along with her."

Gavin's heart did a somersault and landed with a thud in his chest. *What in the hell is going on?*

He glanced at the time. It was 9:35.

He swallowed hard and checked his phone log for missed calls. There weren't any.

I'm going to get the ass-chewing of a lifetime. I'm surprised he hasn't called my number a dozen times like he does when he can't reach me at the office.

After listening to the message again, he dutifully put on his seatbelt and headed back to the courthouse.

The irony of the timing and the turn of events was mind-boggling. *I fabricated the time and meeting with Judge Burton, what a coincidence that a meeting was actually supposed to take place. What could Burton have been given that would warrant calling me at the crack of dawn?*

Suddenly, he thought of Sister Helena's confidence in the power of prayer. He almost smiled as a glimmer of hope ignited inside him.

Could it really be possible that whoever was feeding me information has done the same with the judge?

The notion was almost too good to be true.

Still, he couldn't deny that someone was working on his side to uncover the deceptions.

"Sister," he whispered emotionally, "our visit will have to wait. If you can hear me, keep the prayers coming. Either Heaven or Hell is about to break loose, and I'm going to need all the help I can get."

*****

Maryn slipped in and out of consciousness, waking just long enough to realize she was in complete darkness, before she felt her body fading back into obscurity.

During the brief moment of awareness, her body felt heavy, her limbs refused to obey her silent commands to reach up and remove the covering from her eyes. She wondered if she was paralyzed from the neck down.

With each brief awakening, her senses slowly began to return to her. The sounds of the highway and the near-constant jostling of her body confirmed she was being transported somewhere. The smell of plastic filled her nostrils, confirming the rustling sound of what she believed was some type of garment bag. As she became increasingly aware that she was encased inside what could be a body bag, her eyes flew open in terror beneath the fabric covering them.

In that confused moment, a vision of arriving in hell seemed plausible, especially as the lucid moments increased. Fragmented memories of Lily and Pearl, intermingled with nightmares of recent events, caused tentacles of fear to rise up and choke out all reason, all hope. Still, the fierce mother's love she possessed would not surrender.

Maryn made every effort to get up, but her body wouldn't cooperate. As she thrashed about, the image of a caterpillar struggling inside a cocoon came to mind. With the hope that she could also emerge from her encasement and escape, her efforts increased. As she struggled, strange sounds that could only be her own torturous groanings reached her ears, just before her panicked state was put to an end.

The familiar prick of a needle into her thigh made her realize she was not alone. She arched her back and attempted to scream, but seconds later, tingling warmth rushed through her being, and she slipped back into oblivion.

*****

Just seconds after merging onto the freeway, flashing lights and the wailing sound of a fire engine siren rushed past Gavin, nearly causing his heart to stop.

With one hand on the wheel, his free hand vigorously kneaded his chest until the pain subsided. He wasn't sure whether the pain was due to a heart issue or from nervous acid backing up into his chest. One thing he was certain of, was that he was on the precipice of some sort of resolution that would bring him relief or death to life as he knew it. Either way, he wondered if he would ever be able to drive again without feeling like arrest or death was imminent.

As his gaze shifted between mirrors like windshield wipers, Annie, Lucas, and Brenna, largely occupied his thoughts. His deep love and concern for them made him want to head in the opposite direction one minute and press forward like a warrior and defeat the darkness, the next.

Signaling to exit the freeway indicated that the warrior inside him had won out—at least for the moment and for the present battle, anyway.

He clung to Sister Helena's confidence in God's ability to turn things around. Bolstered with this hope, he turned onto the street that would take him to the courthouse.

Minutes later, Sister's encouraging voice carried him through the parking lot and up the steps. Her unwavering belief in him helped carry him to the elevator and down the corridor to Burton's chambers.

Judge Burton's executive assistant, a middle-aged woman Gavin had met only once before, looked at him with raised eyebrows and said, "You better get in there…he's probably foaming at the mouth by now."

Gavin didn't take time to answer her. He simply nodded and pulled open the door.

The judge was sitting at his desk, facing the wall of windows that overlooked the city.

He's ignoring me. Not a good sign.

"I'm sorry I'm late, Your Honor. I came just as soon as I got your message..."

There was something about the way his head was tilted that stopped Gavin from continuing. In two quick strides, he crossed to him, reached out, and turned his chair around.

The bullet hole was in the dead center of his forehead.

Chapter 34

More than four hours after finding Judge Theodore Patrick Burton murdered, Gavin left the Oakland Police Department and merged into the southbound traffic on I-880.

Numb from the shock of the murder and the lengthy interrogation, but overwhelmed with relief that he'd yet again escaped being arrested for possession, he gave zero thought as to where he would go or what he would do next.

Though he was free for the time being, he felt trapped at the same time. Judge Burton's murder put the exclamation point on the certainty that his only tangible allies in the fight were a young mother of two and an elderly nun who was near death or had already passed away.

Despite the January chill, nervous perspiration rolled down his face. Adding to the feeling of impending doom, his stomach churned like a clothes dryer tumbling around hot coals.

Burton was given evidence about Maryn's case. I was supposed to meet him to discuss it. They're coming after me next…it's just a matter of time.

The police can't help me. They didn't help Roger Townes, they didn't help the Longs, and only God knows how many others.

It was still hard to believe that Burton—a powerful, larger than life judge, was dead. It scared the hell out of him. The frequency and boldness of the murders scared the hell out of him.

They killed Burton in broad daylight in a secured public building and no one saw a damn thing.

The memory of the horrified expression and mournful wailing of Burton's assistant caused him to shudder.

There's no place to hide, no way to feel safe.

His earlier revelation that those behind the evil would fail seemed foolish, irrelevant.

Being right about the bastards eventually tripping up doesn't do the victims much good, or me...dead men don't get to gloat.

In that moment, his greatest consolation was the hope that when they killed him, the world might still learn the truth through the packet of evidence he'd mailed to his uncle.

Though well into his seventies, Wallace Conrad, his mother's brother, and a retired army general, was the perfect and only person Gavin could trust. Without question, he would be willing to carry out Gavin's instruction. More importantly, he had the guts.

In the event of Gavin's death, Wally, as they all called him, was to mail the envelopes to the various news outlets and selected government officials. Gavin had also requested that Wally make provisions to have the instructions carried out upon his own death.

If the situation wasn't so dire, Gavin would have smiled at the satisfaction the old guy would get in helping him. Having served his country for the greater part of his life, Wally had become gravely disappointed in the downward spiral the country was headed. When he learned what was in the envelopes, he'd want to declare war himself.

Gavin's eyes burned with tears of admiration and also in regret that he hadn't talked to Wally since his mother's funeral.

I was too busy messing up my life.

His phone buzzed, startling him from his dismal thoughts.

It was a text from Sylvie. On the way down to the police precinct he'd managed to send her a quick message to let her know what happened and that he was okay. He could only imagine her dismay and fear.

Feelings of despair and worthlessness washed over him as he read her message asking him to call her when he could. In truth, he wanted nothing more than to talk about it all to her—to anyone, for that matter; but the stakes were too high. He didn't dare take the chance. For all he knew, his phone was being monitored.

The precise bullet that sliced the window and blew Judge Burton's brains out gave testament that anything was possible. The killers were pros.

"Think, Gavin…think!" he exclaimed in desperation.

He wondered when he would hear from the mysterious informant again. The absence of any further correspondence made him speculate whether he or she had become another casualty of the unnamed, but very real war.

His thoughts shifted to Maryn, but he immediately pushed her from his mind. No matter how bad he felt about what she must be thinking and how she was suffering, he had to concentrate all his energy on what action to take next. It was do or die now, he was certain. Every move he made would be crucial.

The churning of his stomach matched his swirling thoughts of indecision. With plans to stop at the nearest drugstore for antacid, he exited the freeway.

Traffic lights made him feel the most anxious—like a sitting duck. As his eyes moved back and forth, watching everything, but trying not to look suspicious, his head felt like an oscillating fan on a hot summer night.

While he scanned the horizon, Valley Hope Christian Church caught his eye. For a church with such a promising name, the building looked anything but hopeful. The overgrown, brown weeds rising through the wide cracks in the parking lot seemed to mirror the dilapidated appearance of the building, which, in a different time, had probably been beautiful.

The scene saddened him—mostly because he knew the past years of his life reflected its state.

A lone billboard at the center of the parking lot read:

He leads the humble in justice,
and teaches the humble His way.
~Psalm 25:9

Well, I guess I'm on the right track here. Humiliation has definitely been a part of my life lately.

As he pulled into the drugstore's parking lot, Gavin repeated the scripture aloud. Suddenly, the revelation of the kind of humility the psalm was talking about struck him. There was only one person he knew who lived humbly enough to know the way.

With the revelation, he knew just where he would go.

*****

Gavin's eyes darted back and forth suspiciously as he walked through the hospital corridors. He sincerely wished he was just role-playing in a low-budget thriller, but the dangers were real, the risk high.

As he slipped through the door of the surgical waiting room on the first floor, relief washed over him. The room was empty, just as he'd hoped. Immediately, he punched in Sylvie's number on the phone available for visitors.

While he waited for her to answer, each second felt like an eternity. It was as if he was attached to a ticking time bomb but had no way of knowing when his time was up—when the police would show up to arrest him, or when the bullet would end his life and mission.

"*C'mon* Sylvie...please pick up!" he whispered passionately, full-well knowing that it was a long shot that she would.

No one answers phones from an unknown number these days...including me...

"Hello?"

"Sylvie!"

"Gavin? Where *are* you? Have you heard? I've been going crazy wondering what to do!"

The trembling in her voice was difficult to bear, but there was no way around discussing the inevitable. "Yes...Burton's dead. They killed him, Sylvie...wait...didn't you get my text?"

"Yes! I got your text and it's all over the news! But, I'm talking about *Maryn*. Oh *crap*...you don't know, do you?"

Dread like he'd never felt before filled his entire being. Immediately, he pictured Maryn's thin face and haunted, tormented eyes. "Oh God, *please*...don't tell me she's dead too," he pleaded, holding onto the phone with both hands.

"No...no!" she blurted quickly, "at least I don't think so. I guess she got beat up pretty badly by a couple of inmates who found out why she was there. She's in critical condition."

Gavin almost couldn't process what she was saying. He was so overwhelmed, it took him several seconds to answer. "How did you find out about this? Please don't tell me it's all over the news..."

"No," she interjected, "I found out on my own. After I heard about Judge Burton and knew you were going to be delayed again today, I just couldn't stand thinking of Maryn up there wondering what was going on and where you'd gone to. I decided to call and leave a message for her. When they heard that I was acting on your behalf, they told me she'd been taken to an undisclosed hospital for treatment."

The news was hard to swallow—one tragedy right after another, all due to the evil working in and through some sort of coverup. Gavin rested his forehead in his hand and took several deep breaths to keep his emotions in check.

He fought to keep from shouting a string of swear words long and loud enough to get himself arrested for inciting anger. His tirade would be nothing new to Sylvie—she'd heard it all before, but something inside him wanted to refrain so she wouldn't be as scared.

"Okay," he finally answered, with all the calm he could muster. "As her lawyer I can find out where she was taken, but I might have to get a court order for the release of information from whoever's taking Burton's cases. Problem is, I'm sure it's going to be tough to get a new judge in place...and it's too late in the day for me to do anything now."

After a long pause, Sylvie asked softly, "You okay?"

NO! he screamed silently.

"Yes," Gavin answered confidently. "I just need some time to think. While I'm here at the hospital, I'm going to try and visit Sister Helena and then check into another hotel. I need some time to sort out what to do next. Have you heard anything about Sister's condition?"

"No. I called the church rectory to ask, but all I got was a recording about Mass schedules. The hospital wouldn't release anything to me either. *Believe me*, I tried. I knew you'd be worried."

He smiled weakly. He could only imagine.

"Well, we'll both know soon. I'll text you," he answered with confidence he wasn't feeling.

"Okay...thanks. Gavin...please be careful."

"I will. You do the same. Please don't leave the house unless you absolutely have to. You might even want to consider keeping the boys home from school until this all gets blown wide open. Hopefully, it will just be for a couple of days. I'm still going to expose what I know, but now I have to regroup and figure out how and who to trust."

"Okay," she answered quietly.

Gavin could picture her chewing her bottom lip. He'd give anything to be able to tell her everything was going to turn out okay.

"Well..." Sylvie began again, "I don't know if it makes you feel any better...and actually, it might make you feel worse knowing they're coming from me...with all my flaws, but my mom and I really *are* praying for you and sister too. Tell her that if you get a chance, will you?"

Her words pierced his heart. She sounded so vulnerable. Uncertain, but very sincere. He hadn't ever heard anything remotely like this from her. He hadn't heard from his own kids for days.

He swallowed the lump in his throat and said, "Thanks Sylvie. That means a lot. You never know, your prayers might just be better than anyone's...and I'll take all the prayers I can get right now."

*****

Still reeling from the news about Maryn, Gavin forced himself to put one foot in front of the other and carry on in a fight he was anything but sure he would win. Unlike earlier, when all his steps were purposeful and made in haste, his steps were now leaden.

The information desk was empty, so he decided to go back to ICU where he'd last visited Sister Helena.

With each step that drew him nearer, his stomach tightened, his heartbeat increased.

Please let them tell me she's alive. Please God.

Suddenly, he felt a hand on his shoulder.

"Can I help you?"

His heart fell to his stomach, and he turned around with lightning speed he didn't know he possessed.

The nurse standing before him was clearly concerned by his reaction. "I'm sorry I startled you," she began, "I was a little worried you were going to faint."

Gavin broke out in a cold sweat. He put one hand to his chest, the other across his stomach, and took a deep breath.

He managed a nod and said, "Aren't you the nurse I met the other night? Rachel...if I remember, right. I'm here to see Sister Helena."

She nodded. "Good memory," she answered, giving him a smile. "Yes, I was her nurse. I'm sorry..."

Was? Sorry...

The impact was immediate. Gavin collapsed to the floor and his world went dark.

Chapter 35

The starving masses stood in lines waiting for the food offering their stomachs desperately hungered for.

Despite strong winds that nearly toppled the emaciated crowd, the distribution of food proceeded like a well-oiled machine.

The Distributors were all dressed in white, each one smiling, giving calm words of reassurance to those who came out of great need. It was clear that, for some, the offering would save them from impending death.

Gavin watched from afar as each adult received a basket of bread, and each child, a shiny apple. He smiled as he watched this simple act of human kindness.

He wanted to help. Despite his affluence, he knew what it was like to hunger for love, to thirst for deliverance. With renewed energy, he to the gate.

"I want to help," he declared to the man who appeared to be in charge and was pleasantly surprised when he was ushered to the front of the line without question or hesitation.

"I want to help," he repeated to a woman who looked both young and old at the same time.

She simply nodded and said, "Each adult gets bread. Each child gets a red apple, but to those in that line," she instructed, pointing, "give the yellow apples."

Gavin looked to see to which children she was referring, but their faces were blurred, and the line seemed to be amassing rapidly with each passing moment.

He strained and blinked, trying to clear the fog that grew thicker and thicker around his eyes, but to no avail. For several agonizing moments, he was in the dark, but then the fog suddenly cleared.

Strangely, the children given the yellow apples had disappeared along with the fog. The tearful lamenting of their parents, now wandering aimlessly searching for their children, was near deafening.

Gavin ran to each Distributor and demanded an explanation, but none would answer him. Before long, one by one, the children with the red apples began to fade away and eventually disappeared as well.

The pain of the devastated parents became Gavin's own pain. He shouted and threatened the Distributors with harm if they didn't help him, but to no avail.

The wailing of the parents caused his heart to burn so badly that he fell to the ground and cried out his protest, before his voice would also be silenced.

Gavin lay in agony for some time, before strong arms lifted him from his misery and carried him away.

*****

Gavin basked in the rest and release he needed and longed for, feeling as though he was weightless. Annie wrapped him in a blanket of mercy so soft and warm, that somehow, he knew he must be dreaming.

He hoped to never awaken.

Someone called his name amidst the distinct sound of soft weeping. He became aware of a small, feminine hand holding his own.

Brenna?

Even a slim possibility was enough to coax him out of his peaceful reverie. He made several attempts to lift his heavy eyelids until a blurry face finally materialized.

Sylvie's face was swollen with grief. Her enormous dark-blue eyes were framed with wet, spiked lashes, their poignant gaze matching her mournful expression.

Though Gavin had hoped to see Brenna, his heart swelled with gratitude and fatherly love just the same.

"It's okay, Gavin. You're going to be fine," she soothed. "You just need some rest."

Her words were like salve for his wounded and weary soul. He basked in the attention she was giving him, feeling like a starving man who had just been given his first spoonful of food.

As his awareness increased, he looked around to discover that he was lying in a hospital bed. The peace, he had so recently enjoyed, rapidly faded. Painful memories flooded into his consciousness. He fought to push the images away—Maryn, badly-beaten and alone in a hospital. The faces of little Sophia and the vaccine-damaged children in the files. The pictures of Dr. and Mrs. Long before their demise. Most haunting was the image burned in his mind of what was left of Judge Burton's head.

He closed his eyes to block it all out.

"God help them," he whispered.

At the mention of God, the memory of why he was at the hospital in the first place surfaced, instantly filling his eyes with tears.

"Sister..." he choked, now understanding the look in Sylvie's sorrowful countenance.

"She made it Gavin! She's alive!"

Through the groggy haze caused by his pain meds, Gavin tried to make sense of her declaration. He slowly shook his head as a single tear slipped from his eye. "The nurse said she was *gone*."

"Yes! She was gone from ICU because she was transferred out of intensive care!" she answered through her own tears.

"I don't understand..."

"It's *true*! I finally reached Sister Joanna! I called her to ask for prayers for you and that's when she told me that Sister's heart stopped beating at one point, but when it started again, she improved so quickly Sister Joanna thinks it was a miracle! Sister Helena was moved out of ICU just *hours* before you got here!

His eyes searched her face for any sign that she was making it all up just to spare him. "Are you really telling me the truth?"

"Yes!" she declared happily.

Relief and joy flooded his being so forcefully that it pushed out everything else. Tears dripped from both eyes as he tried to get up. "Then take me to her!" he commanded.

"No...not yet!" she answered with a laugh, coaxing him back down onto his pillow. "You've got some healing of your own to do before you can see her, and besides, even though she's off the ventilator, she's still pretty groggy."

"I'm *fine*," he argued. "I was just exhausted and haven't been eating enough."

"You're *not* fine," Sylvie shot back. "The doctor said you have an ulcer, acid reflux, high blood pressure, and you were extremely dehydrated."

"No big deal. I need to get up...you mean they told you all that?"

"No," she answered with a laugh. "They told Annie. Apparently, she's still listed on your medical files as your emergency contact. She called me and asked if I could come and stay with you."

The fact that Annie sent Sylvie to him instead of coming herself was painfully disappointing, but Gavin quickly pushed it from his mind. His gratitude and joy in knowing that Sister Helena was still alive eclipsed the pain. Moreover, he was not alone. Sylvie was there trying her best to comfort him and make him smile.

A profound and powerful revelation came to him in that moment. He turned his head and looked at Sylvie. She took a big chance in venturing out just to be there for him. Gratitude slowly filled his senses.

I'm alive. For a reason unknown to me, I have not been snuffed out. Sister Helena is alive against all odds. A deadly and ugly truth is about to be revealed to the world, but countless lives will be saved.

His eyes were moist as he said to Sylvie, "The evidence regarding the vaccine dangers has been hidden in plain sight, but so are the good things...and you are one of them. I'm really sorry for the times I didn't realize or let you know how much I appreciate you."

A fat tear rolled down her cheek at his declaration. Choked up, she simply nodded.

"Now," he continued, "I want you to *go home* and take care of your boys. I'm fine. I will do what they tell me…and when this whole thing is out, we'll all be safe."

"I'm not going to leave you here. You won't do what they tell you…"

"I *will*," he assured her, "but my ulcer will only get worse if I have to worry about you. Now go home and *stay put*…and text me when you're there, *please!*"

Sylvie hesitated, slowly shaking her head.

"Go!" he insisted, once more. "I'll be fine. They won't be keeping me here long anyway. They'll give me some meds and send me on my way. I'll contact you just as soon as they do."

"Promise?"

"*Promise*," he lied.

As if on cue, a male nurse, came in to check on the IV line that was pumping much-needed fluids and nutrients into his body. In his hand was a small paper cup containing an antacid and blood pressure pill.

"Hey Gavin, my name's Rick, and I'll be taking care of you tonight. The doc will be checking back on you in the morning. Hopefully, you'll feel better after a good night's rest, so we can kick you out of here sometime tomorrow," he said with a grin.

"See?" Gavin said to Sylvie, raising his eyebrows as he tossed the pills in his mouth and chased them down with water. "I'll be *fine*."

*****

Gavin waited until Sylvie left to press the call button and ask for an extra pillow. When Rick came in with it, Gavin mentioned his acquaintance with Sister Helena, asking if he could find out which room she was in. "She's the reason I'm here in the first place and I want to stop in and visit her when I get dismissed."

"I'll see what I can find out," he assured him. "Your dinner will be coming soon. I figure I better warn you...it's going to be pretty bland. Reduced salt and no spicy food for a while, but you'll get used to it."

Gavin shot him a look that said, yeah right.

Rick laughed. "Okay, so I stretched the truth a little, but it's how you'll have to eat until you get that ulcer healed."

If you had any idea what was going on you would know that my diet is the least of my worries.

Gavin kept his thoughts to himself and offered with a chuckle, "Well, if we are what we eat, it sounds like I'm about to become as enthralling as a traffic court attorney."

Rick laughed. "I'll be back with your friend's room number for you."

"Thanks...I appreciate it."

Gavin had every intention of leaving as soon as possible. There was no way in hell he was going to stay put like a sitting duck. Now more than ever, he was convinced he needed to make contact either with a news-media outlet and possibly one of the several judges he suspected would take the seat on the bench for Burton. How, when, and who that would be, was still very much undecided.

The only thing of which he was certain was his plan to see, with his own eyes, if Sister Helena was alive. Somehow, he felt certain that just being in her presence would help him succeed.

Rick walked through the doorway, quickly putting an end to his thoughts. "Man, I sure wish I could help you with your friend's room number, but I just found out that I can't give it out."

Immediately, Gavin's heart flipped in his chest. "Really? What would be the reason for that?"

"Well, she could have requested it—but last I heard, she was still pretty sedated, so I don't really know. Maybe her family made the decision."

Gavin played it cool. "No problem, I'll just try and reach someone at the convent tomorrow before I leave. I'm sure they'll clear the way. Thanks anyway for checking."

"Yeah, no problem. Anything else I can do for you?"

"No, I'm just going to rest."

"Well…it looks like your dinner's here, and you'll rest better on a full stomach, anyway."

An emaciated food attendant who looked to be anywhere from sixteen to thirty brought in his tray. His skin showed signs of drug abuse. When he spoke, the condition of his teeth confirmed he was a user.

A poached egg, a cup of chicken broth, and a snack-size container of cherry gelatin were the stars of the meal. Unsalted crackers and a couple dried-up carrot sticks played supporting roles in Gavin's food extravaganza.

His eyes lingered on the chipped, black fingernail polish showing through the server's latex gloves, making him wonder who had prepared the food and at what point the gloves were put on.

Good time to lose my appetite—none of this will have any taste anyway.

The second the attendant took his leave, Gavin reached into the drawer attached to his bed tray and grabbed the pen inside. He then rose from the bed and wheeled his IV line over to the closet to get his clothes before heading into the bathroom.

Without any idea as to how long he would have before Rick came back to check on him, he ripped off the tape securing his IV, turned his head, and pulled out the needle. Even with shaking hands, he was surprised by how little it hurt, and more surprised how unafraid he'd been to do it.

Whatever they gave me for the ulcer pain must be good stuff.

The room spun slightly as he worked as quickly as possible to get dressed. Every cell in his body seemed to be screaming both for rest and escape at the same time. His ears picked up every tiny noise, real or imagined, and his pulse increased as he contemplated multiple outcomes—including having to confront Rick or security.

I just might have to leave here without seeing Sister. Something in my gut tells me I need to get out.

Next, Gavin ripped off a sheet of paper toweling and used it pen a note explaining that he was dismissing himself and therefore waiving the hospital of all responsibility for his actions or the outcome of his health concerns. He then placed the note on the closed toilet lid and cracked the door slightly.

The coast was clear.

Hoping that Rick would think he was using the restroom if he checked on him, Gavin turned on the fan, left the bathroom light on, and locked the door behind him.

His heart was pounding wildly as he pulled open the door to the room and peered into the corridor. The last thing he wanted was to be confronted by Rick or any other well-meaning personnel who would coax or demand that he stay.

Several people mulled past, but Rick wasn't one of them. Gavin straightened up and tried his best to look like a visitor rather than a patient. He walked right past a nurse who was fixated on the computer screen of a mobile nurse station. As soon as he turned the corner, he picked up the pace and headed toward the elevator.

Fully conscious of the security cameras that lined every corridor, he tried extra-hard to appear relaxed. Four elevators were available; still, it felt like an eternity before one finally opened. He looked up to discover he was on the 6th floor. Gavin stepped inside.

It's empty!

Elated, he pushed the button to manually close the door and silently pleaded for the doors to quickly shut behind him, so he wouldn't have to make small talk on the way down.

Just before his wish came true, a hand reached out and stopped the doors. It was all he could do to keep from cringing as Rachel, the nurse he'd collapsed in front of rushed to join him.

"I *thought* that was you," she exclaimed. "They released you already? That was quick—I thought for sure you'd at least be staying the night."

Gavin avoided her question and said, "I'm feeling much better. Thanks for helping me earlier."

"No problem! You just happened to pick a great place to pass out," she answered with a grin.

The two were silent for several awkward seconds. In order to avoid potential discrimination citations, Gavin had gotten so used to averting his eyes away from others—especially in close spaces, like elevators, that he almost blew the opportunity that had presented itself.

He lifted his gaze and asked, "By any chance, do you happen to know where Sister Helena was moved? I want to stick my head in and say hi before I leave."

"I don't know what room she's in, but she's probably on the third floor. Most everyone who gets moved out of ICU gets moved there. She's probably still groggy, so don't expect much conversation," she added with a smile.

"Yeah...I don't want to keep her more than a few minutes. Rest is so important. I just wanted to say hello before I leave. I'm just really relieved she made it," he added, honestly.

She smiled. "You and me both! That was really something how she turned the corner so unexpectedly."

"Yeah...well, she's a pretty determined woman," he offered with a sincere smile.

"Have you known her long?" she asked, appearing to be genuinely interested.

He nodded. "For a while...and we have a mutual friend and client."

The elevator stopped, and the doors opened on the first floor. Rachel looked at him and said, "I'd walk with you to the parking garage, but it sounds like you're headed back up to third floor."

"Yeah. Thanks again for all the help today and...well, thanks."

"Sure. That's my job. Anything else I can do for you?"

Hide me, he wanted to say.

He was about to decline when an idea struck him. "As a matter of fact, I was wondering...have you heard about anyone being recently admitted to the hospital under police protection? Apparently, while I was passed out, the client I spoke of earlier was injured at the women's correctional facility and admitted to an undisclosed hospital. It would sure save me some trouble if I found out she was here. As her attorney, my visit would be permitted."

She shook her head. "She wasn't admitted here," she answered confidently.

"You're sure?"

"Yes. If something like that happens, we are all informed."

"I see."

"As a matter of fact," she continued, "we are actually on high-alert right now because of the incident that happened with Sister Helena."

The hair on the back of his neck stood up. "What incident?"

"The stranger in the room—didn't Sister Joanna tell you?"

Gavin's chest tightened. "No. I haven't talked to Sister Joanna since the day of the accident. My executive assistant told me about her heart stopping, but I hadn't heard about anything else. What happened?"

"Well, when I went in to check on her, there was a man there—I didn't even see him at first, but he ran from the room like he was guilty or something."

The blood in Gavin's veins ran cold. "Did you get a good look at him?"

"No, I wish I had, but he was in the shadows before he ran. Must've been hiding behind the door when I walked in."

"You're sure you wouldn't recognize him if you saw him?"

She shrugged. "It's like I told the security officers...maybe if I saw a picture, I could confirm a possibility, but I've never seen him before, that's for sure."

A lightbulb went off inside Gavin's head as he remembered the bug on Sister's purse. "Can you give me just a second? I want to show you something."

"Sure."

Gavin pulled out his phone and did a quick image search on Thomas Pearce.

Bingo! He exclaimed silently, as his gaze connected with a picture of Thomas and Maryn from an online article about Maryn's arrest. Thomas was dressed in full uniform in the picture; Maryn was wearing prison garb. The headline read: Good Vs. Evil—Dedicated Servant, Duplicitous Wife.

The title made him furious, but Gavin played it cool, holding it out to Rachel. "I am wondering...could it have been this man?"

She looked for several seconds and then nodded slowly. "I can't be for certain, but yes, it sure could have been. His face has the same shape. But he's a cop. Why would he run?"

Gavin shrugged. "He's in the midst of a nasty divorce with his wife because of her arrest. Sister Helena and I are her advocates. Obviously, neither of us can say for sure, but it just occurred to me that maybe he wanted to talk to Sister to see what she knew, or maybe even to get some counsel to help put his marriage back together," he offered, though he didn't believe it for a second.

Rachel didn't look convinced. "I don't know...it does look like him, but it sure seems like a weird reaction to me. I didn't get to pursue him because Sister's heart stopped."

Their eyes locked at the exact same time. The unspoken question seemed to hover above them like a cloud of doom.

Gavin could see the fear in her eyes even before she said, "Well, I've probably already said too much, so I'll quit before I get into some sort of legal trouble. Hope you have a nice visit with Sister. Take care of yourself."

Before he could even answer, she turned and headed toward the exit.

Chapter 36

In his quest to find Sister Helena, Gavin walked with purpose down the patient corridors on the third floor. Hearing about the mysterious visitor only added to his over-the-top paranoia, but he was determined to see her before he disappeared—maybe for good.

To be as unobtrusive as possible, he forced himself to refrain from trying to spot the security cameras. Instead, he kept his nose buried in a magazine he'd swiped from the waiting room. Though many rooms were left open enough to allow him a glimpse of the patient inside, he was disappointed that so many were closed.

After the first walk through, he went into the bathroom, waited, and started back through the hallway again. Whenever the nurses gave him opportunity, he knocked on a closed door and waited for an answer before entering. So far, he was 0 for 2—one cranky old man and a sleeping old woman. Thankfully, he'd been able to simply apologize and move on without incident.

His eyes zeroed in on the room almost directly across from the nurses' station; he somehow sensed that Sister Helena was behind the closed door.

Avoiding eye contact with a nurse who looked up briefly as she walked past him, he bypassed the room and continued toward the elevators.

Hoping he'd succeeded in appearing nonchalant, as soon as the nurse disappeared around the corner, he turned and rushed back to the room. After giving the door a soft, swift knock, he pushed it in with a boldness that came out of sheer desperation.

The curtain was drawn around the bed, so he had to walk clear into the room to see who was lying in the bed. His battle-weary heart thundered inside his chest as he peeked around the curtain.

"Sister!" he whispered disbelievingly.

She lay so still, Gavin wondered if she was breathing. He approached the bed with his heart in his throat, silently praying, until his eyes finally saw the gentle rise and fall of her chest.

Yet again, he noticed that her face was without the lines and wrinkles of most people her age. In his eyes, she looked like a sleeping angel. He didn't even care if she didn't wake up for his visit. It was enough to know that she'd made it. He took her hand in his own.

"For such a tough old bird, your hands are as soft as butter," he whispered softly, "just like your heart."

He fought the tears from coming, but they won. He was so damn happy to see her, so tired of the fight, that he didn't even try to prevent them from falling.

For several minutes, he just stood there whispering over and over, "Thank God you're alive."

Muffled voices from outside the room snapped him out of his reverie. It was time to go. Time to face the demons that awaited him—wherever and whoever they were.

"Goodbye, Sister. Thanks for giving a crap about me...I love you," he choked as he turned to go.

"Emm...."

Gavin spun around at the sound of her voice. "Sister?! It's me, Gavin."

Her eyelids fluttered slightly but didn't open. Still, it was obvious that she was trying to lift them.

He patted her hand. "Just rest now, Sister. You're going to be fine..."

"Emmm..." she whispered, so quietly it was nearly inaudible.

"You're doing *great*! You'll be out of here in no time. I'm going to leave now so you can get the rest you need...but I'll be back. I'm sure Sister Joanna will be here soon."

Even with her eyes still closed, Sister knit her brow and slowly shook her head. She tried again. "Em...muh...grunn."

What is she trying to say?

Gavin leaned closer, his ears straining to hear her, but she repeated the same three syllables.

"Emma? Is Emma your nurse?" he asked patiently.

Suddenly, her eyes opened. He smiled broadly at her. "There you are! How are you feeling?"

Initially, she simply stared in response to his question, but then whispered hoarsely, "Emmm...uh...grun...t."

"Who is that Sister?" he asked, searching her face. "I don't know anyone with that name...is she one of sisters at the convent...someone you want me to contact?"

Sister slowly shook her head before closing her eyes once more.

Though he still had no idea what she was trying to tell him, something about the way she had fixed her eyes on him was unsettling, as was the now, completely-silent room. So much so, that he nearly jumped out of his skin when his phone buzzed.

Gavin grabbed his chest and used the bedrail to steady himself. He'd come to fear the sound of his phone going off. He was afraid to look at the text until he realized it was probably Sylvie letting him know she made it home.

He brushed his thumb over the screen and saw that the message was from an unknown number.

Finally! My mysterious ally...

We've got Maryn and are ready to cut a deal.
Show up without the cops and tell us
what we want to know, and she won't get hurt.
All charges will be dropped.
Generous reward for your cooperation.
1115 Centennial Blvd. Back door. One hour.

Gavin nearly dropped the phone. It felt like the wind had been knocked out of him. He took a couple of deep breaths before glancing hopelessly over at Sister Helena. She was sleeping again, but he pleaded anyway, "Pray for me, Sister...and for Maryn...for us all."

Gavin walked as fast as possible to get through the hospital without causing suspicion, but then broke into a dead run through the parking garage to get to the rental.

He was living a nightmare from which he was uncertain he would awaken. Every cell of his body was focused on getting to Maryn on time to save her—though he had no idea how he would do it. Knowing that he was dealing with cold-blooded killers, he didn't believe for a minute they would release either of them, but he was the only hope Maryn had. There was no other way. He couldn't count on the police or anyone else in law enforcement until he figured out who planted the bug on Sister's purse at the correctional facility. Thomas Pearce's actions were highly suspect. If he was involved, fellow officers could also be involved.

Once inside the van, Gavin reached under the seat and pulled out his father's gun—the same gun that was used for law and order and to defend the innocent. The same gun that went undetected by the police earlier that day, and remarkably, when the police arrived on the scene of Judge Burton's murder.

He tucked the gun inside the right pocket of his coat, the St. Michael prayer card into the left.

After keying the address into the GPS, he pulled out of the parking lot, nearly taking the first turn onto the service road on two wheels.

Calm down. Slow down. If you get pulled over, Maryn's as good as dead.

"God, help me," he prayed aloud. "I'm the only chance she has."

He swallowed back his emotion at the thought and continued praying. "If I die today, I ask you to forgive me for all the times I failed you, my wife, my kids, society. Protect them, because I didn't. Protect them now, because I can't. Don't take Maryn away from her kids. There's been enough killing. The children of this world have suffered so much…"

Gavin stopped praying. The dream he'd had just before he woke up in the hospital surfaced.

The children were starving, but what was given to some is not given to others.

"What are you trying to tell me?" he asked aloud.

His question was met with silence.

"C'mon!" he shouted, slapping his hand on the steering wheel.

"What does the dream mean?" he whispered, desperately, trying to keep his eyes on the road, the vehicles behind him, and those on his sides. He wondered when the Lexus would show up, but then realized it would probably be parked at the address he was seeking.

"What does the food represent? Why yellow apples to some?" he pondered aloud, his mind spinning with dozens of thoughts at the same time.

He pictured Sister lying in the hospital, potentially injured by foul play. Immediately he realized that she was trying hard to convey something to him.

"What was she trying to say?" he wondered aloud.

Emma grun...emma grunt.

"What does that mean? Who the hell is Emma Grunt?"

"Never heard of her," he declared bleakly.

Sweat was pouring down his face. His stomach felt like he'd thrown back a shot of scotch laced with broken glass.

In less than half an hour, he'd be facing demons who had murdered innocent people—demons who didn't care about Judge Burton, Roger Townes, Dr. and Mrs. Long, or any of their victims.

Including poor little Sophia Sanchez...Clare Martinez...

Gavin's eyes widened. "Oh my God in Heaven," he exclaimed, "that's it!"

His heart pounded wildly at the revelation of the connection between his dream and what Sister Helena was trying to tell him.

"This is no accident," he exclaimed in awe.

Blessed are you, Simon. For flesh and blood has not revealed this to you, but my Father who is in heaven.

The declaration of Jesus' words spoken to Peter came to him like no scripture had ever come to him before. As a teen he'd become completely disinterested in his religious studies. As an adult, he was a lax, wishy-washy Catholic, yet God was revealing the truth to him for a specific purpose.

Gavin wept tears of gratitude and humility for several moments before feeling a calm resolve wash over him as he exited the freeway.

The time had come. Sink or swim. Do or die. He was in it to win it.

"I have no control over how things go down," he murmured, "but I've got to believe that God is on my side."

He glanced at his GPS.

Two minutes to my final destination...life or death

"God, if I never get another thing, thanks for giving me this revelation and peace, even when I am so unworthy. If I die here today, have mercy on me. Have mercy on everyone counting on me and give me the help I need to at least save Maryn and expose the lies," he prayed as he signaled to turn into the parking lot of what looked to be an automotive supply warehouse or repair garage.

Gavin didn't get a chance to say amen. Flashing red lights appeared in his rearview mirror.

"NO!" he shouted agonizingly, pressing the accelerator to the floor.

Oh God...NO! Help me! He pleaded silently as he kicked up gravel while speeding through the parking lot to exit onto the road behind the building.

Though several car lengths behind, the patrol car followed him through several streets and residential areas before he ran a red light. He swerved just in time to barely miss striking a minivan that looked a lot like the one he was driving.

Gavin cringed at the thought of the innocent family he'd almost injured or killed. Still, he felt he had no choice but to try and outrun the police.

I can't be taken into custody! I can't be late! Maryn's life depends on me.

Before long, he was being followed by two more squad cars. The sight made him drive even faster, the blaring sirens of all three was nearly deafening. He screeched into a parking lot and sped down an alley, knocking over a trash dumpster that spun a full circle before landing in the middle of the alley.

I need to get to the freeway. I can't outrun them here...someone's going to get killed!

He briefly thought about leading the entourage back to the warehouse but then thought better of it.

Even if I had the entire police force with me, I can't trust them—any of them. Thomas Pearce is a cop. He's involved somehow... I just know it.

Gavin felt like he was on auto-pilot, driving like he'd been racing cars all his life. The dumpster in the road bought him a few extra seconds that allowed him to make a U-turn under the overpass and enter the freeway via an exit ramp.

Seeing the traffic coming right toward him didn't deter him. He managed to cross to the far right passing lane, allowing all other traffic to move to their right, but just seconds later, he heard the sound of sirens in the distance, so he made his way back across the lanes, amidst honking, yelling, and cars screeching on their brakes.

With the off-ramp in sight, he maneuvered a U-turn at such a high speed that the van rolled on two wheels for almost a hundred feet before finally slamming back down.

The jolt snapped Gavin's neck back and caused him to temporarily lose his grip on the wheel. Just as he grabbed hold of the wheel and looked up to discover that the police were one step ahead of him. He was heading straight into a barrier line of spikes that would puncture his tires.

Panic like he'd never felt before came over him. Maryn's gaunt, mournful face flashed before his eyes as he slammed the accelerator pedal to the floor and cranked the steering wheel to the right, aiming for the grassy median that lay between the exit ramp and the service road that ran under the overpass.

The realization that he hadn't made the turn on time came with the thunderous exploding of his back, left tire.

Gavin felt the impact in every part of his body as the van rolled over and over and over.

Chapter 37

Gavin roused to find that the van's airbag had engaged on impact, leaving his body feeling like someone had taken a baseball bat to him. He hardly noticed. If anything, he felt a beating was fitting. He'd failed to reach Maryn on time. He'd be arrested now.

Immediately, he wrestled with the idea of sending the police to the warehouse to save her. It was tormenting to try and weigh the chances of success with the potential for more assassinations—including Sylvie and her family, Annie, Lucas, and Brenna.

Surely the thugs heard the sirens and got out of there. I'm sure they had someone watching for me—and for all I know, they could have been tailing me the whole time. Maybe they'll try and contact me again.

Besides, I have no real proof they even have Maryn. No proof she's alive. For all I know...these cops are Thomas' buddies. How else did they just happen to show up at the warehouse? The text could have come from them. I'm not about to tell them all I know until I'm sure it won't do more harm than good.

The revelations helped to calm him a bit, and with no other choice but to surrender, Gavin raised his arms in the air and obeyed every command barked at him. He was cuffed, read his rights, and arrested on multiple counts—one being, possession of a firearm.

Still somewhat dazed, Gavin felt numb as he stared out the back window of the patrol car as it eased onto the freeway to take him to jail. Hot tears stung his eyes. He squeezed them shut and tilted his head back onto the seat's headrest to prevent them from spilling out.

Immediately, however, a myriad of images forced him to open his eyes again. The faces of the victims haunted him. So many had suffered and many more would suffer because of his failure. He felt so defeated. So abandoned. Like a lamb led to the slaughter.

God, why have You abandoned me? Where is the good in this? Why do You allow these bastards to persist in this evil?

With the glass partition separating him from the officer driving, Gavin felt free to let out a roar of lament.

"Where *are* You?" he screamed. "What do You want from me? How can I help anyone from *behind bars?*" he growled angrily, the hot tears returning.

He didn't stop them this time. "I'm worthless," he whispered, woefully. His entire being was filled with anguish.

You are Mine.

The declaration exploded within him.

Unsure as to whether he was losing his mind or had just been given Divine solace, Gavin swallowed hard and tried to calm himself.

Not a single sparrow falls to the ground without My knowledge.

Then what do you want from me? Why are you letting these bastards get away with all this? Don't you care? Maryn's children will be without a mother...

Greater love has no man than to lay down his life.

"Yes! My old man laid down his life and YOU took it!" he cried, stomping his foot in complete frustration.

Greater love has no man...

The explosive shattering of glass interrupted any other thought. Gavin's head shot up. As best as he could tell through the separation glass, the passenger side window had been shattered. The officer was holding his shoulder and appeared to be grimacing, while he struggled to steer.

Just seconds later, the center pane of glass between them opened electronically. "Get down!" he ordered sternly. "We're under fire."

Gavin's gaze shot in the direction of the broken window to see the front half of the infamous black Lexus keeping a steady pace alongside the patrol car.

He didn't need to be told twice. With his seatbelt still engaged and his cuffed hands behind him, he did his best to lower the trunk of his body as far as possible. His heart was pounding so hard, it resonated like a bass drum in his ears.

"Officer down! I repeat..."

The officer's plea for help was abruptly cut off with a grunt. The vehicle immediately began to fishtail.

They got him again!

Gavin dared a glance over the seat to see the officer's neck spurting blood, his head bumping up and down on his chest.

"Oh God...help him! Help *me*!" he cried, amidst the sound of blaring horns protesting the drifting of the car across the lanes.

Though the Lexus had now disappeared, Gavin felt helpless. With his hands cuffed, he was unable to cover his head for protection. Just seconds later, he watched in horror as they drifted in front of a semi-truck. The driver did his best to slow down and miss them but struck the back, driver's side of the vehicle with powerful force.

The vehicle spun in a complete circle and into the path of a pickup that plowed into the rear-end straight on. The impact caused it to flip—end over end—before it came crashing down on the shoulder, rolling down the verge.

Gavin's attempt to keep his head down had been worthless. The force of the first collision had jostled him about, but the seatbelt had kept him from the worst of it. The impact of the second hit, however, caused the back end to smash into the back seat so far that it snapped in two, rendering the seatbelt useless. He was thrust forward onto the partition board, now mostly shattered.

For several seconds, he lay motionless, his entire body on fire with pain. His pounding head and a warm, sticky substance between his cheek and the partition confirmed that he was bleeding.

Certain the ambulance and police sirens would be blaring soon, Gavin wanted nothing more than to keep his eyes closed and just drift away. Still, a greater force beckoned him to open them.

The key to the handcuffs glistened from a ring on the dead officer's belt-loop. His father's pistol and his phone lay on the floor in a clear vinyl bag.

Don't be stupid. You'll never be able to get out of the cuffs and this wreckage before the cops show up.

Greater love has no man than this, than to lay down his life.

"What are you trying to tell me?" he groaned, wanting to sob pitifully. "It's too late to save Maryn now!".

It took several agonizing moments of indecision before he shifted his position and pushed his back against what was left of the back seat. He kicked what was left of the partition into the front seat and then shifted around to use his feet to propel himself, head-first, through the opening.

Glass fragments pierced his clothing in multiple places, causing pain to slice through his chest, but he hardly noticed. All his focus was on retrieving the key.

It was hard to ignore the sight of the slain officer, but sirens off in the distance told him he had just seconds to unlock his cuffs. He gave no thought as to what he would do or where he would go once he was freed, but he was determined to try.

Sweat poured down his face as he made several failed attempts. The task seemed virtually impossible. With his hands behind his back, he couldn't even see what he was doing. The temptation to give up was powerful. He was so tired. Had no real plan.

"Please God...if you want me to get out of here, I need help!" he begged.

The sound of his own pleading made him cringe. *What chance do I really have to escape or to help Maryn?* His panic intensified.

Dizzy, his head fell to his chest.

"I'm too weak," he lamented, just before a bullet whizzed past his ear.

Adrenaline flooded his being, prompting him to try again. The key slid into place like he'd done it a million times. Gavin retrieved his gun from the bag, released the safety, and cocked it.

Another bullet shot past his head.

Through the window, he could see spectators gathering alongside their vehicles at the edge of the verge and the freeway. The lights and sound of patrol cars were getting closer. He didn't know whether to laugh or cry at the sight. The police were either going to be his allies, his enemies, or become victims themselves. He hoped, at least, that whoever was shooting at him was scared off by the amassing number of patrol cars.

Laying low on the seat, he cracked open the passenger side door. The sight of the thick copse of trees at the edge of the verge and parallel to the freeway, elevated his hope of escape. Still, even though the bullets had come from the opposite direction, he worried that the assailant might seek cover there as well.

"God, please help me!" he begged again. "Saint Michael, protect me!" he prayed, as he scooted from the seat and crouched beside the car.

The damp, frigid wind assaulted his face; the sun had already begun its descent. The distance to the trees suddenly seemed much farther, but he had no other choice than to run.

He didn't get more than a few yards from the car before pain exploded in his right shoulder, causing him to stumble and fall to the ground. Instinctively, he rolled behind a rusted aluminum barrel that lay on its side. The black char around the rim told him that it had probably been left behind by one of thousands of homeless persons who used the wooded areas for shelter.

The slamming of patrol car doors and what he imagined was the scurry of ambulance personnel, filled the air. But just a second later, the shrill sound of the sirens stopped; the atmosphere became eerily silent.

The slamming of his racing heart filled his ears. With each pounding pulse, blood seemed to trickle faster from the hole in his shoulder.

He dared a glance around the barrel to see a solid line of patrol cars, but the notorious Lexus was absent. The sight did little to comfort him. The smell of the blood pooling on the ground below reminded him the enemy was near.

Gavin felt like a sitting duck. Despite the tall, dry grass, the glum realization of his vulnerability seeped into his being. The urge to surrender or start crawling toward the trees was fierce, instinctual, but getting the police force to realize his intentions without getting killed would be a challenge. Still, he felt he had to try.

I have to turn myself in...I won't be able to help anyone if I bleed to death.

Putting as much pressure on his shoulder as he could stand, he used his free hand to knock the handle of his gun against the barrel in a rhythmic motion.

Three quick taps. Three solid hits. Three quick taps.

He repeated the SOS sequence his father had taught him as a boy, counted to ten, and then slowly made an attempt to rise.

STAY DOWN.

The authoritative command came from within. Gavin hesitated. Lightheaded, he didn't know whether the command was the voice of wisdom or his cowardly, weary spirit.

The bullet that ricocheted off the top of the barrel gave him the answer. He hunkered back down and covered his head, as a hailstorm of gun fire rang through the air.

All Gavin could do was close his eyes and pray for mercy.

It took several agonizing seconds for him to realize that the barrel was not getting hit.

They aren't shooting at me! Who are they shooting at?

Though the shots continued to ring through the air, Gavin couldn't detect even one coming close to where he lay.

What the hell is going on?

His breaths were coming quickly. He knew his condition was worsening, but the urge to venture a glimpse over the barrel proved too great.

"Cease fire! Stand down!"

The order was shouted by an officer with a bullhorn from behind a shield. Then, just as abruptly as the shooting started, silence came.

"What the *hell!*" he whispered, swallowing hard.

Gavin counted at least six other shields before his eyes came to rest on an officer being held at gunpoint by a man dressed in dark pants, a black sweatshirt, and ski-hat."

The darkening sky overhead and their distance from him made it too difficult for Gavin to clearly see either man's face, but the threat was palpable.

"This is Police Sergeant Wade," the bullhorn echoed, "you are surrounded on the ground and more forces are arriving by air. Lower your weapon and back away from the officer. I *repeat*...lower your weapon and back away from the officer and you won't get hurt."

The assailant was undeterred. Holding a gun to the officer's temple, he pulled him to his chest and slowly began to back away from the line of shielded officers.

Greater love has no man than to lay down his life.

Gavin's body felt heavy; his head was spinning.

The voice inside him came again, only this time, he could see his father standing before him. He could see every wrinkle that framed Joseph Antonio Steele's soulful brown eyes, smell the aftershave his mother bought him every Valentine's Day.

His father smiled at him.

It was all Gavin needed to give him the courage and strength to stand up, take aim, and fire.

Chapter 38

Maryn stood at a distance watching Lily and Pearl chase after the sanderlings that flittered about, scouring the water's edge for food. The wind carried the sound of their giggles and shrieks to her ears, bringing enjoyment and longing both at once.

The familiar feeling of sand between her toes brought back bittersweet memories of her days there with Thomas. Memories that were gone forever.

Still, she was grateful that her babies were so close—almost within her reach. Her arms longed to pull them close and never let them go, but the chains that bound her were too strong.

Over and over, she pondered as to what heinous crime she'd committed for which she deserved such strict confinement. Nonetheless, though an unrelenting wind pushed her back, causing her to stumble repeatedly, she plodded forward, determined to reach them.

With each fall, she winced at the bruising of her arms, her legs, the pounding of her head, as it hit the ground over and over. She was so weary, so weak, she feared she would never get to them.

Maryn began to sob. Her hope had been shattered yet again.

But then a stranger knelt down beside her. One by one, he removed the bonds that held her captive. The blustery wind quieted and became more of a gentle breeze that revived and refreshed her. The man's kindness helped to lessen her tears. He took her hand, caressed it, and called her name.

"Maryn...*Maryn*...it's me. Everything's going to be all right now."

The voice sounded like Thomas. The nightmare she had dreaded every night was upon her once more. Maryn began to cry.

"Please...don't cry, baby. *Please*."

The weight of the man's body pressed down upon her chest. His hand caressed her head. His lips dropped tender kisses over her cheeks, eyelids, forehead, and lips, lingering there for several seconds before she realized that it was not the salt of her own tears she tasted, but his.

Maryn's eyes slowly opened. A face that looked like Thomas was just inches from her own. Fat tears dropped from his eyes onto her cheeks. His tortured expression displayed the depth of his emotion as he spoke the words she never thought she'd hear again.

"I love you, Maryn! Oh God, I *love* you! Forgive me, honey. Please, *forgive* me," he wept, laying his head on her chest.

Maryn was sure she was still drugged or dreaming. The possibility caused panic to rise inside her and spill over. "What is *happening*? I don't understand!"

Confused and dizzy, she pushed at his shoulders. He immediately sat up but reached for her hand and held it.

For the first time, Maryn became aware of the twin bed she was lying on. Her eyes darted about, taking in the details of the primitive bedroom she'd never seen before. Whitewashed stone walls, a single, tiny window high on the opposite wall, one small wooden table next to the bed, and a simple crucifix above the doorway.

When her gaze came back to his face, she couldn't keep the trembling from her voice. The pain was too fresh, the wounds too deep. Maryn was petrified to hope again. To believe again. "Where *am* I?" she demanded. "Is this room part of the prison? Are you really here...is *this real* or just part of another cruel nightmare? Oh, *God*! I can't take another moment of this torment. Please, tell me what is happening!" she pleaded chokingly.

"It's *real*!" Thomas answered quickly, trying hard to smile with quivering lips, tears pouring down his face. "You're out of jail and never going back!" he exclaimed, before pulling her to his chest and burying his face in her neck. "I'm so sorry, Maryn!"

Her entire body trembled as he held her. She wanted nothing more than to melt against him but being deceived again would be too devastating.

"*Why* Thomas?" she asked, pulling away from his embrace, her throat now so tight she almost couldn't get the words out. "You *abandoned* me…you testified *against* me!"

"I didn't know what else to do…there was no other way!" he answered, his eyes pleading.

"You took my *babies*!" Maryn interrupted agonizingly, shoving him further away. "*Where* are my *babies*?" she demanded.

She threw the covers off and tried to rise from the bed. "I can't stay here. I've got to find them!"

Thomas quickly took her face in his hands and brushed at her tears with his thumbs. "They're *here*, honey!" he rushed to explain. "They're *safe,* waiting in a room just down the hall. I needed you to wake up and talk to you about everything before I brought them in…"

The door of the room burst open.

"Mamma!" the girls screamed in unison.

With the force of a tidal wave behind their love, Lily and Pearl ran into her waiting arms. Time ceased to matter in that moment. Hugs and kisses, tears and giggles, silly chatter and whispered words of love filled the room. Each declaration of love, every smile, every embrace, were like tender blossoms coming together to form bouquets of joy and hope, filling the air with the heady fragrance of thanksgiving.

"Pinch me," Maryn whispered to Lily over the top of Pearl's silken head. "I want to know that you're really here with me. This just *can't* be a dream," she said breathlessly, achingly.

"No Mamma," Lily answered firmly, shaking her head. "I don't want to hurt you. Don't worry, Pearly and me are here to stay. Daddy said you are never leaving again and that you're all better now, right? Well, 'cept for the owies on your face…*right?*"

At her declaration, Maryn's heart ached with sincere hope that Lily was right, but she couldn't guarantee her sweet daughter anything just yet. She gave Lily a wobbly smile and said, "Oh Lily, you're right, my heart will *always* be with you and Pearl."

Pearl suddenly scrambled from the bed, only to return just seconds later with a toy doctor's kit she'd received for Christmas. Sporting plastic glasses, a stethoscope around her neck, and holding an empty tube of antibiotic ointment, she climbed on the bed and declared, "I'm gonna fix your owies wight now!" Then, with her face whisper-close to Maryn's, she pretended to smear the ointment on her tear-streaked face.

Maryn drank in every detail of Pearl's sweet face. Once again, she thanked God that her breathtakingly beautiful girls were healthy.

They were dressed in billowy cotton dresses—Lily's was pink, Pearl's violet. Someone had neatly French-braided their silken hair and tied the ends with matching ribbons. But it was the beauty inside them that tugged at her heart and filled her entire being with a love so intense she didn't think she could take another breath. She had no doubt that she would simply quit breathing if she were to ever lose them again.

As much as she never wanted to cry again, tears spilled from her eyes.

"There she goes again, Daddy," Lily offered with a chuckle, grabbing several tissues from the box that Thomas held out to her. Gingerly and sweetly, Lily dabbed at her mother's eyes and still-swollen cheek and lips.

The oversized toy glasses slid to the tip of Pearl's nose, making her look comical and adorable at the same time. "Looks like Doc Pearly is gonna hafta find some med'sin for your leaky eyes, Mamma," she declared confidently.

"You two are all I need to feel better," Maryn answered with a genuine smile.

Thomas stood by in silence. She could feel him intently watching, but she still couldn't really look at him. Too many questions remained unanswered. She needed time. Time to sort everything out. She was certain the wellspring of love she'd always had for him was still there, but the vessel from which she could draw from it and be refreshed was full of holes. Her heart was battered with wounds of pain, disillusionment, abandonment, and betrayal.

It was as if Thomas could read her thoughts. "Girls, Mommy needs a little more rest, and I am sure that Sister Louisa must be looking for you."

"No!" they cried in unison, Pearl wrapping her skinny arms around Maryn's neck.

"Daddy," Lily protested, "can't Pearly and me just lay with Momma while she rests?"

"Yeah, we'll be *super-duper, 'specially* quiet," Pearl added, nodding enthusiastically.

Maryn's heart swelled with love at their determination, yet their insecurity crushed her just the same. They should never have been subjected to the trial they'd just endured; she wondered what the long-term effects would be. Still, she also knew there was no way to get around having a serious conversation with Thomas. There could be no real healing of their family until she was sure of his motives, sure he wasn't deceiving her again.

As if on cue, a fresh-faced nun in full habit appeared at the door. "You little rascals tricked me," she said, laughing. "Come now, let's give your Mamma some time to rest. How about you girls help me fix her something to eat? We'll make something special for both of you too. How does that sound?"

The girls' eyes lit up briefly, but then focused on Maryn. It was clear they were filled with uncertainty.

"We haven't met before," Maryn said, holding her hand out to Sister Louisa.

Louisa took Maryn's hand and pressed her palm against her cheek. "The Lord has heard our prayers. You are alive and safe, and with your children once again," she offered sincerely, pulling Maryn into her embrace.

Maryn felt the woman's genuineness and love clear down to her toes. Though Louisa was younger, her embrace was that of a mother. A friend. An ally. A sister in Christ.

When the embrace ended, Pearl, still wearing the comical glasses on the end of her nose, held up a pair of plastic scissors and a tiny strip of gauze. She turned to Sister Louisa and declared, "Mamma's got leaky eyeballs. I'm gonna hafta do alotta work on fixin' 'em."

She then turned back to Maryn and asked, "Do ya think you can handle that, Mamma?"

Maryn burst out laughing and pulled Pearl into her arms, sure she was experiencing a tiny, but sweet, glimpse of heaven. "Oh my sweet Pearly...you are definitely a rare gem."

"Jim? Who's *Jim*?" she asked, making a face. "I'm your Pearly, silly! Your head bump must be makin' you kinda mixed up."

"Okay, Doc Pearly," Thomas interjected affectionately, "you and your sister go along with Sister Louisa now. Mommy and I need to talk about plans for our family. We're going to get to have some fun just as soon as she feels stronger."

The girls looked at Maryn, and she reluctantly nodded. "It won't take long, and you'll be right back here with me again. Be good girls and help Sister in the kitchen...I'm hungry!" she added, fibbing. She was feeling many emotions, but hunger wasn't one of them. Her stomach was in knots.

After the girls said their goodbyes and scurried from the room, silence immediately filled the space. It was just two of them now, but the room felt smaller somehow.

Maryn was grateful someone had changed her from the prison garb into a pair of gray running pants and a plain, long-sleeved, navy t-shirt. Even so, she felt self-conscience of her dirty hair and haggard appearance. Her heart was beating wildly to have Thomas so close. The love she'd had for him was still there, but the pain of his rejection cast a shadow of doubt that also remained.

To appear more confident than she was feeling, she squared her shoulders, locked eyes with Thomas, and said, "I risked everything because I knew the truth. I'm not going to be taken in by anything but the truth now...so you better start talking."

Chapter 39

"I don't really know where to begin," Thomas admitted, pulling the simple wooden chair up next to the bed. "I'll start by telling you that you are in the convent of the Sisters of the Immaculate Heart, located in a small village just outside Iguape, Brazil. We'll be staying here for the time being, anyway."

"*Brazil*?!" Maryn exclaimed, her eyes searching his face for any hint of teasing or duplicity. There was none.

For the first time, she noticed the deep lines around his mouth, the puffiness and dark circles under his eyes. There was a weariness in them she had never seen before—not even when he worked double-shifts. The realization caused a tiny crack in the wall she'd built around her heart.

"Yes, *Brazil*," he repeated.

"But how can I be in Brazil when I was just in jail? What day is it? How long have I been here? How would I have been able to board a plane? How did you plan all of this in so short a time?"

Hesitantly, he reached over to take her hand but then pulled back, when she quickly folded her hands and put them in her lap.

"I didn't," he went on, as if he didn't notice. "I've been planning for this for more than six months now."

"That's *impossible!*" she interrupted, "You aren't making any sense. I was just in jail, *remember*?! You *chose* to testify against me!"

His eyes misted. "Babe, that was the hardest thing I've ever had to do in my life...*believe* me."

The emotion in his voice and in his expression helped to rein in her indignation, but Maryn still felt the sting of his betrayal. He seemed a near stranger.

"It's *true*. Actually, this journey started even before then...when Pearl had her twenty-four-month shots and she spiked such a high fever—I know you remember."

"Of *course,* I remember! It was *awful*. I had to bathe her in tepid water to keep the fever down. I'll never forget how she shivered and begged me to let her get out."

"Well, you weren't the only one who noticed. After that, I started wondering about whether the vaccines were all they were cracked up to be. I didn't share all my concerns with you because I didn't even know if my worries were even legit at first. I mean, you're a nurse—you work alongside doctors in a country that's supposed to be on the cutting edge of healthcare. I figured that you of all people would *know* if the vaccinations were dangerous for children, and you might even be a little insulted if I questioned them."

He had Maryn's full attention now. Her heart dropped to the bottom of her stomach at the reminder.

As if he sensed what she was thinking, Thomas quickly added, "I'm not blaming you! I'm just trying to explain my reluctance to fully believe anything I'd been worried about. I kept going back to the argument that, as a nurse, you would be aware of the risks versus the benefits...but then I realized that you had been taught by the same institutions that taught the doctors. If I was going to find anything out that would be unbiased, it would have to be on my own and outside of the normal perimeters."

Maryn nodded. "I can't tell you how many times I wondered about the vaccines—not so much before the girls were born, but afterward. An apprehensive feeling came over me each time I took the girls to get them, but there was nothing I could do about it. I told myself that the experts knew what was best—that it was all worth the risk...until I kept having the truth slap me in the face.

"Then, after the Lunatia vaccine began to cause so many issues, I really doubled down on my research. I didn't tell you I was withholding the shots because you would have been forced to make a choice to turn me in or be complicit with my breaking of the law."

Thomas slowly shook his head. "I knew you were torn, and I suspected you were researching, but I also figured it was best to let sleeping dogs lie. Then, just about the time I started to relax a little because the government studies came out touting new safety findings, a call came in on a possible infanticide. It was the second time that *month* that we were called to a home where an otherwise healthy baby had allegedly been found dead in their crib. The first was a two-month-old baby boy."

Maryn closed her eyes and swallowed hard before she looked up at him knowingly. "Poor baby! Did you suspect SIDS? It's been on the rise these past several decades."

Thomas nodded. "Yes. That was the final ruling from the physician on the baby boy—especially because of his age. On the other hand, the mother of the second baby said her four-month-old daughter had been extremely fussy because of the shots she'd gotten that day. The doctors had assured her the reaction was normal, but when the mother went in to get her the next morning, her little baby girl was blue. She'd died in her sleep."

Maryn shook her head sympathetically as he continued.

"As you know, we are trained to treat every case individually, never ruling out an accident or homicide, but after doing policework for so many years, you just start to *sense* when people are lying and when they're not. These parents seemed *very* legit. They followed all the SIDS precautions—non-smoking household, put their baby in the crib on her back, no record of substance abuse, no threat from poverty or related circumstances—it just didn't make sense, so we had to order an autopsy."

"Those poor parents…I can't imagine what they went through," Maryn bemoaned.

"Me either," Thomas answered sadly. "So, that same day, while I was eating my supper in the squad car, I started doing searches on Sudden Infant Death Syndrome and that's when I started to really suspect that the vaccinations could be a factor."

"Did you ever go back and ask the parents of the baby boy if he had been recently vaccinated?"

He nodded. "He'd had his shots the previous day."

"Dear God," Maryn whispered. "Do you realize how blessed we are that the girls are healthy?"

"Yes," he answered woefully, "and that's why I feel so terrible about not warning you to stop vaccinating them. The truth was there all along and I chose to ignore it."

It was hard not to immediately come to his defense, but she remained quiet and let him continue.

"I told myself that the two of us had good genes. I told myself that all the studies couldn't be wrong and that vaccines had been responsible for entire countries surviving," he explained glumly before he continued. "Vaccinations were a big part of your job and how you made a living, just like upholding the law was how I made mine. There seemed to be no way to compromise. I completely dropped the ball and decided to believe all the propaganda—because it was *easier*."

Maryn's eyes misted. She had wrestled with all of the same arguments. More than once she had talked to him about her fears, but he just seemed to shut down, much like she was doing now. In truth, the words just wouldn't come.

"Even after Pearl had her twenty-four-month shots and had that reaction," he went on, "she did seem to recover pretty quickly, so I tried to dismiss it all as hearsay and false rhetoric. I told myself that there had to be other influences, like genetics, pesticides, poor diet...you know, all that...up until the day you told me about the problem with the Lunatia."

Maryn eyes bore into him. "I want to believe you, but I'm still having a hard time with all of it. Why didn't you tell me any of this before? You *knew* how worried I was about the vaccinations! *Dammit, Thomas!* I was all *alone* in the battle...you wouldn't even *talk* about it."

"I *know!*" he lamented. "I'm *sorry!* I look back and it's even hard for *me* to understand!"

He sprang from the chair and began pacing. "From the minute I started looking into what was happening with the Lunatia, I kept uncovering more and more. You know that cops hear things that the rest of the public never gets wind of—like when homicides are called suicides and when someone's been paid off or has strong-armed the media to change the tone of reporting for political reasons.

Despite all the corruption, I've held onto the conviction that even though it's broken, our laws and judicial system are something we *must* fight to uphold. Yet, for these past months, I spent my days fully enforcing the law and fully preparing to break it at the same time!"

Maryn didn't miss the slight quiver in his voice. She could feel his angst, the conflicting turmoil he was battling. "Thomas...I"

"They're *killing* people, Maryn," he said flatly, his expression indicating that he clearly expected her to be shocked by the revelation.

"I *know*," she answered with great anguish. "I have heard this too...but w*ho* is doing the killing? Is it the pharmaceutical companies? They almost *have* to be involved...or is it the government?"

Thomas shrugged and shook his head. "I still don't know who's behind it all...but they are killing natural doctors, nurses, lab-techs, lawyers...Judge Burton."

Maryn gasped. "Judge Burton is *dead*?"

"Yes...two days ago. I didn't realize it was going to go this far, this fast, but whatever the hell they're trying to cover up must be monumental. He was shot in the head not even a day after he received the packet of information I sent him."

"What information?"

"Everything I had collected to date about the vaccines and about the death toll, including the fact that they altered David Adam's autopsy—which I sent to your lawyer.

Anyway...I'll show it all to you later, but for now, I want to make you understand...my intention was to tell you everything I knew and make plans *with* you to protect the girls. I waited because we needed to save as much as possible from both incomes to make a big change. Not to mention, as an officer of the law, I needed to make sure we were right and not just being idiotic anti-vaxers as we are so often called."

Maryn stayed quiet while he talked, but inside she marveled at what he was saying. Still, the pain was too fresh.

"Your arrest changed everything," Thomas continued. "The media was already speculating about whether you had uncovered something about the vaccines, so I had to act fast. I know I put you through hell, but I just didn't see any other way."

Just the mention of the ordeal caused Maryn to tremble again. Tears of anger and rejection kept her silent.

"My fury...the hate speech in court...all of it was to distance myself from you."

At his declaration, her heart sank yet again. He seemed to be talking out of both sides of his mouth. Maryn shook her head slowly, the pain building, spreading through her body.

"Maryn...believe me...I did it for *you*...for *us*. I figured that as long as you were going to be discredited and in prison, you were no threat. Otherwise, we were all potential threats. You know now that the corruption runs deep, and the more I learned, the more I was convinced that anyone with too much valid information would be seen as a threat. I had very few people I could trust, so I had to live the lie even at work, at least for the most part. When I heard Burton was murdered, I knew the time had come to get you out. As terrible as it was that you were beaten up that way, it actually helped us pull it off."

"Who's *us*?" she interjected, still wary. "Who told the authorities in the first place? Was it you?"

"No! I *swear*! I don't know who turned you in, and I didn't dare ask because I didn't want to send up any red flags to indicate I was anything but totally against your actions. If I were to guess, it could have happened because whoever is behind all this was detected hacking into the system to get information regarding David Adam's health records. If that happened, it's possible that the questions began at the top and made their way down to Carol, who felt she had no choice but to point a finger at you."

What he was saying made sense, but he still seemed a stranger. Her trust in him was tissue-paper thin.

"Maryn, there are actually many people helping us right now. It's a network scattered throughout the states and dozens of other countries. I know it seems hard to believe, but I'm not making this up. I was able to get you out of the country only with the help of this secret network."

Maryn stared back at him, her expression clearly showing her skepticism.

Thomas risked her rejection and reached out to take her hand. This time, she didn't pull it away. "Who is helping us?" she asked.

"The network is called S.I.G.H.T. It stands for Saving Individuals from Government Health Tyranny. Its members are doctors, nurses, parents, ex-pharmaceutical reps, scientists, researchers...they come from all walks of life. We are all helping each other any way we can. Lisa Parker is the only person on the force I confided in—I didn't want to tell my partner because if anything went wrong, he would be implicated as well."

"Is this the Lisa who used to work on drug stings with you?"

"Yes. She quit working in our department nearly a year ago, but before she was transferred, we had a serious conversation about the vaccine issue after she miscarried her first baby—I am sure you remember when that happened."

Maryn nodded. "Yes...poor thing. Did she ever get pregnant again?"

"No, not yet, anyway, but she is convinced that the DTAP immunization they insisted on giving her while she was pregnant was what killed her baby. Remember, she was 34 weeks along when the baby died."

"That's *terrible*! I believe it, Thomas. I have heard of more like her."

"Yeah, me too. She actually approached me when she heard about your arrest and asked to meet privately. That was when she told me about her own concerns and offered her support to help us any way she could. Our meeting turned out to be a bigger blessing than I could have imagined, because her husband works at the correctional facility—he was my one and only connection to you. His name is Mack."

"Mack?!" she exclaimed, her expression immediately filling with fear. "He was the one who drugged me!"

"I know, honey. I'm so sorry, but that was the only way we could get you transferred out of there. Mack did the cell check, drugged you, and then made the claim that he found you unconscious after the beating. That way we could transfer you to the hospital. From there, a physician who we'd been working with sent you to the coroners to have your death certificate signed."

"This seems too bizarre to be true…"

"I realize that, but every word of it *is* true, Maryn. I have been working with this network of people to expose the danger and help build your case for exoneration, but the killers are ruthless and again, the coverup runs very deep. Judge Burton must have told someone about the packet of information we sent to him, either that, or his office or phone was tapped. It's also possible that someone who works in his circles is involved."

The onslaught of information was too much for Maryn to absorb at once. The pain was too fresh. The betrayal, too recent.

As if he sensed her torment, Thomas rushed on. "I can't imagine what you went through, Mare. If I could have changed it somehow, I would have, but I felt powerless to intervene. I've spent most of my life upholding the law and defending the innocent, and yet there was nothing I could do to help you without hurting you more."

Thomas eyes glistened with unshed tears. With his voice thick with emotion, he added, "I can honestly say that *no one,* including myself, fully understands what you went through or how you suffered...there is probably only one thing on earth I could relate to your pain, but it wouldn't even come close to being as terrible as what you endured...and that would be the thought of you alone and devastated in prison...the way I felt knowing that you thought I'd betrayed you...the images of our family being picked off, one...by...one."

His voice cracked and tears spilled onto his cheeks.

Maryn's eyes pooled with tears. "You're telling the truth, aren't you?" she declared, rather than asked.

All Thomas could do was nod.

The hope buried deep inside Maryn that had diminished to a mere ember, reignited. But unlike a flame of fire that can both destroy and save, the flame of hope in God had saved her.

Maryn didn't give a single thought to her sore muscles, head wound, or past doubt, she simply reached out and pulled him into her arms. Their coming together was like a magnetic force. The intensity of their embrace, mingled with the past fear, disappointment, rejection, and unrequited longing, welded them together, bonding them together even stronger than before.

Two hearts, one love. Two parched souls, one fountain of hope. Tears of sorrow became rivers of solace, flowing together freely from an ocean of mercy and love.

A timid knock, quickly followed by a barrage of small-fisted knocks, broke the trance of their reunion.

The sound caused Maryn to give a hiccup of a giggle. "I never thought I would ever be happy to be interrupted while you are kissing me, but..."

Thomas cut off her explanation with another quick kiss before dabbing at her face with tissue. "I understand completely. We'll talk more later...please *forgive me.*"

Maryn nodded happily, but her eyes welled up again. "Please forgive *me.*"

Chapter 40

Amidst a spectacular orange and purple sunset, Gavin sat next to his father at the water's edge, watching the waves roll in. It was so good to see him again, to fish side by side, and soak in the sounds of nature around them. Briefly, he wondered why it had been so long since they had spent time fishing together, but then he remembered that their favorite spots had gotten overcrowded with tourists, vagrants, and litter—including broken beer bottles and used drug needles.

Now, the sand beneath his feet felt as soft as down. A gentle breeze rolled off the clean, crystal-blue water, the temperature was a perfect seventy-seven.

Joseph Steele gazed over at him with soulful, brown eyes. "Son, I'm very proud of the man you've become. You laid down your life for the sake of greater good. There is no greater love than this."

Gavin felt embraced by his father's voice, so strong yet gentle, like always. His smile had a way of making him believe that everything would work out in time.

Gavin returned the smile just as his mother brushed back the hair from his forehead, like she did when he was a boy. He hadn't even noticed her arrival until she caressed him. In the breath of a second, she reached out her arms to pull him so close it seemed their hearts were one, beating in perfect unison. Not even the sun could match the feeling of warmth that spread through his entire being.

The love he'd longed for all his life filled him. The peace that had so evaded him, now enveloped him.

"I'm home," he whispered. "I never want to be without you again."

"You will never be without Me. I am with you always."

Gavin looked up from his mother's embrace to see a man standing before him, and immediately fell to his knees in awestruck wonder. Like a child, he laid his head on the ground at the King's feet and whispered, "Lord, I am not worthy," as tears spilled from his eyes onto the sand.

"No greater love has any man than this, than to lay down his life," Jesus answered, bringing Gavin to his feet with His outstretched hand.

All at once, the water split in two. The right side remained as it had been just minutes ago—serene and breathtakingly beautiful, the rhythmic sounds of life encompassing them. In direct contrast, the left side of the divide was dreary; the foliage charred, the murky water, filled with floating debris.

Eduardo's bloated body suddenly surfaced. Judge Burton's body floated up alongside him. One by one, the water filled with thousands of corpses—both male and female of every age, every race. The vultures swirling overhead made themselves heard, but their cries sounded more like Maryn's tearful sobbing.

The sight of sweet Sophia sitting next to the filthy water's edge caused a tear to roll from Gavin's eye and make its way down his cheek. Sophie slowly turned toward him, her eyes void of all emotion and perception.

More tears came as a multitude of children filled the beach as far as his eyes could see. Gavin turned to Jesus. "You're asking me to return," he said knowingly.

"I am with you always, until the end of time."

Gavin turned to find his Mother there. Her beauty and the peace surrounding her was indescribable.

"Do whatever He tells you," she whispered, lovingly.

"Gavin...Gavin...I'm here."

The gentle voice was familiar, but muted, like it was coming from the bottom of a well.

Frustrated, Gavin knit his brow and worked with all his strength to lift his eyelids.

"Try and relax, Gavin. You've been through a lot."

The sound of her voice confused him. After several failed attempts, he finally opened his eyes to discover his ears had not deceived him.

He stared at her, long and hard, drinking in every aspect of the face he knew so well, before he whispered hoarsely, "I must be dreaming...I thought I just left Heaven."

Annie smiled. "No...you just finally woke up."

He stared at her again, noticing her sad expression, the moisture in her eyes.

Suddenly alarmed, he asked, "What time is it? Why are you here? Are the kids okay?"

He tried to sit up, but she gently pushed him back down, saying, "It's okay. The kids are *safe*...thank *God*."

"I'm so confused...are you sure Brenna and Lucas are safe? Where are they? I don't get it..."

"Yes, the kids are safe. You've been unconscious for almost a week, that's why you're confused," Annie offered with a smile.

He looked around the room. "A *week*? Where am I?"

"That's a long story..."

"Well, if you're here, I must be dying, so you better tell it to me quick."

Annie couldn't help but chuckle—his sense of humor was always a way to her heart.

"You're under a physician's care at a guarded, undisclosed location. The kids are here too."

"How...what...where?"

Annie chuckled. "I can't give you the details because I don't know everything. All I know is that your Uncle Wally pulled some strings to get you moved here for the recovery. He contacted me after he couldn't reach you, and before I knew what was happening, he showed up at my door to let me know that you had been shot and that something big was about to go down.

"He was insistent that I go with him and it was better if we all holed up together under military protection. His exact words were: You're going to be in the care of some of the bravest, most trusted men I know."

Gavin was still groggy. Slowly, he became aware of the bandage on his head. He vaguely remembered getting hit in the shoulder but had no idea what the bandage on his head was for.

"If the pain is bad, they can give you something," she offered. "It's going to take some time before you feel yourself again, but you'll get there."

She went on to explain how lucky he was that, so far, the area of his brain the doctors were most worried about was showing signs of full recovery.

Gavin was barely listening. He had to know the truth. The memories were flooding in faster than he could stop them, making his stomach lurch. He swallowed hard to keep his composure.

In order to ask the hard questions he dreaded most, he had to clear the emotion that was choking off his voice. "Sylvie...is she okay?"

"Yes. I just spoke to her minutes ago when she called to check on you."

Tears spilled from his eyes. "So, she and her kids are *safe*?" he asked, his eyes searching her face.

Seeing his tears made Annie blink back her own. "Yes. She told me to tell you she's glad to hear you're alive...and that she's still praying for you."

Gavin almost smiled but couldn't quite bring himself to it yet. "God, I hope so...I hope nothing happens to them."

The obvious depth of his turmoil prompted her to quickly explain, "The world thinks you are dead, Gavin. Apparently, when you shot the man holding the officer at gunpoint, someone else shot you in the head. You flatlined twice on the way to the hospital and the news got leaked to the media. From what I know, there was a neurosurgeon in triage waiting to examine you. He was the one who brought you back and determined that the bullet penetrated the outer left side of your skull and exited the back on the same side. The bullet was removed from your shoulder without any complications. The doc thinks it was the loss of so much blood that caused your heart to stop."

Gavin could only stare as his groggy mind tried to grasp everything she was saying.

"The next thing I know," Annie continued, "Wally's made some connections to get you—all of us transferred here. We left in the middle of the night. He thought it was best to let the media run with the story until everyone involved in the cover-up is named and arrested."

Gavin searched her face. "So, that must mean he sent out the information..."

She nodded. "Yes. That's why I assured you that Sylvie and her kids are safe. They are not a threat to anyone now because the whole dirty secret has literally exploded—twenty-four-hour coverage on most every network, every newspaper source. One thing we can always count on with the biased news media is that they can be bought...and this story is *profitable*."

Still stunned from all he'd been told, Gavin simply nodded. He was quiet for several seconds as he recalled different details of the nightmare. Suddenly, he remembered why his arms were filled with scabbed-over cuts.

The chase from the warehouse...the wreck in the squad car... Maryn!

The thought of her made his head throb. He wanted to ask whether the police had busted the warehouse but was absolutely petrified to ask if Maryn made it out alive. Still, he would never rest until he knew her fate.

"Annie...what happened to Maryn Pearce? Is she..."

He couldn't bring himself to finish.

Annie sucked in a breath and said sadly, "The media is reporting that she died from the beating she took while incarcerated."

"Oh *God!*" Gavin whispered hoarsely. "No...please God, no! I was trying to get to her on time..."

Annie took his hand. "Don't believe the worst just yet. Wally is trying to find out if the report is accurate. The people helping us may have intervened...maybe it was better for her if everyone believed she was dead, too."

Gavin wiped at his eyes. "I sure hope you're right...I feel so terrible that I didn't help her in time. She didn't deserve any of what was done to her."

With tears in her own eyes, Annie nodded. "I'm beginning to understand that. I'm seeing a lot of things differently these days."

"The man I shot...who was he? Is he dead?" Gavin interjected, avoiding her eyes. His confused expression indicated that his mind was racing and struggling to put together the series of events.

"It's being reported that he's dead. They are still withholding his identity, but say that the guy was a rogue, ex-marine who was being paid to take you out. Wally thinks it may take a while before we know if it's true, depending on how the government ends up spinning this whole thing."

"Who hired him?"

Annie shrugged. "I don't know if we'll ever know for sure, but according to Wally's sources, there's evidence he was hired by the CIA."

"Oh, and I'm *sure* they're taking full responsibility," Gavin answered sarcastically.

"Of course not. They are denying all knowledge of it. Their take is that this guy had PTSD and just went off the deep end."

"Yeah sure..." Gavin didn't finish his sentence. His face fell. Anxious lines around his mouth and eyes changed his entire expression.

"Gavin, you saved that officer's life," Annie quickly interjected proudly, "You're a *hero*."

Gavin shook his head and tried to get up, blurting, "Annie, if the CIA is involved, we are not safe on a military base. It's possible there were two assassins there that day—the one I shot and the one who shot me in the head—unless it was one of the cops, I guess. No matter what, the CIA is sure to find out where we are...we've got to get out of here."

She took both of his arms and eased him back down onto the bed. "It's okay, they won't find us. We are being guarded by military men, but this base is *different*...it's located in Argentina."

"*Argentina? What*? How..."

"You've been in a coma for a week, remember?" she offered with a smile. "There is a network of people all over the world helping to hide us."

"A network? What do you mean? Are you *sure* Brenna and Lucas are okay? Did you just say the kids are *here*...in Argentina?"

She smiled. "They sure are—in another room down the hallway, playing video games."

"What about school? Lucas is graduating soon...the kids are really *here...in Argentina*?" he asked, clearly struggling to make sense of all she'd revealed to him.

Annie patted his forearm and smiled. "*Yes*. They're out on funeral leave. The world thinks you're dead, *remember*? They'll be in just as soon as I let them know you are awake. Believe me, they are anxious to see you and are full of questions."

Gavin remained quiet for several moments before he said, "Well Wally better know what he's doing, or the world may just be proven right."

Chapter 41

"It's believed by some to be the greatest, most far-reaching scandal in the history of mankind, but is the Vaccine Warfare Scandal the bombshell it first appeared to be? Leading experts have come forward with evidence indicating that the massive explosion is about to fizzle."

The attractive female anchor on WNBC continued, "Despite the hundreds of thousands of anti-vaccination and human rights protestors marching across the nation, the lack of concrete evidence and solid, scientific documentation are helping to put out the fire that was ignited last week, leading many to believe the VWS was nothing more than a series of unfortunate events."

Laura Townes was hanging onto every word the news anchor was saying. As usual, the intrigue and shocking aspects of the VWS soon became the focus, quickly eclipsing the facts. But even after the latest coverage had ended, her broken heart pounded just as furiously as it had the first time her eyes connected with the picture of her husband and Eduardo Rojas shown on the evening news. Like the rest of the world, she also wondered at the chance of the two meeting, their deaths, just days apart. Her mind raced with potential explanations and suspicions she could no longer deny. Suspicions that only got stronger each time the VWS was discussed, which was nearly around the clock.

More than anything, Laura wished it would all go away so she could pretend she was certain her husband had died of a heart condition. How she wished she could simply carry on with her mourning. After more than three decades of marriage, she'd earned the right to mourn.

The thought of her four children and two precious grandchildren caused hot tears to spill onto her cheeks. If she were to come forward with information, they would suffer right along with her—maybe even more because of their age, the culture, and era in which they would grow up.

Still, she knew what she needed to do. There would be no rest for any of them—in this world or the next, if she withheld what she had suspected for years and was potentially confirmed through the breaking of the VWS and picture of her husband's meeting with Rojas.

Woodenly, she stood up and made her way into the bedroom. The crucifix above the chest of drawers reminded her of her ultimate mission and goal in life—a goal that had gotten buried by the shades of gray morality of the times and the security her chosen ignorance had provided.

As if seeing Him for the first time, she stared at Jesus' countenance as He hung there in complete humility and surrender to the Father's will. Rather than a symbolic work of art or, to some, a superstitious safety net of sorts, in that moment, His crucifixion became real to her. She could almost smell the blood that poured from His wounds, almost hear His ragged, painful breathing as He struggled to take each breath.

Laura fell to her knees and sobbed long and hard. There would be no turning back once she picked up her cross and exposed the truth she believed would surface from her discovery.

I am the way, the Truth, and the Life. No one comes to the Father, except through Me.

The scripture rose up inside her. She wondered at her ability to trust God and move forward. She was no saint. She'd lived her life trying to do the right thing, but like most, she had looked the other way too often and had fallen way short of who she had aspired to be.

The thought of her kids and grandchildren following in her or Roger's footsteps spurred her forward.

She got up, dried her eyes, and blew her nose. Resolutely, she crossed the room to a large, framed picture of their family standing in front of the White House.

Mentally, she did a quick calculation to conclude that the picture had been taken more than fifteen years ago. Their oldest son would have been nineteen, her youngest daughter, just six.

Roger's smile was still genuine then.

The truth nearly made her knees buckle. Still, she had avoided knowing the truth long enough. It was time to act.

Reaching up with both hands, she lifted the heavy picture from its brackets and laid it on the bed. The keypad on the wall safe seemed to stare back at her, as if to say: *This is the point of no return.*

Her hand shook as she reached into her pocket and pulled out the letter that had been delivered by registered mail the day after Roger passed away. Her mind flashed back to the exact moment that she still remembered so vividly...

Hoping to somehow feel a connection with Roger, she had hastily ripped open the envelope. Seeing his hand-writing so soon after his death felt like nothing short of a gift. Her eyes drank in each word.

Within just moments, however, an intense fear she'd never known before prevented her from continuing. Somehow, in the depth of her soul, she knew that what she would find in his words would tear their lives asunder, and she wasn't ready for any of it. She immediately shoved the letter back into the envelope...

Now, in light of the VWS, she could no longer ignore her husband's attempt to atone for his sins from the grave.

Resolutely, Laura smoothed the wrinkled page as best she could. God willing, this time she would read it to the end.

January 23, 2025

My Dearest Laura,

I asked our lawyer to deliver this to you in the case of my untimely death. If you are reading this letter, it means that I have been given the punishment I wholly deserve.

First of all, know that I love you. My love for you has always been real. Never doubt that. You, our children, and grandkids are the greatest gifts I've ever been given. It's a shame that I may be realizing it too late in the game. I am going to do my best to right the wrongs I have been involved in, but if I die before I get the chance, I will need you to do what I was unable to do—tell the truth.

In the safe behind the picture in our room are the documents I want you to mail to Jerrod Browden at CWTN, William Green of CBN, Governor Lynn Danson of Iowa, and Senator Marcus Pritmer of Kansas. The collective efforts of these good people will not be ignored by the media and the exposure to different political parties will ensure that they will not be ignored by the government or the media.

To say I'm ashamed of myself isn't sufficient. I've fallen so far. Swept up in the greed and power that came with my position, I have put lives in jeopardy and am responsible for the death of many because of my cowardice and silence.

You will find the rest of what you need to know in the envelope inside the safe, along with the documents I spoke of.

The code is: 10061991.

I love you, Laura. I'm so sorry. I love you all.

Roger

Laura's fingers were ice-cold as she punched in the numbers on the key panel. A single tear rolled down her cheek at the realization he'd used their wedding date for the code.

Just moments later, she was sifting through the contents of the safe, which included a handgun, four thick envelopes filled with documents and what appeared to be research studies that would take literally hours to read. Lastly, an envelope with her name on it stared up at her.

She crossed to the bed and sat down. Inside was a flash drive and a typed letter several pages long. The signature on the last page was Roger's. She'd recognize it anywhere.

My Sweet Laura,

I am so sorry for all you are going through—and for what you will endure with the revelations I am about to make. My intention was to do all I could to right things before I told you. I sincerely hoped that the good that would surface from my admission of truth would outweigh the injuries I've caused, but if you're reading this, it's game over for me. Still, you deserve an explanation. The kids deserve one. The country and the victims deserve one.

Laura put the letter down and grabbed a tissue. She blew her nose and looked around the room. All that had been so familiar to her seemed to be a lie. Life as she knew it was slipping through her fingers like sand. The innocent faces of her once-happy family stared back at her. Above their picture, the door to the safe hung open, much like an open mouth that mocked her for being completely oblivious to all that had been going on under her nose.

The gravity of Roger's words shook her to the core. It was obvious that whatever he'd done was something bigger than she could have imagined. She'd suspected he was involved in shady behavior for years. Initially, there was money missing from their bank accounts. Credit cards were taken out in his name only. His explanations were enough to put her mind at ease. Then the money seemed to magically reappear, and their lifestyle was improved dramatically.

She'd told herself that she was imagining things—that he was too good of a man to be pulled into dirty dealings. The platform he always campaigned on was politics with integrity. In that moment, Laura wondered if she ever really knew him at all.

A battle for survival of her family, her body, and soul was being waged within her. If she continued reading, there would be no turning back. She'd already come to grips with the reality that her family would suffer because of whatever Roger had done, but the temptation to shove it all back inside the safe and walk away was powerful.

Serious doubts surfaced, quickly colliding with increasing anxiety. Laura wondered whether her home would be taken from her. She wondered at her ability to endure the public outcry, the news-media, the loss of friends and respect in the community and parish. Most painful of all was the thought of her family and how the paparazzi would torment them all once the truth was out.

Images of her precious grandchildren having to be ushered into the car or into school to prevent them from being hounded for comments, or ridiculed for what their grandfather had done, caused her anguish that was more severe than learning that Roger was dead.

As the minutes passed, however, her pain slowly began to be replaced with hot, resentful anger. Her entire body trembled at the injustice of what had been thrust upon her, their children and innocent grandchildren.

Laura was suddenly sure of what was right and just. She would do what her husband had failed to do—protect their family.

She furiously stuffed the letter back inside the envelope and crossed to the safe. Placing the letter inside, she shut the door, and carefully rehung the picture.

And then she walked away.

Chapter 42

Gia Stark's gait was purposeful as she strode through Ministro Pistarini International Airport, located approximately fourteen miles from Buenos Aires, Argentina. Though her flight had been delayed because of a fuel issue, she would still have ample time to complete the next leg of the journey, which would bring her within a few miles of her target destination and completed mission.

While making her way to connect with the pilot who would take her the rest of the way, her phone buzzed. She couldn't help but smile. It was a message from Ronan, her fiancé and fellow-operative, letting her know that he had just landed in Brazil.

The news greatly relieved her. One last assignment and they would be free to settle down and enjoy life in Switzerland—a life they'd only dreamed of until they were offered this high-risk assignment.

Knowing that Ronan had landed safely gave her a confidence she could only describe as impenetrable. Together, they were serving their country and saving countless lives in the process. Pride rose up inside her, helping to squelch any reservations she'd initially had in carrying out the assignment.

They both understood their mission. Both knew the gravity of the consequences should they fail. There was zero room for error.

We'll do what needs to be done...even when it's hard...that's why we will get to live the rest of our lives in comfort.

The vision of their just reward helped confirm that she was doing the right thing in carrying out the targeted termination.

Lives are at stake. The continuation of the world as we know it is at stake. Ronan and I cannot fail.

The pilot's name was unknown to her, but their mutual mission was confirmed with the exchange of the pre-determined dialogue. "Everything's ready for take-off," he offered, in heavily-accented English.

"And I'm ready to land," Gia responded, as she slipped into the passenger seat of the private plane that would take her to the appointed destination.

As fate would have it, one life would end, but two lives would begin anew. It was only a matter of hours now.

"We *won't* fail," she affirmed aloud before closing her eyes to rest.

*****

No one gave the old man with a cane a second glance as he made his way through the busy São Paulo–Guarulhos International airport. Not a head turned his way, as he caught a cab to the hotel booked under his alias.

Once inside his room, relief washed over Special Agent Ronan, but was quickly replaced by a sense of urgency when Gia texted back to inform him that she had also landed. His heartbeat quickened at the thought of her safety. She was a pro, but he still worried. No assignment was without risk, and there were always variables.

Still, the knowledge that they were both one step closer to completing the assignment which would propel them forward into another life and country, both excited him and made him anxious, simultaneously. Staying focused on every detail was imperative. The plan had been calculated with precision; there was no room for mistakes.

Once his clothing, makeup, and hairpiece was removed, he showered and prepared his skin for the reapplication of tinting cream. Knowing it would take time to thoroughly dry before he dressed, he double-checked to make sure his 9mm pistol was fully loaded before placing it and the silencer at the bottom of the canvas bag he would carry with him.

He closed the bag and returned to the task of dressing for the mission. It was just a matter of time before the unpleasant task was carried out and he would be on his way to meet Gia.

*****

Dressed in hospital scrubs and a Padres ballcap, A.J. Brin scanned the space until his target for Phase I was in sight.

Like most everyone who passed him by, his focus was on his phone. He sauntered through the hospital parking garage as if he had all the time in the world. In reality, he was taking in every aspect of his surroundings.

He tilted his head back and vigorously rubbed his neck. The effort allowed him a quick glance up at the garage's camera. He was relieved to see that the lens had been shot out as planned.

According to his sources, the owner of the dark-blue mini-van, a nurse and mother of two, was working a twelve-hour shift and wouldn't notice it was missing for hours because a co-worker was in charge of picking up her school children.

With the government's security program at his disposal, A.J. used his phone to override the van's computer system. He disabled the alarm, unlocked the door, and just seconds later, drove away.

Twenty minutes later, he checked into a hotel room under an alias. Once in the room, he immediately began the tedious, but familiar, task of becoming a woman, which included arm, chest, and facial hair removal, followed by a full application of a facial mask, cosmetics, skin tint, colored contact lenses, and eyelashes.

Next, he stepped into a full-torso, padded, female bodysuit, pink scrubs, and sneakers. To complete his disguise, he donned a brown wig, secured a pony tail, and then pulled the ponytail through the back of a pink, *LA Dodger's Princess* cap. As usual, by the time he was finished, his own mother wouldn't recognize him, and neither would anyone else.

By the time A.J. drove to Mountain Glade Elementary, he was experiencing the nervous anticipation that always came with an assignment.

He took the opportunity to circle the building to check for any unexpected obstacles or potential issues and to locate Section D, parking space twelve, which would put him in the optimal operative position to carry out his mission. It was imperative that he secure perfect access to his Phase II target.

School was scheduled to end in less than two hours. Experience assured him that the wait would seem overly long and much too short at the same time.

More than ever, he relished the idea of having the task behind him. This would be the last assignment he'd accept. Unlike the years he worked in the Marine Force Recon, where he could mull over each task with his fellow comrades, his off-the-record work for the CIA was mostly carried out alone. He was more than ready to put this particular task behind him.

He always hated the killing—he especially hated this assignment. Years of experience had opened his eyes to the fact that things are rarely as they seem. Despite the intel he'd been given, the recent VWS coverage he'd been following in the news had left him with feelings of uncertainty. With each passing day, he began to wonder how much of it was truth and how much was a smokescreen. Either way, he was obligated to do his job; obligated to uphold the oath he'd taken to protect national security.

A.J. checked the timing mechanism on the explosive pack that would blow the van and anyone within a ten feet radius, to smithereens. He hated to have to carry out such an unpredictable mission at a school. It would be a miracle if only his target was killed. Still, he had no doubt that the specifics were chosen so that terrorism would be blamed.

He pushed away the imaginings that came to mind, reminding himself of what he'd been taught so often: Collateral damage was sometimes unavoidable and often necessary to preserve an outcome of greater good.

Having checked and rechecked every wire, he shoved the explosive devise under the passenger seat and headed to the nearest fill station for an iced tea and an overcooked hotdog.

Knowing it could be the last time he'd eat for a while, he chewed slowly, mindfully rehearsing each step of the plan one last time.

*****

Like a starving, lonely dog awaiting the arrival of his master, Danny Barra's whole body shook with anticipation of the high he would experience soon.

Though he was still feeling the effects of his medicinal meth, he lit up a joint and inhaled deeply. He could afford to treat himself—he'd be fixed for quite a while, soon.

As the drugs worked their magic, the hunger he felt earlier disappeared with his cares. Lying across a park bench just blocks from the meth treatment center, Danny felt euphoric, certain his bad luck had just turned around. He laughed aloud at his good fortune in having made such an epic connection with the new worker at the Medicinal Meth Outreach.

"The dude's been there," he declared aloud with a lazy smile. "And what a freakin' genius...workin' where the meth's free and the contacts can pull in big buys. What a *sweet* deal."

His phone went off. It was the text he was waiting for:

Reminder:
Your equipment is waiting in the alley at 8th & Jefferson.
Please return the equipment to this same location when your task has been completed.
Payment will be rendered upon completion.
Remember, our firm offers incentive bonuses.

Danny threw his head back and laughed again. "Freakin' *awesome*. The dude's got it all worked out, just like he said. I think I just may have found my new best friend."

Chapter 43

The near-empty glass slipped from her hand and shattered on the floor. Startled by the sound, Laura Townes woke to find an empty wine bottle in her lap. Grasping the bottle, she made several attempts to set it upright on the end-table beside her. After she'd finally managed the task, she rubbed her eyes and squinted to determine how far the glass shards had scattered on the Brazilian-cherry, hardwood floor.

She glanced over at the clock on the wall.

10:23

Wow...I sure didn't waste any time getting soused this morning. If I play my cards right, I can be drunk again by noon.

She laughed aloud for several seconds before her laughter turned to bitter tears. The pain was back. There was no subduing it. No amount of alcohol or prescription pain killers could numb it. No matter what she did or how far she ran from it, the pain followed her. Plagued her.

She startled at the buzzing of her phone on the table next to her, but she simply stared at it. Communication with most anyone had become something to avoid. It required looking people in the eye—a feat she could no longer accomplish.

The phone buzzed again. This time it was a text from her son, William.

Mom, I've been trying to reach you.
Charlie's in the hospital. His fever is really high
and he just had a seizure. Call me as soon as you can.

Laura's entire body trembled violently at the news. The weight of her silence pressed in on her.

Her mind flashed back to the past weekend's dinner they'd had together. Emily, her daughter-in-law, had mentioned her growing apprehension to giving Charlie the vaccinations he was due to have at his upcoming well-check.

William had reassured her by regurgitating the latest facts and figures about the dangers of postponing immunizations, while Laura remained as silent as a corpse.

Suddenly the words she'd tried to pretend she'd hadn't seen in Roger's letter haunted her. It was if they'd jumped off the page and were spinning about her, coming at her like arrows to pierce her heart, her mind, her soul.

I didn't warn them...even with all my suspicions and fears, I didn't utter a single word of warning to protect my own grandson. The Vaccine Warfare Scandal should have been the topic of our conversation. I should have told them that they should take a wait and see approach.

"I am a despicable *coward*," she mumbled brokenly.

Numbly, she rose from the chair and walked right through the trail of broken glass, giving no attention at all to the pain or the blood that now trickled from her feet.

Grabbing a glass from the cupboard and the half-empty bottle of scotch that Roger drank on occasion, she stumbled back to her bedroom.

With an almost full bottle of prescription sleeping pills in hand, she crawled up onto the bed and took a gulp of scotch. The hot liquid burned her throat and made her cough.

Her nose was running now, almost as profusely as the tears ran from her eyes. Despite her blurred vision, she watched the bright red spot under her feet grew grow larger on the bedspread. She hoped the bleeding would make her death quicker. The pain was too much. Her precious little Charlie was suffering because she was weak. A phony. A failure.

"Oh Charlie-muffin. Grammy is so sorry! Please forgive me!" she sobbed, trying desperately to open the pill bottle.

Her shaking made it awkward, painful. The pain worsened with each attempt; finally, she realized that she had cut her hand at some point. The blood dripping onto the bed matched the steady flow of tears dripping from her eyes.

Undeterred, Laura tried even harder, until at last the lid popped off, spilling the pills all over the bed and floor. She scrambled from the bed. On her hands and knees, she frantically began collecting them, as though they were her lifeline rather than her ticket to hell.

When she'd gathered what she believed was a sufficient amount, she closed her fist and rose to sit on the bed. It had been weeks since she had slept for more than an hour at a time, she was desperate for lasting sleep. More desperate to never wake up.

She tossed back a handful of pills and chased them down with the scotch. Immediately, she gagged and choked like she'd done previously. Some of the pills landed onto her lap and the bed, now rapidly dissolving because of the alcohol and her saliva.

But she was determined.

Laura poured more scotch into the glass and this time she took sips. Slowly but surely, she was able to get it down without choking. As she glanced up for one last look at her family's photograph, she knew she deserved every ounce of suffering she was enduring and more. Though her stomach was on fire, she kept drinking.

"Your parents are despicable creatures," she spat. "We *deserve* death and eternal punishment."

Her vision began to blur. She closed her eyes to shut out the smiling faces of those she loved the most, but immediately, Charlie's little cherubic face materialized.

"Oh God!" she cried, sobbing. "Take my life in exchange for his! He's just a baby! Just an innocent!"

Laura vomited over the side of the bed.

When her stomach had emptied, her eyes scanned the bed to find any remaining pills, so she could try again. The room was spinning, the bed seemed to be moving up and down. Still, she was able to find remnants of at least a half-dozen pills, so she quickly swallowed them and then lay back on the pillow.

The smell of vomit and blood filled the room.

She turned her head to look one last time at the crucifix on the wall. Jesus' eyes seemed to stare sadly back at her.

Laura shook her head slowly.

I'm sorry, Jesus...but I am a monster.

She closed her eyes to stop the tears. Darkness enveloped her this time. She was losing conscience. It would be over soon.

They will all be better off without me. The world will be better off without Roger and Laura Townes.

Chapter 44

Lily and Pearl sat as close as skin to Maryn as she read them, *The Box*—a story about a boy who is greatly surprised on his birthday, when his daddy comes home from military service.

She'd read it to them dozens of times since they'd been reunited; and without fail, each time, one or the other would remind her how happy they were that she "came back, just like the daddy in the story."

As upsetting as the declaration was for her to hear, it could never eclipse the joy and gratitude she felt at being reunited with her family. The peace she'd sought for so long was finally hers to enjoy, but in a much greater capacity than she could ever have imagined. Her girls were in her arms. Safe.

Thomas lay next to her on the beach, one of his arms wrapped protectively around her waist. With him close by, ever-watchful, guarding them in true officer fashion, Maryn found more and more moments of peace. In the nearly two months since their reunion, her physical and emotional wounds had faded to the point that, at times, she was able to completely put the memories from her mind—something she could never have imagined impossible.

They had settled into a simple flat not far from the convent. The property was owned by a successful American physician and member of S.I.G.H.T who had also helped get them out of the United States. His generous offer allowed them to stay until all real threats had been extinguished.

Thanks to exposure of Gavin Steele's information given to the media and congress, the S.I.G.H.T network was growing, both in numbers, and in the ability to empower citizens to speak out and petition for change. This was like salve for her wounded soul.

Knowing the world believed her dead and that Gavin and his family were also safe, helped her to relax while the purging of the government entities continued.

Under a large, blue and white umbrella, the girls giggled as they scrambled off Maryn's lap and repositioned themselves onto Thomas' lap for the next book. The sight of them together nearly took Maryn's breath away.

Thomas looked up and gave her a smile so peaceful it was as if he'd just declared, "All is right with the world."

Their eyes locked for several seconds until Pearl announced, "Daddy, we're ready to start!"

As was her habit, Maryn reached up to twist a strand of hair, to keep her emotions in check, but quickly realized the new length made it impossible. Instead, she tucked her mahogany colored hair back behind one ear and admired the equally short hairstyles and color on her daughters. The new cuts framed their tiny heart-shaped faces perfectly.

Already tanned from their time spent at the beach, Thomas' shaved head didn't diminish his good looks at all. In fact, his blue eyes seemed to stand out even more. It was so good to see him happy again. His smiles were genuine now. They came easily and were no longer followed by a slight knitting of his brow.

Despite the crowds around them, it felt as if they were alone—a complete and private entity of love and family. Though the temperature was a balmy eighty-seven degrees, Maryn snuggled closer to the three.

She bunched up her backpack and covered it with a folded towel. After placing it behind her head, she settled into a comfortable position on her back and slid her sunglasses from her head onto the bridge of her nose. The tint made the scene seem even more perfect, softening the harshness of the sun's brightness, deepening the water's blue color in the bay.

Her eyes grew heavy to the rhythmic sound of Thomas' voice as he read a silly rhyming book about "crocodiles and puppy smiles" for the second time.

Cozy and content, Maryn was just about to close her eyes, when an old man stumbled head first in the sand about ten yards from them. His cane, which he'd lost during the fall, had landed just outside of his reach.

Thomas was on his feet even before Maryn could sit up. She watched with pride as her beloved rushed to help.

*****

La Café Carmelita was brimming with boisterous conversation and laughter. Lost in the moment, Gavin watched Annie from across the table. The brilliant blue sky, laced with soft, white clouds that floated across the massive skylight overhead, still could not compare. Annie's beauty was timeless, her expression priceless, as she laughed and played a trivia game with Lucas and Brenna playing on Lucas' phone.

The scene was surreal, the emotions it invoked, raw and wholly authentic. His life and world had fallen apart, his family had been all but lost to him. His choices, both bad and good, had led him to death's door, yet the mercy of God sent him back to enjoy a life he didn't deserve. His heart nearly burst with love for the three.

"And that's why they call it grace."

Gavin could almost hear Sister Helena's voice. She must have used the phrase at least a dozen times after scraping him off the ground that fateful morning.

If the scene before him wasn't already enough to make him grin like a simpleton, the thought of Sister would have. Several weeks prior, he'd received word, via one of Wally's informants, that Sister was alive and well, back at the convent and "still doing her best to help make sure Heaven was overcrowded."

I owe her so much. She never gave up on me. God, please continue to protect her...and please protect and bless Sylvie.

Thoughts of Sylvie made his heart ache. It had taken him much too long to realize she was a friend and faithful ally, even when he was at his worst.

I hope Sylvie stays in touch with Sister Helena. She needs a faithful advocate to help her with those boys.

Thinking of her boys triggered a painful reminder that sobered him. Nothing yet had really changed regarding any kind of vaccination recall. Last Wally reported, the scenario back in the states was going down just the way he suspected it would.

First and foremost, America came to know the face of Jeremy Wood, the assailant Gavin had taken out while he was holding the officer hostage. Wood, an ex-marine, reportedly dishonorably discharged, was believed to have fired the gun that wounded him and killed Officer Mark Stanton, the officer who was transporting Gavin to jail. Of course, the media paraded Wood's picture across the airways at every opportunity and delved into every aspect of his "disturbed" and "violence-ridden" life.

Not surprisingly, the instant the Vaccine Warfare Scandal broke, Gavin's own status changed drastically. He went from being a modern-day saint for getting killed while intervening on the hostage situation, to being a disturbed, violent alcoholic, who was known mostly as a staunch defender of drug cartel members.

Having been caught with an illegal firearm, it was also rumored that Gavin was involved in gun-running activities, especially when the video of him in the elevator surfaced. The ultimate mission, of course, was to make him out to be a radical, so they only aired a few grainy seconds of him pointing the gun straight at Sylvie's blurred-out face.

With each day, the outrageous plot thickened to include speculation surrounding the assassination of Judge Burton. The story currently being peddled was that the drug cartel ordered the hit in retaliation for a drug and firearms deal gone bad involving Eduardo Rojas, which was also somehow tied to his shootout with the police, since he was Rojas' lawyer. Meanwhile, the incident with Wood and his connection to current FBI and CIA agents was downplayed until it was all but forgotten.

Public service announcements assuring parents that vaccinations were not only safe, but would keep their children from imminent death, increased dramatically. The government, in its usual big-talk and slow-action fashion, assured the American people that every aspect, including the deaths of so many doctors named in the VWS, would be thoroughly examined and allegations taken "very seriously."

Grim-faced politicians came out of the woodwork to assure the American voters that their parties' policies would ensure safety, accountability, and transparency between government agencies and pharmaceutical companies.

Gavin shook his head.

Yeah, and many of those same bastards are scrambling to cut a deal with the pharms and government agencies to sweep their involvement as far under the rug as possible—at least until elections are over, anyway.

I have a hard time believing that no one outside the government frauds has discovered the deeper truth about the Lunatia. If Maryn knew it, others know it too. I guess it's possible that they are still afraid of the fallout—and who could blame them. But if something irrefutable ever breaks, we'll be hearing the screaming all the way to Argentina.

Despite his good mood, the thought was sobering. It was sad to realize that consequences from the deep coverup may not be fully known to the public for years—if ever. The VWS came onto the scene like an iron-fisted warrior, landing beefy punches that dazed the public and government officials; but slowly, the warrior became weakened by the deceitful, low blows of mainstream media propaganda and general self-absorption of the culture; lastly, fear played a role.

Three powerful demons hard to defeat.

If Gavin had to bet, the real issue with the Lunatia would probably never surface. Eventually, the pharms would admit to "some issues" with the vaccine. Then, slowly but surely, "new and improved" Lunatia and other vaccines would gradually make their way onto the scene and the madness would begin again.

Unless those who know the truth come forward.

"Penny for your thoughts," Annie declared with a smile and thoughtful tilt of her head. She was looking at him the way she did when they first met, and it nearly took his breath away. Gone were the lines of uncertainty, pain, and disappointment that had framed her eyes and mouth.

Annie had been a rock for him. She never left his side for the entire duration of his medical treatment. Always encouraging, always positive. Without the alcohol to fuel tension, they fell back into the rapport they'd enjoyed early in their relationship. Their relationship deepened with the long hours of talking and through the endurance of painful physical therapy and frustrating occupational therapy sessions.

Between the head injury and extensive muscle damage to Gavin's shoulder, the control needed for simple tasks seemed near impossible at times. Their "second, first kiss" happened after Gavin succeeded in lifting his arm high enough to shave himself. It was Annie who spontaneously and gleefully kissed his lips with a loud smack when he finally accomplished it, but it was Gavin who pulled her close and kissed her passionately.

The physical and occupational therapy teams left the room, while years of pain and uncertainty were washed away with the embrace.

The minute the kiss ended, Gavin blurted, "Will you marry me...again?"

"We're still married in the eyes of God," Annie had replied breathlessly. "I never got my annulment because I never wanted the divorce in the first place. I never wanted anyone else...I just didn't know how to reach you."

Tears filled Gavin's eyes when he replied, "Annie...you were always the better and I was always the worse, but I still want to say my vows to you again...this time, I know what it takes to keep them...and that I can't do it without God's help."

Just days later, when it was determined that Gavin was physically able to make the move from Buenos Ares to secure an apartment in an unknown location, it was clear to all that the decision was monumental. If he accepted the recommended resettling, the family would either need to return home without him or make the journey with him. Lucas and Brenna could finish their studies via the internet, but their friends, their careers, their futures would be placed on hold—something Gavin didn't want or expect.

On the morning of his discharge from the hospital, when the three showed up to tell him they were all coming with him, it was a moment in time he would never, ever forget. His heart had nearly burst with love and gratitude.

Wally, now a sworn-in member of S.I.G.H.T, explained that due to intel indicating that the VWS investigations were stalling out, the city chosen was Puerto Madryn. Its remote location, beautiful beaches, and the whales visible from the shore during the summer months, made the adventure something they were all looking forward to.

Now, as Gavin sat enjoying a beautiful evening with his family, it all seemed like a dream. The city had not disappointed. Not only was his lovely wife by his side, but his children, who had only recently seemed more like strangers.

In the almost two months since the shooting, Brenna and Lucas had expressed their pride for his brave actions, but what they were most proud of was his sobriety. He was proud of that too. He hadn't had a single drop to drink and had no desire for one.

For the first time in more than a decade, Gavin felt alive—not just physically, but emotionally, spiritually.

Blessed.

The realization made his eyes shiny with tears of gratitude.

He gave Annie a trembling smile and said, "If I never live another minute on this earth, I want you to know how happy I am right now. We're a family. We love each other. That's all that matters to me."

With her own eyes glistening with tears, "Ditto," was Annie's only reply.

*****

Traffic Delay Ahead.

"Noooo!" Sylvie whined, after reading the flashing sign. Nervously, she stretched her neck to check the rearview mirror, praying silently that Clare had fallen asleep. The poor little girl had been extra-fussy all day, so the idea of her screaming while they were stuck in traffic set her teeth on edge.

She let out a sigh of relief to see the toddler was out like a light. "Thank God for that favor," she whispered, "she must be getting her two-year molars."

Along with her mother, Sylvie had been caring for Clare ever since Gavin's departure. They had also taken in a couple of extra infants whose parents were caught in the same predicament. Clare had been the only one up from her nap, so Sylvie took her along to give her mother a break.

While she waited, her thoughts turned to Gavin. Since his departure, he had wired money twice to her, via his uncle Wally—both to pay for her salary until he returned and for Clare's child care as he had promised.

His generosity made her smile, but it quickly faded. She still had absolutely no idea where he was and often found herself wondering when he and his family would be able to return, if ever. Despite his flaws, Gavin had been more of a father to her than her old man had ever been. Deep in her heart, though, she feared that things had changed permanently. Life had changed forever.

Sylvie missed Gavin. She also missed the excitement of her job. Even so, the way her boys responded to the extra attention she was giving them was more than worth it. She was able to spend time with them before and after school and was available for school activities. It was easier to stay calm and be more patient when instructing them to do their chores or helping with their homework. For the first time since they were born, she didn't feel guilty.

Admittedly, however, the days were challenging. She was already of the belief that her mother, Jana, was a saint on earth for all she'd put her through, but never more so than now. She had a certain way with her boys and all the kids they watched. Sylvie was learning to be patient right along with the little ones under Jana's instruction.

Moreover, it was very rewarding to know that she and her mother were potentially saving lives. Admittedly, there were times when the stress of wondering when someone would turn them into the state for providing childcare without a license weighed on their minds. It wasn't the effort of getting a license that was troubling, but rather, the blatant government overreach. The endless paperwork, rigorous house inspections, strict dietary guidelines, and proof of immunizations for every child, were sufficient reasons to avoid becoming licensed, but knowing that she, her mother, Kade, and Jack, would also be required to be fully-vaccinated, including the yearly flu shot and every vaccine on the market, was the nail in the licensure coffin.

"Geez, I hope something gives way soon," she whispered, mindlessly switching the radio station while they were at a complete standstill.

There's so much talk about introducing new legislation, but so far, nothing's been done...and every day they seem to produce a new study and excuse for why kids like Clare, Sam, and Sophia developed the lumps and the symptoms.

"Yeah, *right* it's a Hispanic gene mutation," she grumbled.

There were plenty of vaccine injuries before the Lunatia came onto the scene.

The thought caused her to glance back at Clare's cherubic face. She looked like a sleeping angel. Her rounded cheeks were slightly flushed. Her wispy brown hair fell across her forehead. Long, dark lashes fluttered against her cheeks.

She's so beautiful. No one would ever believe she was vaccine injured if they saw her right now.

Sylvie's throat grew thick with tears. So far, she knew of no cure to fix Clare's roaming eyes and inability to communicate.

Maybe the new doctor Chelsey talked to will be able to help detox the metals out of her system. He at least gave her a little hope.

She wiped her eyes with the back of her sleeve just as traffic began to inch forward.

I hope the boys won't be worried because I'm late. They're so clingy these days. I think they know more than they let on...

Her thoughts were interrupted as the movement came to a halt yet again, and the obnoxious honking ensued.

Hoping to keep Clare from waking, she quickly turned up the radio. She always hated being stuck in traffic but never more than when she was trying to get the boys picked up. A certain feeling, she could only describe as separation anxiety, always seemed to settle into her heart until she had the boys with her.

Well, at least Ricky will be with them...that should keep them preoccupied till I get there. Hopefully, they won't even notice the time, and Ricky will be happy to see his baby sister.

*****

Though the temperature was crisp, Sister Helena soaked up the cozy warmth of the midday sun that filled the garden. The visit from Gavin's Uncle Wally, several weeks prior, immediately came to mind, causing her thoughts and prayers to drift from Gavin and his family to Maryn and her family.

After he had sworn her to secrecy, Wally told her what he knew and what he didn't. The news that Gavin and Maryn were alive brought her immeasurable joy that couldn't be repressed, even with the news that it was possible they would never be able to return to the states. Still, as she prayed, she felt certain she would see them both again, even if it was in Heaven. In the meantime, her prayers for them and all involved in the breaking of the VWS, fervently continued.

Thanks to the "fiery furnace of death miracle," as she and Sister Joanna liked to call her astonishing recovery from the accident, her faith was stronger than ever. Knowing that God had faithfully answered her prayers had greatly expedited her healing and increased her confidence that real change would come in time.

Helena's ears perked up at the ringing of the visitor's bell. Normally, she would have felt a bit reluctant to leave the peaceful garden space, but she'd finished her prayers and sensed it was time to serve.

Sisters Joanna and Mary Frances were off helping to prepare the second-grade communicants to receive the Sacrament of Holy Eucharist this upcoming Sunday. The two novices were also away on retreat, so Helena hurried as quickly as possible to reach the door before the visitor departed.

She peered through the thick door's tiny window to see a disheveled young man staring back at her. His dark brown eyes couldn't hide the fact that his pupils were dilated.

Despite having been cautioned multiple times by the parish priest against allowing unannounced and unknown visitors into the convent, Sister threw open the door and exclaimed, "Hello there, young man! I'm Sister Helena. What can I do for you today?"

He offered her a quick, nervous smile, his discolored teeth giving further evidence to confirm he was a meth user.

"I'm looking for someone to talk to...can I come inside?" he asked.

Helena was torn. If he was an addict, it was possible he was there to rob her blind—or worse. Thoughts concerning her safety raced through her mind in the seconds he stood there, but he was small in stature. Skinny. He looked like he hadn't had a decent meal in weeks.

There was something about him that pierced her heart. Society had contributed to his plight, abandoned him by covering up and denying the root causes of addiction. The misguided compassion of many federal and state programs only served to prolong addictions and promote lack of human dignity that comes through healing and empowerment, rather than enablement. Knowing this made Helena feel more sympathy than fear.

This man needs me for something. If the Good Lord wants to call me home today, that's His business.

She waved him inside. "C'mon in. If you want to talk, I've got two good ears to listen."

Danny gave her a triumphant smile. "I won't keep you long, I promise."

Chapter 45

Laura, wake up. William is calling. Charlie needs you.
I can't.
He's crying. Wake up!
I'm a coward.
You're My beloved.
I'm not strong enough. I can't do it.
You can. I will help you.
Oh God...oh God...

"Oh God!" Laura cried out, before vomiting over the side of the bed once more. This time, the vomit was mostly saliva and bile, a result of her stomach's continued protest of the scotch, pills, and her breakfast of wine.

The phone on her nightstand buzzed. She didn't move. Though the bleeding of her feet and hand had stopped, she felt too sick to cry. Too miserable to do anything but lay there and exist.

The buzzing continued several times before sheer pride caused her to reach over and grab it. She didn't want anyone coming to find her just yet.

Seeing the number of times William had tried to call her immediately pierced her heart.

"Oh God, I'm a wretched human being," she wept. "I cannot do this to him. I can't."

She reached out a trembling finger and pushed the redial button.

William answered on the first ring. "Mom! Are you okay? We are worried sick about you!"

"Y-yes...I'm fine."

"You don't sound fine. Are you sure you're okay?"

"It's just a flu bug," she lied. The room was spinning. "How's Charlie?" she asked, trying hard to sound normal.

"A little better, thank God! His fever broke and he hasn't had another seizure since we got here."

Relief flooded Laura's being. Her chest literally ached. She was certain it was from the vomiting but also from her heart breaking into pieces at what she had put them through, and what she'd almost carried out. Truth was, she still had no desire to live.

"Mom...are you sure you're alright?" William asked again, his voice now trembling. "It sounds like you're crying. Don't worry...I think our Charlie-muffin's going to be just fine."

Laura burst into full-blown tears at the use of her pet name for him.

"Mom, it's going to be okay. We love you...do you want me to come over there?"

She looked up at the crucifix on the wall.

I am patient with you, not wanting anyone to perish, but desiring everyone to come to repentance.

Laura mustered every ounce of maternal strength she possessed to stop crying. She swallowed hard and answered, "No. Your place is with Emily and Charlie...and you know you're going to have to report this to VAERS, right?"

"Report what?"

"His vaccine reaction."

"Do you really think this is from the vaccine? C'mon, you're not really buying into all that are you?"

His voice sounded much more scared than convincing.

"Yes," she replied quietly, but firmly.

"He's had shots before, and this never happened. The doctor thought Charlie was probably just brewing a virus we didn't know about when he got his vaccine, so his fever might have been a little high. Sometimes kids just have seizures with high fevers."

Laura closed her eyes. A dozen thoughts raced through her mind in that moment. She wanted to believe Charlie's doctor in the worst way. She wanted it all to go away; yet there she lay, in her own blood and vomit, spared for a reason.

"Mom?"

"Yes?"

"They are probably going to dismiss Charlie soon. As long as his fever doesn't spike again, we'll be taking him home."

"Oh William, I'm so happy to hear that," she choked. "You have no idea..."

"Mom..."

"It's okay, William...don't worry about me." Her voice cracked.

She swallowed the lump of emotion in her throat and added, "You just take care of my Charlie-muffin...and tell him Grammy will love him forever and a day."

*****

You know my name, but I don't know yours," Sister Helena offered lightheartedly, as she ushered her guest into the visitor's center.

"Uh...Daniel...Danny," he answered nervously, looking around the room in every direction.

Sister smiled inwardly. She could tell he was uncomfortable. She'd come to discover that more people than not felt uncomfortable in spiritual settings. She supposed it was because they reminded them of unsettled thoughts about faith and their own mortality. On occasion, though, she'd welcome in a soul whose spirit was longing for peace, until their eyes fell upon the beautiful images of Christ, His Blessed Mother, and the saints, and they would suddenly feel a connection to God unlike ever before.

Danny appeared to fit in the first group. He was clearly agitated. "Would you like a glass of water or tea, Danny?" she asked, trying not to make him feel like he was being watched like a hawk.

"Uh...yeah...sure. I'm thirsty. *Very* thirsty."

His eyes darted back and forth anxiously.

"Okay, I'll be right back with some tea for you. Do you use anything in it? A little sugar maybe? I have some lemon too."

"Sugar. I like the white stuff," he answered, suddenly giving her a leering grin that unsettled her.

She squelched the nagging feeling and said, "The kitchen's just right around the corner. I'll be back in no time."

When she returned, Danny reached for the glass she offered him and drank like he'd just spent a week in the desert. He set the glass down on the table so abruptly, the sound startled her.

"Is there anyone else here?" he blurted suddenly, rising from the chair and crossing to the stand in front of the wall-length window displaying the garden area.

After giving the space a quick once over, he turned to face her. "I mean...I don't really want to talk unless it's private."

"Don't worry, no one will disturb us here in the visitor's center," she reassured, skirting his question. "Now, what can I do for you today?"

"Do you really believe there's a God and...a Heaven," he asked.

Sister melted inside. "Yes, Danny...I really do. I *know* there is...do you? What is it you believe?"

Danny didn't respond. Instead, a strange look came over his face.

Before Helena fully realized what was happening, he drew a gun from his pocket and aimed it directly at her head.

"Sorry Sister, I don't believe in God...but this way, if you're right, you'll get what you want most, and I'll get what I want most."

"Danny...no...you don't want to do this," Sister pleaded. "Put the gun way..."

The explosion of gunfire was the last thing Helena heard before she hit the ground.

*****

At approximately, fifteen minutes prior to dismissal time, A.J. Brin merged into the line of parent vehicles driving to Section D of Mountain Glade Elementary. It was a surprisingly slow-moving process, as every vehicle was required to pass through the scanning gate which would lift the heavy metal barrier and allow the registered vehicle to pass through. He held his breath and hoped the somewhat worn sticker on the windshield would scan without incident.

As he waited, his heart pounded within his chest. Despite the chilly temperature, he was sweating. He quickly turned off the heater.

Seeing the gate finally lift was a welcome sight but did little to calm his heart rate. It only meant that he was closer to mission accomplished. Closer to the killing.

Behind his oversized sunglasses, his eyes constantly scanned the area, checking for anything that would interfere with the plan or cause him to have to abort the mission.

Even before he'd pulled into the assigned parking space, he could see that his target had yet to arrive. Still, he was undeterred. It was just a matter of time. His mission was to detonate as soon as the subject was in position, and he would not falter. His taxi was scheduled to pick him up a block away at 3:17. His alternative escape plan was to continue walking for just under a quarter mile until he reached the QuickMart filling station, where a fellow operative would pick him up.

Either way, A.J. was certain the mission would go off like clock-work. That remained his focus. He couldn't think about the collateral damage. His job was to succeed.

In just ten minutes, he would exit the vehicle, walk through the throng of parents moving toward the entrance to greet their children, and deftly escape without notice. After it was all over, the security cameras would pick up his image walking away from the vehicle and report that the relative of a known terrorist was responsible. The facts wouldn't matter to most, including the terrorist groups, who would be happy to take credit.

A.J. turned on the radio and opened the latest shades of gray novel he found lying on the passenger seat and pretended to be completely absorbed in its drivel. He was more than anxious to be done and on his way.

*****

Gavin glanced at his watch. It had been more than forty-five minutes since the waitress had taken their order. In his drinking days, he would have already put away several drinks and would never have even noticed the wait; but despite his good mood, his stomach growled in protest.

As if his family heard it above the lively music and atmosphere, all eyes were suddenly on him.

"Man, I hope the food gets here soon," Lucas admitted. "I'm *starving.*"

"Me too," Brenna agreed, tipping the empty tortilla bowl and grabbing the last chip fragment. "The waitress didn't bring near enough of these to keep us waiting this long."

"It surely can't be too much longer," Annie offered, turning to look around for their server.

Gavin did the same, just in time to see an attractive woman headed their way. She was wearing a polo-type shirt that featured the restaurant's logo and looked like management material to him. The tray she was carrying was filled with food.

"Looks like maybe we're going to get something free," he said with a grin and a wink.

Sure enough, she stopped at their table and immediately began to apologize. "I am so sorry for the delay in your food. Your server went home sick, so of course we wanted to prepare fresh plates for you, and your ticket's on the house today."

"Oh...thank you..." Gavin began, as she hastily distributed their plates of food. She was so completely absorbed in who ordered what that he didn't get a chance to tell her that the free meal wasn't necessary.

His was the last plate on her tray. "And this must be yours," she offered cheerfully, placing his meal in front of him.

Her English was so perfect that Gavin was about to ask her where she was from, when she said, "Enjoy your meal, folks!"

"Thank you. I'm sure we will," Gavin answered with a smile.

"Whoops, my shoe's untied!" she blurted suddenly. "Don't mind me while I prevent a face plant," she said with a laugh, squatting down to tie her shoe.

"Ow!" Gavin exclaimed suddenly.

"What the matter?" Annie asked as she spooned pico de gallo onto her entree.

"It felt like something…bit my leg," he answered.

At the sound of his voice, Annie looked up from her task to find that his face had turned white.

"Honey…are you okay?"

"What's wrong, Dad?" Brenna asked nervously.

"He's passing out!" Lucas exclaimed, rushing from his side of the booth to get to his father.

"Somebody call an ambulance!" Annie shrieked, her eyes quickly scanning the room with the hope of getting the manager's help, but she seemed to have disappeared.

*****

Maryn watched as Thomas swiftly retrieved the man's cane from the sand and stretched out his other hand to help him up. Immediately, she breathed a sigh of relief to see the stranger rise to a standing position.

"Our Daddy is such a good Daddy," Lily declared admiringly as they watched the exchange.

"The bestest," Pearl agreed, vigorously nodding her head.

Maryn couldn't agree more. Thomas looked so handsome and masculine, yet his genuine smile and concern made him even more attractive.

"Look girls," Maryn said with a smile as she watched Thomas and the old man walking toward them. "It looks like we are going to be meeting someone new."

"I'm thinkin' maybe he's kinda old not new, Mamma. He's got a cane."

Maryn chuckled. "Some people use a cane because they have a hurt back or maybe a leg that isn't working right. But it's important that we are very kind to people who are older or struggling with an injury."

Lily looked at the two men approaching and immediately reached out to take her sister's hand. The protective gesture touched Maryn's heart. It was clear that their trial had taught them to be there for one another.

In an apparent attempt at discretion, Pearl cupped her mouth with her hand and whispered loudly to Lily, "We might hafta talk really loud in case he's got a lotta hairs comin' outta his ears like Walter."

Maryn couldn't help but laugh. A nostalgic longing for home swept over her. Pearl was talking about their neighbor, Walter. He enjoyed the girls' company so much that he made a gate in his back fence, so the girls could pass through whenever they needed to get their ball, visit his dog, or talk to him when he was out in his garden. Thinking of Walter was a reminder that there were still good people in the world.

"It's not the hair in Walter's ears that makes it hard for him to hear," Maryn quickly explained to the girls, "it's just because he's getting older."

Pearl nodded her head thoughtfully. "Ohhh...*gotcha*. How much longer are you gonna be able to hear good Mamma?"

Maryn laughed again. "Oh Pearly...you are so funny. God willing, I will be able to hear well for a *very* long time."

She nodded. "Mamma, do they make pink canes? I want a pink one when I get old... an' me an' Lily are gonna shave our ears if they get hairy...right Lily?"

Lily didn't get a chance to answer Pearl.

The deafening sound of gunfire exploded in their ears before they hit the ground.

Chapter 46

It all began many years back—with my addiction to cocaine. I always wondered if you sensed that I had some sort of addiction, but even once I'd kicked the habit, I was never man enough to tell you the truth. If this comes as shock to you, I sincerely apologize, but unfortunately, my addiction would be the catalyst for even more scandalous behavior.

Laura Townes wiped at her eyes and nodded her head. "Yes…I wondered. I just didn't know what exactly it was," she whispered woefully.

Speculating at the extent of the scandalous behavior to be revealed, she felt the temptation to bolt again. Instead, she grasped the crucifix in her hands ever tighter and continued reading.

The more cocaine I used, the more money I needed. I got to the point where I needed my own supplier and a way to fund my habit; otherwise, I would have been exposed to you, our children, my colleagues, and the whole country.

Just about this time, in my 3rd year in Congress, I was approached by a member of the FDA, a man named Larry Dowlin who told me he could really use my help in clearing the way for an experimental vaccination that would not only prevent the spread of a new and dangerous virus, but potentially save lives through a method never used before, called "tracking."

Obviously, I was intrigued and agreed to hear him out. Larry immediately set up a meeting that included Chuck Jones of the CDC, and Janet Spool, the CEO of Welprox Pharmaceuticals.

The Lunavirus had just made its way into the states. Jones and Dowlin made the case that Americans were in need of a vaccine to prevent the spread and potential loss of productivity due to sick leave and parents who would miss work to stay home with their children for the duration of the illness. Moreover, considering the controversy regarding whether the U.S. should finish the border wall or open borders completely, there was concern that the influx of unvaccinated migrants would dramatically increase risks to Americans via multiple health hazards.

The FDA and CDC wanted to provide full support to Welprox in developing a Lunavirus vaccine that could be added to the mandatory school schedule. This way, every child, especially those migrating into the country, would receive it. The bigger plan, however, was to develop a vaccine that contained a type of microchip—the smallest they'd ever manufactured, to help track the immigrants and to provide data for future reference.

I was assured that our country would be safer if the CIA, which was also fully-aware of the proposed tracking system, could locate and number every single immigrant in a matter of minutes, and that the microchip was completely safe. The kind of information made possible through this type of program would be crucial to health record keeping and give the CIA data they could share with law enforcement when the need arose to track and locate immigrants who were a threat to the citizens—those involved in drug running, terrorism, etc.

Admittedly, the prospect would prove to be a tricky and complicated venture. Secrecy was critical. We talked at length for nearly an hour until Jones and Dowlin suddenly excused themselves. It was then that Janet Spool told me that I was chosen to grease the wheels because of my reputation for objecting to the development of future vaccines from aborted fetal cells.

I basked in the compliment for all of five seconds before she added, "We see you as the perfect poster child for this project because of your pro-life efforts. Someone with your type of reputation would really help push the mission forward among your colleagues and greatly increase the vaccine's credibility with the news media outlets.

We are fully aware that you have a cocaine addiction. In exchange for your cooperation, we will help keep your secret from going public and compensate you generously."

Laura read the last paragraph several times over. It was almost incomprehensible to absorb the fact that Roger had been involved, to any degree, with such a questionable project.

No wonder he was so rattled at times. It was obvious that the tracking vaccination project was extremely unethical, or they wouldn't have stooped to blackmail.

"Jesus, help me get through this…I trust in You," she prayed aloud before turning to the next page.

Believe me when I say that I wanted to tell them to shove their shady program and their blackmail up their asses. I really did. But the kids were all doing so well in school, and William, especially, looked up to me so much that I just couldn't do it—that and the fact that I had an addiction to coke that was costing me a grand a day at times.

I told myself that maybe there was merit in the program. You know, how we've always talked about the need for immigration reform and securing of our country's borders. I told myself this was a way to track incoming people without making them feel singled-out or discriminated against. I told myself that honorable citizens had nothing to worry about.

I told myself a lot of things in those days. Mostly, I told myself that the truth would destroy our marriage and family, so I needed to just trust the validity of the program. I vowed to blow the whistle the minute I saw anything that looked remotely disturbing.

That was a lie. Just one of many, I am ashamed to admit.

It quickly became clear how imperative it was that the government entities involved promote the vaccination to the public at large, so the news features and public service announcements began immediately. Pictures of dying children lying beneath mosquito nets drew immediate attention, especially to parents. Then, once it was announced that the mosquitos carrying the Lunavirus, previously common mostly to South American countries, had begun to rapidly migrate to the U.S., parents were hoping for a vaccination. Soon, they began demanding one from their government leaders. Lunatia was suddenly in high demand.

PSA's using words like: high fever, chills, body-aches, and potential death from shock, made the writing of pending legislation that would add Lunatia to the vaccine schedule as quick and easy as snorting a line of coke in the bathroom of our own home.

As long as the deception made me feel better and helped the country, no one needed to know the full truth.

That's the lie of addiction. The lie of greed. The lie of corruption.

Laura put the pages down and squeezed her eyes shut, hoping the effort would blot out the image of her husband snorting cocaine in their home—possibly just a few feet from their bed, where she now sat reading his letter of confession.

The urge to cope with alcohol the same way he had used cocaine was powerful, almost paralyzing, at times. As shocking and disappointing as the revelations of Roger's actions were, the past weeks of her increased dependence on alcohol and sleeping pills gave her an unexpected compassion regarding the devastating stronghold of substance abuse.

"Only in God is my soul at rest," she affirmed over and over until the desire for "just one glass" of wine passed. She blew her nose and continued reading.

So, the addict I'd become became convinced that the preliminary trials would prove to be unsafe, and I wouldn't even have to deal with helping to push through the addition of Lunatia to the mandated schedule. This made perfect sense to my addicted soul every time I made another buy and every time I used.

The real problem began when I questioned Janet Spool about the results of the preliminary trials. She informed me that they had done a two-week study on mice, and since there appeared no issues with the vaccine, the FDA gave a preliminary clearance to manufacture the first batches and distribute them to pediatric clinics.

Of course, I was very nervous and appalled that such a short study was done on something that would impact so many and asked to read the reports. But Spool sidestepped my request by assuring me that the trials done were standard then backed me off by saying, "Don't worry, the first Lunatia vaccines won't even carry the tracking capabilities. We just want to test the Lunavirus and adjuvant reactions first and expect them to be much like any other vaccine."

When the first reports of complications came into VAERS, I became very worried. So much so, that I wanted to walk away. I knew that James and Charlie would be required to receive the vaccine once it was mandated, and I finally realized that if the testing on Lunatia was so grossly negligent, then the other vaccines had been approved much the same way. If I stay, I would be helping to push a product that was toxic from the get-go.

I wanted out—in the worst way, so the Lunatia became the deciding factor to not run for another term in congress, and what pushed me to seek treatment for my addiction.

I lied to you about attending that week-long vaccine conference in Switzerland before my term ended. I checked myself into one of the best detox hospitals available there. After I returned to the states, I went to confession, tried to attend daily Mass more, and continued professional counseling. I was willing to do anything to stay clean, so I could extricate myself from the promotion of the vaccine project. I was finally ready to admit to my sins.

The glitch with my plan was that the first Lunatia had already been recalled because of complications, and there was a great deal of pressure being put on Welprox to reduce the high number of adverse reactions coming into VAERS. So, before I could even slow things down, the new and improved Lunatia, supposedly geared to each different ethnic group, came back on the market. As you can guess, this was nothing more than a ploy that would ensure that only those primarily of Hispanic descent would be receiving the tracking chips.

Moreover, an adult version of the Lunatia was contingent upon the success of the pediatric version. This would eventually lead to implantation of these chips into those with specific ethnic ancestries and eventually, could be used to target other "types" of people—those with mental illness, those on government programs, etc. Ultimately, though none would admit it, the goal was to have a way to control the population.

To achieve this objective along with the aim to be illness-free, we were experimenting on our most precious resource—our children.

And little did I know that my nightmare had just begun.

Just a day after I publicly announced my decision not to run for another term in congress, I was contacted by President Moore regarding the VSIPC.

I'll never forget how I felt when he asked me to head up the vaccine safety commission. It was as if he knew I was already fed up with his government entities, and the only way to keep me in the "club" was to appoint me—either that, or he was naïve as hell.

Of course, I should have and would have turned it down, but a little visit from a not-so-friendly CIA agent, Gerald Holt, gave me great pause. Holt strongly urged me to "do my patriotic duty and protect the security of our government policies."

There was no mistaking his implication that there would be "unfathomable and irreversible damage done to the nation, including, possibly, your family" if national security was compromised.

So I kept quiet.

Then yesterday, a man by the name of Eduardo Rojas contacted me. He had been one of my suppliers when I was using, so, initially, I thought he wanted to meet with me as part of the blackmail regarding my appointment to the VSIPC. I was dead wrong.

Rojas was there to plead the case of a family member—a little girl named Sophia, who had been irreparably damaged by the Lunatia vaccine. Sophia's brother would also be required to have the shot once it was mandatory.

Rojas showed me pictures of Sophia before and after her vaccine injury. It was clear that something terrible had gone wrong. Rojas also presented me with something even more frightening—a lengthy list of natural doctors and practitioners who were now dead. The number was astonishing. I knew in my bones that their deaths couldn't possibly be coincidental.

He showed me pictures of the lump on his Sophia's head. It seemed obvious to me that it had been caused from the tracking microchip, which, though smaller than a virus—around 15nm, was programmed to work by traveling through the bloodstream to the brain, where it would register and eventually dissolve. Obviously, little Sophia suffered ill effects from it. There was so little testing done on it, it's no small wonder she's not dead.

I was so rattled after Rojas' visit that I went to the VAERS site to see how many reports had come in since I'd last checked. Much to my shock, they were gone. Wiped clean.

The good news in this whole mess, is that, by the grace of God, I happened to take screen shots of the reports when I first got involved. It was my way of monitoring the improved safety as the project progressed.

After discovering the deletion of the VAERS reports, I knew that those with a vested interest were playing for keeps. I also knew it was only a matter of time until I was found out and realized they would never allow me to leave the project or position knowing what I did, so I breeched security and copied as much information as I could get my hands on.

The screenshots and everything I found are included in the documents and on the flash drive. This information must be made known to the American public. Our kids are slowly being poisoned.

Laura, there will be thousands, potentially millions, of people adversely affected by this vaccine. Not to mention, like the rest of the vaccines, we have no idea as to what harm will come when the Lunatia is added to the mandatory schedule.

So, now you know why you are reading this letter. More than likely, I have become another name added to the list. I can't redo what I've done in the past, but I beg your forgiveness, and beg even more for your cooperation in sending out the information I've left you.

The killing must stop. The deception must stop. The truth needs to be told. Generations have already suffered at the hands of big pharma and corrupt public servants. More will suffer than ever before if the truth remains hidden. If they get away with tainting this vaccination with the tracking, they will experiment further with population control and other unethical practices. I am absolutely certain of this.

Every citizen, endowed by our Creator, is guaranteed life, liberty and the pursuit of happiness. No one should be forced to put a foreign substance into his body—of any kind, or for any reason. This is not freedom! It is tyranny!

1 Corinthians 6:19-20 confirms that our bodies are not our own. We were created by God and Christ paid the price for us. We are to glorify God in our bodies, not destroy them. We have free will.

I realize that what I am asking you to do will cause your life to be turned upside down—even more than it already has been. But believe me when I say that you will be exposed to a much greater version of hell if this information fails to become public knowledge. Our world will become so filled with brain-damaged and genetically damaged people, that it will eventually self-destruct. The population will cease to replace itself. The youth will die or become demented before they ever reach old age. The elderly will die because they have no one to care for them because the younger generation is plagued with auto-immune diseases and neurological damage.

I'm trusting you because you are my good and sweet Laura, my wife, the amazing mother of my children and grandchildren. You are the only woman I have every loved, and the only woman I know, who is brave enough to do the right thing no matter what.

God will take care of you because He is on our side. He is Truth.

I love you, Laura. May God forgive me. May you forgive me.

Roger

Chapter 47

A.J. looked at his watch and then at his phone. Both read 3:10—time to exit the vehicle and move to the playground where he could mix in with the crowd of parents watching their preschool children at play while they waited for their older siblings.

Where is she? He groaned silently, careful to not use the target's name even in his thoughts. Feeling a sudden chill, he zipped the pink sweatshirt up a little higher.

With the detonation phone in one pocket and his cell phone in the other, he plugged in his earbuds and got out of the van, locking the doors behind him.

Casually, but purposefully, he walked between the cars, trying to appear as though he'd done it dozens of times before. By the time he reached the playground, it was 3:12. Like most parents waiting for the bell to ring, he appeared to be glued to his smart phone. Behind his glasses, he watched for a sign of his target; there were still many vehicles trickling in.

By 3:14, he'd walked around the play area and to the edge of Section C, where the youngest children would be picked up, all the while, keeping his eyes on the empty parking stall in Section D.

The minutes felt like hours until the bell rang at 3:15.

He hoped the target would arrive soon. It was easier to get away unnoticed in a crowd, and he was due to be picked up in less than three minutes. His back-up ride at the QuickMart would be gone in less than fifteen minutes.

The seed of worry that had sprouted earlier inside his gut had now blossomed into a full-fledged foreboding. Anxious seconds ticked steadily by, noisily resounding through his being.

At eighteen past three, pickup was well underway. The sounds of children's voices and slamming car doors filled the air. Still, there was no sign of his target.

My taxi will be gone soon.

Just five minutes after the bell, vehicles of all makes and models had successfully picked up their children and were on their way. Section D was emptying fast. The crowd of parents and younger children, who had passed the time on the playground, had all but disappeared. The thinning crowd gave him satisfaction in knowing that meant less chance of collateral damages, but still, he was on edge.

Something's gone wrong.

He checked his phone for a text giving him an abort code.

Nothing.

3:22

Seven minutes past the bell.

By now, his eyes were fixed so hard on the target area that his vision blurred. He blinked to clear them, and after he'd done so, a trio of boys materialized on the curb adjacent to where the detonation van was parked.

They appeared to be about six or seven, and like typical kids of their generation, in just seconds, they'd flung their backpacks off and huddled together to play a game on a tablet as they sat waiting.

Not more than about ten feet from them, the volunteer supervisor for the section chatted with a fellow-parent, completely oblivious to what the boys were doing or saying.

A.J. swallowed hard. He couldn't let his concern for the boys or the bystanders get in the way of his mission. They were collateral damage. Nothing more. Nothing less. Still, his entire body pulsed with apprehension. He checked for a text again.

No abort code.

Inwardly, he shook his head. Outwardly, he continued to appear enthralled with his phone screen while he waited for his child.

3:25

I have five minutes until my ride at QuickMart is gone. I don't think I can even get there in that time.

The last thing he wanted to do was to fail this last mission, but nothing felt right. His target had yet to show.

He watched the volunteer and the parent again, realizing that they appeared to be very agitated about something they were watching on the parent's phone screen.

With a flick of his thumb, A.J. tapped into a live newsfeed. Breaking News was flashing across the screen. He turned up the volume in his earbuds just as the target vehicle rolled through the gates.

Mission underway!

He grasped the detonation phone.

Wait! His conscience screamed. He watched the boys look up to see that their ride had arrived and wished he hadn't seen their faces. They were all so young. He wondered who the third kid was.

Collateral damage.

He punched in the nine-digit code sequence. The push of one last button would end of life of several—the total number of casualties would remain to be seen.

It'll be over for the boys quickly, he reminded himself, placating his conscience.

Subject's pulling in.

Three...two...one...zero!

*****

Huddled in the backseat of a taxi, Annie, Brenna, and Lucas clung to one another in helpless dismay and confusion. Despite being together as they rushed to the hospital to be with Gavin, they were each experiencing a profound sense of aloneness and defeat, as if the fateful news of his death had already come.

It was hard to focus on anything other than what had just occurred; nonetheless, they hung on in hope, fervently praying together that their family, which had only just reunited, would not be torn apart yet again.

If the shock of seeing Gavin collapse before their eyes wasn't enough to shake them, discovering that their first server was found dead in the restroom, was. Like with Gavin, there didn't appear to be a single visible bruise, wound, or mark on her to indicate the cause of her demise.

Annie blinked back the tears in her eyes. She needed to be strong for Brenna and Lucas. At last report, Gavin's heart was barely beating when he was loaded into the ambulance. Still, she clung to the same hope she tried her best to impart to her children.

It was almost impossible to believe that the incidents with Gavin and the server were unrelated—especially considering the fact that the woman who eventually brought them their food had vanished. None of the workers recalled seeing the woman they described as a member of the management team. A handful of patrons saw her, but not a single person could identify her.

Annie wondered if they would ever really feel safe again.

She glanced up at the taxi driver a few feet away from her and wondered if they were really being taken to the hospital. In truth, she was in a foreign country and something cynical had just happened to her husband and possibly, an innocent bystander.

The more she thought about it, the more she realized they were huddled together like sitting ducks. She forced the thought from her mind and silently prayed that God would protect them, protect Gavin, and reveal the evil culprits involved.

"Mom…mom!" Lucas interrupted her prayer. "Sorry, but you're going to want to see this—it's Dad!"

He handed her his phone. "This is a network from the states," he added, as a picture of Gavin appeared, followed by a picture of Maryn Pearce.

Annie's heart fell to her stomach. She wondered if it was somehow possible that the breaking news was to announce that Gavin, already thought to be dead, had just died.

Lucas quickly turned up the volume and the three listened intently.

"New and incriminating evidence regarding procedures and key players of the CDC, FDA, CIA and Welprox Pharmaceuticals has just surfaced. This evidence is believed to fully substantiate the circumstantial evidence that Gavin Steele put into the hands of authorities…"

Just hearing his name made Annie's eyes well up. It became increasingly hard to take a steady breath. Hard to hear anything but the pounding of her heart in her head.

"Mom...it's going to be okay," Brenna soothed, squeezing her hand.

"Shhh..." Lucas hushed. "Listen!"

"According to Governor Lynn Danson of Texas and Senator Marcus Pritmer of Kansas, Laura Townes, widow of the late Congressman Roger Townes, is said to have dropped an evidence bomb of nuclear-fallout proportions, via test-data, transcripts, bank accounts and safety deposit boxes, that will allegedly blow the Vaccine Warfare Scandal wide open. Danson and Pritmer were two of four recipients of the evidence along with Jerrod Browden of CWTN, and William Green of CBN, who just minutes ago confirmed that the evidence appears to be rock solid, and so damaging, there is almost zero chance for the reparation of the American people's trust.

"Included in the mountain of damaging evidence is a list of alleged homicide victims—mostly doctors, health enthusiasts, and other technicians who discovered the vaccine dangers and facts relating to the VWS coverup. According to Jerrod Browden of CWTN, details of the shared information will be made public soon, ensuring that an investigation into these deaths, including the recent murder of Judge Theodore Burton, will be forthcoming. The truth will be exposed no matter how grisly and complicated the revelations."

The taxi pulled up to the emergency room doors before Annie could even fully process what they'd just heard.

She paid the driver and the three rushed through the doors, each wondering in torment, if the breaking news had come just a little too late.

"If I never live another minute on this earth, I want you to know how happy I am right now. We're a family. We love each other. That's all that matters to me."

The words Gavin had spoken to her earlier now haunted her. Annie choked back a torrent of tears.

Oh God...did he say that to me because he somehow knew he would die soon? Did you tell him to say it?

"Hold on Gavin!" she pleaded aloud, as they hurried through the corridors. "Please…hold on!"

Chapter 48

A female police officer stood over Danny Barra's lifeless body while she called for backup and an ambulance.

Amidst the shattered glass from the garden's window, Sister Helena watched her go through the necessary precautionary procedures.

Though dazed, but still in awe at the force that had pushed her to the ground, Helena said a prayer for Danny. Clearly, it seemed that his life on earth was over. The bullet had hit him square in the chest. Still, she prayed for God's will to be done and for mercy on his soul. Suddenly, she wondered where Danny's mother was and how she would take the news. Several tears slipped from her eyes at the thought, causing her to pray for all those who loved Danny and would mourn his passing.

"Sister...I am Officer Lisa Parker," the officer explained, "Are you okay? May I help you get up?"

Still somewhat in shock, Helena stared at Lisa for several seconds before she answered. "I think so. I'm a little stiff, of course...but that's nothing new," she added as she took the officer's hand.

Once she was up, Lisa guided Helena to the sofa on the opposite end of the room where there was less glass scattered about.

"How about you sit here while we talk," Lisa suggested with a smile. "I want the EMT's to check you over just to make sure you're okay. That was quite a hit you took."

Puzzled, Sister Helena tilted her head to one side and asked, "What do you mean—hit? In my mind, I heard a voice warning me that Danny was going to shoot me no matter what I said. The voice warned me to get down, so I did. But I just have to know...where did you come from and how did you know Danny was here? Thank you for saving my life, by the way...you truly just saved my life!" she said tearfully, managing a shaky smile.

"I'd like to take all the credit, but I can't," Lisa admitted, smiling. "To be honest, I don't know if I'll ever be able to explain how I ended up here in time. I know for sure that I'll never get anyone to believe what I saw."

"I'll believe you," Sister answered firmly. "The Holy Spirit warned me that Danny was going to shoot me, yet I am alive. Tell me...I'll believe you."

Lisa's eyes grew shiny. "Years ago, when I worked for the Drug Enforcement Administration, I busted Danny Barra a handful of times. He would do his time but continued to use. Truth was, I hadn't given him a thought since I left—he's just one of many who never dry up and actually end up worse because of the failed rehabilitation system."

Sister nodded. "So many are using drugs, alcohol, and sex to fill the emptiness in their hearts that only Jesus can fill...but go on, I want to hear every detail."

Lisa nodded. "All during the night, I had dreamed of a shooting. I woke up sweating, my heart pounding, and so confused, because the shooting always happened in a beautiful place that I could only have described to be what I thought Heaven would look like."

Lisa then turned her head and gestured toward the garden. This isn't Heaven, but it's as close to Heaven as I have seen in this dismal city in a long time."

Sister nodded and smiled. "Go on," she coaxed.

"This morning, as I was getting ready to go to work, Danny's name popped into my head while I was in the shower—out of the blue, but it was like nothing I'd ever experienced. Like...his name was said inside of me...and *loudly*...like a shout."

"That was the Holy Spirit," Sister affirmed.

"I am unfamiliar with what you are saying, but I was certain, in that moment, that something must be up with Danny."

"But how did you know that he was *here*?" Sister asked, unable to contain herself. "You came from out of nowhere!"

"Yes and no. When I got to the precinct, I called one of my co-workers and asked about Danny. He informed me that Danny was still using and getting his meth from the city's meth outreach clinic. Normally, this wouldn't surprise me at all—except for the fact that within the hour, I received a tip from a fellow member of S.I.G.H.T."

"Sight?" Sister asked, "is that a police department?

Lisa shook her head. "No...S.I.G.H. T is an underground network of people working to save individuals from government health tyranny.

Sister's eyes widened. "A very worthy undertaking!" she exclaimed.

The sound of approaching sirens grew louder.

"We aren't going to be able to talk much longer," Lisa declared, "but I will quickly tell you that the tip I received was to check up on a man suspected to be involved with arranging assassinations on those who opposed the pharmaceutical industry.

S.I.G.H.T sources told me that the guy had taken a job as a volunteer at the meth outreach, so I did a drive by and then decided to park down the street from the clinic during my lunch hour to watch. I guess I hoped to maybe get a glimpse of him...but instead, Danny came walking out of the clinic, and that's when I followed him here."

Sister nodded. "I see. How did you know he wasn't just visiting an old nun for some counsel?" she asked.

"I saw him cock the gun before he rang the doorbell. Initially, I was going to come through the front door, but realized it might scare Danny into action...so that's why I scaled the garden wall and watched through the window. The rest is history."

Sister Helena shook her head in awe.

Two squad cars and an ambulance pulled up to the curb as Lisa looked at her and said, "I can fill in more details for you later, but let me tell you one last thing…you didn't fall to the ground…a big, powerful man with wings grabbed you by the waist and pulled you to the ground in the split second before Danny fired. With you out of the way, I was able to stop him from firing again."

Chapter 49

A.J. walked down the street as fast as his feet could carry him. It would take a series of miracles for him to get away without being caught, and he had long ago quit believing in miracles.

In a matter of minutes, entire networks of people would be searching high and low for him. To say the odds were greatly stacked against him was an understatement.

Still, he couldn't look back. He couldn't turn back the clock. What was done, was done.

He disappeared into the nearest neighborhood. Pretending to bend down to tie his shoe, he snapped off the back of his cell phone and scratched the inside so it couldn't be tracked. Next, he did the same with the disposable phone he'd used for the mission and then slipped it between the grates of the sewer drain at the curb.

On the next block over, he used the equipment from his bag to enter and hotwire a 2018 Ford truck. In just seconds, he was heading toward the freeway. His plan was to drive to the bay and dump the truck in the water and hotwire another.

With one quick motion, he pulled off his cap and wig, then peeled the silicone mask from his face and stripped off the fake eyelashes. Sweat was pouring down his face by the time he'd wiggled out of the pink jogging jacket and replaced it with a flannel shirt.

He used his teeth to remove the fake fingernails. Then, he pulled out a fistful of wipes from his bag and proceeded to remove every trace of makeup on his eyes and scrub at the dye on his arms and neck.

After the tedious task was finished, A.J. donned a pair of Raybans and an Oakland A's cap. From the waist up, he now looked like a middle-aged nobody, which was just what he wanted.

Traffic had slowed with the onset of rush hour, so he took advantage of the slower speed to wiggle out of the pink running shoes and jogging pants. Getting into his jeans was more of a challenge, but doable when traffic stopped altogether.

Behind the dark glasses, A.J. kept his eyes peeled for any signs of being followed or law enforcement. The apathy of the people in the cars around him became his ally. Each person had their own set of thoughts and concerns as they maneuvered through the rat race each day.

No one cares about who's sitting in the car next to them. Most just care about getting home...getting high...getting laid...getting rich.

The realization helped him push all worried thoughts from his mind, until a vision of the three little boys on the curb reminded him of what he'd done. His stomach did a somersault; his hands began to tremble.

Still, he couldn't allow himself to think about them, about his past, about anything but escape. The CIA would hire thugs to kill him when they found out. They wouldn't forgive his moment of hesitation or his decision to abort the mission.

They would come after him. They'd pursue him for the rest of his life. But as the vision of the three boys surfaced again, A.J. realized he was okay with dying for his decision.

He stared at his reflection in the mirror for several seconds and realized he meant it. His life had been lived to bring about honor and justice—without these, life would have no meaning, no real hope.

If I somehow make it through this and ever find out that my instincts were right...that I was sent to assassinate innocent people to protect some greedy pharmaceutical bastards and their corrupt government cronies...

"I'll find a way to expose every last one of them," he avowed.

Chapter 50

Thomas slowly opened his eyes. Despite the pain in his side, he smiled up at Maryn, whose tearful face was just inches from his own. "C'mon now honey," he said softly, "wipe that worried look off your face. Everything's going to be okay."

She tried to smile back, but the corners of her mouth kept turning downward instead. "I know...I'm so happy you're awake...and you *are* going to be okay," she answered, her lips quivering as she spoke.

"You look about as happy as stoner with a joint and no matches," he teased with a grin, before wincing.

Maryn wanted to smile, but the pain he was in did not escape her notice.

"Cheer up!" Thomas tried again. "The bullet just grazed me. The docs have me all sewed up and I'll be good as new in no time. The girls are safe at the convent with Sister Louisa. God protected us all by thwarting the assassin's plan. Any word on who it was yet?"

Maryn shook her head. "No. From what I understand, there has been very little coverage of the incident here in Brazil, and zero coverage back in the states. It just makes me sick to think that he was going to kill the both of us...and in front of the girls..."

Her voice broke.

"But he didn't. He's dead. Thankfully, the S.I.G.H.T network came through for us in time."

Seeing Thomas awake, hearing his voice again, was an answer to Maryn's fervent prayers. He was right, God had intervened through heavenly and earthly angels.

When Thomas' friend and fellow officer, Lisa Parker reported an attempt on Sister Helena's life to her husband Mack, he immediately contacted the S.I.G.H.T networkers in Brazil. An agent was immediately sent to watch over their family. None of them had paid much attention to the man reading a book just a few yards from where they were sitting that day, but it was his bullet that took out the assassin before he and Thomas reached the family. Unfortunately, the bullet grazed Thomas' side.

Maryn finally managed to give him a wobbly smile. The entire ordeal was a lot to absorb. Thomas was unaware of the documents recently turned over by Laura Townes, yet he was still speaking positively, giving God credit where it was due.

Love deeper than she'd ever felt for him rose up inside her and spilled over onto her cheeks.

He reached up and brushed the tears away with his thumbs. "Don't cry, Mare. It's going to be okay."

"I know it will," she answered, covering his hands with hers while she told him the good news about Laura Townes.

Thomas couldn't contain his joy. "This is how justice is supposed to work," he muttered with tears in his eyes.

The sight nearly took her breath away.

Maryn bent and gently touched her lips to his. Thomas cupped the back of her head with his hand and kissed her with all the passion, hope, and love he possessed.

Chapter 51

Annie's heart literally felt like it was in her throat when she left the tearful embrace of her children. Only one person at a time was allowed in the room where they were examining Gavin, so she uttered a hopeful prayer and then followed the nurse down the long corridor.

Pushing away the fear that Gavin's words had been prophetic felt nearly impossible. A vision of the dead waitress back at the restaurant prompted her to prepare her heart for the worst. It would be nothing short of a miracle if he made it.

By the time she was ushered through the doorway, Annie sucked in a deep breath to steady herself.

"I'll go get the doctor," the nurse stated in broken English.

Annie nodded stiffly.

"Oh God...please!" she whispered, crossing to the bed where Gavin lay as still as stone. "Gavin...honey...I'm here. Please wake up. Please don't leave me now..." Her voice cracked.

"Okay," he answered softly, his eyes slowly opening.

Annie threw herself across his chest and wept. "You're alive...oh my Dear God...you're alive!" she exclaimed.

"I think so," he answered groggily, staring at her. "Please tell me I'm not going to wake up to find that you are just a figment of my imagination."

"Oh Gavin!" she gushed, showering his face with kisses, before asking, "Do you remember anything about what happened?"

He stared at her for several moments and then slowly shook his head. "I remember being at the restaurant and waiting for our food, but after that it's a blank. I have no idea how I got here...in this room," he said, looking around cautiously. "Are we still in Argentina?"

Annie nodded. "We are. You're in the hospital. I don't exactly know what happened either, but...oh gosh...I've got to let the kids know you are okay before I explain. They're worried sick. Let me text them and then I'll tell you what I know," she exclaimed through happy tears.

"I love you, Gavin!" she declared exuberantly, kissing him soundly on the lips before she picked up her phone to relay the good news.

Gavin gave Annie a tired smile. Despite her reassurance, he still wondered if he was just dreaming. He felt so groggy that he was unable to determine if the events of the past months had even taken place. In truth, he feared he would wake up to discover he was still a lonely, worthless drunk, running from the demons— both seen and unseen.

The thought was too much to bear.

His eyes drank in every detail of Annie's face as she texted the kids—the creamy softness of her cheeks, now red from crying, the way she reached up to swipe at a wayward tear away before she continued the task.

She's done enough crying over me to last a lifetime.

"Don't cry, Annie," he whispered tenderly, stroking her arm gently.

She looked up and grinned. "These tears are happy tears."

"Then if you're happy, no more tears, okay? I just want to see you smile. I can moon you if you want me to...it'd be pretty easy to do in this paper-thin gown."

Annie burst out laughing and kissed him. Just then, a tall, lanky, dark-haired physician, who looked to be not much older than Lucas, walked through the door.

"Good to see you awake," he said with tired smile, his English thickly accented. "We got your lab results back...you tested positive for benzodiazepine and propofol—two drugs used to induce sleep and short-term memory loss—you know, like when you're having a dental procedure. Any reason in particular why we found them in your system?"

Gavin shook his head. "The last I remember is that we were at the restaurant waiting for our dinner."

"Well, that's to be expected, considering these drugs."

"I am sure the police will be contacting you regarding your findings," Annie interjected, seeing Gavin's confusion. "If not, you will need to report this incident. My husband suddenly fell over at the same restaurant where our server was found dead."

The doctor raised his eyebrows. "I *see*...well whoever administered this drug apparently knew what they were doing—combining it is tricky—and dangerous. Too much of either could have killed you. The good news is that, with rest, you should recover completely."

Just moments after the doctor left, Brenna and Lucas came rushing into the room. Amidst hugs, kisses, a bit of nervous laughter and lots of questions, Gavin experienced yet another joyful reunion of his family. Tears filled his eyes to see their happiness and relief at knowing he was alive. It was more than he could ask for. More than he deserved.

Lucas was ecstatic to fill him in on the latest VWS news regarding the evidence turned over by Laura Townes.

Despite his still groggy state, knowing that the truth could not be covered up again brought even more peace to Gavin's sated, happy heart.

"It's over now," Gavin murmured disbelievingly. "There won't be any more killings because there's no one else to protect. They're all going to be exposed now."

"Do you really think so, Daddy?" Brenna asked, tears in her eyes. "I don't want anything else to happen to you."

She hadn't called him Daddy since she was six. Gavin's heart swelled with love. "I really believe it, Brenna...and don't worry, God's protected me so many times that I'm finally beginning to understand that he wants me around for you."

The two embraced for several seconds before Brenna said, "I want to believe that, but I don't know if I have enough faith...how in the world did you survive another attempt on your life?"

Gavin took her face in his hands and smiled tenderly at her. "In the words of one of the sweetest, most faith-filled, most *determined* woman I know... 'it wouldn't be called faith if we understood it all.'"

"Did Mother Teresa say that" Annie asked.

Gavin laughed. "No...Sister Helena Brandt said it. Someday, I'm going to have to introduce her to all of you. She's like Mother Teresa...on steroids," he added with a laugh. "And the truth is...I'd bet my life that she was praying for me this afternoon. Her prayers are *powerful*—because she *believes*."

"Do you believe in God, Dad?"

The question came from Lucas. From the look on his face it was clear that four years of liberal professors had succeeded in planting seeds of doubt.

"I do believe, Lucas. More now than ever. Good and evil are at war in the world, but evidence of God—and His *truth*, is all around us. No matter what we are questioning, looking for...if we look for the answers with eyes of faith, we are guaranteed to find them."

Lucas slowly nodded. It was clear he was still mulling over the entire concept. Finally, he answered with a boyish grin, "Does that include the answer to finding the best take-out pizza in this city? I am *starving!*"

Gavin laughed. Lucas was always one to find a way to be lighthearted in stressful situations. He was looking forward to making up for lost time and be the father both he and Brianna needed and obviously wanted.

He reached over, took Annie's hand and smiled. "Yeah...it applies to everything."

Annie smiled back with all the love she possessed in her eyes.

"Everything," she agreed.

Chapter 52

Anxious for take-off, Gia impatiently drummed her fingers on the arm of her seat. The mission had gone off without a hitch, but the mixed emotions that flooded her senses after every termination mission were more intense because she had yet to hear from Ronan.

She tried not to think of the previously happy family who were now in throes of mourning the death of their father and husband, reminding herself that the greater good of the world had been at stake. There was no looking back.

That poor waitress I drugged will think twice about passing an extra roll of toilet paper under the stall again—or maybe not. There's a good chance she may not remember any of it.

The plane that would carry her to Switzerland lifted into the air, and within just minutes, the speaker announced that electronics could be turned on again. Gia held her breath as she checked her phone for a message from Ronan.

Her stomach, already feeling as hard as rock, tightened another notch as she realized he had not answered her, had not phoned.

She put in her earbuds to listen to music, but deep down, she couldn't shake the feeling that something was wrong. She could feel it in her bones.

Was he arrested?

The thought prompted her to search Reuters for any breaking news from Brazil.

Nothing so far.

She searched Buenos Aires news expecting much of the same; it was early. But just as she was going to close out the webpage, her eyes caught a headline that caused her heart to plummet:

Server Found Dead at Popular Local Cantina

Server? They have it wrong!

Despite her confidence that the news had been misreported, Gia's mind frantically retraced her mission.

Is it possible I mixed up the syringes?

Her eyes scanned the brief article that failed to even mention Gavin Steele's death, and her anxiety grew.

She then searched Brazilian news outlets again for breaking news of Ronan's mission, but found nothing.

With her heart now slamming wildly inside her chest, she searched the news media in the states for any updates on the missions there. A breaking news video came up featuring the familiar face of the CIA operative who had given them their missions. The tagline read:

FBI, CIA, CDC, and Welprox Execs Implicated in New VWS Explosive Documents.

Gia listened to the report for several moments before she could fully comprehend the fact that she had just killed an innocent bystander, possibly on orders from a corrupt agent. The urge to vomit rose within her.

She stared at the screen and listened until she could bear no more and then yanked the earbuds from her ears.

That means that Ronan's mission was probably corrupt as well.

Fear like she'd never experienced before seized her being. Pain and regret for what she'd done raged through her body like fire spreading across dry grassland. Her head began to pulse violently and a buzzing in her ears made her feel like she could pass out.

At the same time, she wanted to jump out of her seat, for the plane to land immediately, so she could run from the truth, hide from her shame.

She felt trapped, suddenly wondering if those around her would somehow discover who she was and what she'd done.

Gia cautiously lifted her head to look around, just as the plane exploded in mid-air.

The End

Epilogue

Maryn sat on her heels praying, her tears drying almost instantly in the cold November wind.

So many tragic events, so much sorrow to deal with, yet her heart was filled with hope. Thanksgiving was just days away, and she had much to be thankful for.

The evidence turned over by Laura Townes made the entire world sit up and take notice. Each day, new evidence surfaced to collaborate what Gavin had initially exposed. Even Carol, Maryn's past supervisor, stepped forward to testify, that she was approached by one of her superiors and given the okay to omit the Lunatia vaccination from Sam's record. The explanation given was that China had purportedly tainted a batch of Lunatia to destroy the U.S. economy. Moreover, if the adverse reactions caused by the tainted Lunatia reduced overall use of the vaccination, a Lunavirus pandemic was possible.

Still, within forty-eight hours of Towne's exposure, the stock market crashed. Just days later, rioting ensued. With every passing week, and with each new detail exposed, new investigations were launched—and not just in the United States.

Angry citizens across the globe were demanding answers, reporting their own nightmarish stories to the television networks and internet sites, making loud and sometimes violent attempts to force their governments into providing safer vaccines and demanding the guilty parties cough up their admissions of guilt.

The casualties caused by the war on truth were mounting. Rioting violence took the lives of some, others fell because of despair, including Larry Dowlin of the FDA and Janet Spool, the CEO of Welprox Pharmaceuticals, who committed suicide just minutes after warrants were issued for their arrests.

Still, there was no other way. There would always be a price to be paid to keep truth alive.

Maryn said a silent prayer that the heavy price paid by so many would produce real and permanent changes, not just in stopping the vaccine mandates, but in the way people blindly trusted powerful entities.

For too long, many had largely relied on state and federal governments, their agencies, and medical professionals to take care of everything for them, much in the way they trusted the news media to report only the facts.

She prayed the Vaccine Warfare Scandal would go down in history as a reminder that where there is potential for financial gain, there is also potential for great corruption.

Immediately, Maryn thought of Judas and the thirty pieces of silver he exchanged for Jesus' life. She then pondered the ultimate price Jesus paid to bring His Gospel of Truth to the world.

Also choosing to show sacrificial love, thousands of people in the S.I.G.H.T network had risked their lives, their families' lives for the sake of humanity—their numbers were miniscule compared to the opposition stacked against them.

The twelve men Christ sent into the world to evangelize and speak the truth of the Gospel must have felt the same. They were like grains of sand compared to the collective beaches in the world; yet with God's grace and favor, they succeeded in making Christ's love and His message known.

Still, as more than two thousand years passed, the world had fallen away from God's truth rather than holding on tight to every aspect—and the effects of sinful disobedience were evident in every facet of society. Without truth, there could be no real life, no meaningful existence, no genuine compassion.

Thanks to God's grace in action through truth and the vastly increasing members of S.I.G.H.T, the war would be waged now rather than in the years to come, when the population would slowly, but surely self-destruct, and countless souls would perish.

Maryn wiped at her cheeks with the back of her glove.

There is so much to be thankful for.

*****

Gavin walked with purpose through the rows and rows of headstones, his eyes perusing each name. As the gloominess of the scene around him penetrated his soul, his heavy woolen coat couldn't seem to keep the chill from his bones.

As disappointed as I was that Wally's broken wrist would keep him from joining me, I'd have to be cruel to wish this bitter cold on anyone.

He had studied the map Wally had given him enough to know exactly where he was going, but Gavin paused and double-checked it anyway. He was determined to pay his respects before it was time to meet his driver and head to the convention center just outside Philadelphia.

The S.I.G.H.T convention was probably the only thing that could have prompted him to interrupt his stay in Killarney where he would return to spend the holidays with Annie and the kids.

Despite the take down of key players in the CIA, the FDA, the CDC, the AMA, and Welprox Pharmaceuticals, frequent relocation for at least the next two years was recommended by S.I.G.H.T because of pending litigation, including civil and criminal trials.

In truth, Gavin was happy to comply and move from Argentina to Ireland. Touring the castles and taking in the rich history had been on Annie's bucket list for as long as he could remember. The kids were just as excited as she was. His only regret was that it had taken the near destruction of their marriage and his life to make it happen.

Thanks be to God; those days were behind them now. His purpose in life was clear—to serve God, his family, and to honor truth until he drew his last breath. There was no other way for him. No turning back.

He now knew that he was not alone in the mission and looked forward to meeting the brave individuals from all over the world, who would come together under the semblance of attending the annual National Wildlife Protection Convention.

When Wally contacted him about the S.I.G.H.T convention, Gavin was determined to go out of his way to be there and pay respect to them all. They were the real heroes in his book, much like the hero he was determined to honor shortly.

As he drew nearer to the grave he sought, he could see a woman there. Her head was down, so he couldn't tell if she was crying or praying. He had no desire to disturb her, but nothing would stop him from carrying out his task.

Gavin's eyes fell upon the name that had become so familiar to him on the simple white headstone. The woman kneeling there looked up from beneath the hood of her coat.

"Maryn?"

He hardly recognized her with the dark hair and just enough weight gain to make her look like the picture of health.

The tears that had halted earlier, immediately filled Maryn's eyes as they collided with Gavin's.

"Gavin!" she exclaimed breathlessly, "I never expected to see you again."

With tears in his own eyes, he reached out his gloved hand and helped her to rise. The two embraced briefly before he offered her a shaky smile and said, "Normally, I would completely agree...but these days I've learned to expect most anything."

Maryn nodded. "It's a miracle we are both alive."

"Nothing but," he answered, before they turned toward the grave, and Gavin read aloud:

Alexander Jackson Brin
Faithful Patriot
Born: September 11, 1989
Died: April 14, 2025

The two reflected in silence for several seconds before Gavin took out a small bronze crucifix and laid it at the base of the headstone. There were tears in his voice when he said, "I've been told that there were three professional agents commissioned to kill that day. A.J. Brin was the only one who aborted the mission. He saved Sylvie's life. I will never forget him for that."

"And God knows how many others," Maryn added.

Gavin nodded and wiped at his eyes. "You know they killed him, right?" he stated more than asked.

She nodded. "I figured so...too many are dead for me to believe he stepped in front of a car on a crowded street."

"Yeah...let's hope he's the last one to die for the cause of perfect health."

"He won't be," Maryn whispered sadly.

"I know," Gavin answered without pause. "Even with the evidence A.J. left behind that implicated the CIA and FBI members involved, eventually the danger will appear to have passed. The economy has slowly started to recover the past several months, and humanity will continue their quest for the trouble-free life. The names of those indicted, the details of their deceptions, will be forgotten and eventually be replaced by a *new and improved* version of false hope."

"I'm afraid you're right," Maryn affirmed. "We can't control the will of the people. We can only lead them to the truth. They're the ones who have to choose."

"Speaking of truth...are you here for the S.I.G.H.T convention by any chance—you're not living in the States now, are you?"

"Actually, we relocated just weeks ago to a small town in Kansas. Thomas wants to continue working in law enforcement and his fellow S.I.G.H.T members agreed that it was safe to come back. And yes…I'm here for the convention too. There's power in numbers," she offered with a hopeful smile.

Gavin held out his arm. "Then how about we go meet the group of people who are helping us take back our freedom?"

*****

Gavin and Maryn were required to show their invitation and S.I.G.H.T identification number before they were given admittance. Though the truth regarding the VWS had changed public opinion drastically regarding the concept of vaccinations in general, and the number of people who questioned vaccine safety was growing leaps and bounds, there were still factions who hated anyone who stood in the way of, or questioned, what they'd always believed. They remained convinced they could keep their children and themselves disease-free through immunizations. Some of these groups had threatened to carry out violence against any and all who disagreed. So much so, that it was recommended that new identities be adapted if and when Maryn and Gavin came back to reside in the states.

The two walked side by side down a long corridor and then pushed through double doors. A massive banner hanging from the ceiling of a room big enough to house a basketball court welcomed them to the National Wildlife Protection Convention.

Stuffed animals ranging from pheasants to a full-sized brown bear were scattered throughout, but the animals were greatly outnumbered by thousands of concerned, determined citizens gathered there.

Maryn and Gavin exchanged a look of sheer awe as they experienced the raw hope and forcible energy present in the room.

"Not to sound corny, but this really is a sight to behold," Gavin offered with a grin. "It's…*powerful!*"

"I agree. This is what hope feels like," Maryn answered, just before she felt a tap on the back of her shoulder. She turned around to find Lisa Parker standing there with tears in her eyes.

After they hugged and greeted one another, Maryn introduced Gavin to Lisa.

"So, *you're* the officer who saved Sister Helena!" Gavin exclaimed, grabbing her for a bear hug that could have very well coined the term.

Before long, the three were gushing over one another's heroic efforts and attributes.

"How is Sister Helena?" Gavin finally asked enthusiastically. "Have you seen her since the incident? I'm still dying to know how she figured out that the Lunatia was targeted toward immigrants."

Gavin didn't get a chance to hear her answer. A voice from behind him floated right to his heart. "I didn't realize this was the mutual admiration society convention...I must be in the wrong place."

Gavin swung around to find Sister Helena just inches away. Her smile was as bright as the sun, but her glasses were fogged over with happy tears. "All the while I was in a coma, I prayed," she began, her voice trembling slightly. "It was as if the angels pulled me into a safe, warm place so I could hear His Voice without distraction. He showed me the children who were damaged and those who would be damaged if the truth didn't come out. He showed me the suffering masses and then He sent me back...to help them, to love them...including *you*."

Gavin fell into her embrace and wept like a boy in his mother's arms. The two held onto one another for several minutes before Gavin broke the hold and said, "Sorry for the tears...you'd think I was eight years old."

Helena snatched her glasses from her nose and rubbed the moisture from them with the sleeve of her habit. "Gavin Steele, I've been waiting a long time to see the man God called you to be...and he finally showed up. Don't you *ever* apologize for tears! Why do you think the good Lord gave them to us?"

She settled her glasses back onto her nose and added with a grin, "As long as you didn't mess up my hair and makeup, it's all good."

Gavin laughed and shook his head. He pulled a handkerchief from his pocket and wiped his face. "As I live and breathe, you are the funniest, oddest, most faith-filled and *stubborn* woman with nine lives I've ever known."

"Gee thanks…but I prefer to call it *fortitude*," Sister answered with a wink and a chuckle. She then turned to welcome Maryn into her arms and the happy tears began again.

For the next hour or so before dinner and the presentations would begin, they shared their stories, connected the dots, and tied up loose ends where they could.

Along with Thomas Pearce, The S.I.G.H.T members were responsible for much more than Gavin imagined—the text messages, the middle-of-the-night fax, and the picture of Eduardo and Congressmen Townes. He was stunned to discover that the police who followed him to the warehouse had been tipped off by S.I.G.H.T to prevent Gavin's assassination. It was the CIA who'd been following him—mostly to intimidate him into rejecting Maryn's case.

Unfortunately, after Judge Burton received the anonymous packet of information from Thomas, he immediately called his longtime friend, Chuck Jones at the CDC to demand some answers regarding the Lunatia vaccine.

Just hours after the phone call, Jeremy Wood assassinated Burton, and a bribed officer on duty collected the packet of data from Burton's office and destroyed it.

Two days later, the officer shot himself. Sadly, to date, the truth about whether he actually took his own life or was another casualty of the VWS, had not surfaced.

Bit by bit the pieces came together to form a clearer picture of both deliberate and Divine interventions.

The transmitter on Sister's purse was put in place by Mack, as a favor to Thomas, so he could stay connected to Maryn and the meetings with her lawyer.

Sister's car accident was determined to be caused by simple human error that began with the blowout of her tire. Startled, she had slammed on the brakes and gave her steering wheel an over-sharp turn that caused the car to roll. A fuel leak from the impact ignited the fire. The explosion was heard and tracked by the transmitter, which also served as a tracking device, allowing the S.I.G.H.T technician to pinpoint her exact location and send the ambulance.

It was Thomas who had tried to retrieve the transmitter from Sister Helena's purse at the hospital, and it was S.I.G.H.T who intercepted Gavin's phony dialogue with Sylvie. By then, they'd already received information that a hit on Judge Burton had been ordered, so an officer was sent to keep Gavin from his meeting with the judge.

Gavin marveled at how close he'd come to being caught in the crossfire, and how even the things that seemed to be working against him were actually working for him.

Later on, during Lisa Parker's recounting of the powerful guardian angel who had pulled Sister out of harm's way, the knowing smile on Sister's face was a sight to behold. Her smile grew even broader when Lisa admitted to having been a professed atheist until that moment.

With each story and piece of information shared, it became very clear that a force much greater than the human will had aided their efforts. Those who were believers recognized the hand of God and the meting out of His poetic justice; the unbelievers present were left doubting their own disbelief.

By far, the highlight of the evening, happened when little Sophia Sanchez walked on stage holding the hand of her mother, Isabella.

Among those sitting at the table with Gavin, Maryn, and Sister Helena, all eyes were shiny with tears. But, by the time Isabella finished sharing Sophia's story and details of their exodus and journey to safety with the help of S.I.G.H.T, there wasn't a dry eye in the room.

Next, Isabella introduced Sophia's new doctor. Dr. Brent Pelman, a second-generation neurosurgeon specializing in pediatrics and naturopathic medicine, explained his methods for detoxing metals and other toxins from Sophia's body. With the already proven success in multiple patients, Pelman's expectation of improving her brain function and other symptoms, through the healing of brain lesions with the reduction of the autoimmune response, was promising.

"With detoxification, targeted supplements, and optimal nutrition, including organic food and pure water, I believe Sophia and other vaccine-injured children may improve over time," Pelman explained. "To what extent remains to be seen, but one thing is certain...with more natural-path doctors like me and dedicated researchers free to openly share their findings and continued research without being hindered by government regulations and coercive medical conglomerates, there is great hope for all."

Hope.

As the tiny baby in Maryn's womb stirred, the concept took on a whole new dimension. Tears of joy filled her eyes yet again. Knowing she would never be forced to take her healthy child for an injection she didn't believe in was more than she could ever hope for.

Hope.

Gavin had been devoid of hope for so long that he'd begun to believe it was merely a concept that existed only in the mind. As he sat there among so many people who had risked most everything to help expose the truth and take back freedoms that were nearly lost, he experienced a hope that was electrifying, inspiring.

He glanced over at Sister Helena, who sat there watching him with tears in her eyes and a knowing smile. Suddenly, he was sure she was thinking of the many times she'd reminded him of the scripture in Romans 12:12.

"Rejoice in hope, be patient in suffering, persevere in prayer".

Gavin grinned back at her knowingly. He was determined to do just that.

"For nothing is hid that shall not be made manifest, nor anything secret that shall not be known and come to light."
Luke 8:17

Made in the USA
Coppell, TX
24 November 2020